A.F. Smith is an editor of academic texts by day and a fantasy writer by night. She lives with her husband and their two young children in a house that was apparently built to be as creaky as possible. She can be found on Twitter @afesmith and online at www.afesmith.com

Also by A.F.E. Smith

The Darkhaven Novels
Darkhaven

Goldenfire

A.F.E. SMITH

Book Two of The Darkhaven Novels

HARPER
Voyager

Harper*Voyager*
An imprint of HarperCollins*Publishers* Ltd
1 London Bridge Street
London SE1 9GF

www.harpervoyagerbooks.co.uk

This Paperback Original 2016

First published in Great Britain in ebook format by Harper*Voyager* 2016

A catalogue record for this book
is available from the British Library

ISBN: 978-0-00-814174-5

Set in Sabon by Born Group using Atomik ePublisher from Easypress

Printed and bound in Great Britain

Prologue

'So you understand now,' the dark-velvet voice said. 'You understand what you have to do.'

'Yes.' Kai resisted the urge to peer through the shadows cast by the single oil lamp. The Brotherhood kept their identities a closely guarded secret. Seeing one of their faces – accidentally or otherwise – would be a swift route to a slow death.

'Repeat your instructions.'

Kai swallowed a nervous catch that threatened to become a cough. It wasn't the job; that would be the fulfilment of a long-held desire. It was the faceless man who was so unsettling – specifically, the note of implacability in his voice.

'I am to go to Mirrorvale. To Arkannen. I am to find a way into Darkhaven. And once there –' A pause to give proper recognition to the significance of the task. 'I am to kill Ayla Nightshade, the last living Changer.'

'That is not strictly true.' The dark-velvet voice now held a little less velvet. 'It is possible that other Changers live. But they are far from attaining their majority. Do you understand?'

'Yes, sir,' Kai said.

'There is a child in Darkhaven who may be one such. If you can dispose of him at the same time, all well and good, but your focus must be the woman. Again, do you understand?'

'Yes, sir.'

'Good. Then take the weapon.'

It sat on the small table at Kai's left elbow, gleaming gently in the light from the lamp. The question rose up without volition.

'You're sure this can kill them?'

'We are always sure.'

Of course they were. Reining back sudden reluctance, Kai picked up the weapon. It was cold and smooth, surprisingly heavy for something that size. A small thing to destroy a monster.

'You will change your identity, of course,' the man said.

'Of course.' Certainty came flooding back. Kai tucked the weapon into an inside pocket and stood ready to depart.

'Have you considered how you will get inside?'

Kai smiled. 'With respect, sir, I think it best if you know as little as possible.'

'Indeed.' Through the shadows, the silhouette of a man inclined his head. 'Then go. There will be no need to send word when it is done.'

ONE

On days like this – red-gold and glorious – her ability to Change seemed to Ayla Nightshade to be the only thing she could ever require.

As she flew over the forests and fields to the west of Arkannen, she noted the signs of autumn's approach: the turning leaves, the tang of woodsmoke, the crops ripe in their rows. Farmers and labourers, toiling in the afternoon sunshine, raised their arms in salute as she passed overhead. She was aware of their respect, and accepted it as her due, but made no acknowledgement; she was too intent on the sensation of her wings beating the air, the joy of her own swift flight. And so she passed over her people as a fleeting shadow, a cinnamon-scented breeze, a flash of gold against the sky.

She heard the mine before she saw it: the rumble of the atmospheric engines – lifting water from the seam and powering the lifts – carried a long way on a still day, particularly to her sensitive ears. The small town that had sprung up close to the mine came next, a jumble of mismatched roofs, and then she was at the mine itself. Its towers spilled across the ground below her as if they had been extruded from the earth. Up close, the noise and smells were almost overwhelming: soot and steam, the clanking of the coal trucks, the roaring engines. Even the thuds of the miners' picks, down in the tunnels, though she doubted any human ears could hear those at this distance.

The land around the mine was churned up and torn, blackened with coal dust, but beyond it was a small hill – and that was where the people had told her they would wait for her, beside the lookout point at the top. Ayla scanned the hill: just below the summit was a small grove of trees with a clearing at its heart that would make a perfect landing spot, both convenient and secluded. She flew over the mine, snorting at the prickle of the smog against her skin, and descended into the clearing.

As she landed, she Changed; that swirling sensation like pins and needles inside her bones that heightened to an intense explosive *shiver*, as if her entire body were turning itself inside out. Shifting from human to Alicorn was an expansive process, an opening up and a gaining of freedom, whereas Changing the other way always felt like being squeezed back into a skin that was too small. Her bones shortened, four swift legs becoming clumsy human limbs. Her body shrank and softened. Her wings vanished, leaving only the ghostly memory of flight. Yet it wasn't just her physical self that altered. In creature form she retained all her intelligence, but her focus was somehow ... sharper. Less cluttered. Whilst in the air, she'd been thinking about nothing but her immediate goal; if she had been attacked or something had gone wrong, she would have approached the situation with the same single-minded intent. It was only after the Change that she was assailed once more by tomorrow and yesterday and what if and maybe: the complicated web of emotion, memory, conjecture that made up a human life.

She could understand why more than one of her ancestors had retreated into creature form for good.

Still, the desire to do so herself was only fleeting. There was Tomas, for one. And Myrren's child. Besides, a Mirrorvale ruled by a Changer creature in perpetuity would be a starker and more fearful place. That was the balance required of her, of all the Nightshade line. The creature side was for retribution. The human side was for mercy. Her people had to know they could expect both. Only then could they respect as well as fear her.

And respect her they did. Ayla recalled the workers she had passed in the fields, this time with a touch of gratitude. After three years, the people of Mirrorvale were used to the sight of a golden unicorn with feathered wings in the skies above them. After three years, Ayla herself no longer felt ashamed. Her father had done his best to destroy the joy she took in her gift, but time and common sense had rebuilt it. The average Mirrorvalese was as awed by a winged horse as by a Firedrake. Only within Darkhaven had there ever been an obsession with *purity*: the idea that her hybrid form was somehow wrong, that only the five elemental forms taken by her ancestors – Firedrake, Hydra, Unicorn, Phoenix, Griffin – were acceptable. And with the help of her new Captain of the Helm, even Darkhaven was becoming more enlightened.

Ayla was a creature of ice and ebonwood: beautiful, cold, relentless; wise, resilient, self-renewing. And she had finally learned to be happy with that.

She took a deep breath, stretching out arms and legs, feeling her way back into her human form. Everything around her was muted, now: the sounds of the mine a dim roar, the colours of the leaves faded, the smells of soot and steam almost gone. She could no longer taste coal dust in every breath she took.

Of course, her senses were still sharper than most people's, but compared to what they had been just a few moments before ... Ayla shook her head, ears still ringing with echoes. Usually she found her return to human form almost unbearably empty of sensation, for a little while, but on this particular occasion she thought she was probably glad of it.

From the small bag she always carried with her, she withdrew her clothing. It had taken her some experimentation before she'd hit on the perfect outfit – one that fell in the sweet spot between elegance and practicality. The soft trousers and tunic were quick to put on and take off, yet they were made from a high-quality embroidered fabric that proclaimed her status. Most importantly, they emerged from the bag barely more crumpled than when they'd gone in, which meant Ayla could go about her business without feeling self-conscious.

Of course, her father wouldn't have cared. Her father would have Changed in full view of everyone – walked naked through a crowd – held a formal state meeting wearing just a cloak. But though Ayla had learned a lot since his death, that insouciance was a step beyond her. She wasn't even sure she wanted to emulate it. Her father had enjoyed making people uncomfortable; if she wandered around naked in public, the only person she'd discomfit would be herself.

Fully dressed, she stepped out of the grove and looked back down the hill towards the mine. It didn't take her long to pick out the dull gleam of the parallel rails that stretched from the towers that housed the steam engines and lifts to the preparation plant on the outskirts of the town. A steam-powered train. Ayla had already discussed with several engineers the possibility of laying similar tracks all the way to Arkannen; currently coal was delivered to the city's greedy factories by canal, but it was a slow journey. Admittedly a cross-country railway would be far longer than this one – longer, too, than Arkannen's tramways, and with more difficult terrain to cross – but she had hopes that it was possible. Mirrorvale was a small country; to hold its own against its neighbours, it needed to outpace them in industry. For centuries her family had encouraged their subjects to rely on Changer creatures as the only defence they needed against the grasping hands of the wider world, but if the Nightshade line were to fail –

No. She pushed the thought aside. *You don't have time for all that now. Focus!*

Trying to draw on some of her creature-self's single-mindedness, she turned her back on the mine and climbed to the top of the hill. Three people awaited her there: a richly costumed man to one side, a more shabbily dressed man to the other side, and a neat-looking woman between them. Their positioning made it easy enough to identify them. The woman in the middle would be the local magistrate, which made the wealthy man to her left the mine owner, and the man to her right the worker who had laid the complaint.

This sort of thing was usually quite straightforward. Though most grievances could be resolved by local law enforcement, there were always a few people who refused to comply with a magistrate's judgement – at which point, the magistrate had the right to request help from Darkhaven. More often than not, seeing a Changer creature up close was enough to convince the recalcitrant to obey the law. And if that were not so, Ayla could impose harsher punishments than any magistrate. For a start, Darkhaven's overlord was the only person in Mirrorvale who could sign a warrant of permanent incarceration or – if necessary – execution.

Her father had been known to carry out the latter before the ink was dry on the page.

Still, that was unlikely to be relevant here. It was a simple case: the mine workers had laid a claim that the owner was cheating them out of a fair wage, the magistrate had found in their favour, and yet the owner had refused to pay the difference. Ayla was here to convince him otherwise. With any luck, it would turn out to be one of those cases where the guilty party simply wanted to have his sentence confirmed by the highest power in the land, either because he wouldn't submit to a lesser authority or – which was sadly all too common, and wasted far more of Ayla's time than she cared to think – because he fancied a good look at a Nightshade.

Yet as she walked towards the little group, her hope of an easy resolution began to fade. The man she'd identified as the owner was fixing her with a belligerent glare; not at all the conciliatory expression of a man who had been cowed by the sight of a Changer creature. He was a big man in both height and girth, and he was using it to make his presence felt – all folded arms and looming shoulders. She found it rude enough that she deliberately ignored him for a while, greeting the magistrate first and then the worker before finally turning to the mine owner and greeting him in turn.

'My lord,' the man replied. There was mockery in his smile, but Ayla couldn't call him on it. The ruler of Mirrorvale was its overlord; there was no female equivalent. *Which says a lot.* Though most people in Darkhaven had enough sense to address her as Lady Ayla, *my lord* was technically the correct form of address.

Ayla doubted the man before her intended it as a point of etiquette.

She asked the magistrate to set out the case, then listened politely and without impatience as the woman went through the same points that Ayla had already read in the written record. It was important that everyone present should hear the official version of events, to prevent dispute later. When the magistrate had finished, Ayla turned to the mine owner.

'It's straightforward enough,' she said. 'These expenses you have been docking from your workers' pay are unlawful. You have no right to make them pay for the tools they use in your service. Nor for the care of a physician, if they suffer injury in the course of their work. And you certainly have no right to force them to work longer without additional pay. You know the law.'

He scowled. 'Your father –'

'Would have made the same judgement,' Ayla said briskly. And it was true: Florentyn had always upheld the rights of his workers. Perhaps that and his swiftness to punish those on the wrong side of the law were two sides of the same coin. But the mine owner shook his head stubbornly.

'He'd have understood that a man has to turn a profit. And I can't do that if I'm to pay for every damn miner who knocks his elbow or stubs his toe down there.'

'You can if you run your mine efficiently and with the welfare of your workers in mind,' Ayla said. Then, deliberately, she looked him up and down, taking in the embroidery on his coat and the lace ruffles at his wrists – as fine as her own clothing. 'But my guess is that you're too interested in filling your purse to worry about that.'

His face darkened. Taking a step forward, he gripped her by the upper arms as if to remonstrate with her. And Ayla reacted automatically.

Twist out of the way. Knee to the groin. Punch him while he's weakened. The lessons dropped into place without conscious thought. Only when he staggered to his knees in the dirt in front of her did she realise what she'd done, and then it was all she could do not to smile.

After what had happened to her three years ago, she'd insisted that Tomas teach her how to fight. As she'd discovered to her cost, it wasn't always possible for her to Change in order to defend herself, not without causing injury to innocent citizens or bringing a building down on her own head – and in human form, since her father had refused to send her for weapons training as he had Myrren, she'd found herself pretty near powerless. But she'd been determined not to stay that way. If another Owen Travers came along – a man who sought to impose his will on hers through physical strength alone – she'd make damn sure she knew how to deal with him.

And so Tomas had trained her. She was small, but her Nightshade blood made her stronger than she looked; with the right knowledge, Tomas had said, she'd be able to hold her own even against a trained soldier like Travers – or himself. And so it had turned out. Of course, to begin with he'd been gentle with her, even timid, until she'd pointed out tartly that no attacker would be so kind. After that, he didn't hold back, and she went to bed each night with an impressive collection of bruises. Still, it was briefly worth it for the first time she disarmed him on her own merits. She'd whooped and cheered like an excitable child until he brought her back down to earth, quite literally, by knocking her feet from under her.

Never let your guard down, he'd told her sternly, pinning her to the ground with ease. *Even if you think you're safe. Now, let me show you how to counter this grip.*

Since then she'd been practising, and sometimes she could beat him. Admittedly it was more not than often, but at least it wasn't never – and the fact that she didn't make it easy for him gave her confidence now. After all, there was a big difference between Tomas Caraway, Captain of the Helm and one of the most skilled swordsmen of the fifth ring, and a mine owner who'd probably never picked up a weapon in his life.

The question was, really, how far she was going to take it.

Grasping the mine owner's shirt in her fist and giving it a twist to constrict his throat, she looked steadily into his wide, sweating face. This was what her people expected from her: a Nightshade overlord ruled as much through physical dominance as anything else. If anything, she was being kind. Presented with anyone who dared to be this insubordinate, her father would have taken his Firedrake form and ripped the offender to pieces without a second thought – she'd seen him do it to a man in Darkhaven once, all blood-spatter and entrails and high-pitched screaming. In Florentyn Nightshade, the balance between retribution and mercy had been askew. Or was it that Ayla erred too far on the side of forgiveness? Would she lose that hard-earned respect as a result of what could be perceived as weakness?

No. I have to stop comparing myself to my father. He was what he was. I am what I am.

Now, where are those pressure points Tomas showed me …?

She tightened her grip on the man's throat until the hint of fear in his eyes became the predominant emotion. Then, with a shove, she let him go. He sprawled on the ground, gasping.

'Pay your workers a fair wage,' she said. 'I am letting you live for the sake of their livelihoods. If I hear ill of you again, I won't be so lenient.'

'Yes, ma'am.' The reply was hoarse. Ayla looked up and gave the magistrate a nod, which the other woman returned after a moment's hesitation. The workers' representative was staring in unabashed amazement: no doubt one more story would be added to the local people's repertoire tonight. That was no bad thing. In general, the more stories were told about Changers and their abilities, the less likely people were to commit a crime.

'Let me know if you have any more trouble,' she told the magistrate. Then, because one lesson she had taken on board from her father was that it was always wise to leave people a little on edge, she turned away without another word and walked back down the hill.

When she reached the clearing, she undressed quickly and packed the clothing into her bag, before Changing back into creature form. Her body still hadn't forgotten the shape of it from her journey here; she settled into it as if it were a favourite gown. A toss of her horn picked the bag up and settled the strap over her head. Time to go home.

Once she was back in the air, she circled round and flew upwards, following the slope of the hill. The three people at the top were temporarily cast into shadow as her form blocked out the sun. To add to the effect, Ayla flung her head back and sent forth a Unicorn's battle cry: a high, sweet, piercing note that resonated deep in human bones.

That should reinforce the day's events in their minds.

Satisfied, she left them behind with a single sweep of her wide wings, and headed back to Darkhaven.

TWO

It was an easy job, her latest employer had said. Almost an insult to someone of her capabilities. In and out, quick as blinking. A mere stroll. And she'd be paid double her usual fee.

Perched on a window ledge half the depth of her boot and a full five storeys above the ground, her back pressed hard against the glass, Naeve Sorrow suspected he might have been embellishing the truth a little.

She'd known it at the time, of course. Who paid double for easy? The whole point of hiring her was to get things done that no-one else could do. But money was money, her reputation was at stake, and so she'd taken the job despite her suspicions. Probably because of them, to be honest. The more time she spent in Kardissak, the more restless she became – and the more she found herself taking on the dangerous assignments, the ones even other seasoned mercenaries backed away from. She flirted with death like a two-bit whore desperate to make a sale.

The breeze currently whispering in her ear provided a vertiginous reminder that death didn't like to be trifled with.

A light was extinguished in the room behind her, and Sorrow turned her head slowly in that direction. That was the

13

first point she intended to include on the long list she'd give her employer when she returned with the goods and a demand for half again on top of the agreed fee. The mansion was supposed to be empty, the owners away. Yet unless Kardise ghosts could walk around opening doors and lighting gas lamps, there was very definitely someone at home.

Point two: the safe hadn't been in the room specified, meaning she had to go hunting through the house for it.

Point three: once she'd finally found the safe and got it open, it turned out to be empty.

Point four ... she hadn't got that far, because that was when she'd been interrupted by point one.

Still, Sorrow hadn't given up on the job, not yet. She'd managed to close the safe and climb out of the window when she heard the creak of footsteps on the stairs. And whoever the footsteps belonged to clearly hadn't heard her, because he – definitely a *he*, she'd heard him mutter something under his breath – hadn't searched the room or looked out of the window. Nor had he moved the right-hand curtain aside and thereby treated himself to a fine view of her backside squashed up against the glass. As far as Sorrow was concerned, that meant the game was still on. All she had to do was figure out where in this whole ostentatious pile of a place someone would keep important documents, if not in the safe, then get there without encountering the muttering man. She was armed, of course, but she didn't want it to come to that. Clients didn't like it when she left corpses in her wake, unless that was what they'd requested in the first place.

The room behind her had been dark for some time now, and she hadn't heard a sound or caught any glimpse of motion through the shadowed glass. Sorrow began to edge back along the sill towards the open window – then jumped at the sound of a man's voice, loud enough through the still night air that he could be standing next to her.

For an instant she lost her balance. Her body tipped forward – death swirled up from the yawning drop to kiss her cheek with cold lips – but then she pushed herself back against the glass once more, heart thumping, swearing soundlessly but with vigour. She must have made some noise in that moment, she was sure of it. A soft thud on the window, a stifled gasp. Yet when her pulse slowed enough that she could hear over the sound of her own terror, the man was still talking, calmly and evenly.

'Everything is in hand, I take it, with the council for –' but Sorrow didn't catch the last word, because it wasn't one she recognised. Though she spoke fluent Kardise, there were still occasions when the unfamiliar slapped her in the face.

'Councillor Lepont has been paid off.' That was a second speaker, a woman. Cool, a little amused, as though she were humouring her companion simply by being there. Her voice sounded further away; Sorrow judged her to be standing just inside the door of the room, while the man was at the window. 'He was too concerned with his errant son to put up much of a fight.'

'The boy is still missing, then?'

'Rumour has it he has left the country.'

'He was allowed past the checkpoints?'

'Why not? Councillor Lepont is far more persuadable when distracted.' A low laugh. 'Thus the decision falls in our favour.'

'Doesn't it always,' the man said drily. 'And the election next month?'

'The will of the people shall be done. Naturally.'

'Naturally.' Footsteps moved across the floor; Sorrow heard the chink of glass on glass. Probably the decanter she'd seen on the sideboard when she entered the room. 'So there are no outstanding matters of concern within our borders.'

'Nothing of any import,' the woman said. Closer to Sorrow, now, as if she'd come further into the room while the man was at the sideboard by the door. 'The people live their lives, the government play at governance, we do what is best for Sol Kardis. So may it always be.'

'So may it always be,' the man echoed. 'Drink?'

She laughed. 'I don't trust you enough for that.'

'Very wise.'

Silence fell; presumably the man was drinking, the woman waiting. Sorrow realised she was panting silently, as if she'd been fighting instead of standing motionless on a cold window ledge. She forced her breathing pattern back to slow and regular, but she was unable to control the erratic pulse of her heart.

Point four: the Kardise Brotherhood are involved.

She was in far deeper shit than she could have known.

The country of Sol Kardis was nominally a democracy – indeed, they made a lot of the fact. *The will of the people is the will of the nation*: so it was proclaimed above the grand archway that led to the government buildings right here in Kardissak. Every three years, representatives were elected to sit in parliament, but the Kardise people also had the chance to vote on all sorts of other things that affected them, from the local to the national. Yes, a few malcontents sometimes got together and muttered about how the government wasn't really in charge of the country at all, but there were always people willing to see a conspiracy in every corner. Most Kardise were justly proud of their democratic system. *Far better*, more than one of them had boasted to Sorrow, *than being ruled by an unnatural beast like you Mirrorvalese, or a group of bickering lords like those in the Ingal States. At least we have a choice.*

Yet all the same, she had heard stories, and she had seen certain things for herself. It had been enough to make her believe that the conspiracy theorists might be right: all that choice was an illusion. There was a power behind the government. Those in the know called them the Brotherhood. And all the signs indicated that she was listening to two of them talk at this very moment – by moonlight rather than gaslight, to help them conceal their faces from the world.

No wonder the fee for this job was so high.

'I brought the document you asked for,' the woman said. 'I'll leave it on your desk.'

'Thank you.' Footsteps again, two sets this time. Sorrow imagined them circling the room, careful to stay a safe distance from each other at all times. Comical, but at the same time … not. When the man spoke again, he was back at the window. 'I appreciate your support in this matter. Fourteen is recalcitrant.'

'I hold no particular allegiance to either of you,' the woman replied from over by the desk. 'But in this instance, your interests more closely align with my own.'

That answered one question. Sorrow had identified two possibilities: either her employer was a lackwitted fool who'd sent her up against the Brotherhood without realising who he was really trying to rob, or she'd been cast straight into the middle of an internal power struggle. But if the document these two were discussing was the one she was after – and she strongly suspected it was – then that made her employer Fourteen. Which meant, once again, that she was in the shit. Whether she stole the document or not, she'd make a powerful enemy. Maybe two.

Point five: I'll have to watch my back much more closely from now on. Even double-pay-and-a-half isn't enough to cover that.

Still, she didn't see that she had much choice. If she failed to steal the document, she'd have a powerful man after her who knew exactly who she was and how to find her. If she succeeded ... well, she'd have won his favour, and if she could keep it then he'd have no reason to betray her to his colleagues, particularly if he thought she could do more work for him. Besides, with any luck, the two in the room behind her would each think the other a double-crosser, and neither of them would ever suspect there had been someone else involved.

Yes. She was going to have to steal that document.

One of her legs was going numb. Ever so slowly, she shifted her weight to the other leg and flexed the toes on the offending limb. *Come on, come on, lock the bloody thing up in the safe so I can get it out again* – Once again, she nearly fell off the window ledge when the man's voice spoke close by.

'And as payment?'

'Information, of course.'

'Of course.'

'You are involved in the Goldenfire business.' The woman was still over by the desk. Unlikely as it seemed, Sorrow thought she caught the click of her fingernails tapping the polished wooden surface. 'Tell me what you know.'

'I daresay you have heard a certain rumour,' the man said. 'A whisper that the indestructible has turned out to be destructible. Not all rumours are falsehoods.'

A sharp intake of breath. 'You interest me greatly. And your plan is to take advantage of this opportunity?'

'It is more than a plan. It will shortly become a reality.'

'Ah.' The woman's cool detachment had thawed a little, now; hints of bloodthirsty excitement were showing through like the edges of rocks under snow. 'Then the army –'

'Is being readied as we speak. An animal with its heart cut out is no more than meat for the taking.'

'Finally,' she breathed. 'Finally the balance tips in our favour.'

'It will be a victory for enlightened people everywhere,' the man said drily. 'The prevalence of science and reason over the unnatural power of Mirrorvale.'

They're talking about killing Ayla Nightshade. Sorrow's pulse had finally settled, but that sent it straight back into erratic mode. An emotion of some kind squirmed through her guts; she examined the feeling, and identified it as guilt. Because if – as it appeared – the Kardise Brotherhood were arranging to have the overlord of Mirrorvale assassinated, Sorrow herself was the one who had discovered the method for it. Before she wounded Myrren Nightshade with a pistol, three years ago, it had been common knowledge that no weapon in existence could hurt a Changer.

Not that she'd ever told anyone the truth. It had always struck her as too valuable a piece of information to be traded. And she was pretty sure none of the very few other people who were privy to it would have shared it either. But secrets had a life of their own in Arkannen. They tended to come out and play, despite all efforts to keep them locked up. Still, Sorrow could hardly be held responsible for that – nor, indeed, for the discovery itself. She was no more to blame than whoever first uncovered the properties of gunpowder.

As the guilt faded, her usual sense of opportunity was already shivering down her spine. Knowledge of this particular plot could be highly useful to her now that she was tangled up with the Brotherhood – because her involvement with Fourteen was bound to go wrong sooner or later. She would cease to be useful, or know too much, and then she would be disposed of. So before that happened, it would be sensible to arrange a way out. Helping a half-Nightshade baby and his mother to escape Mirrorvale had left her distinctly out of favour in Darkhaven, but what better way to regain that favour than to send warning of the impending assassination? They'd have to welcome her back to the country after that. They'd have to forgive her for the so-called kidnap of Ayla's half-brother Corus.

And in fact, that was another thing. Given the Brotherhood's intentions towards Ayla, if they discovered that Corus and his mother Elisse were living on their very doorstep, Sorrow wouldn't give much for their chances of continued survival. Which meant she was going to have to convince Elisse to take Corus back to Mirrorvale before the damn stubborn woman got the two of them killed. If Sorrow played it right then she'd prevent an assassination, protect her sort-of life partner and kind-of adopted son, and preserve her own skin into the bargain.

Of course, if she played it wrong then everybody died. That almost went without saying. But nor did it matter. None of this rationalisation did. Because though she wasn't a patriot by any definition of the word, and though she hadn't set foot in Mirrorvale for years … it was her country. Arkannen was the closest thing she had to a home. And she'd be damned if she'd let the Kardise tear it apart.

Apart from anything else, it had been years since she'd tasted taransey.

'… look forward to hearing of our triumph,' the woman was saying inside the room. Her voice grew gradually louder;

she was approaching the window again. 'But I have work to do. You will send word when you have further news?'

'Certainly,' the man said from over by the desk. Sorrow heard the muted clang of the safe door. 'For now, let me accompany you to the street.'

'I can see myself out.'

'I'm sure you can. But I would rather not give you the opportunity to prowl through the rest of my house.'

'I doubt you possess anything that could surprise me.' Amusement coloured the woman's voice. 'But if it will make you feel better ...'

'Humour me.'

The man's footsteps crossed the floor, and an instant later the woman's joined them. Sorrow waited for a count of twenty after they'd left the room – too much longer and there was a danger the man would return before she was ready. Then she edged along the windowsill, prised the window further open with her fingertips and climbed back through it, landing on the thick sheepskin rug with as little noise as possible.

Her limbs were stiff, but she didn't dare take the time to stretch them fully. If she were caught here, she wouldn't live to see morning – or else she'd have to kill a member of the Brotherhood, which would carry its own problems. So as soon as her cold, cramped fingers felt flexible enough to work her set of picks, she crossed to the safe and coaxed it open a second time. As expected, it contained a folded, sealed document that hadn't been there last time she looked. Sorrow tucked it into the inside pocket of her coat, then swung the door closed again. With any luck, the man wouldn't check his safe for a day or so. But that still left her with a challenge: how to get out of the building without being caught. She'd come in through the back door, but that wouldn't work as an exit now the owner was at home.

In the end, she took the servants' staircase down to the kitchen, then descended the narrow steps into the cellar. Then it was simply a matter of bracing herself in the coal chute and inching her way up it. If she fell, she'd probably break something and be stuck in the cellar until the next time someone wanted coal, at which point she'd be in a whole heap of trouble. But that didn't happen, and finally – muscles shaking with the exertion – she pushed open the hatch that covered the chute and wriggled out into the street.

She was covered in enough coal dust that she looked as if she'd been sweeping chimneys, but she didn't stop to clean herself up. Instead, she headed off down the street at a run. The sooner she got back to her lodgings, the safer she'd feel – and the sooner she could write a letter to Tomas Caraway.

THREE

Ree stood outside the Gate of Steel and gazed up at the row of sharp metal blades that lined the archway. Here she was. A few more steps, and she'd be in the fifth ring.

As she hesitated in front of the place she'd been dreaming about since she was old enough to read, her doubts all came swimming around her again: a school of sharp-toothed fish, nipping away at her confidence. *You're not good enough. They'll chew you up and spit you out. Girls can't be Helmsmen.*

Stop it, she told herself sternly. *Those aren't your doubts.* Not that it made much difference. They were in her head, whether she'd put them there or not.

She reached into the bag that was slung across her shoulder and pulled out her border pass. Her tutor had explained to her that although people weren't allowed to enter the higher rings of Arkannen whenever they felt like it, youngsters in search of weapons training had always been welcome from anywhere in Mirrorvale. All she had to do was present her identification to the guards at the gate and explain what she was there for. One of them would show her to the quartermaster, who'd enter her details in his ledger and allot her a place in the barracks.

O'course, it's a bit different now, her tutor had said. He was a big, bluff man who looked like he belonged in a field rather than a duelling ring, but he was far more nimble than his appearance suggested. *I hear the weaponmasters've made a few changes. Still, you get there sometime in the week 'fore the next training period starts and you'll be fine.*

Clutching the border pass, Ree took a deep breath and let it out slowly. She'd arrived in good time, on the first day of the sign-up week that preceded the start of training. She had her identification. She just had to step up to the gate and let everything on the other side of it fall out as it would. The thought didn't make a blind bit of difference to the churning in her stomach, but she obeyed it anyway. As she approached the gate, one of the watchmen peeled off from the wall where he'd been lounging and came to meet her.

'Weapons training?' The boredom in his voice reassured her. This wasn't anything out of the ordinary. She was an everyday person doing everyday things. With a mute nod, she showed him the pass.

'C'mon, then.' He turned on his heel, and Ree followed obediently. As she passed beneath the steel teeth of the gate, her heart gave a funny little skip. She'd done it. She was really here.

Just as her tutor had predicted, the guard took her to a building not far from the gate and handed her over to the quartermaster. He, in turn, proceeded to give her a bewildering set of directions: *Your barracks are here. The trainees' mess hall is there. The practice grounds are over there.* She didn't take in any of it, except the final set of instructions.

'From here, turn right and stay on the main street until you see a long, low building with a red roof. That's the central training hall. You'll find the sign-up sheet pinned on the door, along with separate lists for specialist training, like the Helm –' He broke off from his practised recitation long enough to sweep her with a glance. 'Though, of course, that won't be relevant to you.'

At that casual confirmation of Ree's doubts, they swam back in shoals. She bit her lip and didn't reply. After all, the quartermaster was only saying what everyone assumed. There were too many more important battles ahead of her to make it worthwhile fighting this one. All the same, after she'd left him with mumbled thanks and set off in search of the training hall, she concentrated on warding herself against those biting doubts. She couldn't afford to listen to them, not now she was here. She couldn't let anyone make her feel she wasn't good enough. And so she deliberately remembered each and every time she'd been mocked or slighted for her *inappropriate ambitions*, until she was wrapped in a thick blanket of anger that would protect her far better than fear. *I won't let them stop me. I can't. This is what I've wanted all my life.*

As she walked the streets of the fifth ring, trying to stare wide-eyed at everything without seeming amazed at all, she was relieved to see women as well as men. In fact, close to half the warriors she passed were female. The Helm might not include women in their number, but mercenaries, patrolmen and the Arkannen city watch were not so closed.

So why aren't you trying to become a sellsword or a soldier or a member of the watch? Ree asked herself, but she already knew the answer. The fifth ring winnowed out the best potential warriors from across Mirrorvale. The Helm accepted only the best of the best. And if Ree wanted to prove herself to her own satisfaction, she had to be the best of the best of the best.

Do it perfectly or not at all, her mother had always said. Though, of course, she'd been talking about etiquette or embroidery or whatever it was she'd been trying to drum into Ree at the time. Yet the only lesson for which Ree had shown any aptitude was horse riding and then, later – once she'd persuaded her father that a daughter who could fence would provide amusing anecdotes to tell his friends – sword fighting and acrobatics. When she'd surpassed her tutor, he'd helped her to convince her father that with two other daughters to marry off, having a third who could pay her own way in the world could only be a good thing. And thus, despite her mother's opposition, Ree's father had let her come to Arkannen.

You can have a year, Cheri, he'd said. *You're sixteen now, old enough to give it a good go. And if you can't make anything of it, at least you'll get it out of your system.*

He expected her to fail. They all did. Her mother was actively hoping for it. And so Ree had no choice but to succeed so fast and so marvellously that it would be impossible for them to decide it wasn't working out and bundle her off back home like a runaway lamb.

Yet now she was here in the fifth ring, with the training hall only a few steps away, *fast and marvellous* seemed a long way off. Everyone was so big. And so … well worn, making her lovely new training clothes – the ones she'd slunk into an alley to change into as soon as she was off the airship – look silly and childish, as if she were a child playing at dress-up. And the weapons! She'd never seen so many weapons. The people here were adorned with them like the society ladies back home were adorned with gemstones.

Ree looked down at the slim sword by her side, the one she'd had since she was twelve. *We're really not prepared for this.*

Of course we are, she imagined her sword replying.

She raised her head again. To her left was a wall made of sand-coloured stone, into which was set a wide archway. Through it she could see the single-storey building that the quartermaster had described, a long hall with a shallow sloping roof tiled in orange-red. Unlike the buildings down in the lower rings, which were a jumble of ever more fanciful styles from different periods in Arkannen's history, this one didn't look as if it had changed since the city was built. A single set of double doors led into the hall, and windows just beneath the roof ran the length of the building – too high to see in through, but providing plenty of natural light. The hall contained several indoor practice floors, the quartermaster had said, plus as many external grounds at the back.

Between archway and hall was a dirt yard, which appeared to be deserted. Ree took a deep breath and rested her hand on the hilt of her sword, drawing enough courage from it to step through the archway. The walk across to the door felt endless, but finally she reached the sheet of paper pinned to the door of the hall, and the sharpened stick of charcoal tied to a nail beside it, and used one to sign her name on the other. *Ree Quinn*. Not just in the general training section, but in the Helm assessment section as well. She let the charcoal fall, and took a deep breath. *There. Done it.*

'You here for the training?'

So she wasn't the only one who'd turned up on the very first day. Tensing automatically, Ree turned to find a young man standing behind her. Maybe a few years older than her, curly hair, skin a darker shade of brown than her own, cheekbones to die for. Even in her current state of prickle, she noticed the cheekbones. She scanned his face for mockery, but found only a friendly grin. All the same, she couldn't help the defensive note in her reply. 'I just signed up for the Helm assessment programme.'

His smile didn't change, but his eyebrows lifted. 'Setting yourself a bit of a challenge, aren't you?'

'Why?' Ree snapped, a bit of that protective anger she'd summoned finally spilling out. 'Because women can't be Helmsmen?'

'I'm not saying they can't. I'm saying they aren't. There's a difference.'

'And that would be ...?'

'One's a judgement, the other merely an observation. And if there's one thing you need to know about me, it's that I never make judgements about anything. Far too much effort.' He stuck his hand out, his smile growing even warmer, and added, 'I'm Zander. I'll be joining you for the assessment.'

Ree took his hand. Her smile answered his of its own volition; he was clearly a practised flirt. But it was going to take more than a curly-haired boy with amazing cheekbones to distract her from her course.

'If you don't like making an effort, I'm surprised you want to be considered for the Helm,' she retorted. 'It's not exactly an easy life.'

'Physical work, I can handle,' Zander said. 'It's my brain that's lazy. Though not so lazy that I didn't notice you failing to tell me your name.'

'Ree.' *Elements*. He'd won her over, and she wasn't even sure how. Still, she reminded herself belatedly, no point being too antagonistic. She'd never get anywhere if her potential future colleagues decided to close ranks against her.

'Ree,' Zander repeated. He peered at her name on the sign-up sheet. 'Short for ...?'

'Just Ree.' She certainly wasn't going to share *that* secret with him. Hastily she dug up a question from her mother's endless lessons in polite conversation. 'So where are you from?'

He finished signing his name beneath hers and turned, eyebrows raised. 'Why? Because someone with my colouring must be foreign?'

'No, I –' She was already blushing and stammering when she noticed the way his eyes were creasing at the corners … and realised how exactly he'd mimicked her earlier defensive tone. Curse him. For a man who claimed to have a lazy mind, he was pretty sharp.

'I meant where in Mirrorvale,' she protested.

'I know.' The smile that had temporarily retreated to lurk in his eyes returned to his face. 'And my family is from Sol Kardis, originally, as you probably guessed from the way I look. But I was born and grew up in Cardrey.'

Ree relaxed. 'That's not far from my village. Torrance Mill, you know it? I must have visited Cardrey nearly every week when I was a child.'

'What are the chances?' Zander's expression stayed as friendly as before, but she detected a shade of constraint in it. His gaze flicked over her shoulder, then returned to her face. 'Looks like some more victims are heading this way.'

He walked off to greet the new arrivals, but Ree stood lost in thought. *Huh. So he doesn't want to talk about his home town.* Well, everyone had secrets – that was pretty much what made people human. All the same, it was odd.

She turned. Four or five more young men had entered the yard, and Zander was busy charming them in exactly the same way he'd charmed her – with that air of insouciance and a smile that assured his audience how pleased he was to meet them. He didn't just flirt with women, then. For some reason that made her feel better about succumbing to it. She wandered over to join them, arriving in time to catch the tail end of the introductions.

'And this is Ree,' Zander said without a pause, as though he'd planned to include her all along. 'Another masochist for the Helm assessment programme.'

That inspired a few curious glances from the new arrivals. One of them, a short stocky lad, frowned at her and began, 'But she's –'

'A woman. Yes.' Zander clapped him on the back. 'With powers of observation like that, Farleigh, you'll be joining the Helm in no time.'

The others laughed; the one called Farleigh gave him a mock scowl. Unsure whether to be amused or irritated – she was, after all, perfectly capable of standing up for herself – Ree said nothing. *You may not like making an effort, Zander, but you're bloody clever. If only I knew whether you're really as pleasant as you seem.*

She stayed mostly quiet as the boys got to know each other through a mixture of bravado and banter, but her attention kept being drawn back to Zander. He was somehow … more detailed than the others. Like a full oil portrait, when the people around him were mere sketches. Most of the other boys were indistinguishable to her, even after a half-bell spent in their company, but she'd never be able to mistake Zander for anyone other than Zander. Which wasn't to say she was attracted to him, or even that she liked him. She didn't know *what* she thought of him. But one thing was for sure: she envied his ability to make so much impact on the world, simply by virtue of being in it.

Time passed, a few more boys showed up, and after a while the chiming of bells from up in the sixth ring – *Third bell!*

No wonder I'm famished – galvanised them into going in search of food. That was how they ended up in the mess hall, eating something beige that tasted far better than it looked.

'You wait till we get near the end of training,' Farleigh said. 'The food won't even taste good by then. The cooks run out of money and interest after a while.'

Farleigh, apparently, was an expert on the fifth ring and everything therein. An expert on the whole city, in fact. Unlike many of the new recruits, he'd grown up in Arkannen, so he knew his way around. Ree found it a little intimidating to be in the company of someone who knew so much more than she did, but she did her best to bluff her way through it. When he paused for breath, she asked him why he wanted to join the Helm, and he gave her a proud smile.

'It's in the family. I've known I'd be a Helmsman since I was a tiny lad.' The smile turned slightly condescending. 'What about you?'

'I want to be the best,' Ree said simply. 'And the Helm are the best.'

He nodded. 'True. Though just wanting isn't enough, is it?'

Lucky I have the talent to back it up, then, Ree was about to say – but again, Zander got in first.

'Ambition versus family tradition, huh? Wonder which will turn out to be the stronger force.'

Beneath the table, Ree's nails dug into her palms. She wasn't sure why she found his constant deflection of Farleigh's barbs so annoying. He was trying to be kind, after all, whereas Farleigh was clearly attempting to needle her. But perhaps it was because Farleigh's reaction was what she'd steeled herself to expect. She was used to throwaway quips and mocking remarks being aimed in her direction, and she'd learned how to handle it – whereas Zander's behaviour was another thing entirely. Somehow, it made her seem weak even as it tried to strengthen her.

'What about you, Zander?' she asked sweetly, seeking to turn the tables. 'What could possibly have made someone like *you* want to join the Helm?'

The slight, telling emphasis on the word *you* found its mark; Zander's forehead creased as if she'd stung him. Ree suppressed a smile. Maybe she had learned something from her mother after all – though it didn't take long for him to come back with an answer.

'Money. A Helmsman's pay is worth having. And I'm decent enough with a sword.'

Disdain settled on Farleigh's face. 'Is that it?'

'More or less.'

'But surely … you believe in protecting the Nightshade line, don't you?'

Zander shrugged. 'I make a point of not believing in anything too much.'

Farleigh glanced over at Ree, and for the first time the two of them were united in mutual opinion. Because the whole point of being in the Helm was to believe in something. The Mirrorvalese might not have gods, but they had Changers. And as far as the Helm were concerned, it came to the same thing.

'Well,' Farleigh said. 'All I can say, Zander, is that it's a good thing not all aspiring Helmsmen are like you.'

'Really?' Zander's voice remained light, but his gaze was intent as it moved between Farleigh's face and Ree's. 'Seems to me it's believing in things that causes a lot of the world's problems. Believing in something enough to die for it means believing enough to kill for it. And that's when you start putting principles above people.' One eyebrow twitched. 'Look at Captain Travers.'

Three years was plenty long enough for the story of Owen Travers – the man who had been Captain of the Helm until he sought to commit treason against the Nightshade line and was killed in a duel by the new captain – to have reached every corner of Mirrorvale and beyond. So Ree didn't question the point. All the same, she still thought Zander was wrong.

'But killing is part of what the Helm do,' she argued. 'If you're not willing to kill, then –'

'I didn't say I wouldn't kill. If I were a Helmsman, I'd do what it took to protect the Nightshade line – up to and including killing. But I wouldn't do it because I believe Changers are better than everyone else. I'd do it because it's my job.'

'So what makes you any different from a sellsword?' Ree asked. She meant it as a genuine question rather than an insult – mostly, anyway – but his brows drew together in anger, for an instant, before the frown was replaced by his usual cocky grin.

'I told you: I don't believe in anything. At least sellswords believe in money.'

After that, he turned the conversation to less serious things, and the rest of the afternoon passed in a haze of chatter. Yet late that night, lying awake in her unfamiliar bed, Ree found herself thinking about it again. She'd never before met anyone who didn't believe implicitly in the right of the Nightshade overlords to rule Mirrorvale. She thought Zander probably had a point when he talked about the dangers of being willing to die for something, but all the same … wasn't that the purpose of the Helm? How could he *do his job*, as he'd put it, if he didn't have a reason to lay down his life for the cause? If it came to that, wouldn't he just turn and run?

Belatedly she noticed that she was mulling over a philosophical point instead of fretting about the weeks to come, and smiled to herself. It had been a pretty good day, all things considered. Zander and Farleigh and the rest might have tested her, sometimes – just as they'd tested each other, feeling their way into this new social hierarchy – but they hadn't offered her any outright animosity. In fact, after spending a couple of bells with them, she'd felt surprisingly at home.

Burrowing down under the thin covers, she closed her eyes and let herself imagine good things ahead. The fifth ring wasn't so very daunting. Maybe she'd prove her parents wrong after all.

FOUR

To Captain Tomas Caraway of the Helm, Darkhaven, Arkannen, Mirrorvale:

Belated congratulations on your promotion. I gather you disposed of the previous incumbent quite neatly. And concomitant with that, congratulations on your current life of domestic bliss. Something of a change from your former existence, unless the tedium of it has driven you back to the consolation of an ale-cup.

A piece of information has come to my ears that I feel I should share with you, in fairness if not in love: Sol Kardis is preparing for war. It is readying itself for a new opportunity that will soon present itself. And my informant referred to cutting out Mirrorvale's heart as the only way to tip the balance. You may recall my inadvertent discovery of three years ago. Perhaps you might remind your employer/lover of the same.

While you have her attention, you might also let her know that I saw a certain child of our mutual acquaintance last month, and he is thriving nicely.

With admiration, if not respect,
Naeve Sorrow

Postscript: I intend to send this through a man who owes me a favour, to avoid prying eyes. Please do me the courtesy of not arresting him when he hands it over.

Caraway reached the end of the page and glanced back at the accompanying note, penned by a Helmsman whose bewilderment came through in every word. Apparently the letter had been delivered to a Helm safe house in the fourth ring by a wanted pickpocket and petty criminal. He hadn't explained exactly how it came to be in his possession, but it seemed highly unlikely that it had been viewed by officials on either the Kardise or the Mirrorvalese side of the border. The Helm had been all set to arrest him, but the man had claimed immunity by virtue of the fact that he had news of vital importance to deliver from Naeve Sorrow. Since everyone in the Helm knew that Naeve Sorrow had absconded from Mirrorvale three years ago with Ayla's newborn half-brother, the man on duty had immediately sent a runner up to Darkhaven with the letter.

And, as it turned out, with good reason.

Frowning, Caraway raised his head. Ayla was busy spreading honey on her biscuit and very carefully not looking at him, but curiosity radiated off her like the steam rising from her tea. He often received messages related to Helm business, of course, but not so often at the breakfast table.

He hesitated, not wanting to spoil their time together – it was rare enough that Marlon continued to slumber past first bell, giving them a little oasis of peace and quiet before the demands of the day began – but keeping the letter from her would serve no purpose other than to create an argument. So he handed her the single page in silence. Then, because he had far less self-control than she did, he watched unabashed as she scanned it, her dark brows drawing further together with every word.

'Fire and blood!' she snapped finally, slamming the letter down on the table top with enough force to make the crockery rattle. 'How she has the effrontery to –'

'To send us a well-timed warning?' Caraway finished for her. Ayla pinned him with a glare, which reluctantly softened in answer to his smile.

'Surely you don't intend to defend her,' she said, though with less heat. 'She is keeping my brother from me. He belongs here, Tomas.'

'I know. But think of it this way: she didn't have to write at all. Yet she chose to send word of this threat.'

Ayla lifted a shoulder. 'But Sol Kardis has been snapping at our borders for years. Skirmishes break out with depressing regularity. I see nothing new in that.'

'Look past the barbs,' Caraway said softly. 'She refers to her discovery. She refers to cutting out the heart of Mirrorvale. They intend to send an assassin for you, Ayla. And this time, they've found a weapon that can do the job.'

Her fingers curled inward on the table, crumpling Sorrow's letter. 'A pistol.'

Caraway nodded. For centuries, people had thought of Changers as indestructible. They were impervious to steel. They were far stronger than any man. And though in their human form they were more susceptible to damage, killing them in their sleep was the only sure-fire way to do it – because otherwise, even wounded, they could just Change to protect themselves. All that had been common knowledge right up until three years ago, when Naeve Sorrow had shot a Changer creature with the pistol she carried. Bruised it, only. But a bruise was more than anyone had achieved before.

Of course, that Changer creature had been Ayla's brother Myrren, who had later taken his own life with the very same pistol ... so all in all, Ayla had little enough reason to like the damn things.

Three years. It was long enough that Caraway had begun to think they were safe – that word of this unexpected Nightshade vulnerability hadn't reached the wrong ears, and never would. The original secret had been shared by a mere handful of people, none of whom had any motive for making it more widely known. Yet despite that, somehow, a rumour must have crept across the border to Sol Kardis.

The Kardise would have wanted to be sure. No doubt they had carried out tests, though of what kind he could barely imagine. No doubt they had taken the time to train their assassin and improve their technology until they knew, beyond certainty, that a single shot would kill the intended target. The pistol they were sending to *cut out Mirrorvale's heart* would be the best that three years of dedicated work could create. And what did he have to set against it?

Himself. The Helm. None of them were bulletproof, but they would have to be enough.

'We'll make some changes to security,' he said, taking refuge in practicality. 'Let no-one new into Darkhaven. An assassin with a pistol would still need to get close to you – he'd only have one shot, and he'd want to make sure it didn't go to waste – so if you're well-guarded at all times ...'

Ayla didn't reply. Her gaze stayed fixed on her white-knuckled hand; her head drooped. Looking at her, Caraway was seized by a surge of tenderness. She carried the weight of Mirrorvale so lightly, like a wreath of flowers crowning a springtime dancer. It was easy to forget how young she was, and how burdened.

'It will be all right, love.' He knelt beside her chair, drawing her hands down to interlock with his in her lap. 'They won't succeed. I promise.'

With a sigh, she lowered her head until her brow was resting against his. He felt her whisper brush his skin. 'I'm scared, Tomas.'

'I know. But I'm here, and the Helm –'

'The world is changing. You can't stand between me and every pistol-wielding assassin Sol Kardis sends our way.'

Caraway couldn't argue with the first part of that statement. The Helm had confiscated more firearms this past year than in every other year put together. But he could argue with the second part, and promptly did so.

'Of course I can. I'm your Captain of the Helm. If a single bullet reaches you without going through me first, I don't deserve to keep that title.'

Ayla shifted in her seat; her hands twisted out of his grasp, but only to slide up his arms and wind themselves into his hair. Her lips found his, urgent and demanding, and he marvelled – as he did every time, even after three years – at the strange quirk of fate or chance that had brought him here to her side. He would take a hundred bullets for the time they had already shared. He'd take a hundred more if it meant they could have it again.

'You need a haircut,' she murmured against his mouth.

'But if I cut it, love, you wouldn't be able to tug on it the way you do.'

'You make a good point, Captain Caraway.' And she pulled him closer to kiss him again.

He would have been quite happy to explore the situation further, responsibilities be damned, but at that point the door slammed back on its hinges and made them both jump.

'Papa! Papa!' Marlon came hurtling into the room. 'Look! A sword!'

Caraway glanced at Ayla, hoping that today would be the day she went to the boy of her own accord, but blankness had slammed down like a shutter across her face. He knew her retreat was intended to conceal a deep, personal hurt – maybe several. She still mourned Myrren's death. It couldn't be easy to have a living reminder of him in the form of her young nephew, especially when coupled with her longing for children of her own. But Marlon himself was too young to understand any of that. As far as he was concerned, Caraway and Ayla were his parents. And Ayla needed to close the distance between them soon, or she'd regret it later.

'I surrender!' Caraway pretended to cower away from the stick in the little boy's hand. Then he let Marlon chase him around the table, and catch him, and – after a short tussle – bear him to the ground. *I'm capting of the Helm, Papa, and you're the bad man. No!* – clambering up over Caraway's legs to sit squarely on his chest – *no 'scaping!* This went on for a while, until finally Caraway scooped the boy over his shoulder and got to his feet. Marlon's nursemaid, Lori, stood to one side with a smile on her face, and Ayla –

Ayla had gone.

'All right, son,' he said to Marlon – cheerfully, to hide his sudden disappointment. 'Time for me to get to work, I'm afraid.'

He dropped a kiss on the boy's tousled hair, then passed him back to the nurse. Their eyes met, but neither of them said anything – for which Caraway was grateful. He wasn't sure what there was to say. Ayla herself had made it very clear that she didn't want to talk about it, and without her participation, the conversation would just be words. It wouldn't change anything.

With a final farewell to Marlon and Lori, he left the room and set off towards the guardroom. Time to give the Helm their orders. They'd have to make sure Ayla was guarded at all times ... improve security at Darkhaven's gate and maybe the seven city gates, if the watch would cooperate ... keep from employing anyone new here at the tower until the threat was neutralised ... with every step, he came up with something else that either he'd have to do himself or the Helm would need to be told about. Yet through it all, his mind kept returning to Ayla.

Part of it was worrying about the assassination attempt, of course. There had been threats before, but never one of this magnitude. Mirrorvale and Sol Kardis had sat uneasily beside each other for as long as he could remember, so he'd always taken it as given that the Kardise would prefer the Nightshade line weak. That might even be why, misdirected obsession aside, Florentyn Nightshade and Owen Travers had been so concerned with keeping it strong. But it was only in the last three years that anyone had realised it was possible to hurt a Changer creature. And it was only this morning that the threat had become specific and tangible enough to move from a possibility to an outright concern.

Yet that wasn't the only thing he worried about. As he often did in moments of stress, he found himself fretting about Ayla and Marlon. About Ayla and *himself*. About the awkward balancing act he found himself having to undertake, as both Captain of the Helm and Ayla's lover.

When she'd asked him to stay with her in Darkhaven, three years ago, it hadn't been with the stated intent of making him Captain of the Helm. In fact, she'd told him she didn't want to employ him at all. But the position had been vacant, and Ayla in need of a strong Helm to support her through those difficult early days, so Caraway had fallen into taking charge for a little while. Just until everything had settled down. But that little while had lengthened until, one day, he'd realised that six months had passed and the entire Helm was deferring to him without question.

You'd better appoint a new captain soon, he'd told Ayla. *The Helm are getting too used to me.*

She'd given him a look. *Or you could just keep doing a job you do very well.*

But, Ayla … there's us. You and me. I don't want them thinking I was appointed because of what's between us.

It wouldn't be any different from what you do now, she'd pointed out. *They respect you, Tomas. Being given an official title isn't going to change that.*

She'd been right, of course. The Helm didn't seem to care that their captain and their overlord were intimately involved – or at least, their interest lay solely in having something to make ribald remarks about. The only person who worried about it was Caraway himself. And so, after a while, he stopped.

Mostly.

Because it wasn't as if he'd leave Darkhaven, no matter what happened between himself and Ayla – not unless she ordered him out, anyway. He was dedicated to her and to Marlon for life, in whatever capacity she saw fit. But Ayla's own feelings on the matter were far more difficult to determine. Three years ago, she had come through fear and loss to unexpected freedom – a freedom into which she'd thrown herself wholeheartedly. She'd chosen Caraway before she even knew what other choices there were to make. And so, though he knew she cared about him, he couldn't help but wonder if some part of her regretted that haste – especially since the children she'd referred to so glibly back then had yet to arrive, and not through lack of trying. Children and a new future, she'd said; but if the children never came, would she choose a different future as well? One that didn't include him?

We're young, he told himself, as he often did. *There's plenty of time.* And yet he understood her urgency. The Nightshade line had dwindled to a slender thread, a single surviving Changer. If Ayla were to die – he flinched at the thought, but made himself keep on thinking it – if she were to die before any children were old enough to manifest the gift, Mirrorvale would be left vulnerable to the larger countries pressing at its borders. That was why the Kardise had seized the opportunity to make an attempt on her life. That – quite aside from Caraway's own love for her – was why it was so important that the attempt fail.

Of course, even if Ayla were to conceive a child now, close to fifteen years would have to pass before that child could hope to Change. And there were already Nightshade children in the world who would reach their majority sooner: Marlon, for one, and Ayla's missing half-brother Corus. Caraway had tried to point that out before, but Ayla would have none of it.

I don't know what will happen, she'd said. *None of them are full-blooded Nightshades. Corus and Marlon are half each. Our children would be only a quarter. You know that's what I wanted, but all the same, the chances of them being able to Change must surely be decreased. And if none of them can …* She'd shaken her head, turning that thought aside. *The more children we have, the more likely we are to preserve the gift for the next generation.*

As a result, Caraway couldn't help but wonder if she saw their relationship as a bargain he had failed to fulfil. She didn't behave that way – she showed him a passion and delight that surely wouldn't be present in a purely contractual union – and yet …

And yet, he worried.

Do you ever regret it? he'd asked her once, as they lay curled together in the big bed with moonlight streaming through the window. *That you asked me to stay?*

She'd burrowed her head sleepily against the hollow of his throat. *Do you?*

Of course not, he'd answered straight away, and she'd laughed a little.

Well, then.

Then she'd nipped at his skin, a teasing bite, and he'd been too distracted to talk any more. It was only afterwards it occurred to him that she hadn't actually answered the question.

Still, there was no point in thinking about any of that now. It was far more important to focus on preventing her assassination. And ideally he'd enlist help from someone both knowledgeable and reliable – which meant that *ideally*, he'd go down into the fifth ring and speak to Art Bryan. Yet as well as being Caraway's old mentor, Bryan was also the weaponmaster in charge of training, which meant this was one of his busiest times of year. The sign-up sheets for the next training period had been posted a couple of days ago, which meant Bryan would be spending all his time herding youths into the appropriate places.

And one of them could conceivably be an assassin. The thought came straight from the depths of Caraway's own paranoia, but even as he considered it, he couldn't find a way to discount it completely. There were more direct routes to Ayla, of course; but unlike any hiring of staff in Darkhaven itself, which happened as and when it was needed, the twice-yearly intake of new recruits into the fifth ring was as reliable as clockwork. He ought to know: he'd set it up that way himself. And since it became harder to access the rings of Arkannen the higher you climbed, an assassin might seize the chance to secure a place in the fifth with an eye to reaching Ayla later on.

Particularly since it was now common knowledge that after seven weeks, Caraway took those of the recruits he'd selected for further training up to the tower to meet her ...

In the past, youngsters had turned up at the fifth ring whenever they saw fit. The weaponmasters and their assistants would assess them, agreeing to train them if they showed the basic aptitude necessary to become warriors. Only after a year could they formally express their desire to join the Helm – at which point the Captain of the Helm would step in, carry out his own tests and select those he deemed worthy of his attention for further training.

Caraway had changed all that. He wanted a Helm full of lads who could think for themselves, as well as being skilled warriors able to follow orders. And the only way to learn what aspiring Helmsmen were really like was to be involved right from the start – before they'd all been buffed into uniformity by a year of rigorous discipline and drummed-in obedience. But of course, the Captain of the Helm didn't have time to run down to the fifth ring every time a new recruit showed up. So he'd approached Bryan with a fresh proposal: a twice-yearly intake of youngsters, including an initial seven-week period during which the weaponmasters and the Captain of the Helm would work together to assess those who were interested in joining the Helm. That way, the successful students' training could be steered in the right direction from the very start – and they'd be much more likely to be accepted into the Helm once their training period was over.

To Caraway's relief, Bryan had welcomed the idea. He hadn't been sure how Bryan would react; after all, Caraway had been Bryan's student and then his most notorious failure, yet here he was, approaching the weaponmaster as an equal. *So you're calling yourself Captain of the Helm, now, boyo?* he'd imagined Bryan saying. *Wasn't so long ago you'd do just about anything for a cup of ale.* But of course, it hadn't been that way at all. Bryan was both an honourable man and a practical one – and it had never been easy for the weaponmasters to train so many different youths, all arriving at different times of the year with different backgrounds and skill sets. So in the event, his response to Caraway's rather tentative approach had been a brisk nod.

Seems sensible to me, lad. There'll be a bit of awkwardness to start with, 'fore it comes widely known that we only test twice a year. But after all, the young 'uns can still show up whenever they like – even do some preliminary training. They just won't be assessed until the time comes.

And you don't mind me being involved in the testing? Caraway had asked shyly. Bryan shot him one of his penetrating looks – the kind that made new recruits quiver – but all he did was shrug.

No skin off my nose, boyo. It's your Helm.

Which was really all Caraway had needed to hear, because it meant that Bryan accepted him as more than just an ex-alcoholic who'd fallen on his feet. Since then, they'd worked together on several new intakes of recruits, and they'd become ... perhaps *friends* was too strong a word, but on the other hand, perhaps it wasn't. Bryan never hesitated to tell him when he was being stupid, but since he treated everyone the same way, that was hardly an indication of anything. He'd certainly helped Caraway get to grips with a lot of things. How to handle the sudden transition from disgrace to triumph. How to make his mark on the Helm. How to be the person who, after what he'd done to protect Ayla three years ago, everyone seemed to think he was.

On a few dark nights, when it had all become too much for him and *the consolation of an ale-cup* had showed an increasingly tempting face, Bryan was the one who'd talked him back to sanity.

So he wouldn't hesitate to call Bryan his friend, though he didn't know what Bryan himself would think of it. But since Bryan was the only one who hadn't actively sought to hinder him, three years ago, it had been easy to form that bond with him – far easier than the bonds he was still forming with most of the Helmsmen under his command. In some ways, the Helm had accepted him more readily than he had accepted them. He'd often needed to remind himself, early on, that their previous captain had moulded them into something that would take a considerable amount of work to undo. And though they were getting there, it wasn't over yet.

They still called him Breakblade, sometimes, but now it was a mark of respect. Strange, that. He hadn't thought he'd ever hear it without flinching, but it turned out a name was only as hurtful as the intent behind it.

Descending the final flight of steps, Caraway made a conscious effort to push his introspection aside. His convoluted thoughts had brought him as far as the guardroom, but now he needed to focus. The assassination attempt that

Sorrow had referred to was unlikely to happen on the same day he'd received her letter – it could be weeks, even months, before he needed to be fully ready – but he had a lot to get done. He'd talk to the Helm first, set them to improving security in Darkhaven. And in a few days, once the rush of new recruits had died down, he'd talk to Bryan about the possibility of an assassin in the fifth ring.

FIVE

Penn had been in the fifth ring for less than a bell, yet already he despised everyone he had met there.

Of course – and he was perfectly happy to admit it – he had been predisposed to feel that way. Nevertheless, his fellow trainees were pretty vapid, even according to his low expectations. In a way it made his task easier, but it wouldn't be conducive to a very enjoyable few weeks.

More than a few weeks, he reminded himself. *Seven at the very least, and far more likely a year. This is a long-term job.*

The thought was depressing. He didn't want to be around these people for a year. Admittedly they wouldn't all be there for that long, but since he didn't like any of them, it hardly mattered which of them were accepted for Helm training alongside him.

You're assuming an awful lot, he told himself with mordant humour. But really, he had no choice. Although he'd been unable to make a detailed plan before he arrived in Arkannen, owing to lack of information, he was fairly certain that being accepted for Helm training would be a key component of it. As such, he *had* to be accepted. His father wouldn't countenance failure.

He'd deliberately timed his arrival in the fifth ring to fall near the end of the sign-up period; better to go straight into the training than to hang around for a week second-guessing himself. Yet as a result, most of the other recruits who'd signed up for Helm assessment had been there a few days longer than he had, which meant they already knew each other a little. Enough to make him feel like the outsider, at any rate. But then, perhaps it was inevitable he'd feel like that, given his opinion of them and what he planned to do.

He sat in a corner of the mess hall and watched the faces around him. Quite a variety of faces, in every colour of skin and hair and eyes he could think of. Penn wasn't used to that. The village he came from was in northern Mirrorvale: pretty much as far from the borders with other inhabited countries as you could get, and too small to be worth a visit from outsiders. As a result, everyone there looked sort of like him, blue-eyed and fair-haired and light-skinned. He'd never even noticed that homogeneity until he came to Arkannen. And everyone was so loud, talking over each other and over the continuous background roar of the city. In the fifth ring that roar might be muted to a murmur, but it was still audible.

They'd told him their names, when he first arrived. All in a jumble, too fast to take in, let alone remember. First names only, as if he and they were already friends. And then they'd asked him his.

Penn Avens, he'd said stiffly – trying to get used to the name, trying to get used to *them*. He hadn't said anything else, and they'd left him alone after that. One thing to be thankful for, at least. He didn't think he could have coped with a whole afternoon of forced small talk; far better to sit here in silence – watching the people, listening to the noise – and try desperately to come up with a way of living with all this for a whole year.

Currently the boys nearest him were discussing a venture down into the lower rings of the city, though the destination was unclear. For a group of people who were meant to be future Helmsmen, they lacked both decision and efficiency. The one called Farleigh kept pontificating about how his family had been in Arkannen for twelve generations, which apparently made him some kind of city royalty second only to the Nightshade overlords. He enumerated every single attraction to be found between the fifth ring and the Gate of Birth, whilst Penn stared at the floor and let the words wash over him. If only he could perform his task now and let that be the end of it.

Though, of course, he wasn't capable of performing his task. Not yet. That was the point.

'… You coming, Avens?' The voice held an edge of impatience, but then, it had taken him longer than it should have to identify the surname as his own. His mother's name, from before she was married. It was as good a name to go by as any.

'Coming where?' he muttered, glancing up.

'To sample all the delights Arkannen has to offer, of course.' It was that Zander boy, the one who acted like he owned the world. Penn didn't even know his second name, which was irritating, because it meant he couldn't call Zander by it in the same lofty tone that Zander had used on him.

'I suppose so.' He had no desire to spend more time than he had to in Zander's company – in any of their company. But to achieve his purpose here in Arkannen, he was going to need information. And he wouldn't find that lying around in the lonely emptiness of his barracks.

Besides, part of him wanted to know what it was about the city his cousin had loved so much. Loved enough to die for.

'And you, Ree?' Zander asked, addressing the sole female of the group. Penn hadn't expected a girl, not in the Helm assessment programme, but there she was. 'Last chance before training starts. Fancy a night of wine and whoring?'

Ree folded her arms, stern-faced. She had an interesting face. Not pretty, exactly – or at least, it was hard to tell under the boys' clothes and the short mousy hair – but her amber skin and almost feline yellow-green eyes made her striking enough. It was a shame the effect was marred by her tendency to frown. 'I don't think so.'

'I meant it metaphorically,' Zander said with a grin. 'The second part, at any rate.'

Ree's lips twitched, but she shook her head. 'I'd rather get a good night's sleep. That way I'll run rings round you lot on the practice ground tomorrow.'

'So what you're saying is, you need us all hungover to stand a chance of beating us.'

'What I'm saying is, commitment to the training is more important to me than wasting a night on alcohol. And that's how I *know* I'll beat you.'

Ugh. Penn wasn't sure which of them he found more annoying. All that half-meant banter only made him more certain they'd end up sleeping together, like every other love–hate pairing in history. He waited in the background as Zander and Farleigh and a couple of the others said goodnight to Ree. Then he trailed after them as they headed towards the Gate of Steel and out of the fifth ring, listening with less than half an ear to Farleigh's endless boastful facts about everything they passed.

They wound up in an inn, of course. Barely a glance at any of the interesting things that could be found between the fifth ring and the first: the airships and the factories and the beautiful striped streets of the fourth ring. Penn had taken the chance to explore earlier that day, before he signed up for the assessment programme, and so he didn't feel he was missing out; all the same, his estimation of Zander and his cronies went down another notch.

The inn was called the Unicorn, and it was crowded and unpleasant. After he'd finally extracted a pitcher of ale from the overworked bartender, Penn turned and – with some reluctance – looked for the others. Zander was easiest to pick out from the crowd: he'd found a girl to talk to. Someone like Zander always found a girl to talk to. *Forgotten Ree already?* Penn wanted to ask. But he had to admit, this one was pretty spectacular: a tall, slender girl with skin like smooth honey and hair the dark scarlet of Parovian wine. Despite himself, he drifted closer.

'… initial assessment period lasts seven weeks,' Zander was saying. 'Then they decide which of us they think have the potential to become Helmsmen.'

'It all sounds very exciting.' The girl's voice was high and breathless. She even managed an eyelash flutter. Penn wondered briefly if he was doomed to be surrounded by stereotypes.

'What about you, Saydi?' Zander asked her. 'What brings a rare beauty like yourself to a dump like this?'

Rare beauty. Does anyone really talk like that? But Saydi was smiling and blushing and toying with her hair as if she'd never heard such a profound compliment.

'Oh … I'm looking for a job.'

'As a barmaid?' Penn put in drily. Both Zander and Saydi turned to look at him, and for a moment their expressions were alike in annoyance. Though not alike; Zander just looked petulant, whereas narrow eyes and tight lips gave Saydi's face a spark of intelligence. Then it was gone, and her voice prattled on with the same hint of a giggle as before.

'I was up at the tower earlier. Darkhaven. I thought I might get a job as a servant there. But they were turning people away at the gate. Some kind of security threat, they said.'

What? But – Penn reined himself back before he could even finish the thought, because it wasn't possible that a Darkhaven on full alert could have anything to do with him. Still, it wasn't good news. Not that his plans were all that specific, as yet. He just didn't want anything to limit his options.

Saydi was looking at him again, a slight frown between her perfect brows. He wondered what kind of expression had crossed his face, that it had actually shifted her attention away from herself. Or, no, *attention* was probably the issue: he wasn't responding to her with flattery and obvious intent. Her interest in him was no more than a distorted reflection of his lack of interest in her. All the same, he sought for a distraction.

'You should try getting a job in the Helm. I hear the pay is good.'

She stared dumbly at him. 'Women can do that?'

'Apparently,' Penn said. 'At least, we already have one signed up for the assessment programme.' Then, with a certain amount of malice, 'Isn't that right, Zander? You seemed very friendly with her earlier.'

The look Zander gave him said more clearly than words, *Back off – you're not going to win this one.* Still, he nodded and smiled at Saydi.

'If Ree can do it, I'm sure you can. Have you had much weapons training?'

The hint of giggle in Saydi's voice became an outright reality. 'Wouldn't you like to know?'

Ice and shattered steel. Foreseeing the approaching descent into increasingly cringeworthy innuendo, Penn retreated to the bar for another drink. It wasn't as if he even wanted to win that particular contest. He had enough complications in his life without adding an empty-headed female to the mix.

You make sure you get this right, boy, his father had said to him just before Penn left for Arkannen. *You're doing this for family, remember.*

For family, Penn had echoed. *I won't fail you, Papa. I promise.*

Yet already, it was clear that keeping his word wasn't going to be as simple as he'd expected.

When his fellow trainees decided to move on – not to anywhere interesting, of course, only to a different inn – he excused himself on the grounds of tiredness. He stood outside the Unicorn, watching them whoop and stagger down the street, Saydi's red hair distinctive among the dark and brown and yellow heads of the boys. Sudden homesickness clutched at him, then: a desire for familiarity and comfort. A desire to be back in a place where he didn't have a difficult task to perform or a load of strangers to navigate, just the minor dull chores of everyday.

But of course that was stupid. He'd known since he was fifteen what he'd have to do, when he was old enough. It was three years since being at home had been the peaceful idyll he was imagining now; for three long years he'd had his father's bitterness in his ear. At least once he'd done his job he'd be free of that.

The quickest route back to the fifth ring was to his left. He turned away from it, and went in search of a shrine.

It was one of the few useful pieces of information that Farleigh had provided on the way down here, amongst the boasting and the bluster. The trainees of the fifth ring weren't meant to visit the great temples of the sixth ring uninvited, but if they wanted to give thanks or make a supplication, there were plenty of small shrines in the lower rings. *Usually near something related*, Farleigh had said. *Like the shrines to Flame and Steel by the smithy. Makes it convenient for the workers.*

Though Penn's family always made sure to follow the seasonal observances, they had no particular devotion to one element; yet Penn himself had always been drawn to Air. *You'd be better off choosing Steel*, his father had told him. *It's what you'll need in the end. No man ever defeated his enemies with a breeze.* But though Penn had nodded and agreed, he'd kept up his own small, private relationship with the lightest of the elements. It brought him luck – or if it didn't, it brought him the idea of luck, and that was just as good. Maybe if he found a shrine and took a moment to centre himself, it would be easier to get through the days ahead.

Yet to start with, he wasn't sure where he should be looking. Perhaps he'd have to retrace his steps after all, go up to the third ring – because there were bound to be shrines to air and wind at the airship stations, to let travellers request swift journeys. But then he reached the top of some steps and saw sails on a nearby roof. They belonged to the screw pumps that drew water from the river to flush through the sewers, driven by a combination of wind power and manual labour. No doubt the workers often made dedications to Air, hoping for a good wind that would make their task easier.

Reaching the pumping station through the maze of streets wasn't as easy as it had looked, but finally Penn arrived outside it. Sure enough, there was a shrine a little way down from the workers' entrance: a simple recess in the wall, like a doorway leading nowhere, with a cushion on the floor and a light curtain to draw between the supplicant and the street. The walls were decorated with fragments of coloured glass, and at the back of the shrine was a smaller alcove that held nothing more than a mirror attached to the wall. Air meditations tended to concentrate on the regulation of breathing rather than any external aids.

Entering the shrine, Penn closed the curtain behind him. Then he knelt down and tried to focus. *This is the most important task you'll ever complete. Your family is relying on you. Just suffer these stupid people for as long as it takes.* Yet other thoughts kept creeping in, despite how he tried to banish them. *It's going to be hard. You'll probably fail.* And worst of all, *Are you sure it's the right thing to do?*

After a while, the last question began to drown out all the others – *Great, now even Air has deserted me* – and so with a muttered curse he left the shrine again. He found a man waiting outside: rather scruffily dressed in a sort of patched-up robe, unshaven, and with a blue smear of dye in the centre of his forehead.

'Sorry,' Penn mumbled. 'Did you want to –?'

The stranger smiled at him. 'Don't worry. I'm only 'ere to tend the shrine.'

'That's a job?' *Oh, come on, Penn, you could at least try and restrict your rudeness to people who deserve it.* 'I mean … I didn't realise anyone tended them.'

'Keeps 'em nice. I don't get paid for it, of course, but I earn enough of a livin' in stories and advice.' He grinned.

'For the weighty matters, ask a sixth-ring priestess, but if you've a small question or just want to hear a fable, the priests of the lower rings are 'appy to oblige.'

'Oh.' Penn wasn't sure what else to say. He nodded and made as if to depart, but the self-styled priest stopped him.

'So? You want some advice? If you don't mind me sayin' so, you seem like a lad with somethin' on his mind.'

'No, I ... no. Thank you.' What would it be like, to unburden himself to this stranger? Penn found the very prospect of it terrifying. Not so much the part where he revealed his purpose in coming to Arkannen – that could only be a relief, given how it burned inside him – but the possibility that he might be talked out of it as a result. With another nod, he turned and hurried away.

'Then 'ere's somethin' for you free of charge!' the man called after him. 'Which is crueller, wind or steel?'

That was close enough to Penn's earlier thoughts to give him pause. He pivoted slowly on his heel, and the priest raised his eyebrows.

'Ah, that caught you, didn't it? And no doubt you'd say steel.' He barely waited for Penn's confused nod before shaking his head. 'But you'd be wrong. Cold steel cuts with intent, for the sake of justice. But a cold wind cuts innocent and guilty alike, because it doesn't know how to differentiate between them.'

Ice and shattered steel – but his usual oath was too apposite to be comfortable. Not knowing how to respond, Penn turned back around and kept walking, ignoring the man's calls: *That spoke to you, boy, didn't it? That spoke to you! If you want more advice, you know where to find me.*

It was just a coincidence, he told himself as he hopped on the tram that would take him round to the Gate of Flame.

The sort of general platitude that the priest might offer to anyone. Yet the words buzzed at the insides of his ears, like bees trapped in his head, all the way back to the fifth ring.

It was only when he reached the barracks that he realised his entire coin-purse was missing, and by that time he was too despondent to care.

SIX

Miles was still asleep when Bryan got up. Nothing out of the ordinary there: it was barely light outside, and an academic's schedule was very different from that of a fifth-ring weaponmaster. Bryan tried to move quietly, but it was one thing for a man of his size to be light on his feet in the wide-open space of a duelling ground, and quite another to creep about in a warp-floored bedroom barely big enough to contain a closet as well as a bed.

'You are doing that on purpose,' Miles mumbled without opening his eyes, the third time a particularly loud creak cut through the early-morning hush – which, for Arkannen, meant a background hum as opposed to the midday roar. Bryan rocked from foot to foot, eliciting another groan from the protesting floorboard, and grinned.

'It wouldn't be disturbing if you were already up, Milo.'

'Some of us live life at a more civilised pace.' Miles kept his eyes closed, but now a smile touched his face too. The faint twang of his accent still lingered, even after several years at the city university. It was what had first attracted Bryan to him – that voice, across a crowded street, even before he saw the face behind it.

'True, if by civilised you mean lazy.' Bryan turned to fetch a belt from the drawer, only to be hit squarely in the head with a cushion. He spun back round, but Miles didn't appear to have moved from his previous position. Bryan's return throw sent the cushion sailing over Miles's head to hit the wall on the far side of the bed.

'Lazy or not, I am a better shot than you,' Miles murmured.

'You just keep thinking that.' Bryan crossed to the bed and brushed a kiss across Miles's lips. 'See you tonight.'

He popped into their tiny galley kitchen to grab a sweet roll, before letting himself out of the apartment and beginning the short walk from the Ametrine Quarter to the fifth ring. Miles would get up around second bell and eat a leisurely breakfast before strolling down to the university. By the time he started his teaching day, Bryan would have been out on the practice ground long enough to need a break. And by the time Bryan arrived home, aching and weary, his throat sore from the constant volume he needed to penetrate the cotton-stuffed ears of whichever youths he'd been training, Miles would have been back for at least a half-bell.

Of course, that also meant there'd be a meal ready on the table – and it seemed alchemy worked in the kitchen as well as in the laboratory, because the meals more than made up for the disparity in their working days. In fact, on the odd occasion when Miles became so caught up in his research that he only stumbled back in the pre-dawn chill of the following day, Bryan found himself staring into his larder with the vague helplessness of a stranger in a new city. Apparently a lifetime of fending for himself meant nothing compared to the eighteen months or so that he and Miles had been living together. In fact, recently, when Miles had left Arkannen for a week – as he did on a semi-regular basis, to visit his family back in Parovia – Bryan had lived almost entirely on street vendors' fare. Not, of course, that he'd ever tell Miles that.

He passed through the Gate of Steel with a hand lifted in greeting to the watchmen, and headed for the training hall. The sign-up sheet was due to come down this morning, which meant he and the other weaponmasters would spend the rest of the day sorting out groups, schedules and rotas. Exactly the kind of day he detested, but it was necessary for the smooth running of the fifth ring. Bryan suspected that none of the young people who grew up with a romantic dream of being trained by the legendary weaponmasters of Arkannen's fifth ring realised quite how much tedious paperwork was involved behind the scenes. And the other weaponmasters had it worse than he did. At least he got to work with Captain Caraway and the recruits who wanted to join the Helm, which meant that if any of them weren't up to standard he could simply send them off to basic training. The rest of the weaponmasters would have to deal with a far wider spectrum of trainee: from those who were already skilled and simply sought the prestige that fifth-ring training would confer, to the usual contingent of youngsters from wealthy families who were determined to buy what nature hadn't seen fit to give them.

Admittedly, the latter group wouldn't get very far. Everyone who came to the fifth ring went through a testing process, and only those who had the aptitude for it were allowed to stay. That was how the fifth ring both paid for itself and maintained its reputation. Every warrior who trained there, whether he became a Helmsman or a sellsword or a bodyguard, sacrificed a proportion of his wage to the weaponmasters in return for his past training. And that was why the weaponmasters admitted only those they thought would be able to pay their debt.

The list on the door of the training hall was full, which was good, but Bryan spared it no more than a brief glance. He had a few outstanding tasks of his own, and with the rest of his day already spoken for, this was the sole opportunity he'd have to complete them. Yet when he stepped into his small office just inside the hall, he found Tomas Caraway waiting for him. The grave expression on the lad's face told Bryan without the need for further words that his unfinished tasks were going to remain that way, but he offered a cheerful greeting all the same.

'Morning, Caraway. You ready for tomorrow?'

The captain gave him a distracted nod. 'But I need to talk to you. Is now a good time?'

'No worse than most,' Bryan said drily.

'I thought, since the sign-up period is over ...'

'Paperwork, boyo. Mountains of bloody paperwork. But I'm not so enamoured of it that it can't wait.'

'The truth is, I need your help,' Caraway said. 'There's been a threat made against Ayla's life, and I don't trust myself to think of everything.'

No wonder he was worried. An assassination threat was serious business – assuming it was genuine. 'Reliable source?'

Caraway contrived to look both embarrassed and defiant. 'Naeve Sorrow sent me a letter.'

'What, *the* Naeve Sorrow? Darkhaven's most wanted?' Bryan snorted. 'I wouldn't set much store by anything she has to say.'

'I don't have any reason to doubt her information,' Caraway said. 'And I've been implementing all the security measures I can think of, but ...' He hesitated, then asked rather diffidently, 'Can you grill me? Only I'm sure I've forgotten something.'

Bryan looked at him and wondered, as he did from time to time, why the lad had so little sense of his own worth. It would be a different matter if he had no skill in weaponry, but he'd killed Owen Travers – a highly competent swordsman at the peak of his game – with only a broken blade and his own two hands. And that was after years of dulling his wits with alcohol. Since then he'd got back into a proper training regime, and Bryan would be surprised if his better existed anywhere in Arkannen. Bryan himself could stand up against him on the duelling floor, but only because his superior size and weight made up for his relative age and lack of agility.

And yet, even now, Caraway lacked confidence in his own judgement. Bryan would have thought that fulfilling a Helmsman's duty against overwhelming odds, three years ago, was enough to bolster it – particularly since he'd then been unofficially elected as Captain of the Helm by the very men who had previously denigrated him. He performed the role with a quiet proficiency that made him both respected and liked. Yet still, always, he was unsure of himself.

It was the same when it came to Ayla Nightshade. On the few occasions that Bryan had seen her with Caraway, it had been pretty damn clear that she loved him – so why Caraway didn't take the necessary steps to formalise their relationship into marriage was a mystery. Of course, there was her bloodline to contend with; Bryan had always viewed Nightshades as a force of nature, to be deferred to rather than reasoned with. But for all her status and her unpredictable power, Ayla's feelings for Caraway had remained constant for three years. And yet he didn't think he was good enough for her.

Really, the question was whether the lad would ever prove himself to his own satisfaction. He'd grown used to fighting the world's opinions; yet now, the only opinion he was struggling against was his own.

'All right,' Bryan said. 'Tell me what you've done.'

'We were due to hire a few servants, a second nurse for Marlon, and some temporary workers to carry out repairs on the tower – but that's all cancelled now. No-one new will be allowed into Darkhaven until this is over.'

'So you've closed the gates,' Bryan said. 'What else?'

'The Helm are on double patrol. Ayla is guarded at all times. It means she can't go flying, which she isn't very happy about –' a rueful smile – 'but she understands.'

'Good. What else?'

'I suppose the next step is to consider it from the assassin's point of view. He comes to Darkhaven, thinking to enter by deception or by stealth, but there's no way in. So what does he do?'

'I'm asking the questions,' Bryan reminded him. 'You tell me.'

Caraway shook his head helplessly. 'I don't know. Finds another way in somehow. Finds a hole. But if I knew what it was, I'd already have filled it. How can I guard against something I can't predict?'

They were silent for a time. Then Bryan sighed.

'Thing is,' he said, 'assassins are wily bastards. Stands to reason you need another wily bastard to catch one. And let's be honest, Breakblade –' he gave Caraway a knowing look – 'neither of us are that. I'm just an old soldier, and you, Captain, are almost painfully straightforward. Beats me how you've survived as long as you have.'

Caraway looked as if he wanted to object to that, but after a moment he admitted, 'I've written back to Sorrow, requesting her aid.'

'Really?' That did surprise Bryan, and he didn't mind showing it. Caraway raised his eyebrows, feigning surprise at Bryan's surprise.

'You wanted wily. She's about as wily as they get.'

Bryan regarded him doubtfully. 'You sure this isn't her way of messing with you, boyo? Delayed revenge?'

Caraway's glance was swift but stricken. He hadn't thought of that at all. *Straightforward*. Bryan suppressed a sigh.

'Or worse,' he said, 'she's the assassin. Warns you so you'll trust her, then claims she has some piece of vital evidence she needs to show you in person ...'

'No.' This time there was no uncertainty. Bryan shrugged.

'Why not? She's a sellsword, ain't she? And the Kardise would pay damn well for Lady Ayla's head.'

'She made no attempt to be conciliatory in her letter,' Caraway said. 'In fact, she went out of her way to be rude. And besides ...' The hint of a smile touched his face. 'She's set herself up as Corus's protector, and she's in love with his mother. That ties her to the Nightshade line whether she likes it or not.'

'How do you know?'

'I have spies of my own.' His expression turned serious and a little shamefaced. 'I know where Corus is, Art. I've known for months. I've just been trying to work out the best way to get to him before –'

'Before you tell Ayla.'

Caraway nodded. 'If she finds out I know where he is, she'll want to send people straight over there to get him. It could be disastrous.'

Bryan didn't reply to that, because the lad was right – though he didn't want to speculate on what Ayla would say about it when she found out. Instead, belatedly putting two and two together, he asked, 'The boy's in Sol Kardis?'

'Yes.'

'Dangerous.'

'Even more so, now,' Caraway agreed. 'Yet even harder to get him out without tipping off the Kardise or giving them an excuse for war.' Reflectively, he added, 'But Sorrow isn't stupid. She'll be aware of the danger. It's entirely possible she may end up being the one to bring him back, just as she was the one to take him in the first place.'

Bryan didn't say anything to that either. He would usually consider relying on a sellsword, and particularly Naeve Sorrow, the hope of a fool. Yet Caraway seemed very certain about it, and whatever else Caraway was, he was no fool. Bryan was well aware of that.

'Right,' he said instead. 'I'm going to take a look at the sign-up sheet. Find out how many clumsy oafs we'll be dealing with this assessment period.'

Caraway nodded. 'Actually, I wanted to ask your advice on that. Because it occurred to me … well, it's another way in, isn't it?'

'What, assessment?'

'Yes. I thought if the assassin couldn't get into Darkhaven straight away, he might play the long game and sign up for training. Because everyone knows that after the first seven weeks, I take the group who've been picked for Helm training up to the tower. Ayla even comes out to meet them! So maybe, if the assassin is patient …'

Bryan considered that, and gave him a respectful nod. 'You're right – it's one of the few holes left open. Though it would be a damn difficult balancing act to pull off. A competent assassin should have the skills to get himself selected for further training, but he must know we'd be watching.'

'It would be difficult,' Caraway agreed. 'But just to be safe … do you think I should cancel that part of the process this year?'

'Unless you want to use it as a trap,' Bryan suggested.

'Risky.'

'Might work, though.'

'It might.' Caraway sighed. 'I suppose I'll make that decision when I come to it. There are far worse possibilities. I mean, if we're going to talk about *playing the long game* … I only found out about the assassination a few days ago, but they could have been planning it far longer. The required knowledge has been in the world for three years, after all.' He met Bryan's gaze, brown eyes troubled. 'What if the assassin was put in place well before now? He gets close to us, gains our trust, awaits the signal to act …'

Bryan nodded. 'It's possible. In which case, all you can do is make a list of the people who've joined you in Darkhaven since Lord Myrren's death. If they're Helmsmen, don't assign them to Lady Ayla's guard. If they're servants, keep them on duties that don't require them to attend her. And stay vigilant.'

'All I can do,' Caraway echoed. 'You know, I don't like this. Being on the defensive. I'd far rather there was some way to attack.'

Bryan grinned. 'That's because you're straightforward. We'll think of something, boyo. In the meantime, I'll keep my eye on the new recruits. And if you come along to the first day of training tomorrow, you can too.'

After Caraway had gone, Bryan got on with his own tasks, but without much accuracy. Though he'd presented a positive front to the captain, he was distracted and alarmed by the possibility of an assassination attempt – because the consequences of a successful assassination would be dire.

Mirrorvale and Sol Kardis would go to war. Hundreds, maybe thousands of people would die. And although Mirrorvale hadn't been officially at war since Bryan was born, he'd seen enough men killed during his time as a border patrolman that he'd do anything he could to stop it now.

Besides ... on a personal level, the weaponmasters would be among the first called to take a leading role in any conflict. Aside from the patrolmen, who watched over the borders and so were necessarily the first line of defence, the warriors who worked in the fifth ring were the closest thing that Mirrorvale had to an army. Who else was there? The Helm's role was to protect Darkhaven and its overlord. The city watch had a basic level of ability with weaponry, but tended to be the kind of people who didn't have the potential for more rigorous training. And the rest ... sellswords, personal guards, merchant crews and bargemen. They were good fighters, no doubt about it, but they weren't used to working alongside each other. It would be the weaponmasters who were called upon to marshal them into something approximating the kind of army that Sol Kardis had at its disposal.

Not for the first time, Bryan found himself thinking that maybe it wasn't such a good idea to rely wholly on the Nightshade overlords as a deterrent against invading forces. An indestructible Changer creature was still only a single person, when it came down to it. And a destructible one ...

Finally, he gave up on his paperwork and set it aside with a half-hearted resolution to do it later. He was just about to head out to the yard to check the sign-up sheet when someone knocked on the door, then pushed it open without waiting for an answer.

Damn students. Think they can just – But Bryan's bellow died unvoiced when he saw Ayla Nightshade standing on

69

his scuffed wooden floor. Behind her, a sheepish-looking Helmsman lurked in the doorway.

Bryan didn't really see the point of the guard. It wasn't as if the poor man could do anything to defend against a pistol-wielding assassin, unless said assassin were incompetent enough to stand up and announce his presence before firing. Really Ayla ought to stay within the tower until the threat was neutralised. Still, he'd be damned if he was going to be the one to tell her that.

'Good morning, ma'am,' he said with a stiff nod.

'I need your help,' the overlord of Darkhaven said, unconsciously echoing Caraway's words from earlier. 'This assassination business –'

Bryan wondered uneasily whether he was already meant to know about it. Caraway hadn't said his visit was a secret, but he'd certainly given the impression that elements of his plan to combat the threat were not to be widely shared. Such as, for instance, the continued involvement of the woman who'd removed Ayla's half-brother from Darkhaven.

'I'm sure Tomas has told you all about it,' Ayla said, and Bryan gave in to the inevitable. *Beats me how he ever keeps anything from her.*

'He did mention it, ma'am, yes.'

'And no doubt the two of you have come up with various schemes that are none of my concern.'

Bryan shifted uncomfortably. 'I wouldn't put it that way myself, but the Helm –'

His voice trailed into silence. *Damn Nightshades.* Ayla eyed him in silence, before her expression softened.

'I know Helm business is not my business. I don't care what the two of you are planning; I'm sure Tomas will tell me anything I need to know. But your plans are not enough.'

Bryan opened his mouth to contradict her – in the most tactful way possible, of course – but she shook her head.

'I mean for me, personally. This is a threat to my life, yet there's nothing I can do to stop it. Tomas has taught me to defend myself, a little, but against a pistol ...'

She stopped, biting her lip, and for perhaps the first time he saw her as wholly human. He opened his mouth again, planning to say something comforting, but again she got in first.

'I can't sit up in Darkhaven doing nothing about it. I know Tomas, and the Helm, and you are my best possible defence. But if somehow this assassin slips through the net, I need to be ready for him. And so I was wondering ...' She glanced down at her hands, locked tightly together, and then back up at his face. 'I was wondering if your partner might be willing to help me.'

Dumbfounded, Bryan stared at her. She stared back. Finally he gathered his wits enough to say faintly, 'Who, Miles?'

'We all know there's no armour that can defend against a pistol,' Ayla said. 'Not even Changer hide is thick enough to shield me from a bullet. But if brute force won't do the job, I thought perhaps alchemy ...'

It had never occurred to Bryan that alchemy might be of any use in defence. If he were honest, he'd never really thought it had any practical use at all. Miles might talk with great passion about strengthening metals and sharpening blades and making things explode, but that's all it had ever been. Talk. Bryan had yet to see any of the alchemists' grandiose ideas come to fruition.

'After all,' Ayla added, 'it is the same power that runs through my veins. We have alchemy in our blood; that's what makes the Change possible. So if there's any science that can find a solution to my current vulnerability ...'

Changers were powered by alchemy: that was a new one on Bryan. But then, he'd never much concerned himself with how the Nightshade line worked. Like the force of nature he'd compared them to earlier, they just *were*. He forced himself to meet Ayla's expectant gaze.

'I'll talk to Miles this evening. Ask him to attend you at the tower tomorrow. Will that be soon enough?'

'That should be fine.' She offered him a smile. 'Thank you, Art.'

Bryan was rendered speechless again; he hadn't realised she knew his first name. She further confounded him by taking one of his hands between both of hers.

'You know, I never found a moment to speak to you before. Tomas told me it was you who let him through the fifth ring when Travers kidnapped me, three years ago. If it hadn't been for your intervention ...' Her fingers tightened. 'Anyway, I'm grateful. Thank you.'

'You're welcome, Lady Ayla,' he managed. Then, before he'd stopped to think, 'You're more like your brother than I realised.'

Her face changed in an instant, sorrow and yearning washing over it in a relentless tide. He tried to retreat, muttering half-formed words of apology, but her grip on his hand remained firm.

'You trained him, didn't you?' she whispered. 'Can you tell me?'

'I'm sure you knew him far better than –' he began, only to be cut off by a shake of her head.

'I never saw him fight. I asked to be allowed to train alongside him, but my father ... Anyway, it was a side of him I didn't know, and I want to. Please.'

'He was the most talented swordsman I ever taught,' Bryan said softly. 'He was ... driven, in a way no-one else was.

He could take on anyone in the fifth ring – and I tell you, some of the sellswords who stop by are vicious buggers. Er. Pardon my language. But Lord Myrren was better than the best of them. Polite, too, not like some of the cocky bast— um, types we get here. Maybe when you're that good you don't need arrogance. I don't know. To me it always seemed –' Bryan hesitated, before finishing the thought. 'It always seemed he was looking for something.'

'Yes.' Finally Ayla let go of his hand. Tears shone in her eyes, but her jaw was set in fury. 'You know, Weaponmaster Bryan, if he hadn't killed our father then I'd be bloody tempted to do it myself.'

And with that startling statement, she was gone, her guard scuttling in her wake. Bryan watched the door swing on its hinges. He thought he understood where she was coming from, but all the same …. Nightshades. *Force of nature*. He didn't envy Caraway one bit.

On his way out of the training hall, he almost mowed down a girl. She staggered back from the force of the impact, lips parted in surprise.

'Watch where you're going, girlie,' Bryan said, though without any heat – his thoughts still lingering on everything that Caraway and Ayla had said to him. The girl tucked a strand of dark-red hair behind one ear and blinked up at him.

'Sorry. I – am I too late to sign up for training? Only someone told me last night that it closed today, and I didn't know whether he meant morning or evening, but I thought I'd better come and see in case I still had a chance …'

She didn't look like a warrior, or sound like one for that matter, but Bryan had learned not to judge anyone until he saw them with a weapon in their hands. He could tell a seasoned fighter, all right – even at a distance – but trainees

73

… after the number of times he'd seen a promising-looking lad become stiff and awkward with a sword in his hands, or a gangly youth transform into something far more impressive as soon as he was armed, Bryan's only rule about trainees was that it was impossible to tell a damn thing about them just by looking. So he simply jerked a thumb in the direction of the training hall door.

'I was just about to take it down. Go ahead and add your name if you want to.'

'Thank you!' She had a pretty smile. Pretty girl in general, Bryan thought with detachment. She'd turn some of the lads' heads. And it would do them good, because they had to learn not to let themselves be distracted. The best warriors he'd taught weren't put off by anything, be it bruises or taunts or an attractive face.

He let her sign the sheet and move away, before unpinning it and scanning the list. Inevitably his gaze snagged on the final name – and then he noticed that she hadn't just signed up for basic training.

'Saydi!' he called after her, in too much of a hurry to use *girlie* or any of his other usual epithets. 'Did you mean to sign up for the Helm assessment programme?'

She glanced back over her shoulder. 'Oh, definitely, sir. If I'm going to do it at all, I might as well do it properly.'

Bryan grunted a reply and let her go. He'd spotted another girl's name at the top of the list. He was used to training female warriors, of course, but attempting to join the Helm? That had never happened before. And not one but two of them. Bryan's face split into an evil grin, thoughts of the assassination threat temporarily flown from his mind as he imagined Caraway's reaction.

This was going to be interesting.

SEVEN

To Naeve Sorrow, care of Elisse Mallory, Caltor, Sol Kardis:

My thanks for your letter. I assume from its contents that you are close to some well-informed people. As such, I would be most grateful for any further news of this kind.

Of course, it would be a dangerous undertaking. But you are well known for dangerous work. And I think, perhaps, you owe it to my employer.

As for her brother: if what you tell me is correct, he had better come home sooner rather than later. If necessary, I will fetch him myself.

With respect, if not admiration,
T.C.

'I don' get it,' Elisse said. 'If he knows where I live, why hasn' he sent the Helm ta take Corus?'

Sorrow lowered the letter far enough to look at her over the top of it. The dark-haired woman sat very upright in her chair, arms folded, but her eyes betrayed her unease. At her feet, three-year-old Corus played with a wooden horse.

'It wouldn't be easy,' Sorrow told her. It was a relief to speak her native language again; that was one of the things she liked about visiting Elisse. One of the many things. 'He'd have to do it by stealth, else the Kardise could accuse Mirrorvale of sending troops across the border.'

'So why –'

'It's just his way of letting me know he can find you, if he wants to.'

'Yeah, and I don' like it!' Elisse said. 'He's talking about us going back ta Mirrorvale. I thought we were safe here, Naeve.'

Sorrow shrugged. 'Times are changing. The Kardise are going after Ayla Nightshade directly. And if they succeed at that, you can be sure they won't hesitate to dispatch her relatives.'

'But –'

'Listen, Elisse.' Sorrow leaned forward. 'If they find out about Corus, they'll take him away from you. Execution if Ayla dies, bargaining chip if she lives. Either way, it doesn't end well for you. Whereas if you return to Mirrorvale on your own terms –'

'Mama?' Corus was tugging on Elisse's sleeve, eyes wide. Hair even darker than his mother's, skin even fairer, and those deep, deep blue eyes: one glance at him and virtually anyone in the world would be able to make a good guess at his origins. 'Who's gonna take me away?'

'No-one, sweetheart,' Elisse said fiercely. Sorrow met her glare and sighed.

'I'm on your side. You know that. But the balance of risks has tilted the other way. If I do a bit of spying for Caraway, I daresay he'll be open to bargaining with you about Corus's future. But even if he isn't ...' She hesitated only a heartbeat before saying the words Elisse didn't want to hear. 'Being forced to live in Darkhaven has got to be better than being used as a disposable tool by your country's opposition.'

'Yeah, but the Kardise don' even know he exists. Do they?'

'I didn't think they did,' Sorrow said. 'But now, I wouldn't count on anything.'

Elisse was silent for a long while, looking down at the top of her son's bowed head. Then she lifted her troubled blue gaze to Sorrow's face. 'What should I do, Naeve?'

Sorrow suppressed another sigh. It wasn't that Elisse was weak, or needy – far from it. In fact, Sorrow was constantly surprised at her resilience in the face of the many challenges that confronted her as a single parent in a strange country. But the other woman had an almost religious belief in Sorrow's own capabilities. As far as Elisse was concerned, Sorrow had all the answers. And it wasn't as if Sorrow minded that, exactly. It just left her feeling constantly as if she had something to live up to. Before she'd met Elisse, no-one had ever expected anything of her.

Not anything good, anyway.

Elisse was different. Elisse didn't seem to care what Sorrow did for a living. Elisse teased her and confided in her and trusted her to help look after a small child. And that was why Sorrow kept coming back. Sometimes without warning. Sometimes not for months at a time. But all the same, she came back.

Despite the many reasons why it shouldn't work, they were a team. And that was why any decision Sorrow made had to involve Elisse as well.

'We have two choices,' she said. 'We can leave now. Tonight. Flee back to Mirrorvale – or to another country, I suppose, though Parovia isn't exactly Mirrorvale's greatest ally either, and the Ingal States are dangerous for different reasons. Anyway, you might be able to live for a few more years in peace, somewhere in the wilds of Mirrorvale, before Caraway finds you again. Though since he tracked you here, I wouldn't bet on it.

'Or, we stay for a little longer. I try and obtain the information Caraway wants. And *then* we return to Mirrorvale, and use that information as leverage to agree a future for Corus that both you and the Nightshades can live with.'

'S'not much of a choice,' Elisse said. 'Either cling ta safety, knowing it could end any time, or gamble with all our lives for the chance ta extend it.' She looked at Sorrow, biting her lip. 'Spying'ud be dangerous for ya. If they caught ya –'

'They won't catch me if I'm cautious,' Sorrow said. 'Believe me, I won't risk my life for Tomas Caraway's sake.' *Though maybe I would for yours*, she didn't add. Apart from anything else, she wasn't yet sure if it were true. Almost sure, but not quite.

'I don't think they know where you are,' she said instead. 'Otherwise they'd have moved in on you by now. A child of Darkhaven would be too valuable a tool for them to leave unguarded.'

Elisse glanced down at her son again; one hand rested briefly on his hair. 'We didn' think Caraway knew where I was, either.'

'True. Like I said, I wouldn't count on anything.' Sorrow studied the other woman's face, searching for some indication of her decision. 'So what do you want to do?'

Elisse reached a hand across the table as if it were inevitable that Sorrow should offer her comfort; after a moment, Sorrow took it. They sat in silence for a bit, while Corus sang a tuneless and half-formed song at their feet. Then Elisse looked up and attempted a smile.

'Not sure yet. But I'm glad ya here.'

Later, they went for a walk in the cottage grounds. Corus ran ahead, hiding and climbing and picking up anything that looked interesting, whilst Elisse showed Sorrow what had changed since her last visit. The autumn crop was coming along nicely, squash and beans and tomatoes in their rows. Elisse had fixed the loose stone in the flight of steps that led to the upper garden, and a new woven barrier of green branches blocked the hole in the hedgerow where the cow had once got stuck earlier that year. All very domestic and satisfactory, yet Sorrow found herself paying less attention to Elisse's words and more to her surroundings.

The cottage crouched halfway down a hill, on a little patch of land carved out from the slope. Behind it, the meadow that held the cow and a few chickens fell steeply down to a stream at the bottom; above it, the walled vegetable patch and the smaller bramble meadow were reached up a short flight of stone steps. A dirt track ran past one side of the building, the way out to the nearby village and civilisation beyond, but other than that it was completely surrounded by trees. No-one came here unless they meant to; there was no passing traffic on foot or on wheel, and the steep wooded hill concealed it from above, too. It was hidden. Safe.

At least, so Sorrow had always thought.

But now, she found herself looking at it through new eyes – and she didn't like it. Because although it was difficult to stumble across by accident, if anyone did find out where it was and who lived there, it was the perfect place for an ambush. The dense forest meant that the cottage could be approached and surrounded without its inhabitants noticing. And while the track might pose an attack team with a problem, being too rough and narrow for any large vehicle, Sorrow knew that the top of the hill was bare. A small airship could land there easily enough, releasing its occupants to sneak down through the trees.

'You'll need to be careful, Elisse,' she said, interrupting what the other woman was telling her about the harvest. 'If you see anyone coming you don't recognise, get out of here. Don't stop to chat.'

Elisse nodded. 'I thought we'd hide in the hay store till they're gone. No-one'd find that without knowing where ta look.' She grinned. 'No need ta look so surprised. S'only sensible ta think about it.'

'Jump!' Corus yelled. He'd climbed up onto one of the low walls that bordered the vegetable plots. Sorrow grabbed his hands and swung him back down to earth. Elisse tousled his hair, but her expression was serious.

'How long d'ya think it'll take, Naeve? Ta get the information Captain Caraway wants?'

'I don't know,' Sorrow said. 'As long as it takes. So you think I should do it?'

'Yeah.' Elisse dropped a kiss on her son's head, then straightened. 'I don' want Ayla Nightshade ta take Corus from me, but she's his sister. Like it or not, I have ta do everything I can ta keep her alive.'

'Funny, isn't it?' Sorrow said. 'I didn't think I had any loyalty to Mirrorvale. Not having loyalty to anyone is one of my specialities. And yet ...'

'And yet,' Elisse echoed. 'That's the problem, isn' it? We're like pigeons.'

'Why pigeons?'

'Well. 'Cos no matter where we go, we can't help but return home in the end. And if there weren' any Nightshades ...' She shrugged. 'I s'pose there wouldn' be any home left ta go ta.'

'Speak for yourself,' Sorrow said. 'I'm not so attached to the idea of Changers that my world would end without them.'

Though Elisse did have a point, she allowed privately. After all, she herself had always gone back to Mirrorvale, even after weeks or months spent in other countries. Or at least, she had before she met Elisse. Maybe it wasn't ever possible to pull oneself up by the roots. Maybe a person's country always had a place somewhere deep in their heart – in their bones – whether they admitted it to themselves or not. And Mirrorvale *was* its overlords. Mirrorvale meant Arkannen, and Arkannen meant Darkhaven, and Darkhaven meant Changers. Everyone knew that.

Maybe in another life, Sorrow would have joined the Helm.

But that idea was so far-fetched that it made her laugh aloud. She was far too good at breaking the law to want to keep it. Let Tomas Caraway fit himself to the shape the Helm required. Naeve Sorrow would rather bend the world to fit around *her*.

'What's funny?' Elisse asked.

'Nothing. You still have my spare pistols?'

'Course I do.'

'Then let's do a bit of target practice before I go.' Sorrow smiled grimly. 'You might need it.'

Dear Sirs –

You asked me to keep you updated with respect to the Goldenfire business, and so I must inform you that Darkhaven is on alert.

Perhaps I should have expected it, but I didn't. You have, after all, conducted this affair with the utmost secrecy; no reason to suspect the tower would be on guard. And yet, somehow, a hint of the truth has whispered its way here.

As a result, the Gate of Death admits no-one. Every visitor is turned away, no matter their purpose. The Helm control access to Darkhaven and the creature within, and they view the rest of the world with suspicion. I don't yet know if they comprehend the nature of the threat, or its source, but either way it makes my task more difficult.

Nevertheless, I believe I have found a route past the watchdogs. It will take longer than I hoped, but as long as it culminates in the eventual completion of my goal, I feel sure that we will all be satisfied. So I have set it in motion, and we shall see where it takes me.

Be assured that I will send this letter as soon as I find the appropriate means of doing so.

Respectfully yours.

The room was small and bare, but Kai was used to that. A narrow bed, a plain cabinet, a battered old table and chair: it was all much like the preparation facility back in Sol Kardis, except that the wood was darker. No doubt military accommodation was the same the world over. But the room was clean, and the single window admitted a bright beam of evening sunlight, and that was enough.

The task ahead – *Goldenfire* – wasn't going to be straightforward. It would require patience and cunning. But Kai had confidence that everything would go according to plan. There was, after all, no purpose in *not* believing that. Too often, doubt created its own downfall. Admitting to the possibility of failure could make cracks appear in even the strongest situation: like threads of ice through stone, waiting to break it open. Better not to let it in.

All the same, maintaining a constant façade was exhausting – probably more exhausting than the actual training would be. Outside this room, Kai wore someone else's face, someone else's name, someone else's life. It was more than being an actor, playing a part on a stage; it was an act of immersion. Taking on a new character so fully and completely that the truth was no longer there to be revealed by a careless word or an accidental gesture. It was difficult that way, but it was necessary. And it had the additional benefit of subduing the past's vicious sting.

When Kai was alone, it was a different matter. Because that was when the memories came crawling out.

The man stood alone in a desolate wasteland of stone. His back was straight, fists clenched at his sides. He was shouting something, but the words were carried away on the wind.

In front of him, the monster rose up to its full height, blocking out the sun. Vast red eyes glowed with unfathomable malice. Vast sharp teeth gleamed yellow in the shadows. A rumble like the end of the world shook the flagstones, and the man stumbled. He looked small. Fragile. Easy to snap.

A sudden flare of fire lit up the sky, dazzling and terrible. The monster lifted one giant clawed foot to tear at the screaming man. Blood sprayed in a bright arc, covering the flagstones, covering everything. Too much blood –

Kai woke in a cold sweat, heart pounding. The monster – the man –

Nightmare. It was only a nightmare.

Yet the vision of blood still lingered, colouring the faint light of dawn with a scarlet haze. Kai blinked it away, forcing it down. Fear would do no good, nor would succumbing to the relentless tugging tide of memory. All that mattered was the present. All that mattered was a single-minded focus on the task ahead – because only once that was completed would the nightmares stop. Slay a dragon, and there was no longer any need to be afraid of fire.

Of course, that monster was gone, leaving no more than ashes behind. It would be stupid to fear him any longer. But though he might be dead, another remained – and it was that one's duty to pay for her father's crimes. Kai might not be able to kill the old Firedrake, but his daughter …

His daughter was there for the taking.

EIGHT

Ayla stood unnoticed in the doorway to the nursery and watched her brother's child. Marlon looked exactly as she imagined Myrren had, at two years old: slight, dark-haired, restless. As if he were constantly burning energy, even when sitting still. Not that he was ever still for long. *Jumpier than a basketful of frogs*, his nursemaid Lori would say. *Wants to explore everything and then some.*

Two years, and still Ayla felt uneasy in his presence.

It wasn't as if his birth had been a shock – she'd known of his existence well before that. His mother, Serenna, had sent word only a couple of months after her own departure from Darkhaven. Ayla remembered the message primarily for its matter-of-factness. *I must inform you that I am carrying Myrren Nightshade's child. Please advise.* Like a merchant requesting instruction from his investors.

Yet when Ayla had visited Serenna in the Altar of Flame, she'd found something altogether different.

'Thank you for coming to see me, Lady Ayla.' Serenna's voice was colourless, her eyes downcast. The thick veil covering her fiery hair made her into an effigy, remote and lifeless.

Ayla couldn't see any hint of her supposed pregnancy.

'You sent for me.' Ayla wasn't sure of the priestess's intentions, even now they were face to face, so she'd decided to say and do as little as possible until she'd worked it out.

'Not exactly,' Serenna murmured. 'I didn't want to presume. I just hoped – but now you're here.'

So what is it you're trying to tell me? Ayla screamed at her in the silence of her own mind. *That you're keeping Myrren's child? That you're … not?* She didn't think she could handle either option. Despite herself, she fidgeted a little on the bare stone floor. Serenna glanced up, and they stared at each other like statues until Ayla finally snapped.

'It's not long enough since my brother's death for me to be able to play games, Serenna. You've told me you're pregnant and the baby is Myrren's. You must have told me that for a reason. So spit it out.'

Serenna's eyes widened. 'I – I just wanted to –' She took a deep breath, shoulders lifting, and the blank expression settled back on her face as if she'd drawn her veil across it. 'If I keep this baby, I'll lose my whole life here. They forgave me what I did, but this – it's too much. A baby has no place in holy life.'

Ayla said nothing.

'And I'd be afraid for the child, growing up in Darkhaven. I saw how Myrren's life there scarred him. Your father –'

Still Ayla said nothing. An edge of desperation coloured the monotone of Serenna's voice.

'So I wondered if I should call a physician. Ask for something to end it –'

Ayla clenched her fists. '*Why are you telling me all this?*'

Finally Serenna looked up, eyes brimming with confusion and guilt. 'Because I need your help.' A few tears fell down her cheeks, but she wiped them away with the back of her hand. 'I don't know what to do. I cared for Myrren a great deal, but – I knew him a week, Ayla! I've been a priestess since I was twelve. The choice should be simple, and yet I don't know how to make it. I want to stay here, and I want Myrren's child to live, and I can't reconcile those two things.'

It was impossible to remain defensive in the face of such naked distress. Ayla sat down beside her and took her hand. 'What do you want me to do, Serenna?'

'I think … I think I want you to take the child. Promise to raise it as your own. Promise to love it, whether it has the gift or not. I know I have no right to ask –'

'No,' Ayla said. 'But I'll do it, all the same.'

Serenna stared at her, speechless – and in truth, Ayla was equally surprised at herself. Yet she couldn't regret the decision, however hasty. *Myrren's child.* That was all that mattered. Preserving this little piece of Myrren that still lived.

'There are few enough Nightshades in the world,' she said aloud. 'I would count it a gift if you were to carry this one. And I'll make it right with the high priestess.'

'I'm not sure it will be that straightforward.'

'I am the overlord of Darkhaven,' Ayla said with some asperity. 'I don't expect her to object. And besides … most objections can be overcome, if the donation is large enough.'

Belatedly, it occurred to her that she'd made this decision without consulting Tomas – whose life would undeniably be affected by the arrival of a baby into Darkhaven. Their relationship was still new, and still uncertain; she'd always imagined that love would be like a dance, easy and beautiful and synchronised, but sometimes it felt more like a duel. Two of them, testing each other's limits, trying to work out where they could dominate and where they should yield.

Which wasn't to say she didn't love him, and sometimes she could see how the fencing might become dancing, but all the same ... this was a huge decision to make without talking about it first.

She knew that, and yet it didn't matter. Because this was Nightshade business. This was *Myrren*. And whatever Tomas thought about it, she was going to bring this child home.

'Are you well?' she asked Serenna. 'Do you need anything?'

'I'm fine. Sick, sometimes, but I've been able to hide it well enough.' The priestess looked up, meeting Ayla's gaze directly. 'Are *you* well? You must miss him terribly.'

It was rare for anyone to talk to Ayla about Myrren so openly. Even Tomas wasn't sure how to broach the subject. Perhaps they were afraid to keep the wound fresh, but the truth was, nothing could make it worse. Certainly not skirting around the subject as though even saying his name were a forbidden act. She felt a strange rush of gratitude towards Serenna for acknowledging the simple truth: Myrren was gone, and it hurt.

'For a long time, it was Myrren and me against the world,' she said. 'After my mother died, he was the only person I could turn to. It feels like I've lost half of myself.'

Serenna nodded. 'I'm sorry. I really am. I know you blame me for his death —'

'I don't. Not any more.' Serenna might have handed Myrren the pistol that killed him, but the cause of his death had been laid down a long time before that. 'I'm glad you sent for me, Serenna.'

The priestess nodded. She was crying again. And then, somehow, Ayla was crying too. They were a relief, those tears. Maybe it was only possible to grieve for a person properly when you were with someone else who'd loved them.

Whatever the reason, when the storm finally passed she felt fresher – *cleaner* – than she had in a long time, as if some of the dark emotions that had been lingering in the corners of her heart had been washed away.

'I have to go,' she told Serenna. 'But I'll speak to the high priestess. And ... I'll visit you again, if I may, before the baby is born.'

Serenna nodded. 'I'd like that.'

They smiled at each other, rather tentatively. Then, as Ayla turned to leave, Serenna spoke again.

'One more thing, Lady Ayla. Will you – would you mind calling him Marlon? That's my father's name.'

That made two of them, Ayla thought. Corus named for his maternal grandfather, and Serenna's child for his. Neither Corus nor Marlon was a Nightshade name. But she'd broken too many Nightshade traditions already to mind very much about that one. More importantly ...

'What if it's a girl?'

'It's a boy,' Serenna said. 'I just know it.'

Ironic, now, to remember that Ayla had been worried about what Tomas would think. Because as it turned out, he'd taken to Marlon as easily as if they truly were father and son. He'd been the one to collect the baby shortly after birth and bring him back to Darkhaven under escort; upon arrival, he'd presented the cloth-wrapped bundle to Ayla and said with no trace of sarcasm or bitterness, *Here's our boy*. He'd made it clear that helping to raise another man's child was no hardship to him – that he was willing to love Marlon unreservedly. And in the event, it had been Ayla who had to turn away with a lump of conflicting feelings lodged in her throat.

Even now, those feelings were impossible to reconcile.

In a way, it would be easier if the Nightshade blood hadn't shown up so strongly in the boy. If Marlon had inherited his mother's red hair or grey eyes, her freckled brown skin, maybe Ayla would have been able to accept him as a person in his own right and not a constant reminder of her brother. As it was, she could barely look at him when he was in her company. That was why, despite the comfort it had brought her to talk about Myrren with someone who understood, she'd failed to continue her visits to Serenna after Marlon was born – why the most she ever gave the mother of her nephew was a quick note informing her of his progress. Because she'd promised not just to raise the boy, but to love him as her own. And she was breaking that promise.

Marlon looked up suddenly, as if he'd sensed her gaze on him. Ayla took one noiseless step backwards, then another, before hastening soft-footed down the corridor. Guilt and misery tangled in her throat, but she choked them down. It was nearly halfway through second bell; Miles Tarantil was due in Darkhaven to talk to her about alchemy. She couldn't linger any longer.

What could be more important than making things right with your brother's child? a little voice inside her asked reproachfully.

For now, staying alive, she told it, and forced the subject from her mind.

Miles was already waiting in the main hall. Ayla studied him swiftly as she stepped forward to greet him. Dark hair cropped close to his skull; a long, clever face that currently wore an expression of frozen alarm, like a rabbit in a trap. Clearly not a warrior – he was wiry rather than muscular – but light on his feet, though Ayla didn't suppose he ever exerted himself further than a brisk walk to and from the university. He had an academic's stoop, and his ochre skin had a sallowness to it that spoke of days spent indoors. Altogether, he was about as different from his bluff, weathered partner as it was possible to be.

Once they'd exchanged pleasantries, she took him to the library. Perhaps rather an obvious ploy to set him at his ease, but it seemed to work all the same. Besides, the library was one of her favourite rooms now that she'd changed things round a bit. Her father's desk with its single chair had been relegated to a corner of the room – she never intended to confront anyone across it like a teacher with an errant pupil – and instead, she'd installed soft armchairs that were perfect for reading in. Miles settled into one of those and looked around with some interest.

'If I had known you possessed such a fascinating collection of books, I would have angled for an invitation sooner.'

Ayla blinked at him. 'We don't entertain much,' she said faintly.

'No, I suppose not.' He glanced sidelong at her, and some of the tension returned to his shoulders. 'Sorry, was that rude? I am not used to associating with royalty. And for a small woman, you are really quite intimidating.'

Does he always say exactly what he's thinking? Ayla stifled a giggle. Her father would have hated the man, but she was enjoying herself. Which was odd, because she didn't usually tolerate much in the way of insolence. As Miles had said, she was a small woman, and that meant she had to assert herself if she wanted to be taken seriously. Of course, her ability to become a vast winged unicorn with a horn that could cut through steel tended to help with that. Yet she had no desire to put Miles in his place. He was so very earnest.

'Did Art tell you why I summoned you?' she asked, and he nodded.

'Someone wants to kill you. And you think I can help.' A fleeting pause, before his expression changed comically. 'Help you, I mean, of course. Not them.'

'Quite,' Ayla said. 'You may be aware that for hundreds of years, it was thought that no weapon in existence could harm a Changer creature – until firearms came along. Now I have been informed of a possible attempt on my life, and I wondered if there might be something in alchemy that can protect me.'

Miles nodded again. 'It is certainly possible. Art said that you said ...' He stopped, grimacing. 'Sorry. That sounded like playground gossip. But I gather the Change is in some sense an alchemical reaction?'

'I suppose so.' Ayla hesitated – yet she would have to tell him everything she knew, if she wanted him to help her. Shoving aside her doubts, she plunged ahead. 'Actually, I think the important part is that alchemy is how Changers were created in the first place.'

'Really?' Miles leaned forward, a spark of interest brightening his voice, his entire demeanour changing in the pursuit of knowledge. 'Your bloodline was altered by alchemy? Can you tell me how that happened?'

He wasn't Mirrorvalese by birth, Ayla knew that much – so he had no reason to be familiar with Changer history. Truth be told, most Mirrorvalese weren't either. It was one of those things she'd had to learn at her father's insistence: Nightshade secrets she'd been convinced she'd never need to know. Maybe he'd been in the right, on this point at least.

'I can't tell you much about the science,' she said. 'From what I understand, the first Nightshade overlord killed the alchemists who made the discovery, to make sure it wouldn't be shared.' Catching Miles's almost imperceptible flinch, she added, 'I feel I should reassure you that I have no intention of doing the same, whatever you find out.'

He smiled, but it wasn't altogether convincing. Still, he'd relax as he got to know her. Probably.

'In those days, Mirrorvale was divided into fiefdoms,' she said. 'A bit like the Ingal States, I suppose, only the lords were at outright war with each other. And none of them had any perceptible advantage over the others, so their armies kept fighting and dying for nothing. A woodland here. A handful of fields there.

'Like the rest of them, my ancestor wanted Mirrorvale for himself. So he gathered together as many alchemists as he could, from across the country, and set them to work. Yet instead of immortality, he was seeking indestructibility.'

She paused, but Miles was listening with rapt attention, so she went on.

'He got what he wanted, more or less. Through the alchemists' work, he became a Firedrake the size of which has never been seen again, with a wingspan capable of blocking out the sun. And he hunted down all his rival lords and rained fire upon their armies until they were utterly defeated.'

'Strange, that you should be proud of such a history,' Miles murmured, then blushed. 'I mean –'

He doesn't hold back, does he? Beginning to see why absolute bluntness might be a wearing characteristic to have around all the time, Ayla gave him a tight smile. 'My father considered it one of the greatest moments in the Nightshade annals. I don't claim the same, but I don't regret it, either. How could I? If my ancestor hadn't triumphed, his line would have ended and I would never have existed.'

'Of course. Yes.' Miles lowered his gaze. 'I apologise. Please go on.'

'There isn't much else. He executed the alchemists who had helped him. He had Darkhaven built as the new seat of power in Mirrorvale. Over the generations, Arkannen was laid out according to his design.'

'I expect it was the alchemists' design, rather than his,' Miles said. 'I had already noticed that Arkannen is built upon alchemical principles, and that would explain it.'

Ayla hesitated, torn between renewed offence on her progenitor's behalf and sheer raw curiosity. But her desire for knowledge outweighed the need to defend a centuries-dead forebear, and so she echoed, 'Alchemical principles?'

Miles's smile transformed his rather lugubrious face. 'Well, Lady Ayla, it really is fascinating. You know, of course, that Arkannen's seven rings correspond to the seven alchemical elements –'

'I thought there were five,' Ayla said stupidly. 'Flame, ice, wood, wind and steel.'

'Those are the five material elements, but there are also two spiritual. *Boros* and *auros*, or creation and destruction. Birth and death, if you will.'

'Then Arkannen's seven gates –'

'Are named after the elements of alchemy,' Miles finished for her. 'And each gate incorporates the alchemical substance that represents its element. Not only that, but the gates are set at different points around the circle in such a way as to counter-balance the influences of the countries surrounding Mirrorvale.'

That was far too abstruse for Ayla. She managed a faint, 'Oh?'

'Certainly! We have Parovia to the east, held in tension by the Gate of Steel to the west. Sol Kardis balanced by the

Gate of Flame ... I must say, Lady Ayla, it comes as some surprise to me that these details are not intimately known to your bloodline.' He met her silent stare, blushed again, and added hastily, 'That is, I mean to say –'

'It's all right,' Ayla said, taking pity on his obvious discomfort. 'I'm sure you're right. We should know these things. But I fear that over the centuries, my ancestors have focused more on concrete power than abstract knowledge.'

'To their detriment,' Miles agreed, but so enthusiastically that it was hard to take offence. 'Knowledge is what leads to power, after all.' Then a thought seemed to strike him, and he leaned forward in his chair.

'Tell me ... if an alchemist created Changers, what is to stop someone repeating the process? After all, hundreds of years have passed since then. We know more about alchemy than we ever have.' He frowned, gaze turning inward; his voice fell to a murmur. 'In fact, I find it highly improbable that no-one has made a similar discovery since. There must be more to it than that.'

He was an intelligent man, even if he did have a knack of putting his foot in his mouth. Ayla could remember asking the very same question of her father, back before her mother died and Florentyn became focused on his children's flaws to the exclusion of all else.

The other part of it is Darkhaven, he'd said. *Darkhaven and the city that upholds it. We are tied to it, and it to us. If one falls, so does the other.*

Given what Miles had just said about Arkannen being built on alchemical principles, he was halfway to working that out for himself. But Ayla didn't think she should tell him, all the same. The conversation had already cut close enough to the heart of the Nightshade family's secrets. And besides, it wasn't as if she really knew what it meant for her bloodline's fate to be so closely bound to Darkhaven's – only that the tower and the city enhanced Changer power. Somehow.

'All right,' she said. 'That will do, for now. We've discussed my family history and its connection to alchemy. You know something of what I am. Do you think you can help me?'

'I believe it is possible,' Miles said cautiously. 'I would need time to talk further with you, to perform some tests, and to think ... but what you ask is not beyond the bounds of possibility.' His eyes unfocused again. 'It will certainly be an interesting experiment.'

When it seemed he would say nothing more, Ayla prompted him, 'Good. Then how often can you come?'

'What? Oh.' He spread his hands. 'I have my work at the university, my teaching, and I will need time to think about the problem you have set me ... perhaps every week? I am not sure that visiting you any more frequently will help me come up with a swifter solution.' He hesitated. 'Though I realise it is urgent, so if necessary I could give up my job ...'

'No need,' Ayla said quickly, swallowing her disappointment. She'd hoped he would be able to work faster than that – perhaps come up to Darkhaven every day until an answer was found – but she couldn't ask him to abandon his livelihood. Not when they didn't even know whether their research would bear any fruit. 'I'll see you this time next week.'

After he'd left the tower, she sat for a while and thought back over their conversation. She couldn't tell yet whether it would come to anything more than an interesting diversion, but one thing was for sure: it *would* be interesting. And with any luck, it would be more than that.

At least she could feel that she was doing something to preserve her own life.

'I met Bryan's partner – Miles – when I was walking down the hill this morning,' Tomas said later. He and Ayla were sitting together in the music room, one of the smallest of Darkhaven's formal rooms and the one that had always felt most comfortable to them. At least, Tomas was sitting. Ayla lay sprawled beside him on the chaise longue, her cheek resting on his thigh. She was surrounded by so much ritual and structure, so much deference, that she took her freedoms wherever she could find them.

'He told me you'd asked him up here,' Tomas added, playing with a lock of her hair. She turned her head to look up at him.

'I thought he might be able to find a way of shielding me. You don't have any real defence against a pistol, so maybe alchemy ...'

His mouth drew down at the corners, and it dawned on her that she'd essentially just told him he couldn't do his job. But he didn't dwell on it for long.

'It's sensible, I'm sure. The more we can do to protect you, the better.' He tucked the stray lock of hair behind her ear and added gently, 'When were you going to tell me?'

Ayla bit her lip. She wasn't even sure why she hadn't told Tomas about her plans with Miles. It wasn't as if she'd wanted to keep them a secret – and even if she had, she wouldn't have been able to, not with Tomas and Bryan working so closely together. Not with the Helm searching everyone who came through the gate.

'To be honest,' Tomas said, 'I wish you hadn't brought someone new into Darkhaven without mentioning it. Even if it is Miles. We don't know him, after all.'

This. This was why she hadn't told him.

'Bryan does,' she said softly.

'Yes, but I just … eighteen months isn't long enough to really know someone.'

She smirked at him, thinking of the bare week they'd spent together before she invited him to live in Darkhaven. 'Hypocrite.'

'Point taken.' His answering smile was reluctant, but at least it was there. She hoped that was the end of it. Yet after a while, he took her hand and laced his fingers through hers. 'The thing is, Bryan and I were talking about this only yesterday. The idea that an assassin might have been sent here years ago to insinuate himself into our lives, awaiting the command to act. And Miles isn't Mirrorvalese, is he? In fact, Bryan told me himself that he leaves the country on a regular basis.'

'I thought he was Parovian,' Ayla said doubtfully.

'Yes. So did I. But if he really is playing a long game, he'd know how to set a good cover story.'

Ayla sighed. 'In that case, who's to say it isn't you?'

She meant it as a flippant remark – *obviously* – but he frowned at her as if he feared she might be serious. That drove her to sit up and face him head-on.

'Tomas. Honestly. Of course I don't really think –' She shook her head, words deserting her, and finished with, 'Just *stop* it. You can't keep suspecting everyone.'

'I have to,' he said. 'Better to be too cautious than not be cautious enough.'

'You really think someone would go that far? Form a lasting relationship with the sole purpose of getting closer to me? Surely you trust Bryan's judgement better than that.'

For a moment Tomas was silent. Then he said thoughtfully, 'I heard a story, once. Back when I first came to the fifth ring, before I even joined the Helm. There was a mercenary here from one of the Ingal States, and he told us how the second son of one of the lords there won a neighbouring state for his father. He spent fifteen years working his way up from boot boy to butler, just so he could win a place as a trusted servant in the rival lord's own demesne. And then he spent the next ten years sending information back to his father.' He shrugged. 'If anything, forming relationships with people is the mark of a good spy … or a good assassin.'

Ayla couldn't argue with that. Oh, she didn't believe it: she found it simply impossible that awkward, earnest Miles Tarantil, dedicated academic and long-term partner to one of the fifth ring's most respected weaponmasters, intended to kill her. But she couldn't argue with Tomas's determination to prepare for all eventualities.

'All right,' she said. 'I'll be careful. And it's not as if he'll be able to sneak any weapons past your guards, anyway.' Then, because she couldn't help herself, 'Though you realise I sent for Miles. He didn't suggest it himself.'

Tomas nodded. 'Then what gave you the idea that an alchemist might be able to help you?'

'You did, actually. You told me something once about …' She stopped, then added more slowly, 'About Bryan's partner Miles and what he does at the university.'

'Hmm. It's tenuous, but it can't be discounted.'

More than tenuous. If Miles really were an assassin, he'd gone about his task in so roundabout a way as to be almost incomprehensible. But Tomas was frowning at nothing again, looking so careworn that she reached out a thumb to rub the deep line from between his brows.

'I'm not going to give up on this, Tomas,' she said softly. 'I think the potential benefits outweigh the risks. But I will be careful. I promise.'

His gaze refocused on her. 'You'll do whatever you must to be safe?'

'Of course.'

'Then please ... stay in the tower. Keep talking to Miles if you want to, but please don't come wandering down to the fifth ring with only a single guard for protection.'

So Bryan had mentioned that. Ayla let her hand fall back down to her lap. 'I'm beginning to feel as if you don't want me to do anything. You want me to lock myself away and let the *men* take care of everything for me.'

'That's exactly what I want,' Tomas said. 'And if your father were still alive, I'd be requesting the same thing from him.'

She released her breath in something that wasn't quite a laugh. 'You think he'd have listened? More likely he'd have torn you apart.'

Tomas shook his head. 'Whatever else he may have been, Lord Florentyn was a just ruler.'

'Really?'

'In many ways.'

He was serious. Ayla shook her head in disbelief. 'But after what he did to you –'

'What he did was fair,' Tomas said softly. 'Your father could have executed me on the spot, after your mother died. It was his right, and well within his capabilities. But even in grief, he understood it was an accident.' He gave her a rueful smile. 'Your father never killed people for things they couldn't help, Ayla. Only the choices they made.'

She was silent. She'd never thought of her father that way before. But if there was one lesson she really should have learned by now, it was that people usually turned out to be more complex than she gave them credit for.

'So what would you say to him, then?' she asked. 'If it were his life under threat?'

Tomas met her gaze. 'I'd say, *you can't die*. You're the single most important person in this country. You have to do whatever it takes to stay alive.'

Looking at him, Ayla felt the weight of resignation settle in her bones – because he was right. Of course he was right. It was just hard, after three years of relative freedom, to have it taken away from her again. A prison always seemed smaller the second time around.

'All right,' she whispered. 'I'll stay in Darkhaven. But Tomas ...' She leaned forward until her forehead touched his shoulder and she felt his arms enclose her. 'I hope you find this assassin soon.'

'So do I, Ayla,' he said, and kissed the top of her head. 'So do I.'

NINE

On the first morning of training, Ree woke before dawn. She was still tired, but as soon as the significance of the day hit her, she knew she'd never get back to sleep. Her blood was fizzing too fast through her veins for that. So she lay in her narrow cot bed – standard issue for all new recruits – and gazed out of her tiny window at the night sky. She still wasn't used to that sky. She was used to deep, deep black punctuated only by the tiny crystalline twinkles of the stars. But the sky above Arkannen was thick with grey smoke and yellow with the light from the street lamps. She wondered if there was a single shred of real darkness anywhere in the city.

This is the day. She'd been trying not to think about it, but it was there all the same. *Today is when you find out whether you've created yourself an impossible dream, or whether maybe, just maybe ...* But she ruthlessly squashed the rest of that thought, because she didn't dare to hope. She kept imagining the weaponmasters – or worse, the Captain of the Helm – taking one look at her and telling her to go home. Or perhaps she'd get as far as the first sparring session, make an utter fool of herself against a far better opponent, and get kicked out straight away. Because the trouble was,

she had no way of knowing how good she was. She'd only ever fought her tutor. Maybe they'd both been labouring under a delusion.

The poor man had tried, of course. He'd suggested to her father that Ree would benefit from practising with some of the other merchants' sons. But Ree's mother had put her foot down. *It's one thing for you to indulge this nonsense in the privacy of our home, Cheri. It's quite another to make a spectacle of yourself before the whole neighbourhood.* Ree suspected that the only reason her father had been able to overrule her mother on the subject of training in the fifth ring was that Arkannen was too far away from Torrance Mill for Ree to embarrass the family. It didn't matter to Ree's mother that plenty of women made a good living out of weaponry. Ree's mother didn't think *ladies* should make a living at all.

The difficult part, Ree thought ruefully, was that her mother wasn't at all an unpleasant person. If she'd been cruel with her words, harsh in her strictures, then Ree could have hated her and that would be that. But no, she delivered her criticisms as plaintive suggestions, peering at Ree all the while as if she couldn't work out where this odd, independent child had come from. She simply wanted the best for her daughters – and as far as she was concerned, that was aping the wealthy, with their etiquette and their social functions and their pallid, soft daughters whose sole purpose in life was to make a good marriage. She'd grown up in poverty herself; no doubt that was why she was so anxious to see her children established in comfort. And no doubt that was also why Ree found it so hard to convince her that *safe and secure* would never be enough for a gi who would rather overcome an exhilarating hardship th wallow in stifling luxury.

Easy for you to say, she told herself guiltily. *You've never had to suffer real hardship*. Yet she was convinced she'd suffer almost anything rather than be married off to someone she barely knew, or endure her mother's constant gentle comments on what she considered was the only way to lead a good life. After what had happened when Ree declared that she never wanted to have children – the tears, the recrimination, the subsequent skirting around any issue that might cause a similar reaction – those conversations were a particularly gruesome form of torture.

Outside the window, dawn was beginning to extend pale fingers across the smoke-streaked sky. Ree abandoned her bed and headed to the bathing room for a wash. Though it was early, a couple of other girls were already in there. She nodded and smiled at them, trying to conceal the fact that she didn't remember their names. None of them would be training alongside her, because none of them had been crazy enough to sign up for the Helm assessment programme. They'd be taught by different weaponmasters in a different part of the fifth ring. Briefly, Ree wished that she was going to be joining them – that she didn't always feel the need to put herself under such pressure. She could have made friends with other girls like her, girls who were more interested in swords than sewing. She could have relaxed a bit and enjoyed herself, instead of going into training with the knowledge that she'd have to prove herself every step of the way against a group of boys who were expecting her to fail.

But someone has to be first, she told herself, *so why not me?*

All the same, by the time she'd finished washing, her stomach was churning too much to let her eat breakfast. She didn't think she could face the mess hall anyway, not with all the excited chatter and the speculation over who'd

stay the course and who'd drop out into ordinary training. And since the first bell had barely begun, it was far too early to show up at the training hall. So instead, as soon as she was dressed, Ree left the barracks and walked down to the archery stands. She'd never been very good with a bow; she didn't have the eye for it. But she'd been practising this past week, just in case she got tested on it, and there was time to fit in one more session before training started.

To her surprise, she wasn't the only one to have had that idea. One of the boys who'd be training with her was already at the stands, a bow in his hands and a rack of arrows beside him. In contrast to the girls in the bathing room, his name came to her with ease: *Penn Avens*. Unlike the other boys – Zander and Farleigh and the rest – he was very much a second-name sort of person. Though he'd only showed up the day before yesterday, that was clear enough. Ree suspected he wouldn't welcome any interruptions for the sake of mere politeness.

She collected her own bow and arrows and took her place a couple of stands down from him, but after a while she found she was watching Penn rather than concentrating on the practice. Because though she hated to admit it, he was far better than she was. His arrows were clustered neatly at the centre of the bull's-eye, whereas hers – Ree bit her lip, glancing over at her own target. *Inconsistent* was too kind a word. The arrows that had actually hit the woven straw circle were scattered randomly across its face like a handful of dropped pins.

'Don't let them see that,' Penn said. She turned her head. He'd lowered his bow and was standing there watching her, a sardonic curl to his lips. 'You'll be out before you can blink.'

Blushing, Ree made no attempt at an answer – simply rested her own bow on its stand and went to collect her wayward arrows. When she got back to the shooting line, she found that Penn had abandoned his own equipment and crossed the empty stands to join her.

'I take it you haven't done much archery before,' he said, arms folded, watching her from beneath close-drawn brows. She resisted the urge to make excuses – *My tutor had no talent for it, and my mother decided that one teacher in weaponry was more than enough, so it was really a case of the incompetent leading the useless* – and merely shrugged.

'I'm better at other things.'

'Let's hope so,' he agreed.

Why, you rude, obnoxious, self-important –

'I don't see why it makes any difference to you,' she said, swallowing the insults with an effort – though she couldn't keep the heat from her voice. 'Worry about your own skills, and leave me to mine.'

Penn brushed the mop of sandy hair out of his eyes, all the better to glare at her. His eyes were a very pale blue, like a cloudy sky. 'I'm only telling you the truth. You have to be good at everything, or exceptional at something. Otherwise the weaponmasters and Captain Caraway –' for some reason, he gave that name a bitter twist – 'will show you the door.'

Ree's stomach plunged. 'Is Captain Caraway going to be there today?'

'I don't know.' Penn's eyes narrowed and darkened with the force of some angry thought. 'But I really hope he is.'

Without waiting for a reply, he turned and walked away, leaving his abandoned bow and arrows where they lay. Ree heard the door slam as he left the building.

Well. That was interesting.

The encounter had left her surprisingly shaken, and it took her a few more rounds of not very good archery practice before she'd calmed down enough to focus again. Then the assistant weaponmaster at the archery range poked her head through the door and said, brusquely but not unkindly, 'You're going to be late.'

Shit. The silence hit Ree like a brick. No-one else was around. They'd all gone up to the training hall. And if she didn't hurry –

'I'll put your equipment away,' the woman said. 'Worth it just to see a girl in trainin' for the Helm. But you'd best be quick.'

Heart pounding, Ree stammered out her thanks. Then she put her head down and ran.

She arrived in the practice yard, panting slightly, a little before the second bell. To her panicked eyes, the whole place seemed full of people; yet when she centred herself enough to look more closely, she realised there were only forty or so, standing in loose rows about six to a row, facing the door where the sign-up sheet had been pinned. Still, forty competitors for only a handful of places in the Helm meant the odds weren't in her favour ... and the squirming in her stomach returned with full force.

To distract herself, she looked around. The boys she'd been getting to know over the past week were there, all in various shades of hungover – with the exception of Zander, of course, because Zander was the sort of person who never, ever looked the worse for wear. And there were also a few new faces, stragglers who must have signed up just before the list came down. A broad-shouldered lad, a gangly one – and then the world froze around her. Because standing demurely in the front row was a girl. A tall, red-haired girl dressed in beautiful, immaculate clothes with lace at the cuffs, for all the world as if she'd just stepped out of one of Ree's mother's soirees. As soon as she saw Ree, she broke into a beaming smile and said loudly, 'At least I'm not the only one!'

Ree flinched as a dozen heads turned her way. She could see how they expected this to go. Either she and the other girl would become great friends and form their own exclusive little circle separate from the rest, or they'd be bitter rivals who constantly vied to beat each other in training. Those were the only two narratives open to her. That was what happened when you were part of a minority: to everyone else, your identity was intimately bound up with the group you belonged to. And now, however much Ree longed to be an individual person, a trainee like the rest, she'd forever end up being compared to some ridiculously attractive redhead – just because they were both female.

At least I'm not the only one, the girl had said; but as far as Ree could see, it was much worse being one of two than it had been on her own.

She realised that the girl's smile had faded, and that she herself was scowling. Hastily she smoothed the scowl away – it wasn't the girl's fault, after all. It was just the way things were. But Ree didn't go and stand in the front row, all the same. She wove through the ranks until she found a place where she wouldn't be so visible. From there, she glared at the back of the red-haired girl's head until the door at the front of the yard swung open and the assembled recruits fell silent.

The man who walked out to face the group was unmistakably a warrior: broad-shouldered, shaven-headed, skin roughened by the elements. He stared them all down as though he wouldn't hesitate to kick the lot of them out if they didn't behave themselves. And when he spoke, though he didn't appear to be trying to shout, his voice carried into every corner of the yard.

'I'm Art Bryan. One of the weaponmasters here. I'm the one who'll be training your sorry behinds.'

He was *big*. Seriously big. He looked as if punches and blades alike would bounce off his impervious hide. Ree's confidence ebbed a little further. Compared to this man, she was a twig next to a mighty trunk: far easier to snap.

Still, there was no-one with him wearing a Helmsman's striped coat, so at least she wouldn't have to impress Captain Caraway today. That was something.

'During this first week,' Bryan went on, 'my colleagues and I will assess your basic skills. And if any of you have wasted our time by signing up to be considered for the Helm before you're even competent to swing a sword –' he glared indiscriminately around – 'you'll be out on your ear and you won't be allowed back. So if you have any doubt at all that you're in the right place, you'd better leave now.'

He waited, arms folded as if waiting for them to run, but the yard was utterly silent. Ree couldn't hear anyone breathing, much less moving.

'Good,' Bryan said. 'Then if you are found to be at an acceptable standard after the first week, we will continue to assess you for another six weeks – after which time, the best of you will be selected for Helm training with Captain Caraway and myself. Do you understand?'

Again there was complete silence. Bryan nodded as if he'd expected nothing less.

'As new members of the fifth ring, you will be expected to adhere to our Code at all times,' he said. 'You will not fight in anger. You will not use lethal weapons outside the training grounds. You will not settle your differences with your fists. And if you do, you'll be out on your arse. Got it? Let me hear you this time.'

'Yes, sir!' The chorus was loud and fervent. Bryan's stern expression cracked into a rather sadistic grin.

'Good,' he said again. 'Then let's get started.'

As he continued to speak, giving them a short recap of the key people they'd be dealing with and the locations of certain facilities in the fifth ring, Ree risked moving her gaze, ever so slightly – just as far as the two men standing behind the weaponmaster. One – the shorter and older of the two, who Bryan introduced as the armourer – fairly bristled with assorted steel. In contrast, the second man carried a sword at his hip, but other than that he went unarmed. Ree frowned at him, trying to work him out. He wore nondescript clothing, like that of any labourer, and his brown hair was slightly too long and rather scruffy. Not a warrior, then. Or perhaps he had arrived late for the training – albeit he was rather too old to be an inductee – and was now awaiting an unobtrusive moment to slip past Bryan without being dressed down for his tardiness.

Ree was quite pleased with that bit of deduction, right up until Bryan ordered the new recruits to pair up and spar – at which point, the stranger wandered over to lean against the wall. A new assistant weaponmaster, then, come to learn the ropes? Though his behaviour seemed too casual for that. It was all rather odd.

'Want to pair?' Zander's voice said in her ear, and she turned quickly.

'You want to spar with me?'

'You promised to run rings around me, remember? I must admit, I've rather been looking forward to it.'

She still couldn't tell if he was mocking her or not, but she was so relieved not to be paired with the other girl – because *that* would have confirmed their status as outsiders – that she merely nodded. Zander grinned and handed her one of the two wooden swords he was holding.

'There you go. I don't want to run the risk of being spitted on my very first day.'

She glared at him. *Stop patronising me. Stop –*

'Hey, Zander!' called one of the other recruits as he passed by with his own practice weapon. 'Let me know when you've finished messing about with her and I'll give you a real match.'

Ree spun on her heel, lifting her wooden sword, opening her mouth to insult him in kind – but as always, Zander was there first.

'Sorry, Timo. I might not survive this one.'

'Will you stop that?' Ree snapped. 'I don't need you to rescue me!'

He looked at her with raised eyebrows. 'I was just trying to be helpful.'

'Then don't!'

'Fine.' Smile gone, he paced away from her until they were the right distance apart, then stopped and turned. 'Come on, then. If you can.'

Ree clutched the practice sword, anger surging in her blood. She welcomed it; she'd been angry often enough when sparring before to have learned how to use it. How to channel it down from a vast cloud of feeling into something precise and vicious. She offered a short, jerky salute in response to Zander's more graceful one – and then, without waiting any longer, she went for him.

He was a decent swordsman, she discovered as she went through the patterns of attack and defence. Maybe a little better than her, but not by much. Not enough to matter. In fact, in some of the forms she had the edge. If she could just use that to her advantage ...

She pressed forward, and had the satisfaction of seeing alarm rise in his eyes. He was stumbling backwards, sword wavering, unable to escape the blade that was rising towards his throat – and then, suddenly, he moved in an odd twisty motion, knocking her sword arm aside and coming up right in front of her. Close enough to kiss, had she felt the slightest desire to do so. His foot hooked her ankle, the flat of his sword pushed her back – and she was falling.

Her head bounced against the dirt, and for an instant her vision blackened. Once she'd blinked it away, she found Zander crouched beside her with a concerned expression on his face.

'Ree, I –'

She struggled into a sitting position. 'Don't you dare apologise.'

'But –'

'Zander, I mean it.' She couldn't stop the smile that was spreading across her face. 'That was brilliant! I've never seen anything like that before, you'll have to show me how –'

'You're not angry?' he interrupted.

'Of course not! This is what I came here for!' She lifted a hand to the back of her head and winced at the sore patch she found there, grinning all the while. Finally, *finally*, she was among people who could teach her something new. 'I'd only be angry if you'd held back on me.'

He studied her face a little longer; then the anxiety in his eyes vanished and he answered her smile with an insouciant one of his own. 'You're a very strange girl, Ree Quinn.'

'I know.'

'All right, you two!' The bellow made them both jump. They looked around to find the weaponmaster standing a short distance away, arms folded across his massive chest.

Ree grabbed Zander's proffered hand and used it to scramble to her feet. *Don't blush. Don't panic. Don't blush.*

'Names?' Bryan demanded. They told him, and he nodded. 'Good. You, Zander –' a finger stabbed in Zander's direction – 'are inventive. I like that about you. But you're also lazy. You take shortcuts in your stances, in the way you hold your sword. And that might work for you now, but later on you'll regret it. Because once you get on to advanced training, you'll find yourself with a bunch of bad habits you're too old to break. Being accurate now might be harder, but it'll pay off in the long run. Get it?'

Zander nodded, looking more serious than Ree had yet seen him. Not that she had much attention to spare, because now Bryan was turning to her.

'Ree. You held your own against someone bigger and more knowledgeable than yourself. Someone's obviously taught you how to compensate for your size. And what Zander here lacks in precision, you have in bucketloads. Your main problem ...' His eyes narrowed fractionally as he assessed her, before concluding, 'Inflexible. You didn't adapt to his style. You assumed you knew what he'd do – based on your own past experience, I assume – and acted accordingly. But every swordsman is different. Every *person* is different. You learn your opponent in every fight, and learn fast, or else you lose.'

Ree nearly objected that she'd only ever fought one person before, so it was hardly as if she'd had much opportunity to be flexible – but she restrained herself. Because the weapon-master was right. He knew what he was talking about. And if she were to have any hope of progressing beyond this point, she had to learn from everything he told her. So she simply thanked him, and heard Zander echo it. Bryan studied both of them a moment longer, then nodded.

'You're both decent enough for first-timers. I don't utterly despair of making something out of you. And to that end ...' He stood back, expression challenging. 'Let's see you do it again.'

After that, it was nothing but fun. Bryan corrected Zander's grip, and showed Ree how to counter that unusual move, and then they fought each other again. All the while her smile lingered on her lips, despite how it made her cheeks ache. This was exactly what she wanted. What she'd hoped for. And she never wanted to go back.

They might make you, said the small voice of doubt inside her, but she suppressed it sternly.

I am never *going back.*

Too soon, the session was over. Bryan lined them back up before taking his place at the front of the group.

'All right,' he said. 'None of you are being shown the door today.'

The collective sigh of relief in the yard was audible. Though Ree tried to stop it, her gaze slid to the red-haired girl. *You were hoping she'd fail, weren't you?* her conscience whispered. *You're a horrible person.*

'We will continue to monitor your basic skills throughout the week,' Bryan went on. 'Those of you who survive it will go through an intensive training and assessment process in all varieties of combat: armed, unarmed, single and melee. You will learn and be tested on the standard forms of swordplay and rudimentary battle tactics, as well as wrestling and archery.' Ree's stomach plunged. 'After seven weeks, Captain Caraway will assess you one-on-one and identify those of you he feels have the potential for further training. Any questions?'

Again, utter silence gripped the recruits. Then one of them, braver or more foolish than the rest, spoke up.

'Sir, I understand it's traditional to learn the forms. But are they really that valuable, when the people we'll be fighting aren't likely to know them – or if they do, won't necessarily stick to them?'

'Don't look down on the classical training,' Bryan said. 'The fashion these days is to fight as a sellsword fights, quick and dirty. But the best swordsman I ever taught could have wiped the floor with any sellsword and still had the stamina to spar with me afterwards.'

'Who was he, sir? Your pupil?'

'Lord Myrren Nightshade,' Bryan said. 'He could have been the best in the world. But sadly ...'

Ree ducked her head, uncomfortable. Everyone had heard the rumours, but given where they were, no-one liked to ask any questions.

No-one except Farleigh.

'Sir, is it true he murdered his own father?'

'Killed, yes.' The words dropped softly into the sudden silence. 'Murdered, no.'

Ree had almost forgotten the scruffy brown-haired man. She glanced up; he hadn't left his place by the wall, shoulders resting casually against the stone.

'What does that mean?' Farleigh demanded.

'It means that in some circumstances, a man's intentions can outweigh his actions.'

'That's just an excuse,' Penn put in, the habitual frown deepening on his face. 'I don't know where you're from, but I was always taught that murder is murder. *Killing is wrong except in law or at war* – that's pretty much the first lesson my parents ever taught me.'

Ree shook her head. *Yet he's joined the assessment programme ...*

'It's not that simple, though, is it?' she said. 'There's self-defence. Or defence of someone you're sworn to protect. Like the Helm with the Nightshade line,' she added pointedly.

'Exactly.' There went Zander, leaping to her aid again. Well, maybe *leaping* was the wrong word. Sauntering, perhaps. She found she didn't mind it so much this time. 'I mean ... by your standards, Avens, Captain Caraway murdered Owen Travers. Traitor or not.'

'Which is obviously nonsense!' Farleigh added. 'No-one could call Captain Caraway a murderer. He was a hero!'

The brown-haired man had been listening to their conversation with a grave, interested look on his face, but at that he shook his head. 'Tomas Caraway was no hero, believe me. He was a bit of an idiot who happened to get lucky.'

Farleigh scowled. 'What do you know about it? Who are you, anyway?'

The stranger gave him a faintly apologetic smile. 'Tomas Caraway.'

But – but where's his coat? Ree bit her lip, hearing her stunned embarrassment reflected in the shuffling feet and unnecessarily cleared throats around her. This was Captain Caraway. The man who'd discovered the previous captain's treasonous plans and single-handedly rescued Lady Ayla from false imprisonment. The man she'd have to impress if she were to have any chance of achieving her dream. And she'd been standing there judging him on his *hairstyle*.

'The best that can be said of me is that I never lost sight of what the Helm is for,' Caraway said into the silence. 'First and foremost, we aren't warriors or kingmakers or law enforcers. We're protectors. If you want to join us in Darkhaven, you'd do well to remember that.'

He glanced over at Bryan, who gave him a nod. There was respect in it, but also something else. Shared history, maybe. A mutual wry acknowledgement of ... something.

'Quite so, Captain Caraway, and thank you for coming along,' the weaponmaster said. 'See any promise in this bunch of reprobates?'

Caraway shrugged. 'I'm sure a handful of them will do well in Darkhaven – once they've learned that there's more to being a Helmsman than wearing a striped coat.'

He didn't even look in Ree's direction as he said it, but the blood heated her cheeks all the same. Awareness of it doing nothing to improve the situation, she flushed even hotter and dropped her chin to stare steadfastly at the ground once more. Curse her thin skin. She'd bet none of the others were blushing like awkward teenage girls.

'Want to show them how it's done, boyo?' Bryan said. Not the proper way to address the Captain of the Helm, but she heard Caraway's grin in his voice.

'Why not? I can probably get in a defence or two before you disarm me.'

At that Ree had to look up, despite her embarrassment. Bryan and Caraway were facing each other in the centre of the yard, swords in the ready position. They exchanged a nod, the salute of men who spared little time for frivolity. Then Bryan lunged, brutal and heavy, nothing like the careful practice lunges he'd demonstrated so far – Caraway caught the blade on his own and wrenched it aside – and Ree forgot everything else, because they were *good*. This was nothing like watching the other trainees spar, or what she'd been doing with Zander. This was a kind of art.

After an intent, breath-holding interval, she realised that as well as engaging in a genuine attempt to disarm each other, they were demonstrating the forms. Never the same one twice. It was like that game Ree had played as a child, where you took it in turns to name cities or birds or trees as quickly as possible, and if you repeated one you were out; a grown-up version, played at swordpoint. She found herself naming each form under her breath: Firestorm, Red Dawn, Harvest Corn, one she didn't recognise – and then Bryan went for a Cascade of Ice, and even as Caraway twisted nimbly out of reach she was biting back a protest –

'Well?' Bryan turned to her suddenly, eyebrows raised. Hard to tell how he could have heard that quickly suppressed cry above the general cheering and clamouring, but he had. 'Excitement getting too much for you, girlie?'

Her spine stiffened. *But he called Captain Caraway 'boyo',* she reminded herself, *it's not aimed just at you ...*

'No, sir,' she said aloud. 'It's just, I – I believe you already did the Cascade of Ice. Sir.'

Bryan stared at her without speaking; beyond him, a slow grin was dawning on Caraway's face.

'Glad to see someone's paying attention,' the captain said. 'My round, Bryan?'

The weaponmaster snorted. 'Looks like it. You'd better keep an eye on this one, Breakblade.'

'I intend to.' Caraway glanced at Ree with approval, and she felt herself blush again – but this time, she didn't care.

Later, buzzing with the feverish energy that had been ignited in them by the day's events, most of the trainees found their way to an inn. This time, buoyed by praise, Ree went with them. Inevitably the conversation lingered on everything that Bryan and Caraway had said and done, and in particular their duel. It had inspired everyone, Ree realised. It was probably meant to. They'd been given a glimpse of what they could be, if they were good enough. And from there, talk moved to the surprise appearance of the captain himself.

'Why did Weaponmaster Bryan call Captain Caraway "Breakblade"?' the red-haired girl – Saydi – asked with a pretty frown. She'd come along with everyone else, all giggly and fluttery; still riding on the crest of the day's excitement, Ree was able largely to ignore the minor aggravation of her presence. 'It's an odd kind of name to give the Captain of the Helm.'

'They call him that 'cos the weapons of his enemies shatter when he fights them,' one trainee suggested, but another shook his head.

'Nah. S'because even when his sword breaks in half, he's still better than the other guy.'

'I'll tell you the real reason,' Penn said. 'Tomas Caraway was known as Breakblade because his sword was broken in half when he was thrown out of the Helm. And he only got back in because his *lover* put him there.'

Silence fell amongst the trainees. Then one of them said, 'Well, I heard Captain Caraway killed Owen Travers with a broken sword –' and with that, the lively discussion started up again. Ree stayed quiet, watching Penn. He was glowering into his ale cup, face dark with loathing – but she couldn't tell if it was directed at Captain Caraway, his fellow recruits or the whole damn world. Either way, she couldn't see why on earth he'd want to join the Helm if that was how he felt.

'Doesn't like us much, does he?' Zander's amused voice said in her ear. 'More wine, Ree?'

'All right. Just a little.'

He reached across the table for the bottle, and she spotted the design tattooed on the back of his left wrist. She'd noticed it earlier, but she'd been too busy concentrating on the lesson to really take it in. Now, she caught his arm for a closer look.

'This is pretty,' she said, touching it with a fingertip. The pattern was like an abstract flower, eight petals with small circles in between them, picked out in black ink against his brown skin. Zander raised his eyebrows at her in mock disapproval and removed his wrist from her grasp.

'Pretty, no. Attractive, I'll allow you. Or striking, at a pinch.'

'Sorry,' she said with a grin. 'So what's the significance of your extremely rugged and manly tattoo, Zander?'

'Family tradition. My father has one the same.' He smiled back at her, but she detected that same hint of constraint that had coloured his voice when they spoke about their home towns. And, sure enough, after a moment he pulled his sleeve down over his wrist and turned the conversation to another topic. Very adroitly – she didn't think anyone else would have noticed – but again, she found it odd.

Soon they were talking about the weeks ahead, comparing notes on the different disciplines they'd be studying. Once some of the boys had admitted their own weaknesses, Ree didn't feel so bad about her archery – even when Penn tried to needle her about it. What did bother her, though, was Saydi. Time and again, the other girl made remarks that showed her ignorance of combat and weaponry, until Ree found herself wincing along in sympathy. And so, once they were back in the fifth ring and she and Saydi had peeled off from the group towards the women's barracks, she couldn't help interrupting the other girl's flow of chatter with the question that was burning in her throat.

'What are you doing here, Saydi?'

'Me? What do you mean?'

'I mean, this is important to me. I've wanted it my whole life. But you ...'

You make me look bad, she wanted to say. *The boys don't take you seriously, and that means they don't take me seriously either. You're ruining this for me!* But Saydi was already looking hurt, so Ree shook her head.

'Never mind. It doesn't matter. Just ...' She hesitated, then took the plunge. 'You didn't set out to join the Helm, or even become a warrior. You obviously have some skill, or you wouldn't have got through the first day, but why don't you start with ordinary training and see how it goes? I mean, you're obviously not prepared for this ...'

Saydi giggled, though more nervously than usual. 'How do you know?'

Because you have perfect fingernails, you're covered in lace and you don't know a feint from a faint. 'The conversation back there ... have you ever trained before?'

'My father taught me a bit, before he died. After that I taught myself.'

Elements. Ree shook her head. 'You're going straight in at the hardest level. No point making it more difficult than you have to. If you want to be accepted as part of the group and not some kind of – of sideshow –'

She bit her lip, immediately knowing she'd gone too far. But Saydi didn't retaliate. They'd reached their corridor by now; the other girl mumbled something, then hurried off towards her own room without even looking in Ree's direction. Ree felt guilty for an instant, but only an instant. Because what she'd told Saydi was true: this was the most important thing she'd ever done, and she couldn't let anyone ruin it. Particularly not a girl who was exactly like every one of the silly marriage-obsessed females she'd left behind. She'd had enough of that kind of thing in her life already.

Yet somehow, the evening had lost its lustre.

Once the new cohort of recruits had left the yard, Bryan and Caraway ambled around it picking up all the practice weapons – because every wooden sword would need checking for notches and flaws before it was used again. The whole point of a practice weapon was to leave no more than bruises, not to embed a cloud of splinters in some hapless youth's face. Of course, this kind of thing wasn't Bryan's job, and certainly not Caraway's; yet the captain always claimed he liked to carry out mundane tasks every so often, to give himself time to think, and Bryan himself had a very particular reason for wanting to stay behind.

He was hoping that Caraway would bring up the subject first, but the lad remained frustratingly silent all through the process of gathering the weapons. Once they were stacked up, he settled down to check them over; Bryan stood off to one side, arms folded, and waited.

And waited.

Until finally, he didn't have the patience to wait any more.

'So, what did you think of the new lot?' he asked, keeping his tone deliberately noncommittal. Caraway lifted a shoulder without looking up.

'No better or worse than any other intake. Hard to assess much beyond basic skill on the first day, you know that.'

'True. But we've never had an intake quite like this, have we?'

'Have we not?'

'I'd say not, given that it contains two girls.'

'Were there girls? I didn't notice.' Caraway's head was bent, but Bryan caught his lurking smile.

'Damn it, Tomas!' he snapped. 'You could at least take this seriously!'

The smile faded. 'What makes you think I don't?'

'Because you're acting like it's nothing out of the ordinary, when you know damn well it is!'

Still crouched on the ground surrounded by wooden swords, Caraway glanced up at him. 'You thought it would unsettle me, didn't you? You thought I'd see those girls and start fretting over it, wondering how to tell them without being cruel that they were in the wrong place – because I'm a nice lad who doesn't like to hurt people's feelings, but there's no way a woman can perform the tasks required of a Helmsman.'

Since that was exactly what Bryan had thought, he could only nod.

'Sorry to disappoint you,' Caraway said, returning to his task. 'But I see no reason to turn them away.'

As simple as that, eh? Bryan ran a hand over his scalp, unsure whether to be amused or exasperated. 'You think they can do the job?'

'I don't know. But I don't see the harm in letting them try.'

'Owen Travers would have thrown 'em out straight away,' Bryan muttered, and Caraway cast him another glance.

'In case you hadn't noticed,' he said with deceptive mildness, 'I'm not much like Owen Travers.'

Bryan dismissed the obvious with a flick of his fingers. 'I know you want to do things differently, Breakblade, and I respect that. But I still think you're not allowing this issue enough weight.'

'Why not? Why do a couple of girls make so much difference?'

'Because the Helm are men! Always have been! If one of these girls is good enough to pass the training and you end up accepting her into the Helm, it'll cause chaos in the ranks. Surely you know that.'

'Actually, I don't,' Caraway said. Pushing the last practice sword aside, he got to his feet. 'Women have been training alongside men in the fifth ring for much longer than you or I have been here. It's not as if a female warrior is a new idea to any of my Helmsmen.' He frowned at Bryan's sudden grin. 'What?'

'Nothing. 'S just the first time I've heard you call them yours.' *And about bloody time too.* Obscurely heartened by that small show of confidence, Bryan clapped him on the back. 'All right, boyo. You want the girls to train, they train. They've as little chance of success as anyone else, so you may never have to put *your* Helm to the test. And in the meantime, let's hope the lads who've come to try their skill will take to the idea as easily as you have.'

'I don't see why they'd object.'

'Yes, Captain Caraway,' Bryan said patiently, 'but that's because you're an idealist. Just you wait and see.'

TEN

A few days after starting on the assessment programme with the latest intake of Helm hopefuls – one of whom was quite possibly an assassin – Caraway realised that he'd been neglecting Ayla's own training as a result. Which was stupid, because she needed to be able to defend herself now more than ever. With that in mind, he took her off to the small hall within Darkhaven they'd been using for the purpose so that she could get some more practice. Yet with every new grip, every new throw, he became increasingly frustrated. She was good, by now. She learned quickly, and her Changer blood made her nearly his equal in strength. And yet it wasn't enough. He was still beating her, much of the time. And if he could beat her, other people could too.

Come on, Ayla. Grip, lift, slam. *Fight me off.* Grip, lift, slam. *Don't let yourself be caught unawares –*

'Tomas!' She put both palms in the centre of his chest and shoved him as hard as she could. 'Enough!'

He stumbled back a step, focusing properly on her face. She was flushed and breathing fast, but her eyes were narrow with anger.

'I'm sorry,' he mumbled.

'Surely you know this isn't doing any good,' she said, still cross. 'Even if I improve enough to throw you off every time, that won't help me against a bullet.'

'I know.' He scrubbed his hands through his hair. 'That's the problem.'

Her expression softened. 'Tomas, you're doing everything you can. We both know that. I'm as scared as you are, but we'll come through this together.'

'I'm sorry,' Caraway said again. 'It's just ... the other day, I said you had to stay alive for Mirrorvale's sake. But the truth is ...' He looked away, unable to meet her gaze. 'The truth is, I need you to stay alive for mine.'

Silence. It was too much, he knew it was. Showing her the extent of his need for her could only cause her to retreat. But then she said gently, 'Why does that make you ashamed?'

'Not ashamed. Not that. But I shouldn't ...' Eyes still downcast, he struggled for an explanation. 'You're the one in danger. I'm supposed to reassure you. Not let my own fears show.'

'Tomas. Look at me.'

He did. Ayla looked back at him steadily, a gentle downward curve to her mouth. Not sadness, exactly. Something softer and more subtle than that.

'You're allowed to be afraid on your own behalf,' she said. 'In fact –' and here a gleam of mischief entered her eyes – 'I'd be offended if you weren't.'

He had to laugh, and that made the tightness in his chest ease a little.

'Now,' Ayla said, still mischievous, 'try it again.'

Mistrusting her expression, but willing enough to go along with it, Caraway reached for her. Instead of twisting away, she ducked under his arm and came up close against him. Her hands grabbed the front of his shirt. Her head tilted as she stretched up on tiptoes to touch her lips to his. Completely disarmed, Caraway released his hold and kissed her back.

'I didn't hurt you just now, did I?' he murmured when they came up for air. She caught his lower lip between her teeth, hard enough to make him wince, then smiled.

'No more than that.'

And she hooked his feet neatly from under him.

After she'd finished laughing, she appeared above him with a smirk on her face. '*Never let your guard down*, Captain Caraway.'

'I admit, it wasn't the kind of thing I ever prepared for in training,' he replied. 'But now I know *that* kind of move is allowable between us …'

Ayla retreated, laughing again, as he jumped back to his feet and advanced on her. And one thing led to another.

Later, he watched her trying to smooth her rumpled hair back into place without a comb and reflected ruefully that he'd just confirmed everything the Helm thought about his training of Ayla. Not that they'd ever said it to him, and certainly not to her. But he'd overheard a handful of them speculating with salacious glee about what, exactly, their captain taught their overlord twice a week behind closed doors. He'd let them get on with it; soldiers were soldiers, after all, and they'd talk whatever he said to them. It wasn't as if anything they said had really been offensive to him or, more importantly, to Ayla. But the irony was, there'd been absolutely no truth in it. Whatever the two of them might get up to at other times, their training sessions had always focused on genuine fighting skills – until now.

'I think we may have just become a cliché,' Ayla said, turning to him in a half-echo of his thoughts. 'Still, at least now the Helm can indulge their gossip in the righteous glow of truth.'

Caraway reminded himself that she knew far more about what went on in Darkhaven than he gave her credit for. She had, after all, been part of its rather odd community all her life.

'Do you mind?' he asked anxiously.

'Mind?' Apparently giving up on her unruly hair, she let her hands fall. 'Why should I mind? It's not as if you and I are a secret.'

'But –'

'If they have nothing better to talk about than what two grown adults get up to in private, I say let them get on with it.' She crossed over to kiss him, a mere brush of the lips this time, then rocked back on her heels so that she could look up into his face. 'I'd better go and meet Miles. He's returning today so we can start our investigation.'

Her expression was challenging. Caraway decided not to rise to the bait, only saying equably, 'I'd like to greet him myself. Do you mind if I join you for a few moments before I go?'

As he'd hoped, she couldn't really argue with that.

Yet once the two of them and Miles were sitting together in the library, Caraway found himself doubting his own doubts – because he couldn't think of anyone less likely to be an assassin than the man in front of him. Miles didn't appear to have the ability to dissemble in any way whatsoever, even when it would make other people – or indeed, himself – far more comfortable. If he wanted to kill someone, he'd probably tell them precisely why he wanted to do it first.

Still, it wasn't as if assassins came with a warning sign. The best person to carry out an assassination was always the one who no-one could imagine doing it.

'I would like to start by learning exactly what you can do,' Miles was saying now, after some introductory and rather awkward pleasantries. 'You can Change; that goes without saying. But some of the stories I have heard about your father ...'

Caraway felt Ayla tense beside him, but her voice remained calm. 'Go on.'

'They say he had certain powers even in human form. That he could see in the dark. That he could control fire. That he was faster and stronger than an ordinary man, and healed more quickly ...'

Ayla nodded. 'True, true and true.'

'Oh. Then you –'

'I can see in the dark. I'm stronger than I should be for my size. As for controlling fire ...' She looked away. 'Florentyn was a pure creature of flame. As such, he had powers I don't have. Small things, really. He could light the lamps without having to touch them. Incinerate a piece of paper to ashes. No more than that.'

'Of course, you would have no power over flame,' Miles said calmly. 'It is not your element. Something your father might have burned, you would be able to freeze. Did you ever attempt anything like that?'

'I –' Ayla hesitated. 'To be honest, I never thought of it. My father tested me with fire, when I was younger, and when I failed, he told me –' She swallowed, then finished carefully, 'He told me it was because I was neither one thing nor the other.'

Caraway heard all the words she wasn't repeating, and squeezed her hand. She threw him a small, grateful smile.

'With the greatest of respect to your father, he was not an alchemist,' Miles said, oblivious to the unspoken. 'I would

129

expect a hybrid to be stronger, alchemically speaking, than a single element. He was simply giving you the wrong test.'

Ayla stared at him. 'You mean ...'

'Your elements are wood and ice,' Miles explained. 'So if you have any powers such as those you described of your father's, they will take those forms. The power to freeze water, as I said. And as for wood ...' He spread his hands. 'You may be able to snap it. Bend it. Encourage it to grow. I really have no idea which.'

'I've never been able to do anything like that before,' Ayla said doubtfully, and he nodded.

'Nevertheless, I think it is worth a try. After all –' a sympathetic glance – 'if you fail, you will not have lost anything.'

Not oblivious after all, then. Caraway suppressed a sigh. He could see why Ayla liked the man, but he still wished she hadn't brought someone new into Darkhaven. As he'd said, he would have expected an assassin to be personable.

'Here.' Miles held out the glass of water from the table beside him. 'Try this.'

'Now?'

'Why not?'

Ayla took it, her expression a mixture of fear and resolution. She bowed her head, knuckles whitening briefly. Then she looked up and fixed the water with a steady stare.

Nothing happened.

'I told you,' she said, lowering the glass to glare at Miles over the top of it. 'I'm not –'

'It would be very surprising if you could achieve it on your first attempt,' Miles said calmly. 'But perhaps, if you practise ...' He looked thoughtful. 'Tell me, how did your Changer power first manifest itself?'

To start with, Caraway thought she wasn't going to answer. She bent her head once more, running a fingertip around the rim of the glass – but then she spoke in a low, soft voice.

'It was my birthday. I was turning fourteen. I'd been dreading it for months, because Myrren still hadn't made the Change, and my father had grown increasingly violent towards him since – since my mother died. And I knew I couldn't win. If I failed to Change, I would only add to my father's fury. But if I succeeded, it would put all that burden of failure back on Myrren's shoulders.'

Caraway had never heard her talk about it in that way before. He wanted to hug her, but settled for reaching across to squeeze her hand again. Ayla glanced at him, then at Miles, and her defensive, wounded expression eased into amusement.

'There's no need to look so tragic,' she said. 'It's ancient history now. The point is, I didn't want to Change that day. I didn't want the day to come at all. But when my father took me out into the courtyard and assumed his creature form, to see if I would do the same, it just ... happened. The power was there, and I used it before I even knew what I was doing.' One corner of her mouth curled ruefully. 'As you can imagine, he had some words to say about the kind of creature I turned out to be, but that's another matter.'

'I see,' Miles said. 'In that case, it may be that your other powers find you in a similar manner. Alchemy is, in some sense, at the intersection between knowledge and belief. You had no idea of your potential, and so that door was closed. But now that you are aware of the possibilities ...' He peered at her face as if trying to assess her level of openness to new things, then concluded, 'I think on this one, Lady Ayla, we will just have to wait and see.'

She nodded. Despite her attempt to reassure him, Caraway could still see a hint of pain in the curve of her mouth. She might claim that what she'd described was ancient history, but it was still part of her. He found himself hoping that Miles was right, that she would discover these new powers over wood and ice. Maybe then she would be able to lay her father to rest for good.

'Miles,' he began, thinking to ask the alchemist whether there was anything he himself could do to help Ayla – but then a sharp rap on the library door made them all jump. The Helmsman who entered gave a respectful bow to Ayla and a nod to Miles, but his attention was focused on Caraway.

'You'd better come quickly, sir,' he said. 'There's been a shooting.'

Strictly speaking, an unlawful death in Arkannen fell under the jurisdiction of the city watch, not the Helm. Unlike his predecessor, Caraway had no desire to extend the powers of the Helm beyond Darkhaven itself. They existed to protect the Nightshade line: that was all, and that was enough. But on the matter of firearms, the boundaries were less clear. The watch were ill equipped to deal with the sudden rise of illegal weaponry in the city; they didn't know how to handle and store a confiscated pistol, how to use one, how to defend themselves against it. The truth was, very few people in Arkannen did. What knowledge there was lay underground. A few sellswords of Naeve Sorrow's ilk – those who were skilled enough and deadly enough to be largely above the law. The black-market traders who smuggled firearms and powder into the city. Perhaps the odd wealthy specialist who gained pleasure from being able to buy and own something no-one else had ...

And Miles Tarantil.

The thought presented itself apparently from nowhere; it took Caraway a moment to place the memory behind it, Bryan telling him that if he ever needed advice on the Helm's store of confiscated firearms then he could do worse than call on Miles. Because apparently, Miles knew how to use a pistol. *Why*, Caraway hadn't asked at the time – but now, with his and Ayla's previous discussion fresh in his mind, it took on a more suspicious hue. And Miles was in Darkhaven with Ayla right now ...

Caraway hesitated, toying with the idea of returning to the tower. But Miles would have been searched before entering Darkhaven. Everyone was, now, even those who had lived there for years. Even Caraway himself, to make the point that no-one was above suspicion. And the keys to the very secure, nigh-indestructible, *certainly* unpickable safe that contained the pistols were currently hanging around Caraway's neck. Yes, assassins were cunning, but they weren't *that* cunning.

Besides, the watch were expecting him – which brought him back to the original point. The watch didn't know what to do with firearms; it made sense for the Helm, the most highly trained soldiers in Mirrorvale, to take charge of unusual and dangerous weaponry. In addition – though he hadn't revealed it in his conversations with the watch – Caraway had been aware for the past three years just how much of a threat a pistol could be to national security. And so he and the Captain of the Watch had agreed between them that if any crimes occurred in the city that were related to firearms, the Helm would attend the scene to lend their expertise and possibly take charge, depending on the crime.

Of course, usually it was smuggling or illegal possession. Murder was a new and unwelcome development.

The incident had taken place in the first ring, in one of the more disreputable inns that edged the Night Quarter. One of Caraway's old haunts, in fact. Chances were, he'd brawled on the premises himself at some time in his life – though of course, the difference was that he'd never killed anyone in the process. Still, as he stepped over the threshold, he was uncomfortably aware of just how fine the line was between himself and the crimson-spattered lad who sat with an expression of glazed shock between two members of the city watch. The pistol lay on the table in front of them, looking deceptively innocuous.

'Caraway,' the Captain of the Watch greeted him. She was waiting by the door: a tall woman, older than him, stern-faced. The rest of the inn was empty, even the bartender absent from his post. No doubt the witnesses had all been sent away or taken in for questioning.

'Larson.' They exchanged salutes. 'What happened?'

'See for yourself. We haven't moved him yet.' She jerked her head back over her shoulder, and Caraway stepped around her to see, for the first time, the man lying on the floor. There could be no chance that he was still alive. The pool of gore that surrounded his body was far too large for that, and the vast, gaping wound that had obliterated a good portion of his back left little room for doubt.

Fire and blood, Caraway thought – then almost laughed, though it wasn't funny, because that was what the room smelled like. Death and gunpowder. He'd never smelled the two together before, but there was no mistaking either. *So that's what it looks like when you shoot someone.*

Fleetingly he saw Ayla in place of the dead man, and his vision swam. It was no wonder that a pistol could do what other weapons couldn't, and harm a Changer creature. The victim's insides appeared to have exploded out of him.

'Several people saw it happen,' Larson said. 'So you've no need to be involved in the investigation, such as it is. Just thought you'd want to take charge of the weapon.' She eyed the pistol with dour suspicion.

Caraway nodded. 'Do you mind if I speak to the suspect?'

'Be my guest.'

He crossed to the table and leaned both hands on it, looking down at the killer's bowed head. 'Can you tell me what happened?' he asked, not ungently.

The lad clasped his shaking hands and looked up. 'I – I shot him. In the chest. He owed me money and wouldn't pay, so –' An audible swallow. 'But I din't know what would happen – I –'

'Then why pull the trigger?' Caraway's voice lifted, torn between anger, exasperation and just a hint of sympathy. 'Why carry an illegal firearm if you *don't even know what it does?*'

The lad shrugged. *Lad* was the right word. He was younger than Caraway, though fear had aged him. No older than some of the new recruits, up in the fifth ring. 'Gave me a reputation, din't it. Made people back off.'

And there was the problem: pistols were becoming more common than the knowledge of how to use them. A handful of years ago it would have been fists or a knife – both of which could be lethal, of course, but the point was they didn't have to be. Whereas a pistol, in the close quarters of a bar-room brawl ... whoever it was aimed at didn't stand a chance. Rumour didn't lie when it said they were the deadliest weapons around, and in some circles that made them *fashionable*. Which meant you ended up with idiots like this one, carrying fire around in their pockets because they didn't realise it could burn. If the watch or the Helm didn't find a way to stop it soon, they'd only end up with more deaths on their hands.

Caraway couldn't see the dead man's face, but no doubt he was just as young as his killer. And that was a tragedy, whichever way you cut it.

He picked up the spent pistol and slipped it into his pocket. Perhaps he should try to persuade Larson to go easy on the lad. It had been a mistake. Just the stupid act of a young fool drunk on bravado and a sense of his own invincibility ...

But someone had died. That had to be paid for.

'You took two lives today,' he told the trembling boy. 'His and your own. I hope you remember that.'

Then he nodded at the guards, thanked Larson, and slipped back out into the fresh air of the street. He'd suggest to Ayla that a sentence of permanent incarceration would be more appropriate than execution in this case. Everyone deserved a second chance. Maybe over time, the boy could earn the right to commute his sentence to banishment and make a new life for himself elsewhere.

When Caraway got back to Darkhaven, he went straight to the armoury and unlocked the safe with the keys from around his neck. It had always been a general store for rare or dangerous weapons; these days, the vast majority of it was taken up by firearms and everything that went with them. Caraway pulled out the slotted tray from the central shelf and added the newest pistol to the collection. After that he stood there, just looking at the weapons. Twenty of them. Twenty, where three years ago there had been one. Somewhere among them was the pistol that had killed Lord Myrren. Another had killed a man today. Any one of them could kill Ayla.

Twenty. In another three years, would there be hundreds?

'Are you all right?' Ayla said softly behind him. What was she doing in the armoury? Spreading his hands in a futile attempt to hide the open safe and the tray of weapons, he turned.

'I'm not sure you should be in here, love.'

'What?' she said, only half teasing. 'Restricting me to Darkhaven isn't enough for you? You want to restrict me *within* Darkhaven as –'

But then she got close enough to see around him to the pistols, and her face visibly drained of colour.

'I'm sorry,' Caraway said quickly, bundling the tray back into the safe and slamming the door shut. She shook her head.

'It's all right. I can't hide from them forever. It's just ...' She hesitated, then finished in a low voice, 'They already took my brother. When I look at them, I can't help wondering if this is where my family ends.'

Caraway reached for her hands. 'It won't be that way.'

'I wish Myrren –'

'I know.'

They stood in silence for a while. Then Caraway sighed, still thinking about the influx of firearms, and said, 'The trouble is, I don't think we can stop it.'

She looked up at him in alarm. 'Then you think it's going to be that hard? To catch the assassin?'

'Oh – no, not that.' He drew her closer and kissed the top of her head. 'We'll find him, no doubt of that. But the guns ... I don't think we can turn this tide, Ayla.'

'Then don't try,' she said. 'We have to live in the world we have. If we can't stop firearms coming into Mirrorvale, the next best thing is learning how to use them.'

He nodded. 'I'd a similar thought. If the Helm were fully trained in the use of pistols ... if they understood their capabilities and limitations ... but there's danger in it. It would only take one rogue Helmsman to bring down the Nightshade line.'

'As it stands,' Ayla agreed. 'But I'm placing my trust in alchemy. If Miles can find a way to enhance my strength against a bullet, the problem goes away.'

Caraway didn't answer immediately. He shared Bryan's reservations as to the efficacy of alchemy in achieving anything practical. He suspected that Ayla's conviction was born largely of the need to feel as if she were doing something, rather than any concrete foundation. And besides ...

'You know,' he said casually, 'Miles knows how to use a pistol.'

Ayla pulled away from him, regarding him through narrowed eyes.

'Oh, really?' she said with dangerous sweetness. 'I'll have to ask him to show me.'

'Ayla —'

'Tomas.'

Rather than be dragged back down into the quicksand of their ongoing argument, Caraway decided not to press the point further. 'You know I have to consider everything, love,' he said gently. 'It's my job.'

'I know.' To his relief, she rested her cheek against his chest again. 'But I like him, and Art cares deeply for him. That should be enough.'

'Yes,' Caraway said. 'It should.' *And in an ideal world, it would be.*

ELEVEN

It wasn't until near the end of the first week of training that Ree found herself paired with Saydi during assessment. She had been doing her very best to avoid the other girl, partly because she didn't want to give the boys any more fuel for their mocking remarks, and partly because she still felt guilty for what she'd said last time they'd talked. But today she'd stayed behind after her archery training session to ask the weaponmaster about the possibility of extra lessons, so she didn't have time to reach the main yard early and find some boy who thought that sparring with a girl would give him an easy win. By the time she arrived, the recruits were already pairing up – and Saydi, standing near the gate, turned with a beaming smile at her entrance and said, 'Ree! I've been waiting for you!'

Great. But Ree did her best to muster an answering smile, because she knew she wasn't being fair. Clearly Saydi could have held a grudge against her, after their previous conversation; just as clearly, she hadn't. Which probably meant she was a better person than Ree, and certainly meant that Ree ought to be nicer to her.

That resolution lasted right up until one of the nearby boys turned and saw them squaring up to each other. 'You gonna give us a show?' he called with a wink and an obscene gesture.

Saydi giggled. 'Only if you give us one first.'

Elements. Ree fought the urge to slap them both, settling for a general scowl. The boy sneered at her.

'Looks like Ree isn't too keen on the idea. But then, I guess she wouldn't know how.'

'Just you and me, then, Timo.' Saydi blew him a kiss. He laughed and turned away. Seething, Ree barely waited for him to start talking to his sparring partner before glaring at the other girl.

'What are you doing?'

Saydi looked confused. 'What?'

'It's like you don't *want* them to take you seriously!'

'I was just trying to help.' Saydi bit her lip, looking hurt. 'You're obviously not comfortable with that sort of thing, Ree, so I thought – I mean, better to deflect it than make it into a big deal. Isn't it?'

Ree didn't answer: partly because it hadn't even occurred to her that Saydi had been flirting for her benefit, and she didn't know whether to feel guilty or disbelieving; and partly because here was *another* person trying to protect her. First Zander, now Saydi. Why couldn't they all just accept that she could take care of herself?

'Come on,' she mumbled, picking up her practice sword. She might not have the ability to produce easy innuendo, but she could at least claim superiority in the things that mattered. 'We'd better get on with it.'

When they started sparring, however, Ree finally understood why Saydi hadn't been thrown out on the first day. Indeed, if she hadn't been so determined to avoid the other girl, she probably would have seen it sooner. Because Saydi might not look like a warrior, and she might not know what anything was called, and she might have next to no training in the classical forms – but she was a reasonably decent swordsman. A little awkward, and lacking in polish, but she had potential. Even Ree could see that. And if Ree could see it, Captain Caraway and Weaponmaster Bryan certainly could.

Ree knew she should be relieved at that. She had worried that Saydi would reflect badly on her; now that she knew Saydi wasn't so incompetent as to make a mockery of the very idea of a female Helmsman, she should have been able to relax. Yet instead, she found herself disappointed. She had been assuming that Saydi would leave after the week was over, she realised, but that was no longer anything close to a certainty. Which meant that Saydi might pass the seven-week test, go on to be accepted for Helm training, compete with Ree for a place in the Helm itself. And the two of them would continue to be defined as much by each other as they were by themselves.

'Well?' Saydi panted. 'Do you still think I should join basic training?'

Ree said nothing.

'I'd like to be your friend, Ree, if you'll let me.'

Ree wrenched her sword aside. 'I didn't come here to make friends.'

'No, of course, but –' Saydi hopped awkwardly back as Ree went in for the attack. 'Everyone needs friends, don't they?'

She managed to parry Ree's lunge, but her expression was hopeful. Unlike Ree, she obviously hadn't had the chance to get used to the loneliness of swimming against the current of expectation. She didn't want to be Ree's friend, so much as she wanted Ree to be hers.

And despite the fact that she really had no interest in being Saydi's friend, Ree didn't quite have the heart to say no.

'Fine,' she said – and took Saydi's momentary lapse of concentration as an opportunity to disarm her. 'But that doesn't mean I'll go easy on you.'

Saydi giggled. Again. 'I'm counting on it.'

At the end of the first week of training, Bryan and Caraway got together to compare notes on the recruits. As always, they were able to identify a few youngsters who weren't quite secure enough in the basics to make it worth putting them through the rest of the assessment. Those, they took aside and spoke to individually, before calling the rest of the group together.

'Right,' Bryan said when he had them in something approximating ranks. 'We've called you here because you passed the first week of assessment.'

A murmur of relief went through the group, along with several sidelong glances at Saydi; some of the others had expected her to go, but Bryan and Caraway agreed that she'd proven to be a fast learner who deserved a chance. Nevertheless, there was surprise, and Bryan let them indulge in it for a short while before adding, sharply enough to silence them, 'But if you thought this week was hard, the other six weeks are gonna kill you. Each of you has weaknesses that you need to work on, and if you don't work on them to our satisfaction, you'll be out. Got it?'

He paused, fixing each of them in turn with a hard stare while he gathered his wits. Then, with a sidelong glance at Caraway, he made the announcement they'd discussed earlier: the one that was intended to get them talking, and maybe letting something slip in the process.

'In the meantime, all of you are required to undergo a search of your barracks before you start the next stage of training.'

That evoked another murmur, this time of confusion. It wasn't standard procedure. From time to time the quartermaster might drop into the barracks unannounced, particularly if he'd heard rumour that one of the more exotic substances available in the lower rings had found its way up to the fifth. But it was rare that wider, more formal searches were carried out simply because the recruits were moving from one phase of training to the next. Bryan and Caraway had hoped that would mean they'd be bold enough to ask questions, and sure enough, Zander jumped in.

'If you don't mind me asking, sir, what exactly is going on? We've all heard they're turning people away from Darkhaven, and now with this search –'

Caraway nodded. 'We've received a threat against Lady Ayla's life.'

'An assassination?' Farleigh's eyes grew rounder. Bryan didn't appreciate his prurience, and it seemed neither did Caraway; his voice was a shade cooler when he spoke again.

'Yes, Farleigh. So I apologise to all of you for the inconvenience of the search, but I'm sure you understand the necessity.'

'But, sir! Are you saying you think it could be one of us?'

'I don't think anything yet,' Caraway said. 'I'm simply covering all possibilities. That's my job.'

The recruits were silent; Bryan thought several of them looked scared. Apparently Caraway agreed, because his expression softened.

'There's no need to worry. Remember, protecting the Nightshade line against this kind of thing is what the Helm is for. We've always had to live with the possibility of assassination. It's nothing new; it just happens to be a more specific threat than usual.'

'Damn Kardise,' Bryan growled, then wondered if he should have said it. When he and Caraway had discussed having this conversation, they hadn't mentioned revealing the source of the threat. He knew and therefore Miles knew, Caraway and Ayla knew, but did anyone else?

'So it's a Kardise threat?' Farleigh piped up again. He was giving Zander the side-eye, Bryan noticed. In fact, a few of the recruits were.

'Oh, sure,' Zander drawled. 'They're really going to send someone who looks as obviously Kardise as me.' But Bryan thought he seemed rattled, all the same.

'Stop that, all of you,' Caraway said, sharper than before. 'The Helm work as a team. If you let suspicion come between you, this assassin will have achieved a different kind of destruction. Be vigilant, yes. We can't afford to take any chances with Lady Ayla's life. But at the moment, all we have to go on is a rumour. And a rumour isn't enough to convict anybody.'

They waited, but no-one said another word; after a while, Bryan nodded. 'All right. You're dismissed. I'll speak to you once I have the quartermaster's report, Captain Caraway.'

Back in his office, he let out a long breath. *Flaming Luka*, as Miles would say – and as Bryan wasn't allowed to say. He could still remember vividly the first time he'd used the phrase, having picked it up from Miles in the same way that he'd picked up any number of colourful oaths from the mercenaries who came to train in the fifth ring. Miles had been genuinely offended, and asked him not to use those words again.

In Parovia we believe that using the name of our god as a swear word is blasphemy, he'd said very seriously. *The priests would have you doing penance for it if they heard.*

But you say it all the time when we're at home, Bryan had objected, and Miles had flashed him a sudden smile.

That is because Luka the great Sun Lord is my god to blaspheme against.

Bryan still didn't really understand the whole thing – but then, the very concept of a god was alien to most Mirrorvalese. They had Nightshades, and that gave them more than enough powerful and capricious beings to deal with. Of course, Arkannen had absorbed the idea of deity-based religion as it absorbed everything else that came to live within its walls; somewhere in the sixth ring, alongside all the older temples to the elements and the seasons and the other natural forces, there were newer shrines to the Parovian Sun Lord and Maiden of the Moon, the Ingalese god Shabet, and whatever it was the Kardise worshipped. But that was Arkannen. Outside the city, the average farmer would listen with polite incomprehension to any talk of gods – and, no doubt, be mighty amused at the suggestion that a creature that strong could be harmed by words.

Bryan had made that very same suggestion to Miles. *Surely, if Luka is all-powerful, it won't care if you talk about it.*

He, Miles had replied – still smiling, but with that hint of implacability behind the words that very occasionally showed itself. *And it is a matter of respect. You would address your overlord by her title, would you not?*

Only if she could hear me, Bryan had muttered, and Miles had laughed.

That is the point. Luka hears everything.

Bryan had ended the conversation at that point, because he didn't want to offend Miles. It wasn't as if it made any difference to him what Miles believed, after all. But it was Bryan's personal opinion that since the world as he saw it and the world as Miles saw it were identical, save for the addition or subtraction of an all-knowing invisible creature, his version achieved the same result with far less stretching of the imagination. Why believe in a sun god when the sun itself was there to be worshipped?

Of course, Miles always told him he didn't *have* an imagination, so maybe that had something to do with it.

Still, he was going to have to use the imagination he didn't have, now, because that's what he'd agreed with Caraway. They'd talk to the trainees, give them a little more information about the threat, then consider their reactions alongside everything else they knew about them. Bryan wasn't sure he'd have anything to tell Caraway that Caraway hadn't already noticed for himself, but the principle was sound: two sets of impressions were better than one. So he sat back in his chair and began to run through his latest roster of students in his head.

First Zander. The others had looked askance at him, and it was easy to see why. He had what you might call Kardise colouring: curly brown hair, skin several shades darker than the average Mirrorvalese. But that was hardly an indication of anything, these days. Despite the ongoing unsettlement between Mirrorvale and Sol Kardis, people had been crossing and recrossing the border for decades. Come to think of it, Caraway himself could pass for Kardise at a glance, and Bryan was hardly going to add him to the list of suspects. The point was, you couldn't tell where someone came from by what they looked like, not any more ... except a Nightshade, of course. They were still pretty damn distinctive.

Anyway, Zander. He looked obviously Kardise, and that – as he'd pointed out himself – probably meant he was too obvious to be the assassin. Unless it was a double bluff, but that kind of thing made Bryan's head hurt. As he'd said to Caraway, he wasn't a wily bastard.

Penn, then. That one was like a kettle constantly on the verge of coming to the boil. Like a foundry, all sparks and churning molten metal. Something to prove and an angry way of showing it.

Or there was Farleigh. His hero-worship of Caraway would make as good a smokescreen as anything. It seemed a more likely cover for an assassin than Penn's open antagonism.

Bryan sighed. As they'd said all along, the new intake of recruits was only one of the possible places in which to look for the assassin. There were other ways for a determined killer to get close to Ayla, even under tightened security.

Still. He'd continue to keep an eye on them, just in case.

Dear Sirs –

This is going to be harder than I thought. Not only are the Helm aware of the threat, but they know what kind of threat it is and where it comes from. They will be trying to find ways to guard against it.

Still, at least I now know what they know – and that makes it clear to me how I should proceed. I will have to be careful, but I doubt the people I have met here will see through me. In fact, a couple of them may very well turn out to be useful.

In the meantime, in accordance with your instructions, the first step must be to visit a firearms dealer. I am in possession of the list you sent me, so my intention is to set that part of our arrangement in motion right away. I will write again when there is further news.

Respectfully yours.

The dealer was easy enough to find. Kai had been given a list of streets in the first ring, each of which contained one of the black-market traders operating within Arkannen who were controlled by the Brotherhood. And in this entire row full of dingy-looking shops, the vast majority of which were probably fronts for one form of illicit activity or another, only one door displayed the Brotherhood's sign.

Time for a little persuasion.

Kai sauntered across the street and into the marked shop, letting the door swing closed with a rattle. Inside, the dust lay thick on shelves crammed with so-called antiques that no-one would ever buy. The man behind the counter, short and balding with a pair of thick glass lenses perched precariously across his nose, looked up with eyebrows raised in enquiry. 'Can I help you?'

'I understand you sell firearms,' Kai said.

In an instant, the man's expression changed from polite and interested to utterly blank. In fact, he couldn't have looked more suspicious if he'd tried. 'You understand wrong. I –'

His words cut off as Kai leaned forward to show him the ring that identified its bearer as an agent of the Brotherhood. When the trader looked up again, his face was pale and sweat stood out on his brow.

'I've paid my dues. I've sent back what information I could. Please –'

'I'm not a collector,' Kai said. 'I'm here on other business.'

The man didn't ask what business; the Brotherhood had its own methods of discouraging too much curiosity. Instead he asked, far more carefully than he had the first time, 'How may I help you?'

'By staying quiet as I give you your new instructions.'

'What do you mean?' The trader had paled again. 'Surely you aren't gonna cut me off? Not when I have a family to feed –'

148

'I doubt that very much,' Kai said crisply. 'But I'm not here to cut you off. Not unless you *keep interrupting me*. Now shut up and listen.'

The trader opened his mouth, then closed it again. Kai nodded.

'Good. Now. I want you to remember that today, someone came in here asking for a gun. I want you to remember that you sold him one. And when the Helm call round, sometime in the days ahead, I want you to tell them all about it.'

'But –' the trader began, before pressing his lips together to cut off the rest of the sentence.

'There's no need to admit to the sale,' Kai answered the question in his eyes. 'But you do need to be able to describe the customer in some detail.'

I don't understand, said the trader's eyes – but the trader himself said nothing. Kai rewarded him with a smile.

'Good. Then let me tell you everything you need to know.'

TWELVE

Another day, another nondescript meal. Penn sat in a corner of the mess hall, shovelling food methodically into his mouth without thinking too much about what it was, and listened to the others talk. They were talking about their families and the lives they'd left behind; even after three weeks of training, they hadn't tired of that conversation. Yet Penn didn't want to talk about his family. If he did that, the hatred that simmered hotter inside him with every day he spent in the fifth ring would come bubbling to the surface. But he couldn't avoid listening to the others expound at length on all the tedious details of the lives they'd left behind. And because he didn't want to switch off, in case he missed something that might actually be useful, he couldn't help taking it all in.

Farleigh boasted a lot. He always boasted a lot, and about the most mundane things, too: his parents and his sisters and their home in the Serpentine Quarter of Arkannen. Farleigh was a city boy, and very obviously proud of it. His father was a merchant, something to do with wool or fur or skin – Penn glazed over at that point – but Farleigh's uncle and his grandfather and his great-grandfather had all trained in the fifth ring in their time, all gone on to become Helmsmen.

150

Family tradition, Farleigh said with a smug smile. *The eldest son always joins the Helm.*

Saydi came from southern Mirrorvale, where her mother had been a teacher until succumbing to a wasting disease that stole her strength, her sight and finally her life. *My father died years ago*, Saydi said. *It was just Mama and me. So when I lost her, too, I decided I might as well come to the city.* Penn found himself empathising deeply with her, but the feeling soon dissolved as she prattled on about the various places she'd tried and failed to get a job. He strongly suspected she was unemployable. Yet against the odds, she'd turned out to be decent enough at weapons training – *My father taught me before he died*, she'd told them all, more than once; *I just never thought I could use it* – so maybe she'd finally found a vocation where her constant chatter about trivia wouldn't become a problem.

Ree said little, and what she did say was defensive. Penn found her defensiveness just as wearying as Saydi's endless nothings, but at least it wasn't as jarring on the ear. He noted idly that Ree came from somewhere over to the west, near the Ingalese border. And she had a mother who was apparently obsessed with decorum, to the point where she'd locked Ree in her room for a week for wearing trousers. That was sort of funny, given that he'd never seen Ree in anything *but* trousers. Yet Penn didn't learn much about Ree herself. He wasn't even sure there was anything more to her than the desire to prove a point.

Zander ... well, Zander was a little more interesting than he usually was, because he talked less. He came from a town not far from Ree's village – apparently. But he couldn't be drawn on anything more than the vaguest description of his home life and what his parents were like. Mention his father, in particular, and Zander stonewalled: smiling, turning the question aside with his usual ease, but Penn detected a hint of urgency behind it. Zander's keen desire not to discuss his family connections put Penn in sympathy with him for probably the first time ever, and it lasted right up until Zander glanced at him, eyebrows raised, and remarked, 'You're very quiet, Avens. Want to tell us all about why you came to Arkannen?'

Backstabbing bastard. Penn glared at him, but now the others were looking interested too.

'My cousin trained in the fifth ring,' he muttered. 'I figured I'd follow in his footsteps.'

Farleigh perked up at that. 'Maybe he was here at the same time as my uncle. What's his name? Is he an Avens too? I assume he didn't join the Helm, or you would've said, so what does he do now?'

'He's dead,' Penn said shortly, with a swift glance around the table. If he hadn't been simmering with resentment and suppressed fury, he would have laughed at the shocked faces staring back at him.

'I'm sorry,' Ree murmured; and Saydi, after one quick look at his expression, began to chatter about the day's training. A successful defence, so far as it went. Yet Zander just kept watching him, dark eyes steady, until finally Penn snapped.

'What, Zander?'

'Nothing.'

'Spit it out. If you have something to say –'

'I was just wondering,' Zander said slowly and precisely, 'how your cousin died.'

'None of your business,' Penn shot back, and Zander shrugged.

'Not usually, no. But when a threat has been made against the overlord of Darkhaven, and at the very same time there's a new recruit in the fifth ring who's clearly got a chip on his shoulder about something –'

Penn wasn't aware of having moved, but suddenly he was standing, fists planted on the table, glaring at Zander. 'What are you saying?'

'Nothing,' Zander said again. 'Only if I were Weaponmaster Bryan or Captain Caraway – and thank all the little gods I'm not – I don't think I'd have to look far to find a suspect.'

By now, everyone else at the table had fallen utterly silent. Ree started to say something in a low voice to Zander, but Penn – fairly spitting with rage – spoke over her.

'I think you're right, Zander. Only I'm not the one they'd be interested in. Because you're the one who looks like a damn Kardise spy!'

For a moment, Zander said nothing at all. Then, very deliberately, he pushed back his chair and got to his feet. His smile glittered like a drawn blade. 'Want to practise, Avens?'

Thrown by the unexpected question, Penn only stared at him. 'What, now?'

'Why not? We all want to join the Helm, don't we? So the more practice we do, the better.'

That dangerous smile whispered that it wasn't practice Zander had in mind: he was after a fight. And that suited Penn perfectly. In fact he'd have taken them all on, given half a chance, but Zander alone would have to do for now.

'Fine by me,' he said, anger crystallising into a cool determination that matched Zander's own. 'I assume you don't want to use the wooden swords.'

'Why use swords at all?' Zander returned. 'We're starting on hand-to-hand combat tomorrow. I say we get a head start on everyone else.'

So, not even a duel: a brawl. Better and better. Penn began to edge round the table. 'Perfect. Then I assume you want to head out to a practice ground and –'

Zander punched him.

The blow knocked him backwards into his abandoned chair, which in turn tripped him to the floor. His vision blurred, shifting as if his eyes had been spun round in his head. Dimly he heard a single laugh, cut off short; he thought it had been Farleigh. Then Zander appeared above him, holding out a hand to help him up.

'Lesson one,' he drawled. 'The fight starts when your opponent says it does. Maybe from now on, Avens, you'll stop being such a –'

Penn grabbed his outstretched hand and yanked him down and to the side. Even as he scrambled to his feet, his own punch finished the work of knocking Zander to the floor in his place. He went in for a kick, but Zander rolled nimbly and stood. A few paces apart, they circled each other. A thick stream of blood ran from one of Zander's nostrils, and he was no longer smiling.

'There's your lesson,' Penn said. His left eye ached in its socket; he imagined it would swell closed by the end of the evening. 'Don't gloat.'

Zander wiped the blood from his upper lip with the back of his hand. 'What makes you such a misanthropic bastard, Avens?'

'I don't know,' Penn retorted. 'What makes you such an insufferable prick?'

Unexpectedly, Zander laughed under his breath at that. He darted forward and threw another punch, which Penn blocked, and then they closed on each other, firing off blows with wild abandon, grappling without success to throw each other down. All very ineffectual, some detached corner of Penn's mind had to admit. They could do with that hand-to-hand training.

'Will you *stop* it?' someone hissed in his ear. Someone had a tight grip on the back of his shirt, hauling him away. He caught a glimpse of Saydi's red hair out of the corner of his eye, then Ree glaring round Zander at him. The fight was being broken up by *women*. Only Farleigh remained at the table, his expression a mixture of fear and glee.

'Weaponmaster Bryan said if he heard of anyone fighting outside training, he'd kick us out – remember?' Ree snapped. 'It's in the Code. So do you two want to join the Helm or not?'

She had a point. And she and Saydi could easily have sat back and let him and Zander get themselves into trouble. Yet Penn's frustration didn't leave much space for being reasonable. He looked at Ree and sneered.

'Don't be such a *girl*.'

At that, she elbowed Zander aside and stormed towards him. Saydi let go of him just in time for him to receive his second punch of the evening. It didn't knock him down, this time, but it still bloody hurt. He staggered back into Saydi, who caught his arm to keep him on his feet. Not that it did him much good. Ree grabbed him by the shirt front, brought her knee up sharply into his groin, and then – as he doubled over, eyes streaming – punched him *again*.

This time, he didn't even try to remain standing. He sat down hard, ears ringing, face throbbing in time to his heart-beat. Ree, Saydi and Zander ranged themselves in front of him, looking down in scorn. At least, Ree and Zander looked scornful. Saydi's expression was more thoughtful.

It's not fair, he wanted to say. *He started it*. But why bother? It wasn't as if they cared.

'Want to carry on?' Zander asked. 'I think Ree's made her point fairly decisively, but I'm sure she'll make it again if you ask her nicely.'

'No, I get it,' Penn mumbled. 'Ree doesn't like being called a girl.'

For some reason, their scorn dissipated at that. Zander's face creased in amusement, while Ree rolled her eyes. 'I've had it with all of you. I'm going to bed.'

Zander's eyebrows twitched. 'Mind if I join you?'

She rolled her eyes again, though a smile tugged at the corners of her mouth. 'Put some ice on your nose, Zander.' Her gaze moved to Penn, and the smile became a grin. 'And Penn ... you might want to ice your whole face.'

Her voice held laughing sympathy, rather than malice – and she hadn't called him Avens. Penn looked away, made more uncomfortable than he cared to admit by that slight token of ... what was it? Not friendship, exactly. Camaraderie. Complicity.

'She's right, you know,' Zander said, as Ree's footsteps receded. 'Weaponmaster Bryan'll take one look at us and know exactly what we've been doing.'

Penn didn't reply, or even glance at him. After a pause, Zander spoke again.

'I could use a drink before bed. Want to come?'

Still Penn stared at the floor and said nothing. He didn't understand what was happening. They'd beaten him up, pretty much, and now they were behaving as if he and they were all the best of friends? It made no sense. He didn't like any of them any more than he had before.

'Saydi? Drink?' Zander offered, after another pause.

'I think I should stay with Penn,' was the unexpected reply. 'Make sure he's all right.'

'Fine. See you in the morning. C'mon, Farleigh.' Penn heard Farleigh scramble out from behind the table, then two sets of footsteps. But before they reached the door, Zander's voice added, 'Goodnight, Penn.'

Still no Avens. Apparently by losing to them in a fight, he'd earned the right to be addressed by his first name. To be honest, Penn thought bitterly, he'd rather have won the fight and still be thought of as the enemy. He didn't want any of them to like him. That would just make the whole thing harder.

Saydi crouched down beside him and put a hand on his arm. Despite himself, he looked up. The two of them were alone in the mess hall, now. Saydi was clutching a damp cloth, which she dabbed against his swollen face. Penn tasted blood. That last punch from Ree must have mashed the inside of his cheek against his teeth. He hadn't even noticed before.

'Are you all right?' Saydi asked. She'd lost all her silliness and her chatter. Her expression was one of gentle concern. 'I'm sorry I didn't help you more. I was scared … I just wanted to stop the fighting …' She bit her lip, glancing away, then added quickly, 'But I thought it was really unfair. What they did. I mean, I *like* Ree – Zander, too – but all the same …'

Penn's wavering emotions solidified back into hot, furious resentment. She was right. Zander and Ree had outnumbered him. Bullied him. And all that supposed affability at the end had simply been their way of savouring their victory.

'Do you want a hand back to your barracks?' Saydi asked softly. 'We can try and minimise the swelling from those bruises.'

At least one person had seen through the whole thing, even if it was only a silly girl. Penn nodded. 'That would be helpful. Thank you.'

As they walked slowly along the short route between the mess hall and Penn's room, Saydi glanced up at him.

'I hope you don't mind me asking, but what happened to your cousin?'

Penn glowered. 'He was killed.'

'I'm sorry. I – I didn't want to say in front of the others, but my father was murdered, too. So I understand how you feel.'

Penn looked down at her fiery head and felt a pang of guilt for his earlier uncharitable thoughts. He'd done nothing but mock her, albeit not to her face, and here she was showing him genuine concern. Plus she preferred his company to Zander's, which improved his estimation of her a thousandfold.

'Thanks,' he muttered. 'I'm sorry about your father, too.'

She sighed. 'It's good to meet someone else who lost a loved one … *that way*. Well, not good. But you know what I mean.'

He nodded, and she sighed again.

'Did they ever catch the person who murdered your father?' he asked her softly, suddenly curious. Suddenly wanting to know if justice was ever done. But she shook her head.

'No. The murderer died before he could be made to pay for what he did. Sometimes I wish …' She hesitated, then said in a rush, 'Sometimes I wish he was still alive, so I could kill him myself.'

'You think you could do it?'

She shrugged. 'It would be just like killing a monster.'

Killing a monster. Penn frowned. He couldn't see it in quite such stark terms, despite what his father would have him believe. People who did bad things were still people. Yet he knew what she meant. Once you thought of a man in terms of a single unforgiveable act, instead of a bundle of human complexity, he became flat. Two-dimensional. Like the thin wooden figures the recruits sometimes used for target practice. And a target could be knocked down without even hesitating, because morality was no longer an issue.

'What about you, Penn?' Saydi asked. 'Did they catch whoever killed your cousin?'

'Catch?' It was a bitter echo. 'He was rewarded for it.'

He looked down at the top of her head again, wondering if he could trust her. But he longed to talk to someone, and she'd understand. After what had happened to her, she'd understand.

'That's why I came here,' he said softly. 'To make it right.'

For an instant, she froze. Then she lifted her head, gazing intently into his face. 'Tell me about it.'

The man Sorrow knew as Don Pieter Callero, and whom she had now identified as Number Fourteen in the Kardise Brotherhood, lived in a house very similar to the one he'd asked her to burgle. So similar, in fact, that he'd been able to give her detailed descriptions of the layout of the other house, despite never having set foot in it. Perhaps all the Brotherhood lived in them: tall, thin houses with steps climbing from the street to each front door – a strange conceit, that – and long, narrow gardens at the back. In Arkannen, where space was at a premium, they would have been terraced; here, narrow alleys separated each building from its neighbours. As far as Sorrow could see, those alleys served no other purpose than to provide concealment for miscreants like her.

As she neared the house, she felt someone's gaze on her and glanced across the street to find a woman watching her from the opposite window. People were far more suspicious in Kardissak than they were in Arkannen. No, that wasn't quite true: the citizens of Arkannen were as big a bunch of bloody suspicious bastards as could be found anywhere else in the world, but they suspected everyone indiscriminately. Whereas here, *not looking Kardise* drew a disproportionate amount of attention. Not that Sorrow looked anything else, either. Though she was Mirrorvalese by birth, she was a little bit of everything by blood. Literally: her mother was half Ingalese and half Kardise, while her father – himself born and bred in Mirrorvale – had possessed more than one Parovian ancestor. A mongrel, then, and proud of the fact. It gave her a unique position in any setting: not quite part of it, but not so different as to be out of place, either. She'd always found it worked to her advantage, but this was one of the rare occasions when she wished she had a more forgettable face.

Turning her back on the prying neighbour, she climbed the steps to the front door. Most of the houses were painted white, here, which was another oddity. Any white building in Arkannen would have become grey very quickly. But in Kardissak, the centre of industry was on the other side of the river from the residential quarters, and downwind. More than once, Sorrow had been forced to stifle a laugh when she heard a wealthy Kardise complain that the prevailing wind had shifted and the smell of factory smoke was getting into his house. In Arkannen, factory smoke was *everywhere*. Only the sixth and seventh rings escaped it, and that only by virtue of their height above the factories.

Sorrow hadn't realised, before, quite how much she compared other places to Arkannen.

Inside the building, a servant took her weapons without any reaction whatsoever – which spoke volumes for either the excellent training of the staff or the kind of people Don Callero usually welcomed to his house. Sorrow kept a knife up her sleeve, though. This was dangerous territory, and she wasn't certain of her welcome. Thus armed, she followed another servant down the hall and into Callero's study, where she was announced with restrained dignity. The man himself was sitting behind his desk, working on something or other; he gestured her to a chair, but didn't speak until the servant had left and they were alone in the room.

'Well, Naeve?'

They all called her by her first name, here. It was irritating, but she'd had to let it slide. She reached into the inside pocket of her coat. 'I have your document.'

He took it from her and scanned it – unhurriedly, but his grip on the paper was taut and pale. When he looked up, there was genuine surprise in his face, and possibly grudging respect as well. He hadn't expected her to succeed, then.

'I'm impressed,' he said, and Sorrow nodded as if that were no more than her due.

'I hope this is a satisfactory enough outcome that you'll consider employing me again. Though first, we need to discuss the matter of my pay.'

'Oh?'

'There were some … unforeseen complications,' Sorrow said. 'And given their nature, I'd argue that triple pay would be a fairer recompense than double.'

'Oh?' Callero said again. He wasn't giving anything away – but then, even that gave *something* away. She pressed on.

'For a start, the house wasn't empty.'

'Really?' This time, though he sounded surprised, she could tell he wasn't. She'd seen the real thing just a few moments earlier, after all.

'The owner was meeting with a woman there.' Sorrow watched him from under her lashes as she added, 'They called you Fourteen.'

Concealed behind the desk, she slid the knife from her sleeve. If he reacted badly, she'd at least have a chance of defending herself – but he was smiling.

'And you knew what that meant?'

She raised an eyebrow. 'I could hazard a guess.'

'Yet you came back,' Callero said thoughtfully. 'Why did you do that, I wonder?'

'It seemed the safer option.'

'Completing the original job was the safer option,' he agreed. 'That doesn't explain why you came back for more.'

He was sharp. He would be, of course. But Sorrow was ready for him.

'I came back,' she said evenly, 'because as long as I'm useful to you, you have no reason to kill me.'

He nodded. 'True. But the more you do for me, the more of my secrets you will hold in your grasp. And one day, I will have no further use for you.' One finger tapped a quick staccato rhythm on the arm of his chair. 'It might have been wiser to return to Mirrorvale while you still had the chance.'

He knows where I'm from, said a small, nervous part of Sorrow that she usually did her best to ignore.

Of course he does, she told it with a mental eye-roll. *Everyone does.*

Yes, but now Sol Kardis is officially at war with Mirrorvale – Sol Kardis is secretly at war with Mirrorvale. Callero doesn't know I know that. Given the state of mistrust between the members of the Brotherhood, I'm not even sure Callero knows that.

'I had my reasons for leaving Mirrorvale, Don Callero,' she said calmly. 'And they were such that I have no desire to return there. It's entirely likely that returning to Mirrorvale would be even more hazardous for me than remaining in your employ.'

'So to you, I am the lesser of two evils,' he said, and she shrugged.

'More like the least of many. I can't go back to Mirrorvale. Now that I've stolen from ... the people I've stolen from, I'd rather not stay in Sol Kardis without protection. And besides – as I said, now that I've proven my capabilities, I hoped you might have more work for me.'

He regarded her in silence. Sorrow gripped the knife and presented him with an impassive expression. But when he finally spoke, it wasn't what she had expected.

'Tell me why you left Mirrorvale.'

'What?'

'If you are to carry my secrets, Naeve Sorrow, I must also carry yours. Tell me why you left Mirrorvale.'

She thought about it – but only for a heartbeat, because hesitation at this point would be fatal.

'I took something from Darkhaven,' she said. 'And they want it back.'

'Valuable?'

'Yes.'

'Well hidden?'

Apparently not, given that Tomas bloody Caraway knows the address. 'Well enough.'

She braced herself for more questions – *What is it? Where is it?* Most difficult to evade of all, *Can we use it against Mirrorvale?* – but none came. Whatever he'd been trying to get out of her, it seemed he'd got it already.

That made Sorrow uneasy, though she didn't show it.

'All right,' Callero said. 'I have another job that may suit you, given that you are aware of the ... situation between me and certain of my colleagues. The man whose house you broke into last, Eight –' he gave Sorrow a quick, knowing

163

glance – 'he tried to take the document that was rightfully mine. I need to know what he planned to do with it. I want you to pay a visit to his warehouse, down by the docks, and steal his shipping ledger.'

So she was going to be caught between two factions of the Brotherhood again. Well, she'd expected it. And since he was giving her a job, he probably wasn't going to dispose of her on the spot – so she slipped her knife back into its hiding place.

'I think I can manage that, Don Callero.'

'I'm sure you can,' he said. 'But Naeve, please bear in mind that whilst I appreciate you using your initiative in the previous case, this is a different matter. It's important that you do as I've asked without deviation. If the ledger isn't where we expect it to be, or you stand even the smallest chance of being caught by Eight, you need to come away with the job incomplete. Do you understand?'

Sorrow nodded. She understood perfectly. The stakes were higher, this time round; if she got caught, she'd land Callero in it as well as herself. And if there was one thing she really didn't want to do in her lifetime, it was piss off a member of the Brotherhood.

'That's fine,' she said. 'I won't let you down.'

She began to rise from her chair, but he raised a hand to stop her.

'We aren't finished yet,' he said. Sorrow's pulse accelerated despite all her efforts to remain calm.

'We're not?'

His eyebrows lifted. 'I assumed you'd want to discuss your pay.'

Of course. How had she forgotten something so important? Another slip as big as that, they'd be sending her home to

Mirrorvale in a box. Naeve Sorrow *never* forgot what she was worth in coin.

'I thought that went without saying,' she said coolly. 'We've established you'll be paying me triple for the last job. I'll want the same again.'

'No more?'

'I'm not greedy, Don Callero.'

'Then triple pay it is.' He smiled at her again – quite kindly, but for some reason she shivered. 'I look forward to learning of the result.'

THIRTEEN

A few weeks into training, Ree had become disillusioned. She'd expected to have to fight for acceptance every step of the way; that was how it had been all her life, so there'd been no reason to believe the fifth ring would be any different. And in fact, on the whole, her teachers were better than she could have hoped for in that respect. A couple of the weaponmasters had looked askance at her – a couple had laughed at her outright – but with Captain Caraway and Weaponmaster Bryan showing no sign of turning her away, the attitude had largely been one of bemused willingness. *So they have girls training for the Helm, now*, she'd overheard one of them saying to another. *No idea if they're up to it, but that's Captain Caraway's problem.*

The boys she was training with were a different matter.

To be fair, some of them were all right. A few, like Zander, were as welcoming of her as they were of anybody else. And a few more didn't appear to have the imagination to realise she was anything unusual. But to the rest, even after several weeks in their company, she was exactly what she'd called Saydi: a sideshow. An aberration. The punchline to a joke. She spent every available moment practising. She did everything she could to convince them to take her seriously. And yet no matter how well she fought, some of them still mocked her. It was as if the more she did to prove herself physically their equal, the more they tried to take her down with words.

Every morning, she told herself not to let it get to her. That she'd been facing the same problem since she was old enough to pick up a sword. That their words were only words. And every evening, she returned to her barracks a little more drained. Somehow, although she'd known how it would be, some small part of her had secretly hoped that Arkannen would be different. That anyone who came to the fifth ring – a place that prided itself on training *the best warriors*, not just *the best men* – would have far less difficulty accepting the idea of a girl in the Helm than anyone back home.

Turned out, even people in elite places were still people.

She tried very hard to keep her temper, or at least channel most of that anger into the official training sessions. She was well aware that she'd been lucky not to get into trouble along with Zander and Penn, after the night they'd fought; she knew Weaponmaster Bryan had put them on some kind of punishment detail, and she also knew – since she wasn't polishing blades alongside them – that Penn hadn't let on where half the bruises on his face had come from. Perhaps he simply hadn't wanted to admit he'd been knocked down by a girl, but she was inclined to give him more credit than that. Most of the boys wouldn't hesitate to drop her in it, which was why she was doing her best not to get in any more fights.

Unfortunately, they didn't always make it easy for her to stay calm.

By now, as part of their hand-to-hand training, they had moved on to fully unarmed combat – which only made things more difficult. Fighting at close range with batons and knives had been intense, but no worse than swordfighting when it came to the other trainees' reactions to sparring with a girl. But wrestling and martial arts ... the intimate physicality of it had increased some of the boys' suggestive and disparaging remarks a thousandfold. Maybe they were trying to drive her out, make her uncomfortable enough that she'd quit of her own accord. Maybe they were trying to prove to her that she was in the wrong place. Maybe they simply thought it was funny. Whatever the reason, it was gradually working.

This time she was paired with Timo, which was close to her idea of utter misery. As one of the most vocal critics of the fact that she and Saydi had been allowed onto the Helm assessment programme at all, he never missed an opportunity to tell her exactly why it was impossible for a woman to do a Helmsman's job – and today was no exception.

'Look, Ree,' he said with mock kindness, as they stood waiting for the signal to begin. 'Thing is, you're not exactly big. Yeah, weapons can close the gap a bit, but when it comes to close-quarter fighting like this, a man'll beat you every time.'

Ree gritted her teeth, said nothing, and wondered how she could ever have thought *Zander* was patronising.

'I know it,' Timo went on. 'The others know it. Even Weaponmaster Bryan and Captain Caraway know it. You're just wasting everyone's time, trying to turn yourself into something you're not.'

'I passed the first week, didn't I?' This time she couldn't help retorting, although – with a massive effort – she kept her temper in check. 'So that means I have as much chance as anyone else.'

He rolled his eyes. 'They went soft on you, 'cos you're a girl. Everyone knows that. Doesn't mean you'll end up in the Helm.'

They didn't. Did they? Sudden fear prickling at the back of her neck, Ree wrapped her arms around herself. 'No-one went soft on me,' she insisted, trying to convince herself as much as Timo. 'What would be the point? They need people who can do the job properly, so –'

'Exactly!' He grinned triumphantly. 'They let you and Saydi through to make it look fair. But when it comes to it, any new positions in the Helm'll be filled by men. You'll see.'

The sparring started at that point, and Timo got her in a headlock while she was still trying to come up with a decisive rebuttal.

'It's like fighting my little sister,' he laughed in her ear. She drove an elbow back into his solar plexus, as hard as she could, and had the satisfaction of hearing a groan as his grip loosened. Pulling away and spinning to face him, she lifted her hands into the defensive position.

'Fuck your sister,' she spat. 'And fuck you.'

He shook his head, pulling a face of mock regret. 'Sorry, Ree. You're not my type, and you're certainly not hers.'

They closed with each other – and though Ree hated to admit it, he *was* stronger than her. Not a huge amount. Not as much as he might have thought. But enough to make the difference.

Maybe he's right. Maybe Captain Caraway will never really let women into the Helm, and he's just being kind to me –

The thought made her falter slightly, and Timo seized the advantage. Before she knew what was happening, he'd gone in for the throw. She landed hard on her back, the breath knocked out of her lungs. He landed on top of her. Temporarily forgetting all her training, she thrashed wildly, and managed to land one good kick before he succeeded in restraining her.

'This is why women can't be Helmsmen,' he sneered, breath hot on her face. 'You're just not strong enough. Nothing to do with fairness, simply a fact of life.'

Ree could hear some of the others laughing and cheering above them. She wasn't sure whether they could hear what Timo was saying, but it only made her more determined to win.

She grabbed his forearm with both hands, pinning it to her chest. Then she hooked a foot over his calf and pushed upwards with her hips, pivoting the two of them until she could swing her other leg across to sit astride him – and now she was the one holding him down. He tried to throw her off in turn, and then – failing that – he smirked at her.

'Oh yeah, Ree, that feels really good ...'

She headbutted him in the face.

Later, once Timo – his lower face covered with a mask of blood – had been escorted away by one of the fifth-ring physicians, Ree found herself standing in Weaponmaster Bryan's office. The weaponmaster himself sat on the other side of the desk and studied her without speaking. His expression was grave, rather than angry, yet Ree began to quiver all the same. *He's going to throw me out. He's going to send me home. I've failed.*

'Sir, I –' she began, about to attempt some form of defence, but Bryan held up a hand to silence her.

'Ree, you broke his nose,' he said. 'You were sparring, so it wasn't against the Code, but still ... you didn't need to do it. You already had him beat.'

She scowled. 'He deserved it.'

'Why?'

'He said I shouldn't be here.'

'So what, girlie? Not like he has any actual say in the matter. Captain Caraway and I –'

'He said you went easy on me because I'm a girl.' The words caught in her throat. 'Is that true?'

Bryan looked at her a moment longer from beneath heavy brows. Then he said, 'Sit down, Ree.'

She sat. The weaponmaster frowned across the desk at her as if trying to work out the best way to explain some fundamental fact of life.

'If anything, I'm going to be harder on you because you're a girl,' he said at last. 'That make you feel better?'

'Harder?'

''Cos you're an unknown quantity. Don't get me wrong, I've trained plenty of women in my time. Had my arse handed to me by a few, too. But Helm training ...' He spread his hands. 'That's different. I have to be sure you can take it. Have to be sure the others can take it, too.'

'The others?'

'The boys.' Bryan planted a finger on his desk for emphasis. 'Because you know what the difference is between a Helmsman and any other warrior?'

'He's better?' Ree faltered, and the weaponmaster barked a laugh.

'They'd like you to think so! No, the difference is one of trust. The Helm have to trust each other. Utterly. Completely. How you work with these boys is just as important as your skill with a sword. So if you can't win them over –' He made a gesture that suggested *instant death* but probably just meant *the end of your chances*, and added surprisingly, 'You could learn from Saydi in that respect.'

'From *Saydi*? But they laugh at her!'

'They did,' Bryan said. 'But now they're starting to respect her. She may not be as proficient as you, Ree, but she works hard. And she doesn't treat the others as an obstacle to overcome. If you weren't so busy trying to avoid her, you'd have seen that.'

'But she does nothing but flirt –'

'She's settled down,' the weaponmaster said sternly. 'She's knocked some of her own corners off. Maybe you could stand to do the same.'

Ree bit her lip, cheeks hot, and said nothing. She wasn't sure what was worse: that Bryan had noticed her avoidance of Saydi, or that he thought she could learn from her. As usual, her instinct was to defend herself, but she fought it back. Whether she liked it or not, she had to listen.

'Look,' Bryan said. 'I know they give you a hard time. And if I thought it was anything more than words, I'd stop it. But that's what soldiers are like, girlie! Men and women. They rip the piss out of each other, but they have each other's backs. The Helm most of all. And if you want to be a part of that, these lads have to know you have theirs.'

Ree nodded mutely, a little overwhelmed, and he raised his eyebrows at her.

'Here's a secret,' he said. 'You all think it's a contest, and in part you're right. In terms of skill, you've got to be one of the best. But when it comes down to it, anyone who succeeds by stepping on the backs of their fellows ain't gonna be welcome in the Helm. Maybe the old Helm,' he added reflectively, 'but certainly not Captain Caraway's. Got it?'

'I don't want to step on anyone,' Ree mumbled.

'I'm not saying you do. I'm saying, you have to find a way to become their colleague, not their competitor. 'Cos like it or not, they ain't going to make the effort on your behalf.' Bryan looked at her sternly. 'And in case you were in any doubt, Ree Quinn, breaking their noses is *not* the way to do it.'

172

'No, sir.'

'All right. Then go away, and don't do it again.'

As she stumbled back to her barracks, tears of hot frustration stung her eyes. It wasn't fair. She was going to fail, not because she wasn't skilled enough at weaponry – which, until she came to the fifth ring, she'd considered her only potential downfall – but because she wasn't skilled enough at getting a bunch of boys to like her.

It wasn't *fair*.

The tears threatened to overwhelm her completely, but she blinked them back. She had two choices: she could let them beat her, or she could keep fighting. And she wouldn't have come here in the first place if she hadn't been willing to fight.

She simply had to find a different way of doing it.

Ayla had begun to think of Miles's visits as the one time each week when she felt as if she were achieving something tangible in the drive to preserve her own life. Today, as she waited for him to climb the hill to Darkhaven, her impatience was more acute than usual. It had taken several weeks of conversation – Miles finding out what she could do, what it felt like, what she *was* – but he was now ready to start the practical side of their investigation.

Darkhaven had been built to accommodate Changer creatures, so she and Miles could have done their work anywhere, but Ayla had decided that the two of them should use the transformation room. No-one was likely to walk in on them, there was room for her to Change as well as a screen to preserve her modesty, and there was enough space for Miles to have all his alchemical equipment set up without her wings knocking it over. She hadn't expected so much equipment, to tell the truth. She'd thought alchemy was more of a spiritual discipline than a physical one: all arcane rituals and ceremonialism. But Miles had alembics and flasks and tubes and pipes, a small fortune in glass-blowers' wages.

In a way, it was amusing. The Helmsmen at the gate had carried out a thorough search of all that equipment when Miles had first brought it up to the tower, looking for concealed firearms. They'd opened every crate, handling all the delicate glassware with care whilst Miles hovered anxiously in the background. Of course they hadn't found anything, so they'd admitted the lot. They'd even helped to wheel the little cart to the transformation room. And all the while, it hadn't seemed to occur to anybody that if Miles wanted to hurt Ayla, he could simply smash one of his flasks and slit her throat with it. An alchemist's equipment was a potential armoury of viciousness.

To be fair, a shard of glass was unlikely to do her any damage in creature form, so she'd be able to Change to get away from it – whereas that wouldn't help with a bullet. Still, it was quite frustrating how everyone – even Tomas – had fixated on the idea of an assassin with a pistol, the blithe assumption being that if she were attacked in any other way, she'd be quick enough to escape. They might have forgotten what had happened three years ago, but she hadn't. Being a Changer didn't help if the room was too small for her creature-self, or if someone incapacitated her before she could react. That was why she'd wanted Tomas to teach her how to fight – and that was why, now, she was putting her trust in alchemy.

She met Miles at the gate, and they walked to the transformation room together. Once there, he set to work with barely a word, selecting glassware and mixing substances and ... Ayla wasn't sure, but whatever he was doing, it didn't involve giving her an explanation. So she walked slowly along the far side of the long table, examining the half-emptied crates with some interest. Most of them were old battered things, but one was newer: a small chest carved with what looked like the alchemical symbols Miles occasionally scrawled on a piece of paper.

'This is pretty,' she said, risking an interruption. He glanced up to see what she was referring to.

'Yes. I bought it from someone in the fifth ring. It seemed perfect for this purpose, because there is a schematic of Arkannen in the lid.'

'Really?' Ayla opened it. Inside, the thick walls of the chest took up a considerable amount of space, leaving a compact cavity that Miles had filled with packets of different powders. Yet it was the lid that held her attention. As he'd said, seven concentric circles were carved into the wood, with the gates clearly marked on the boundary walls and a tiny heptagon at the centre to represent Darkhaven. It wasn't just Arkannen, either. Around it was the outline of Mirrorvale, disproportionately small in comparison to the city, and the edges of the other countries beyond.

'See?' Miles leaned across the table to point at the design. 'How the gates are joined by dashed lines to the countries surrounding Mirrorvale? Each gate is on the opposite side of Darkhaven from its corresponding country, meaning that the lines cross each other right in the centre of the circle.'

'Where Darkhaven is,' Ayla said. 'So what's at the other end of each line, Miles?'

'As I said –'

'What I mean is,' she interrupted, 'the lines join each gate to a country.' That was still a strange idea in itself. 'But a country is a massive thing. The lines could have been drawn connecting gates to countries without meeting at Darkhaven at all. So if there's any truth in this idea, and it's not just some esoteric theory, there must be something at the other end of each line. Otherwise ...' She shrugged. 'I could draw any shape I liked over Arkannen and claim it revealed some deep-hidden secret, but that wouldn't make it true.'

He bent forward to peer at the diagram. 'It is hard to tell at this scale, but I think the line connecting the Gate of Steel to Parovia ends at Rovinelle, the King's Seat. And it is possible that the Kardise line terminates in Kardissak.'

'So capital cities,' Ayla said. 'Centres of power. But the Ingal States have nothing like that – or rather, they have a dozen. Unless ...' She touched the spot with a fingertip, glancing up at him. 'The old imperial palace?'

'Where the sovereign lords of Ingal once ruled before the country splintered,' Miles agreed. He straightened up and smiled at her. 'You would have made a good alchemist, Lady Ayla.'

She nodded absently, still thinking about the diagram. It all seemed very strange, close to unbelievable – and yet, it was widely held that the temples of the sixth ring kept the natural powers of the world in balance. If that were true, she saw no reason why the gates of Arkannen couldn't have a similar effect. But to what end? *To counterbalance the influences of the countries surrounding Mirrorvale*, Miles had said before; yet she suspected there was more to it. Again, she thought of her father's words: *Darkhaven and the city that upholds it. We are tied to it, and it to us.*

'I never noticed before, but I think the Altar of Flame is positioned on a direct line between Darkhaven and the Gate of Flame,' she said aloud. 'Likewise, the Spire of Air and the Gate of Wind. And no doubt others ... It's amazing, Miles!

The more I consider it, the more I'm convinced that every part of this city was built with alchemy in mind.'

He nodded. 'I am sure of it. That is the difference between a city that grows out of a smaller settlement, and one that was built wholesale for a specific purpose.' Turning away, he returned to the bottles he'd been working with before and picked up a flask of water that sparkled with silver glints. 'I am ready to begin now, Lady Ayla.'

Ayla closed the chest and eyed the flask with some trepidation. 'What exactly is that?'

'Distilled crystal. I thought we would start with your own elements.'

'All right. Then … before we go any further, can you explain how the whole thing works? I mean, it doesn't seem possible that just a few everyday materials combined can achieve … well, anything. It's not even as if you're using the actual elements, flame and wind and whatever. Just symbols.'

'We use both,' Miles said. 'When we make a solid object, we need something to make it out of. So we use the representative materials – the symbols, if you like. But you are correct: a thing made out of glass and crystal and amber and wood and steel is just a thing. The alchemy comes from three principles: the order the materials are combined, *how* they are combined – so we might use flame to heat them, for instance, or wind to scatter one into another – and the addition of the two spiritual elements. It really is quite fascinating –' He visibly caught himself, blushing. 'I am sorry, Lady Ayla. You have no desire to listen to this. For a moment, I thought I was back at the university.'

'Not at all,' Ayla said. 'I'm interested. If alchemy is in my blood, it seems wise for me to know as much about it as possible.' In fact, given the number of other useless subjects she'd had to cram into her head when she was younger, she was surprised her father hadn't hired a tutor in alchemy alongside the rest. But then, Florentyn had always approached the subject of their family's origins with a caution bordering on paranoia. Along with his conviction that the bloodline must be kept pure had come an equally strong insistence on secrecy. Exclusivity. Detachment from the common folk. The Nightshades were special, and they were to be kept that way, and no-one else in Mirrorvale should be allowed to know more about their overlords than was good for them. Even, apparently, Ayla herself.

She wondered if Myrren had known any more about it. He'd been brought up as their father's heir, after all. Or had Florentyn thought it was too dangerous a topic for anyone to mention? After all, there was that question Miles had asked. *If an alchemist created Changers, what is to stop someone repeating the process?* Ayla could imagine very clearly what her father would have done if someone had said that to him.

'So you use representations of the elements to create a material object, and the elements themselves in the process of creation,' she said aloud. 'What of these spiritual elements you keep talking about? Birth and death? I can't imagine how you ...' She bit her lip as an unpleasant thought struck her. 'Don't tell me you add *living things* to these mixtures.'

Miles laughed. 'We are not sorcerers, Lady Ayla. Birth and death – *boros* and *auros* – are simply the driving forces that animate our work. Without them, we would have nothing but inert objects on our hands.'

'That doesn't really answer the question, Miles.'

'That is because I have no answer to give you.' He was still smiling, but now she sensed just a hint of dogged steel behind it. 'Some things must remain a mystery.'

She gave him a sly glance. 'Is that what you tell your students?'

'Yes, actually. At least until the fourth year. If alchemy were possible to understand in a morning, Lady Ayla, I would be out of a job.'

'All right. Then if we've gone as far as we can with the theory –' she smiled back at him to show she understood – 'do you want to tell me exactly what you're planning to do in these experiments?'

His lips quirked. 'Better that I show you. If you could just drink a little of this for me ...'

He held out the flask. Ayla hesitated. Never mind slitting her throat; he could dispatch her without any violence at all, simply by offering her poison. He wouldn't even have to touch her. Admittedly, only a handful of poisons could actually kill a Changer – but if anyone had the necessary knowledge, it would be an alchemist.

Still. She had to trust him. Else why were they even here?

'All right.' Before she could change her mind, she lifted the flask to her lips and swallowed a mouthful of the contents. Immediately her throat constricted, sending her into a coughing fit. 'F-fire and blood, Miles! Th-that's horrible!'

He nodded. 'Unfortunately, Lady Ayla, that was only the beginning.'

After that, it was relentless. He got her to drink different concoctions of water mixed with powdered substances – *Only tiny amounts*, he said, *they probably will not make you sick. Ah ... Changers have strong stomachs, do they not?* He asked her to hold various items – an ebonwood wand, a chunk of amber, a carved metal ring – while he measured her pulse rate, her breathing, her swiftness of reflex. He took samples of her hair and set fire to them, sprayed a fine mist into the air and told her to breathe it in, put a blindfold on her and asked whether particular materials felt cold or warm to the touch. And all the while, he got her to Change. Back and forth, back and forth. Woman, creature, woman. Until she was dizzy and breathless with it. He didn't seem to notice her nakedness, so after a while she didn't either.

Finally, back in human form, she grabbed her robe from where she'd flung it over the abandoned screen and sank down onto the floor. 'No more, Miles, I beg you!'

'My apologies, Lady Ayla.' He was already holding another flask, half filled with murky greyish liquid. He began to extend it towards her, then – at her look – lowered it back down to his side. 'You are correct, of course. That is more than enough for today.'

He turned back to the table and began busying himself with his equipment. Ayla gazed up at his back. Strong Changer stomach or not, she still felt sick.

'Did you learn anything?' she asked plaintively.

'Oh, I think so,' he mumbled to the glassware. 'It is all most interesting. Did you know, your hair is almost impossible to burn? Fascinating.'

'Miles.'

He spun on his heel to look at her, then folded himself gracelessly onto the floor beside her.

'I learned plenty,' he said – a soothing note in his voice that she found more amusing than otherwise. 'Your ability to shift shape is not affected by anything in the air, or by anything you ingest –'

'So no more disgusting potions,' she interrupted. He smiled.

'No more disgusting potions. If I had a way to introduce small amounts of an element directly into your blood ... but no matter. I think the most promising avenue for investigation will be to create something you can wear. Even just holding certain raw materials, you became quicker and stronger. Not by much, but enough to make me think that if I can find the right combination ...'

'Good.' Ayla was overtaken by an enormous yawn. She wiped her eyes and grinned at him. 'Do you want something to eat? I'm starving.'

Once the food arrived, she proceeded to prove that by eating three-quarters of what was there – and being fully aware of their overlord's requirements, the kitchen staff hadn't skimped on the meal. Miles watched her with unabashed curiosity.

'Hardly surprising, I suppose,' he remarked. 'Alchemical reactions require energy. Tell me, are you and Captain Caraway planning to marry?'

It was such an abrupt change to such a personal subject that she choked on a mouthful of bread. Once she'd finally swallowed it down, wiped her eyes and got her breath back, she shook her head reprovingly at him. 'You can't ask questions like that, Miles.'

'I am sorry. It is just that Art always says –' He broke off, blushing. 'Never mind.'

Ayla narrowed her eyes at him. 'What does Art always say?'

'He says he does not understand why Tomas does not ask you,' Miles mumbled, looking down at the piece of fruit in his hands. 'He thinks Tomas is afraid that –'

Suddenly not wanting to hear any of this indirectly, Ayla held up a hand to stop him. 'It's not up to Tomas. As over-lord of Darkhaven, I'm the one who would do the asking. And I'd appreciate it if we didn't mention this subject again.'

'Sorry. I – sorry.' He looked so mournful, and so uncomfortable, that Ayla softened towards him. She turned the conversation back to alchemy by telling him about the various unsuccessful attempts she'd made at freezing water, and the rest of the meal passed without incident.

Yet once Miles had gone, she found herself thinking about his question again. To tell the truth, it was one that had been on her mind a great deal. As she'd said, it was up to her to do the asking. She wanted to do it. And yet she couldn't find the words.

Tomas, I want you to stay here for good.

Tomas, remember when you told me that with my father gone, I could marry whoever I wanted?

Tomas, I love you. I love you …

But she still recalled, very vividly, how painful it had been the last time. She'd offered him herself as well as, indirectly, her hand in marriage – her future children – everything she had. And he'd turned it down. Of course, it had taken her less than a day to realise that reaction had been built on a misunderstanding. But even then, the sting of rejection and the choking down of wounded pride had been hard to overcome. She didn't think she could bear that again.

You're a coward, Ayla Nightshade, she told herself. *And unnecessarily so. You know he's devoted to you.*

For some reason, she found herself remembering their very first night together. It had been a mess, not at all the glorious pinnacle of passion she'd imagined. Not that she'd had anything to go on besides imagination. She'd been awkward, unsure of herself, and miserable with the loss of her family besides. Somehow she'd expected Tomas to take all of that away, but of course that wasn't fair. It was in her head, not his. And so they'd fumbled their way through it, and afterwards she'd burst into tears.

It made her wince even to think about it, now.

Yet the one thing she'd carried with her from that night was how deeply Tomas admired her – not just as a person, but as a woman. His hands on her body had been gentle, but never hesitant; he'd touched her as if it were an act of worship, a giving of thanks to one of the great powers. And that hadn't changed once it was over, as she'd half expected it to. Even through her tears, she'd been aware of him holding her as tenderly as ever. It was the memory of his touch, the *kindness* of it, that had given her enough confidence to try again.

And again.

Until, suddenly and startlingly, it had all made sense – and it had kept making sense between the two of them ever since.

Faced with memories like that, how could she doubt the depth of his feelings for her?

And yet she was afraid. Probably, she admitted to herself, because she knew she'd only have one chance. If he turned down her proposal, she'd never have the courage to offer it again. And so rather than risk that decisive rejection, she held herself back from even trying.

Part of the problem was how deeply he was entwined in every aspect of her life: Captain of the Helm, Marlon's surrogate father, the only man she wanted to share her bed. Which was silly, of course, because those were also some of the reasons she loved him. But he'd been afraid, three years ago, that she was turning to him out of gratitude and loneliness rather than genuine feeling. She could just imagine how he might make that mistake on a far grander scale, now, and assume she'd been swayed mainly or entirely by how useful he was to her.

Don't be ridiculous, she told herself sternly. *Just talk to him about it. You talk to him about everything else.*

Yet once he was home and they were finally alone, she found herself approaching the topic in the most roundabout way possible.

'Tomas, if I die ...'

'You won't die.' The response was swift. She squeezed his hand in tacit acknowledgement of his determination, but went on stubbornly.

'Just listen ... if I die, you'll need to hold Darkhaven until Marlon comes of age. You are his father, to all intents and purposes, and –'

'Of course,' Tomas said softly. 'I'll look after him, you know that. Though without a Changer to defend us, I can't guarantee to hold Darkhaven against the might of Sol Kardis. Better, perhaps, to flee the country and conceal Marlon –'

Temporarily diverted from her purpose, Ayla shook her head. 'He has to stay in the tower. The Kardise may take the rest of Mirrorvale. They may even take the rest of Arkannen. But as long as there is still a Nightshade in Darkhaven, it will all come right in the end.'

'How?'

'The family and Darkhaven. My father always said that if one falls, so does the other; but after some of the discussions I've had with Miles, I believe it's more. I believe it's also the case that one *can't* fall without the other.' Reading the doubt in his eyes, she added, 'It would be something to hope for, at least.'

'Twelve years is a long time to cling to a hope that slender, love.' He brought his other hand over to cover their clasped fingers, looking steadily into her face. 'But I'll swear to it, if that's what you want. It's not as if I'd do anything different, if it came to it. You and Marlon have my dedication, forever and always. You know that.'

And just like that, they were back to the point. Ayla could feel the words on her lips: *And you have mine. I love you, Tomas. Marry me.* But even as she opened her mouth to say them, he spoke again.

'Ayla … are you sure it's wise, to be discussing such things with Miles?'

Not this again. 'I can hardly avoid it. We talk a great deal.'

'About the vulnerabilities of your entire bloodline?'

'The whole point of working with Miles is to find a way to shield my vulnerability,' Ayla reminded him. 'We can hardly do that if we don't talk about it.'

'Well, I don't like it,' he said stubbornly.

Frustrated by their return to the same old argument instead of the very different conversation she'd intended, she snatched her hands away from him. 'Tomas, will you please just *stop* –'

A loud cracking sound made them both jump and look round. At first neither of them could identify the source, until Ayla discovered a new crack running across the top of the table beside her. Wordlessly she beckoned Tomas over, and they both stood gazing down at it.

'Did you do that?' he asked softly. 'After what Miles said …'

'I don't know.' She ran her hand over the wood, feeling the jagged line that split the surface. Had she sensed something new happening, in that instant of frustration? Had the power that Miles had promised finally manifested itself? She wanted to believe it, but she suspected it was just wishful thinking.

'Try it again,' Tomas said.

How? she wanted to ask. *Even if I did it, there was nothing deliberate about it.* But his expression was one of expectant pride, lifting the flicker of hope she felt herself to a small but steady flame. She took a deep breath, centring herself, then tried to extend her thoughts towards the wood. *Break.*

Break now. But nothing happened. Why would it? She didn't know how to make her will become reality. She kept trying until eventually, she had to shake her head in defeat.

'I can't do it. I don't know how I did it before, if I even did.' Her nails dug into her palms. 'Ugh! If my father had just *told* me –'

This time the crack was deep enough that the tabletop bowed. They stared at each other.

'All right,' Tomas said finally, breaking the stunned silence. 'So you can only do it when you're angry.'

She nodded, still trying to process it all. 'Looks that way.'

He gave her an affectionate smile. 'Lucky you have me around to keep you in a constant state of irritation, then.'

'Oh, Tomas.' She rested her cheek against his arm. 'Why can't anything ever be straightforward?'

'Where would be the fun in that?' He kissed her. 'You're a step closer. Think of it that way. Keep trying, and ask Miles about it next time you see him.'

'So I'm allowed to talk to Miles about this, then?' She'd intended it teasingly, but the question came out with an edge to it. Tomas sighed.

'You're the overlord of Darkhaven. You're *allowed* to do whatever you want.' He looked down at her, attempting another smile, but it was weary. 'Just try not to get yourself killed.'

FOURTEEN

Penn might not have liked the inhabitants, but he couldn't deny the lure of Arkannen itself. Albeit reluctantly, he was beginning to understand why his cousin had loved it so much.

He wandered through the sixth ring in a state of almost perpetual astonishment. He wasn't meant to be in the sixth ring, of course – he wasn't a citizen. The people of Arkannen were allowed to visit the temples a certain number of times each year, to celebrate whichever occasions or elements they'd chosen to honour, or to seek advice from those temples that were open to such things, but outsiders were barred. Even if Darkhaven hadn't been on high alert, that would have been the case. Citizens had certain privileges that others did not, one being permission to leave the lower rings. And though trainee warriors were an exception to that rule, they were admitted to the fifth ring only under strict conditions. They certainly weren't allowed beyond it, unless Captain Caraway or Weaponmaster Bryan or one of a handful of other key figures accompanied them.

Penn had considered these points very briefly, and decided that since he had no intention of staying in Arkannen – or even, necessarily, of surviving beyond the end of training – he wasn't going to miss the opportunity to see everything he could. Some of the Helm were using the duelling floors, even this early in the morning; he'd simply walked past, grabbed one of their striped coats and sauntered through the Gate of Ice. The watch hadn't paid him any attention, which didn't say much for their security. No doubt it was different up at the tower, where every Helmsman's face would be recognised ... or maybe it wasn't. Maybe Penn could walk straight in and do whatever he wanted.

Still, he wasn't ready for that yet, so he'd taken off the borrowed coat as soon as he was far enough away from the gate, turned it so the lining was uppermost, and draped it over his arm. Then he'd ignored the shorter route to the Gate of Death and gone the other way instead.

It was the first spare time he'd had in a fortnight. The morning after their silly fight in the mess hall, Weaponmaster Bryan had given him and Zander a single, sweeping glance, then ordered them to polish all the weapons in the armoury. *I want to see my face in every blade. And if you ever do anything like this again, lads, you'll be out. I don't like it when people ignore my rules.* It had been a relief not to be barred from the fifth ring, but cleaning all that metal had been a long and tedious task. It had taken almost every bell of daylight that wasn't spent on training or practice. The only benefit had been that Penn had become sufficiently acquainted with Zander's mannerisms, while they sweated over polishing cloths together, that he was just about able to tolerate them.

'*Fun job,*' *Zander said, straightening up and wiping his forehead with the back of his wrist.* '*This is all your fault, Penn.*'

'*My fault?*' *Penn said indignantly.* '*You punched me first, remember?*'

'*You accused me of being an assassin.*'

'*You accused me first!*'

Zander stared at him, before – suddenly and surprisingly – a grin spread over his face. '*Guess we're as bad as each other, then.*'

Penn thought about it, then touched his fingertips to Zander's to seal the bargain. '*I can live with that.*'

And Penn's evenings had been equally busy, full of Saydi and reluctant socialising. She'd told him – giggling, but with an edge to it that suggested she really meant it – that he needed to behave like a fully functioning member of society, not a petulant child. As a result, he'd squandered more time than he cared to think on chatter and drink with a bunch of people who'd hate him if they knew what he was thinking. He'd tried to express that to Saydi, but she'd only shaken her head. *If we all knew what everyone else was thinking, civilisation would collapse in a heartbeat. As far as I can see, life is based on people lying to each other.* It was one of the things he found himself liking about her: hidden amongst the inconsequential chatter were a few precious coins of wisdom. Yet despite that, he felt as if his entire life had become too full. He needed a place to breathe.

Up here in the sixth ring, he'd finally found it.

For one thing, there were fewer people. It wasn't a celebration day, so the citizens of Arkannen had no reason to be present in any great number. Those he did pass were mainly priestesses, gowned and veiled, going about their business with barely a glance at him. They knew they had nothing to fear from any stranger; no man or woman of Mirrorvale would harm a sixth-ring priestess. And somehow Penn found that calming. He'd grown up with weaponry, and he was more than competent to use it, but he hadn't realised until he left the fifth ring how exhausting it was to be around it all the time. During training he was always on his guard, whereas here he could relax. It was as though the weight of expectation the fifth ring placed on his shoulders simply melted away, leaving him free to enjoy his surroundings.

And there was no denying that his surroundings were very enjoyable. Each temple he passed was more fantastic than the last, yet none of them gave the impression of being ostentatious for the sake of it. In fact, every single one seemed to have been designed perfectly to encapsulate the qualities of the power it revered. The Cathedral of Trees, for instance, was a vast structure made entirely of living trees: their woven branches formed the roof and walls, their trunks the supports and internal pillars, giving the impression of both a worship hall and a sacred forest. Penn didn't have to walk into it to feel the sense of peace it exuded. And the dazzling bronze structure of the Sun Shrine was topped with a circular dish that somehow trapped and reflected light, making it too bright to look at directly, even on an overcast autumn morning like this.

When he reached the Spire of Air, he stopped. The spire itself – a tall, thin shard of glass that looked sharp enough to cut the sky in half – was impressive enough on its own. He could make out the walkway that spiralled partway up the outside of the spire to a platform bordered only by a single rail: the closest thing this particular temple had to an altar. Yet the spire rose out of an equally stunning building, made entirely of glass and carved into a series of shapes that reminded him of birds taking flight. The entire temple gave the impression that it was trying to float up into the sky where it belonged. Penn hadn't made much of his private dedication to Air since his unfortunate encounter with the itinerant priest in the first ring, but suddenly he found himself thinking – for the first time in weeks – that his situation wasn't so very overwhelming after all. Funny, how being in the presence of something much bigger and more enduring than himself could bring him solace.

'Not one of my favourites,' a voice said behind him. 'It's a vicious-looking thing, don't you think?'

Penn turned. Captain Caraway was standing a short distance away, looking up at the spire just as Penn himself had been.

'It always strikes me as the perfect place for a heroic last stand,' the captain went on. 'I can just imagine some desperate man barricading himself at the top of that walkway and fighting off all comers. It has that ... *combative* look about it.' He glanced at Penn, a wry twist to his mouth. 'The Water Garden is much more soothing. Have you visited?'

Torn by confusion and incoherent hatred, Penn shook his head. 'I'm not supposed to be here at all.' Then he winced. *Why did I say that? Like a child confessing to a crime* – But Caraway only shrugged.

'You don't appear to be doing any harm.'

'Not yet,' Penn muttered.

'It's like that, is it?' Caraway looked amused. How did he manage to make Penn feel so ... so *young*? It wasn't as if he were all that much older than Penn, really. Just more experienced – better trained –

'You don't like me much, do you?' Caraway asked, and Penn realised he was scowling. Hastily he smoothed his expression. *You're far too transparent*, Saydi had told him when he'd first confided the truth to her. *You'll never get anywhere if you let your feelings show on your face.* And, of course, she was right. Caraway would never select him for Helm training if he couldn't find a way to suppress his hostility, and that would ruin all his plans. He had to be chosen. *Had* to.

'I don't like anyone much,' he said honestly. Then, because the situation required it, 'But I don't mean to be rude.'

Caraway nodded. 'I understand. It just happens, right?'

That startled a smile out of Penn, but when Caraway smiled back at him he had to look away. *Stop it. He's acting pleasantly enough, but you know the truth.*

'You know,' the captain said, 'it's funny how many people come to the fifth ring in search of something.'

'What do you mean?'

'Well, when I started this job I assumed the teaching part would be straightforward. I'd been through the training myself, so I thought I should be able to pass it on to other people easily enough. But as it turns out, people are complicated.' He grinned. 'More often than not, they're not here simply because they have an aptitude for the blade and they think they could make a steady career out of it. They're here because they want something else. Something less tangible. And before I can assess whether any of them would make good Helmsmen, I have to untangle their skills from all that *wanting*.' He glanced sideways at Penn, before adding lightly, 'But don't worry. I'm not going to ask what you came looking for.'

And I wouldn't tell you, even if you did. Penn frowned. 'What about you? Did you find what you wanted?'

The question had an edge to it – he couldn't help it – but Caraway didn't appear to notice.

'I got it, and I lost it. But I was given a second chance. I try to remember that.'

'You always wanted to be captain of the Helm?'

'I always wanted to be of use to the Nightshade line.' His smile was bewildered. 'I wouldn't have dreamed I'd be where I am now. But there you have it.'

192

Penn's nails dug into his palms. It was only with considerable effort that he held himself motionless instead of turning the full force of his seething hatred on the man. *You're a murderer, Tomas Caraway. You don't deserve it. You don't deserve any of it.*

Though he was trying his very best not to let the emotion show, something of it must have come through. Caraway took a step closer, gaze intent on Penn's face. His lips tightened. For a moment, Penn thought he was going to demand the truth – and who knew what would come pouring out, faced with that demand? – but in fact, when he spoke, his voice was surprisingly soft.

'Penn ... do you want to talk about it?'

Penn shook his head, not trusting himself to speak. Caraway waited a little longer, then nodded in resignation.

'All right,' he said. 'I'm here because the watch sent for me, because one of my students had entered the sixth ring unsupervised. It's not their job to stop you. It's mine, or Weaponmaster Bryan's. But I'm not going to.'

Jolted from his anger, Penn stared at him. 'What?'

'I'll tell them to let you through,' Caraway said. 'You'll have to leave your weapons at the gate, of course. And resist wearing a Helmsman's stripes before you've earned the right to them.' His amused glance rested briefly on the coat draped over Penn's arm. 'But if you like it here, I see no reason to keep you from it.'

For the space of a heartbeat, Penn's world tipped on its axis. Because that was an act of kindness, no more and no less. Under conditions of increased security and with Ayla's life under threat, Caraway had every reason to send Penn back to the fifth ring with a stern admonishment not to do it again. Allowing him the freedom of the sixth ring could only increase Caraway's workload. And Penn couldn't reconcile that with his own opinion of the man.

Of course you can, the dark part of him retorted. *Beneficence suits his inflated sense of self-importance. He's acting like he owns the whole city* – and just like that, his resolve hardened again.

'Right now, you'd better get back to the fifth ring,' the captain added, oblivious to Penn's internal debate. 'Else you'll be late for practice.'

They walked in silence back to the Gate of Ice. When they reached it, Caraway turned to Penn with an easy, sympathetic smile, as if he were completely oblivious to Penn's antipathy.

'I'm not going to pretend to have all the answers. But if you have anything you want to get off your chest, you know where to find me.'

Penn mumbled something, then watched as the captain walked back up the street in the direction of the Gate of Death and Darkhaven. It was only after he was out of sight that Penn found himself wondering why he hadn't tried to stab the man. Obviously Penn couldn't yet hope to beat him in a fair fight, but just now he'd had the chance to catch him off guard. Why hadn't he taken it?

But to that, he could return no satisfactory answer.

Ree wasn't looking forward to the training session that her hand-copied schedule referred to as Teamwork and Tactics. Her tutor had been a competent swordsman who'd been able to convey enough of the basics in other areas of weaponry that Ree could hold her own now, but one thing he'd never touched on was any form of strategy. It hadn't been necessary: their sparring had always been one-on-one, with a tactical aim no more lofty than disarming the opposition. But the

Helm had to be able to formulate battle plans, and they had to work together to carry them out – and Ree didn't have the slightest confidence in her ability to do either.

The recruits were divided into teams of seven or eight, each with an assessor: Captain Caraway, Weaponmaster Bryan or one of the assistant weaponmasters. Ree had hoped to be put with Zander, but instead she found herself on a team with Farleigh, Timo, Penn and Saydi, plus a handful of other boys. Her disappointment surprised her: somewhere along the line, she'd stopped finding Zander's constant defence of her annoying, and begun to rely on it as reassurance that at least one of her possible future colleagues took her a little bit seriously.

In which case, she told herself, *it's probably a good thing we've been separated.*

She stood in stoic silence, ignoring some of her team-mates' grumblings about being stuck with the girls, until the tutors began to lead the teams away in different directions. Ree's team was under the supervision of Weaponmaster Bryan himself; he took them to one of the practice floors that made up the interior of the training hall, then unlocked the door and stood back in silence to let them inside. Ree wasn't sure what she'd expected the room to contain, but it wasn't this: two high wooden platforms, each with steps leading down to the ground, and between them … it looked similar to the balance beams they trained with during agility classes, only rather than being rectangular in cross-section, this one was round. A long, cylindrical pole, almost like the branch of a tree.

'Bet that bugger rotates, doesn' it,' one of the boys muttered.

'Certainly does,' Bryan said cheerfully. 'You gotta use your imagination here, lads, assuming you have any. This isn't a practice floor but a river you need to cross, and with you –' he reached into the bag at his side and pulled out a floppy cloth doll – 'is this poor, helpless baby. You start on that bank.' He gestured at one of the platforms, then across to the other. 'You finish on that one. You have to use the bridge – no imaginary swimming.' He glared around at them, and some of the boys laughed.

'Once you've come up with a strategy, you can test it as many times as you like, but you only get one shot with the baby. If you drop it or fall with it, that's the end. Baby dies.' He grinned, reached out to the large sand-timer by the wall, and swung it until the bulb full of sand was uppermost. 'Your task is to get the baby, and as many of your team as possible, safely to the other side.'

They waited, but he didn't say anything else.

'That's it?' Timo asked. His nose was still purple-red and swollen, Ree noted with an inward wince.

'That's it,' the weaponmaster agreed. He raised his eyebrows at them. 'And you're already losing time.'

The trainees scrambled into action. About half the boys went straight for the near platform, where they discovered that the 'bridge' was even harder to cross than it looked. It spun at the slightest touch; anyone who walked too slowly was tipped straight onto the mats below, while anyone who tried running it soon lost their balance and fell off anyway. Ree tried it for herself, but found it impossible to get further than a few steps. *Then how* …

One of the boys found a coil of rope in the corner of the platform, and suggested that they tie themselves together – but that only made things worse. A single person with good enough agility might be able to make it across to the other side, but put more than one person on the bridge at a time and they ended up knocking each other off. They'd have to step in perfect unison, Ree thought, and even then it would be a close-run thing. It would take days to get it right, not just however long was left in the top bulb of the timer.

The three boys who'd roped themselves together began to argue about each other's mistakes, until Farleigh suggested that it might be possible to cross by clinging to the underside of the bridge with arms and legs. The pole turned out to be so highly polished that he couldn't pull himself along as easily as he'd hoped, but by hooking his knees and elbows over it, he succeeded in dragging himself all the way to the far platform. Yet there was no way to climb back up from pole to platform. As soon as he tried to do it, he ended up falling just like everyone else.

Finally, one of the boys managed to cross the bridge, nearly falling off near the end but throwing himself bodily onto the platform instead – and that was when they discovered a new problem. As soon as any weight was put on the far platform, their destination, the end of the pole that rested lightly on it came clattering down, effectively breaking the bridge. At that, Bryan came over to the apparatus and hooked it back into place with a grin.

'Did I forget to mention that? Soon as you make your real attempt, you don't get to rebuild the bridge once it's down.'

As he walked back over to his vantage point beside the sand timer, Timo scowled. 'S'impossible. There's no way we can get our whole team over there. We can't even get one person over there!'

'It must be possible,' Farleigh retorted. 'The weaponmasters wouldn't give us a task that was impossible.'

'Maybe they would. Maybe they wanna see how we crack under pressure ...'

They started arguing again, but Ree ignored them. She was busy studying the setup: the rope, the rotating pole, the platform that released the bridge as soon as anyone stepped on it...

'We're doing it all wrong,' she said softly.

'What?' She hadn't realised Penn was at her elbow until he spoke. She turned to face him.

'We're doing it all wrong! *As many of your team as possible*, Weaponmaster Bryan said. But what if it's not possible to get more than one of us across there? What if that's the point?'

Penn's eyebrows drew together, but he said nothing. Beyond him, the rest of the team were listening too.

'That's stupid,' Farleigh said. 'This exercise is about us working together. How is it working together if we don't even get across?'

A couple of the other boys mumbled agreement, but she cut across them.

'Because that's what would happen in real life, sometimes. Isn't it? If this doll was a Nightshade baby, and we had to get it to safety, it wouldn't matter how many of us were left behind.'

They looked doubtful. Ree glanced across at the rapidly diminishing sand in the top bulb of the timer, and did her best not to fidget. But then Saydi said, 'You know, I think she's right.'

'Conspiracy of women,' Timo muttered, and Farleigh laughed. Saydi frowned prettily at them.

'I'm not agreeing with her because we're both female,' she said, as if explaining something to a pair of children. 'That would be stupid. I'm agreeing with her because she's making sense.'

Ree suppressed a grin, because it wouldn't have helped, and pressed the point home while she had the chance.

'It's not as if we've found a way to get all of us across, anyway. Our time's nearly up, so getting one person and the doll to the other side has to be better than nothing at all.'

Timo rolled his eyes at her. 'And I suppose now you're going to say it should be you, because girls are better at looking after babies.'

It was so obviously an attempt at provocation that Ree didn't bother to argue with it, simply rolled her eyes back at him. 'Actually, no. It should be Penn.'

That shut them all up. Almost as one, they turned to look at Penn, standing to one side in silence. He crossed his arms defensively.

'Why me?'

'Because I've seen you in agility training,' Ree said simply. 'You get across the narrow beam every time. And we already know that anyone who tries to get across there is going to need a really good sense of balance.'

No-one argued with that; Penn might be difficult to get on with, but there was no denying his skill. Saydi held out the doll, and Farleigh said, 'We can tie it onto your back.'

Penn took it. For once, he didn't look at all angry, only young and rather bewildered. After a moment, he looked up and gave a quick nod. 'All right.'

His acceptance of the task seemed to energise the other boys. They crowded round him, trying to find the best way to secure the doll. Ree hung back, and so did Saydi; they glanced at each other, and Ree found they were sharing a smile.

When Penn was ready, he climbed the steps to the near platform. The rest of the team followed close on his heels, jostling together in a space that wasn't really big enough to hold them all, so they could see the result of their gamble. Penn cast them an irritable glance over his shoulder.

'Give me some room, will you?'

They backed up. Ree saw his shoulders rise and fall as he took a deep breath. Then, as if he'd been doing it his whole life, he ran lightly across the rotating pole. When he reached the far platform, he tugged the doll from his back and – ignoring the clatter of the falling bridge – turned to flash a grin across the gap. Ree had so rarely seen Penn smile that she found it oddly touching.

'Baby's safe!' he called, rocking it in his arms, and the boys began cheering and clapping. Ree looked over at Saydi, wanting to convey tacit thanks for her support, but the other girl was gazing at Penn with an arrested expression on her face, as though she'd suddenly thought of something important. Yet then she blinked and shook her head, turning away, leaving Ree to wonder if she'd imagined it.

'Time's up!' Bryan called. 'And I see you're all so fond of Penn Avens that you've made him your sole survivor.'

The boys clattered back down the steps to the floor, clamouring to know if they'd got it right. Ree herself was longing to find out how they'd done compared to the other teams. Yet Bryan only shook his head.

'We'll give you the results tomorrow,' he said. But when Ree caught his eye, he gave her the ghost of a smile – and suddenly, she was certain that she'd done the right thing.

By the time Miles next visited the tower, Caraway had managed to infuriate Ayla into breaking a wooden practice sword, but she still couldn't access the elusive power without using some kind of emotional response to drive it. Since he was as anxious as she was to solve the problem, he went along to her meeting with the alchemist, and the two of them together explained what had happened.

'Interesting,' Miles said. 'I am not sure, but if I had to guess ...' He frowned. 'Do you remember I said that the power might come to you once you were aware of the possibility of its existence? And that alchemy is at the intersection between knowledge and belief?'

Ayla nodded. 'I don't remember the exact wording of everything you say, Miles, but yes.'

'Well, I think what is happening here is that you *know* the power is within you, but you do not really *believe* it. Anger allows you to break down that barrier temporarily. But if you want to break it down for good ...' He gave her an abashed smile, as though he knew he was about to ask the impossible. 'You need to believe.'

'And how do you propose I do that?'

'Again, this is guesswork, but I would say you need to start thinking of yourself as a real Changer. For years, you were told that the form you take is impure. You have come to terms with that by convincing yourself that purity is not a goal worth pursuing. But the fact is, Lady Ayla –' he leaned forward earnestly – 'in alchemical terms, a combination of elements is no more or less pure than a single element alone. That is not how alchemy operates. If we were to work only with single elements, we would never achieve anything! Your hybrid nature is a strength, not a weakness.' He shook his head. 'Really, your ancestors have a lot to answer for.'

That was uncomfortably perspicacious, Caraway thought, and Ayla's widening eyes showed that the observation had hit home. Still, she recovered quickly.

'That's all very well, Miles, but you're asking me to believe something to order. Surely you know it's not that easy.'

'All the same, will you do something for me? Will you try it again, now?' He held out a glass of water similar to the one she'd tried and failed with before. She pinned him with her fierce gaze, clearly trying to decide whether to reject the suggestion, then – reluctantly – took it.

'Close your eyes,' Miles said, and she obeyed. 'Breathe slowly. Empty your mind. And then gently ... ever so gently ... reach out to the water, and tell it to become ice.' He smiled, though she couldn't see him. 'Alchemy is as much spiritual as it is physical; you have been forcing it, but really it is a matter of coaxing.'

Ayla's shoulders lifted, then fell, as she released a long breath. Caraway watched in love and fascination as she visibly battled with her own need for control. But then her face softened, her white-knuckled grip on the glass easing –

With a small crackling sound, the water froze.

Ayla yelped and nearly dropped the glass, her eyes flying open again. She examined the ice carefully, as though making sure it was real, before raising her gaze to Miles.

'Well,' she said. 'That's new.'

Caraway wasn't fooled. He could see the smile trembling at the corners of her mouth, the brightness in her eyes. She was giddy with joy. And why not? It wasn't every day a person found out they could freeze things through willpower alone.

Given that he didn't seem to be reacting to it at all, he rather suspected that he himself was in a state of mild shock – either that, or spending three years in close proximity to a woman who could turn into a winged unicorn had dulled his sense of wonder.

By the time he left them, she'd managed to freeze another glassful of water, and Caraway himself was feeling more optimistic than he had in a long time. He was proud of Ayla, he realised. Even after three years, she still kept finding ways to surprise him. But more than that ... this new power she'd discovered might be the weapon they needed to defend her against an assassin.

He could only hope.

FIFTEEN

Bryan folded his arms and looked sternly at the assembled trainees on the other side of the table.

'Today,' he announced in a voice that brooked no argument, 'we'll be doing something rather different.'

He glanced over at Miles, who was waiting quietly at the side of the room. They'd discussed the whole thing the previous night. Miles had been reluctant at first; it was another commitment that took him away from his work at the university, and he already spent his one free morning a week up at the tower with Ayla Nightshade. But he had the knowledge that Bryan himself didn't have – and besides, he couldn't deny that it was a good idea, even if it had come from an unlikely source.

I've received another communication from Naeve Sorrow, Caraway had said the previous morning, handing over a scrappy piece of paper. *This time it came with a shipment of Kardise ore on what I strongly suspect is a smuggler barge. She's resourceful, I'll give her that.*

Bryan had taken the message and scanned the scrawled words: *I've accepted another job on your behalf and will send on what you need as soon as I have it. You can pay me later. In the meantime, see how they react when you mention guns.*

In fact, I didn't say anything about paying her, Caraway had added. *Still, that's sellswords for you. So, do you think you can do it?*

What, mention guns? Bryan had considered it, before grinning. *You did say you wanted the trainees to start learning about firearms, didn't you?*

That in itself had been an interesting discussion. Caraway had been adamant that it was a good idea, but Bryan himself had offered plenty of doubts. In the end, though, he'd been forced to admit that if a Helmsman wanted to kill Ayla, he'd find a way to do it with a pistol or without one. The Helm were the only people aside from Caraway himself who were close to her on a regular basis, so they had plenty of opportunity, and they were skilled enough that they could probably incapacitate her before she had a chance to react. But the whole point of the Helm was that they were dedicated to Ayla. Training them in the use of firearms would give them no more likelihood of killing her, and it might give others less.

Of course, that was the Helm proper. Offering the same training to a bunch of hopefuls, most of whom wouldn't end up as Helmsmen, was a step further – and might be a step too far. But Bryan had agreed that it was worth it, on this occasion at least, in case it gave them a vital clue as to the identity of the assassin. *See how they react when you mention guns.* He had considered being subtle about it: dropping a remark about black-market weaponry into the conversation and seeing where it went. But since subtlety wasn't one of his strengths, he'd gone in the opposite direction.

He whisked the piece of cloth off the table in front of him to reveal what lay beneath. An array of pistols, varying slightly in shape and size, but all with the same lethal shine.

This was the Helm's entire cache of illegal firearms, confiscated over three years from smugglers and mercenaries. Until recently they'd sat unused in the armoury, separated from the world by multiple barriers with multiple locks. And now they were being handed over to a group of people that might contain an assassin.

Now that Bryan had actually reached that part, it didn't seem like quite such a good idea as it had when he'd discussed it with Miles last night.

'Firearms are banned in Mirrorvale,' he said, pushing his uncertainty to one side. 'But they get through all the same. In the past, the Helm have kept them locked up where they can do no harm. But it's Captain Caraway's belief that ignorance is no use in the face of a very real threat to public order. He has decided the Helm should know their enemy. Therefore, those of you who are selected for the Helm programme will be trained in the use of firearms alongside every other kind of weaponry.'

He tried to read the murmurs and exchanged glances that followed that announcement, but got nowhere. After all, it was natural for the trainees to be excited, intrigued, even a little daunted. They were in the fifth ring because they had a natural liking and aptitude for weaponry – yet most of them had never even seen a pistol, let alone handled one. They must feel like hunters who'd been tracking a rare and elusive beast for years, only to stumble across an entire nest of the buggers.

'Today, you will examine these pistols,' Bryan went on. 'They aren't loaded, so it's quite safe. I just want you to familiarise yourself with them. You will *not* take them out of this room. You will *not leave* until I'm satisfied that every piece has been returned to me. And once I have them all back, my colleague Miles Tarantil –' he jerked a thumb at Miles, still waiting by the wall – 'will perform a short demonstration. Understand?'

A ragged mumble.

'I said, do you understand?'

'Yes, sir!' The chorus rang out. With a brisk nod, Bryan stepped back and gestured the trainees forward. As they surrounded the table, chattering amongst themselves in hushed but somehow heightened voices, he watched them. Any signs of familiarity with the weapons would be worth noting – as would, he supposed, excessive awkwardness. But nothing in particular struck him. The trainees handled the pistols with caution, and a considerable degree of interest, but that was all.

Bryan imagined himself trying to convince a stranger that he'd never picked up a sword before. He'd probably over-compensate wildly, grimacing and fumbling and dropping it on the floor. But if he were wily enough to be an assassin, he supposed he'd exercise restraint. Watch the others, copy what they did. Try not to stand out.

Yet if he were suddenly put in a position where his reflexes were bound to kick in – if, say, another swordsman attacked him without warning –

'Excuse me, sir?' Ree glanced up from the table. 'Can you show us how they work?'

Right. Hold that thought. Bryan joined the trainees and began to explain the different parts of a pistol – at least, as far as he understood them himself. Miles clearly found the vague descriptions frustrating; he edged closer to the table, putting in a word or two of correction. After a while, with Bryan's encouragement, he had taken over the explanation completely – at which point, Bryan was free to stand back and watch their faces once more.

'Are pistols dangerous to everyone, sir?' Farleigh piped up. 'I mean ... even Changers?'

Well, now. That was an interesting question. Did it betray too much knowledge? Or did it show an assassin's hand too clearly to be an assassin's question? Or was that, in fact, what an assassin would want him to think ...?

Stop that, man. Just remember everything they say and hand it over to Caraway to sort out later. For now, the most important thing is answering *the damn question.*

'Changer creatures are impervious to all weaponry,' he said, taking refuge in the rote response. 'But you're right to ask. As a Helmsman, you would need to know what might threaten those you were sworn to protect.'

Farleigh nodded. 'Though I was really thinking of Changers in human form. After all, they say Lord Myrren died by –'

'That's enough,' Bryan said sharply. *Lad doesn't know when to keep his mouth shut.* 'Lord Myrren's life, and Lord Myrren's death, are none of your concern. But yes, you are correct: Changers are more vulnerable when human. Maybe not as vulnerable as the rest of us, but vulnerable all the same.'

There was a pause. Then Penn said with a frown, 'But I heard that Changer creatures *aren't* impervious to firearms.'

'Me too,' Timo put in. 'They talk about it sometimes in the lower rings. A pistol can kill a Changer, and that's why guns are banned in Mirrorvale.'

Penn nodded. 'I assumed that was why Darkhaven is on lockdown. Because you said the threat is from Sol Kardis, sir, and everyone knows that's where firearms come from.'

None of them knew when to keep their mouths shut. *Just like every other group of callow youngsters I've ever taught*, Bryan admitted to himself. Now, should he deny the rumours? Or would it be better to admit the truth and see where that led him?

Before he could make up his mind, Saydi unwittingly came to his rescue.

'I'm not sure I understand. How do these illegal pistols get into Mirrorvale? Don't they search people at the borders?'

Bryan opened his mouth to reply, but she was already talking again.

'And anyway, I don't see how anyone with a pistol would even get close to Lady Ayla. Security is very tight here. I mean, we're a whole two rings away from Darkhaven, and we still had to give up our possessions to be checked before we were allowed to move into the barracks, and then again after the first week. So if one of us was an assassin –' she giggled – 'you'd already know it, Weaponmaster Bryan.'

'Right,' Bryan said. 'And since the Helm are searching everyone who enters Darkhaven, there isn't any way an illegal weapon can be smuggled in. So I suggest you all stop worrying about the possible effects of firearms on Changers and concentrate on learning how the damn things work.'

Yet his brain was whirring. Saydi was right: what with the initial search upon admittance to the fifth ring and the more recent search of the barracks, all the trainees and their belongings had been vetted far more thoroughly than they as travellers would have been at the borders or the airship stations, before the assassination threat came to light. So if one of them was the assassin, he would have to procure a pistol somewhere in the city before he could carry out his task. In which case, it might be worth suggesting to Caraway that he question some of the known or suspected black-market traders – try and find out if anyone new had come in search of an illegal weapon recently. Of course, the average trainee would have no idea where to go in Arkannen to buy a pistol ... but a Kardise assassin would.

'All right,' he said aloud. 'Move back from the table now. Leave all the pistols there.'

Once the two of them were satisfied that no firearm or even part of a firearm was missing, Miles began to prepare the one he'd use for his demonstration whilst Bryan locked the rest away in the portable safe. Then a thought struck him. *Before we go any further ... time to test their reflexes.*

He held out his hand for the pistol. 'Can I borrow that for a moment, Miles?'

Once he had it, he went through the motions of loading it, but without actually adding any powder. Then, holding the weapon so that it pointed loosely in the direction of the trainees, he frowned.

'Funny ... the mechanism's sticking ... if I just –'

He bent his head to fiddle with the pistol, waving it in their direction without appearing to be aware of it. And as his finger tightened on the trigger, he watched them covertly.

Miles, of course, flinched away in alarm.

Most of the trainees stared dumbly back at him.

And Zander dived aside as if he'd been shot in truth, pulling Ree with him.

'That's better,' Bryan said. 'Lucky I forgot the powder, eh? Better let the professional handle it, I think.'

He turned away to return the pistol to Miles, trying not to let his inward smile show on his face. *Well, what do you know? That was pretty damn wily.*

Miles gave him a suspicious look, but took the firearm and loaded it properly. They'd set up one of the archery targets on the far wall – *The bullet will probably get all the way through*, Miles had said, *but the straw will slow it down at least* – so Bryan herded all the trainees out of the way, leaving Miles a clear line of sight to the target.

Bryan had seen Miles use a pistol several times before, so he was used to the sudden noise and the violence of the impact. He'd hoped that since the trainees didn't have that level of familiarity, he'd notice some difference in their reactions when it came to that crucial point. Yet when the bullet tore through the centre of the target, the overwhelming response was cheers and applause. They were excited by the damn pistol. Hardly surprising, given their interest in weapons as a whole, but it didn't make it easy to pick out a divergent reaction in the group.

Miles's eyes met his, a question in them. Bryan shook his head slightly: *No idea.* The demonstration didn't prove anything either way.

Still, he had something to tell Captain Caraway, at least. Because of all the recruits, only one had exhibited any awareness of what a pistol could do *before* he was shown it in action.

'So now we're alone,' Zander said, 'what did you make of today's lesson on firearms?'

He'd joined Ree as the recruits headed back to the mess hall after the day's training, and they'd ended up talking all through the meal and beyond – until they were the only two of their cohort left, even Farleigh having given up and wandered off to seek other amusement long ago. Ree had enjoyed the whole evening more than she would have thought possible a few weeks ago. Ever since the Teamwork and Tactics session, the rest of the boys' attitude to her had changed – because it had turned out that her team was the only one to complete the task successfully, and she had played a key part in that. Of course, the difference was minor; it wasn't as if anyone was going to switch straight from despising her to admiring her unreservedly. But the teasing had lessened, or maybe her perception of it had simply changed, and for the first time she and her fellow trainees felt like comrades, not competitors.

Of course, Zander had always been welcoming to her; and now that she'd got over her defensiveness towards him, and he was managing to restrain himself from riding to her rescue at least some of the time, she was well on the way to thinking of him as the closest friend she'd ever had.

Now, not sure what he was getting at, she frowned at him. 'What do you mean?'

'Well, other than the fact that I saved your life –'

'What?'

'You know. Kept you from being shot in a freak accident. Unless, of course, you think our weaponmaster was actually trying to murder you –'

'Oh, stop it.' Ree elbowed him in the ribs, laughing. 'It wasn't even loaded. You dragged me onto the floor for nothing.'

'Other than the fact that I *saved your life*,' Zander repeated, feigning an injured expression, 'I wondered what you thought about the whole thing. Firearms have never been taught in the fifth ring before, to the Helm trainees or anyone else.'

'Weaponmaster Bryan said that Captain Caraway said –'

'I know what they said,' Zander interrupted. 'I was there. But I just thought there might be something else to it.'

Ree considered that. 'You mean, like trying to get the assassin to give himself away?'

'Yes.' Zander looked both admiring and a little alarmed. 'Exactly like that.'

'Well, if that's the case, you made yourself suspect number one,' Ree said. 'Seeing as you're the only one who reacted to

211

the danger implied by that pistol. None of the rest of us even realised there *was* any danger.' She bumped his shoulder with hers. 'Still, it's only a problem if you really are the assassin.'

She was joking, but the shade of alarm in Zander's eyes grew more pronounced. 'Do you think that's what people will believe?'

'You're worried about this.' She peered at him. 'Where *did* you get your knowledge of firearms, Zander?'

'Not worried, exactly. Just a little unsettled. No-one likes to be falsely suspected.'

He'd completely ignored the question, Ree noticed.

'Don't worry,' she said. 'I can vouch for the fact that you don't believe in anything strongly enough to be an assassin.'

'Aw, thanks, Ree.' The teasing expression returned to his face. 'I'm so glad I saved your life rather than anyone else's.'

'What about Saydi?' The words were out before she could stop them, and instantly she wanted to take them back. They sounded too much like jealousy. But Zander only shrugged.

'What about her?'

'I just thought – she and you might –'

'Gods, Ree. Have you really not noticed – no. Clearly you haven't.' He winked at her. 'Unless I'm much mistaken – which never happens, obviously – she and Penn are enjoying each other's company right now.'

Ree stared at him. 'Saydi and *Penn*? Really?'

'Why not?'

'He hates people!'

'Apparently not her.'

'Oh.' Ree didn't know what to say to that. Saydi might talk too much about insignificant things and be far too ... well ... *girly* for Ree's taste, but at least she meant well. After seeing her struggle to improve every week, Ree could even afford her a measure of grudging respect. Whereas Penn ... Ree never would have put Penn with Saydi. She never would have put Penn with *anyone*. Penn was the angriest person she'd ever met.

'Do you really think he's the assassin?' she asked curiously. 'That night when the two of you fought, you said –'

Zander shook his head. 'Not really. I can't imagine an assassin being furious all the time. Assassins have to be calm. Steady.'

'You mean, like you?' Ree suggested, but Zander only laughed. She would have pressed further, but at that point, the caretaker came over to throw them out of the mess hall so that he could lock it up for the night. With muttered apologies, they made for the door.

Outside, it was already dark. The moon was close to full, an irregular orb veiled in the gauzy tracery of smoke that was Arkannen's permanent blanket. Ree breathed the night deep into her lungs and thought, as she often did, how different the city smelled from the countryside. It wasn't something people often thought about, but even without the use of eyes or ears she'd still know she wasn't in Torrance Mill any more. A sudden swift homesickness came over her, but she suppressed it. Nostalgia, no more. Strange how memory could gild her childhood with that wonderful, melancholy sense of long-lost time, even when she had absolutely no desire to return to it.

'So.' Zander grinned at her, breath steaming in the cool air. 'You coming back to my room?'

By now it was a running joke between them. He always asked. She never said yes. But this time, unexpectedly, she found she was considering it.

A lady does not share herself around like a pot of ale between stablehands, her mother had said when she caught Ree kissing one of the neighbours' boys at the age of twelve.

If you will not conduct yourself as befits something rare and precious, you cannot expect others to treat you that way. She'd brought Ree up in the belief that sex should be restricted solely to marriage, and since Ree never intended to marry, she'd always assumed it was a part of life she'd never experience. Yet she'd defied her mother in everything else, so why hold on to that? As far as her fellow trainees were concerned, sex was just something you did to relax – nothing to do with love, and certainly not with marriage. Maybe if she tried it, she'd stop acting like such a mooncalf over … other people.

'Fine,' she said, before she could overthink it. 'Why not?'

It was almost worth it for the sheer dumb surprise that flashed across his face. But that soon faded, to be replaced by rueful amusement. 'You don't have to look so depressed about it.'

Ree realised she was frowning and smoothed it away, trying for a smile. 'Sorry.'

'You know,' Zander said, 'this isn't obligatory. If you're doing it just because I've badgered you into submission, that's a horrible reason and you should walk away now. Maybe punch me first.'

As always, she couldn't tell if that puppy-eyed sincerity was totally genuine or if it was all part of the act. But in the end, it didn't matter. It was her choice. She'd be using him as much as he'd be using her.

'Oh, no, it's nothing to do with you –' she began, then stopped at his chuckle.

'I hope it is a *little*.'

She couldn't help smiling back at him. 'Come on. It's cold out here.'

Afterwards, she wandered around his room wrapped in a sheet, looking at the sketches he'd tacked to the walls and feeling pleasantly ... floaty. A little sore, maybe, but certainly not like the damaged goods her mother had described. Nor, indeed, did she show any sign of falling in love with Zander, which had been her own fear. No – she still liked him well enough, but that was all.

Altogether a very satisfactory experiment, she thought, and giggled. Then clapped a hand over her mouth, because she *never* giggled. Giggling was for the Saydis of the world. Not her.

'What's the joke?' Zander asked. He was lying back on his elbows in bed, bare-chested, watching her lazily. Good mood already dissipating, Ree shook her head.

'Nothing.'

Lowering her gaze, she caught sight of the corner of a wooden box poking out from under the bed. The part she could see was carved all over with an abstract design that reminded her vaguely of the tattoo on his wrist.

'That's a pretty box,' she remarked.

Zander nodded, but she noticed a hint of caution in him – the same as when he mentioned his family or where he came from. Plain curiosity led her to add, 'What's in it?'

He smiled. 'Secrets.'

'Will you show me?'

'It's locked.'

She gestured impatiently. 'Then unlock it.'

'I can't,' he said. 'I threw away the key.'

Oh, really? She raised her eyebrows at him. 'Then why keep the box?'

'I still use the box.'

'Stop talking in riddles, Zander! There's no way the quartermaster would have let you in here with a mysterious box that could contain anything –'

'Oh, but he did.' Now Zander was grinning. 'I told him I lost the key on my way here, and asked where in the city I could get another made. To tell you the truth, I think I made him feel sorry for me.' Suddenly the grin disappeared, and he looked at Ree with big, sad eyes. '*It's just so frustrating! That box contains all the keepsakes I brought with me to make my new lodgings seem like home. Honestly, sir, I'd rather have lost anything else but that.*' Just as quickly, he dropped the regretful voice he'd been putting on and switched back to his usual cocky smile. 'But in reality I just pick the lock, when I need to. I decided that was probably safer than having a key I could lose or anyone could steal.'

Doubly fascinating – and a little disturbing, too, since she hadn't realised Zander was such an accomplished liar. She longed to know what was in the box, but there were even more pressing questions. 'How on earth did you learn how to pick a lock?'

'I taught myself.'

'So you break into things,' she murmured. 'You lie to city officials. And yet you want to join the Helm.'

'Why not?'

'Your skills seem more suited to crime than law enforcement. That's all.'

He smirked at her. 'Want me to show you how?'

'What for?'

'Well,' he said. 'For one thing, you never know when you might need to become a criminal in order to catch one. And for another, it would be fun.'

'If I get it right, do I find out what's in the box?'

'The box's secrets die with me,' Zander said. 'But I can teach you with the door lock, if you like.'

Ree weighed her desire to learn more of his secrets against her desire to learn new skills, and came down on the side of the latter.

'All right,' she said. 'But I'll figure you out one day, Zander, I promise you that.'

'There's really nothing to figure out,' he said lightly. 'Now come on over here ...'

It took her a while to understand how to manipulate the tumblers, but once she'd learned how to feel for the slight differences in pressure that indicated movement, she turned out to be surprisingly proficient at it. Zander was an excellent teacher, patient and encouraging – not at all what she might have expected, had she given it any thought at all.

'There,' he said finally. 'You're just as much a criminal as I am, now.'

She smiled at him. 'You should do this for a living. If you don't join the Helm, I mean.'

'What? Pick locks?'

'Teach people. You'd make a great weaponmaster.'

He lifted a shoulder. 'Thanks, but it sounds like an awful lot of work.'

Why does he always do that? Ree had begun to realise that despite his cocky exterior, Zander was hiding just as many insecurities as everyone else. It was something of a revelation. But she didn't think he'd appreciate her calling him on it, so she just grinned. 'Bet the pay's good, though.'

'I like your thinking, Ree Quinn.' He bumped her elbow with his and nodded at the set of lockpicks in her hand. 'You can keep those, if you like. I have more.'

She looked at him quizzically. 'Aren't you worried I'll try to open that box by myself, some other time?'

'I trust you,' he said. 'Anyway, who says there'll be another time?'

Barely managing to suppress her flinch, she lowered her chin and pretended to be very interested in the floor. 'Of course.' *Was it that bad? Was I –?*

'Ree.' She glanced up to find him watching her. 'I was kind of hoping there'd be another time,' he said softly. 'I just didn't want to ... you know. Assume.'

'I see. Um ...' *Elements*. She was blushing again. 'I'd like that. If you want.'

'Oh, I want.' He reached out to unwrap the sheet from around her shoulders. 'How about we start right now?'

SIXTEEN

Penn's previous conversation with Captain Caraway, up in the sixth ring, had shaken him more than he cared to admit. Not that he'd changed his mind about killing the man; that would never happen. Apart from anything else, his father would disown him. But he was beginning to have serious doubts about his plan to achieve it. Because for an instant, talking to the captain had made him wonder if he'd got it all wrong. And if a single encounter could weaken his resolve, however temporarily, what would happen after he'd been trained by Caraway for a full year? It was possible that when the moment came, his own guilt at playing the double agent for so long would choke him. He needed to find a way of ridding himself of that guilt in advance.

In the end, he left the barracks and went down into the lower rings of the city, back to the shrine of Air he'd visited when he first arrived.

He waited by the shrine for nearly a full bell, ignoring the curious glances of its occasional visitors, before the itinerant priest he'd met before came into view. The man stopped when he caught sight of Penn, a wavering expression crossing his face as if he might run.

'Don't go,' Penn said. 'I'm not here about my coin-purse, if that's what you're worried about.'

'Coin-purse? What coin-purse?' The priest took a few steps closer. Penn gave him a disbelieving look, but made no further comment on the disingenuous question.

'I came for some more advice,' he said. 'I think you owe me that much.'

The man's frozen countenance eased into a half-laugh. 'All right, lad, if that's what you want.'

He glanced into the shrine and, finding it empty, gestured Penn inside. The space wasn't really big enough for two people; they knelt side by side facing the decorated alcove, shoulders touching, curtain drawn behind them to provide the illusion of privacy.

'Right, then,' the priest said. 'What can I help you with? Women, is it? Young lad like you, it's usually women.'

'Not women.'

'Men, then? Not sure as I can advise you so well there, but I'm willing to give it a shot.'

'Not men, either.' Penn paused, but he couldn't resist adding acidly, 'Not every problem in the world revolves around sex, you know.'

The priest gave a crack of laughter. 'More'n you'd think, boy. More'n you'd think. So what is it, then? Spit it out, I'm a busy man.'

'I came to Arkannen to kill someone,' Penn said. 'And now –'

'You're wondering if it's the right thing to do?' the priest put in. 'That's an easy one. *Killing is wrong except in law or at war.*'

Odd, to hear his own words replayed to him. But of course, that principle applied only to the original act of murder.

Executing the murderer was simply upholding the law where the law itself had failed. An act of justice.

'No,' he said coolly. 'I already know I'm going to kill him. What I'm trying to decide is whether I need to feel bad about it afterwards.'

He felt the priest tense beside him. The priest's voice said, with an edge of unease to it, 'I'd imagine the answer to that one is an unequivocal yes.'

Penn shrugged. 'Ah, but you don't know much, do you? You told me the wind is crueller than steel. But the truth is, steel can choose whether to strike or turn aside, and that's what makes it cruel. Choice. Whereas the wind simply acts according to its nature. It has no choice but to blow. And without choice, how can there be cruelty?'

'Listen,' the priest said anxiously. 'I don't know who you are or why you want to kill this man, but people aren't like the wind, nor steel neither! That was just something I made up, and I never meant –' He breathed heavily, perhaps searching for words, before concluding, 'We always have a choice. There's no power under the sun can make a man commit murder unless he decides of his own free will to do it.'

'Apparently you don't know my father.'

The priest fidgeted beside him. 'This isn't a joke!'

'I'm not laughing,' Penn said. 'And you haven't answered my question. A man killed my cousin. I intend to take his life in return. Should I feel guilty once the deed is done?'

There was a long pause, before the priest sighed. 'I understand the desire for vengeance. Believe me, I do. But that's why we have the city watch, or the Helm. I can't condone you taking the law into your own hands.'

'Says the man who makes a living from theft,' Penn put in drily, and the priest shook his head in stubborn denial.

'If you're looking to me for absolution, lad, I can't give it to you.'

'Fine,' Penn said. 'Good. That's all I needed to know.'

He began to clamber to his feet, but was stopped by the priest's hand clutching his sleeve. 'Where are you – what do you mean?'

'You've put my mind at rest,' Penn told him. 'Now I know I can't be forgiven for what I have to do, it doesn't matter how I do it. I'm putting myself beyond the pale anyway, so I needn't have any scruples whatsoever. That's actually quite comforting.'

Straightening up fully, he drew the curtain aside to step out into the street, then cast a glance over his shoulder at the wan-looking priest.

'Thanks for your help,' he said. 'I hope you enjoyed my money.'

Once she'd discharged her duties as Darkhaven's overlord for the day, Ayla spent the rest of the afternoon freezing water. It was exhilarating – as exhilarating, in its own way, as the Change itself. That was a large power, a vast shift in her entire being, a remaking into something new. Whereas this ... it was more like discovering a hidden talent that had been lying dormant but fully formed inside her, like waking up suddenly able to speak a different language or play complicated music. A smaller power, but the fact that it belonged to her human self rather than her creature form made it extra satisfying. She was used to being able to do wonderful things when she Changed; it was good to have something to set against that, however slight, when she was in her human skin.

Even if Miles did turn out to be an assassin, she'd still be grateful to him for leading her to this.

She'd started with glasses of water, just like the ones she'd tested with Miles. Once the novelty of that had worn off, she'd turned to the tap in her bedroom, and discovered that a basinful of water was no harder to freeze than a glassful. She'd found herself wondering if it would be possible to freeze all the water in Darkhaven's pipes in one go – and that was when she'd dragged her guards out to the central square. It had rained the night before, and she couldn't cause too much chaos with puddles.

The summoning of the ice was becoming easier each time. She'd learned the trick of it, now: *coaxing rather than forcing*, Miles had suggested, and he'd been right. She just had to relax her mind, ask the water to change, and it obeyed. Not only that, but she could shape it as she changed it: a small pool of water could become a delicate ice tree, rising up out of the ground like a real growing thing. Amazing to think that she'd had this capacity inside herself for ... years, probably, and she'd never even thought to look for it. That was how strongly her father had convinced her of her impurity.

The thought saddened her, but it also reminded her that she had two powers to play with, not one. Ice was so much fun that she hadn't got around to testing whether she could now control wood without needing to work herself into frustration to do it.

Crouching down on the ground, she scooped together some of the twigs blown in by the autumn winds and regarded them through narrowed eyes. She'd try and snap one without touching it. That was a simple enough task. But she'd have to concentrate, or she'd end up freezing them instead ...

The twigs snapped, one after the other, with a series of sharp pops like breaking bones. And then they froze, instantly, tiny ice crystals appearing across the surface of each one.

Ayla leapt to her feet and, temporarily oblivious to her stoic guards, did a triumphant dance.

Yet she stopped abruptly mid-spin, because she suddenly realised she had more company than the Helmsmen. Marlon and Lori were standing on the far side of the square, watching her gravely. Usually the boy would be taken for a walk outside the tower every afternoon, but since the assassination threat he'd been restricted to Darkhaven – which meant this was the only place that Lori could bring him for a bit of fresh air and freedom.

Ayla dropped her arms to her sides. She extended her thoughts to the ice-tree, trying to turn it back into a puddle, but the gift didn't work like that. She could freeze water, not melt it again. Before she could work out what to do next, Marlon trotted over to her with Lori trailing behind.

'Did you make this?' he asked, peering at the little tree.

'Yes.'

'How?'

She didn't want to have this conversation. Not now, maybe not ever. But he was waiting for a reply, so she answered shortly, 'It's what Nightshades can do, Marlon. Summon ice, or fire or wind. Bend wood or steel.'

'Can Papa?'

She thought he meant Myrren. She thought he was asking what Myrren had been able to do, and she was already groping for the words that would allow her to explain to a two-year-old that a vital part of Myrren's gift had been missing – and that she'd only just discovered this aspect of her own – when she realised he meant Tomas. She wasn't sure whether that left her more saddened or relieved.

'Your papa isn't a Nightshade,' she said softly. 'Just us.' Then, to forestall any more questions, she pointed to the far side of the square and ordered the boy, 'Fetch me another twig and I'll show you.'

He dashed off, returning with a waterlogged stick clutched in one fist. She took it from him, held it at arm's length, and coaxed the wood round into a circle. Then she spun the water from its surface into a delicate pattern of ice-threads that spanned the centre like a cobweb. Marlon watched wide-eyed.

'Is it real?' he whispered.

'Yes.' She handed him the pretty thing, watching as he touched the filaments of ice with a careful finger. 'When you're old enough, you'll be able to do it too.' *I hope*, she didn't add. Because who knew what Marlon might become? He might take the form of a pure Changer creature. He might be a hybrid. He might not Change at all. Or he might be like his father, possessed by a dark and lethal creature that took over his conscious mind without leaving a trace of memory behind ...

Sudden grief rose to catch in Ayla's throat. She swallowed, squeezing her eyes shut for an instant to force it back, then managed a smile. 'You stay out here and play, Marlon. I have work to do.'

He looked disappointed, but nodded obediently enough. No doubt he was used to her fleeting appearances in his life. Evading the nursemaid's gaze – for either reproach or compassion would have undone her – Ayla turned and hurried away across the square.

Dear Sirs –

You will be glad to learn that I can see what I have to do, now. And indeed, I will have to do it fast, because I betrayed myself in today's lesson. I revealed what I knew. They were already watching me with suspicion, because of the way I look, so now that I have shown my hand ... the best thing I can do is act.

Still, it doesn't matter that recent events have precipitated this action, because everything is ready. I have the pistol. I have the way in. Now all I have to do is put my gun between Ayla Nightshade's eyes and pull the trigger.

Expect to hear word of my success very soon.
Respectfully yours.

Kai looked down into the keyless box that was usually kept under the bed. *Perfect. Absolutely perfect.* Every single item would make its contribution. And when the inflammatory weapons inside the box exploded into the light, the long-awaited death of a monster would be one step closer to becoming reality.

Kai read over the papers one final time, before slipping them back into place. The pistol itself followed. Bryan's little game with the firearms had been informative, but the conversation that had taken place between himself and Captain Caraway afterwards had been even more so.

Saydi made a good point, Bryan had said after the recruits left the training hall – looking all around him uneasily, but not moving close enough to the open window to spot Kai standing beside the wall. *Our assassin needs to get hold of a weapon from somewhere. I thought if you visited some of the usual suspects –*

Yes, Caraway had agreed. *If any of them have sold anything to ... anyone we know, that answers the question. And if not, I can cut them a deal for notifying me of anything that happens in the future.* He'd clapped Bryan on the back and made for the door. *I'll go tomorrow.*

At that point Kai had slipped away, gripped by a fierce excitement that made it hard to walk casually. They were going to the gun sellers. And that being the case, the time had come to set the first phase of the plan in motion.

The time had come to make use of the pistol in the box.

With a smile, Kai slid the box back under the bed and left the room.

SEVENTEEN

Caraway's list of known and suspected gun smugglers wasn't a long one, but he knew it would take him an entire day to work through it. For a start, the people on the list were naturally wary of a visit from any kind of law enforcement. They were the kind of people who were able to continue their own particular trades solely because no-one had ever found enough evidence to convict them of a crime, so their instinct when faced with the Captain of the Helm would be to say as little as possible. His first challenge would be to get them to talk to him at all. And even if they agreed to that, it was hardly likely they'd admit to selling an illegal weapon.

The one advantage he had – and he'd never dreamed at the time that it could possibly be classed as such – was the years he'd spent drunk and destitute in the lower rings of the city. He might not have broken the law in any significant way, back then, but he'd done enough stupid things to see the inside of plenty of jail cells. To Ayla and the Helm he might be a man who'd fallen from grace and regained it, but to at least some of the criminal underclass he wasn't far off being one of their own who'd made good. That – coupled with the fact that he had little authority over the city except as it related directly to Nightshade business – meant that in the past, certain parts of the city had opened up to him more readily than they would to the Captain of the Watch.

All the same, it wasn't an easy task. By the time Caraway had navigated three prickly, defensive conversations without learning anything of use, he was ready to call it a day. But he knew he had to get the whole job done as quickly as possible, before they started talking to each other, so with barely a sigh he moved on to the fourth suspect on the list.

Klaus ran a small antique shop that was widely rumoured to be a front for weapons dealing. To begin with he was as closed off as the first three, opening his mouth only to provide a strenuous denial of any illegal activity; yet when Caraway asked him very tactfully if he'd had any new customers recently – *Perhaps looking for an unusual weapon? One you wouldn't normally find in the city?* – something flickered in his eyes. When Caraway pressed him, he hesitated before giving a quick nod.

'I might've had someone in here asking about a pistol, not so long ago. Not that I was able to oblige,' he added hastily. 'But as a responsible citizen of Arkannen, I thought you might like to know about it.'

'I see,' Caraway said drily. 'And what could possibly have led this person to believe that you'd be a good source of illegal firearms?'

Klaus shrugged. 'I'm sure I don't know. Took me a while to understand what he was asking for. But I soon sent him about his business once I worked it out.'

Restraining his scepticism with a mighty effort, Caraway nodded. 'So what did he look like?'

'Curly dark hair. Skin the shade o' yours, more or less. Bit like old Miko who runs the scrap metal business over on Canalside.'

It took Caraway a while to place old Miko, but when he did, the description made rather too much sense in the light of the current investigation. Miko was a Kardise immigrant who had lived in Arkannen for close to twenty years.

'Kardise, then?' he said, just to be sure.

'I dunno. Prob'ly. He was a young man. Smiled a lot. Had a design on his left wrist ... something like a flower.'

Zander. It was like swallowing a hot stone, painful but undeniable. Caraway had seen that tattoo more than once during their training.

Maybe it's a Kardise tradition, he told himself, though he didn't remember seeing anything similar on Miko the scrap metal seller. And besides, Zander had claimed he was from Mirrorvale ...

'Like this?' he asked, using a fingertip to sketch the design in the dust on top of one of the ancient cabinets that Klaus kept purely for show.

'That's the one,' Klaus said. 'You know him, then?'

'Yes,' Caraway replied slowly. 'I do.'

He made his way back to the fifth ring almost in a state of trance. He liked Zander. *Everyone* liked Zander. He found it almost impossible to believe that Zander could mean any harm.

And that's what makes him the perfect assassin, his cynical side replied.

He couldn't look at any of the recruits when he reached the training hall. He walked straight to Bryan and asked to speak to him alone. Then he fidgeted on the sidelines while Bryan instructed his assistant and left her in charge. All the same, he forced himself to wait for Bryan to be out of earshot of the group before spilling everything he'd learned. He didn't want any hint of this to reach the wrong ears before the appropriate moment – if that ever came.

'Calm down, you blinking imbecile,' was Bryan's first response. 'You're letting far too much of it show, and you really should know better.'

I deserved that. Caraway took a deep breath, let it out gradually, then said with only a trace of his former urgency, 'But what do you think? It feels wrong to me, Art. And not just because I liked – *like* – Zander.'

'There's only one way to find out,' Bryan said. 'If he did go and buy a pistol, he can't be carrying it around with him. It must be somewhere in his room.'

'Surely not. That would be asking for trouble, particularly after we searched the barracks. He'd hide it somewhere else –'

'What, in Arkannen? You name one place that can lie undisturbed in this city for more than half a bell and I'll call you a liar. Anyway, it's a start. Even if we don't find a pistol, we might find something.'

As it turned out, they found *something* all right. Upon application of a prybar, the locked and keyless box under Zander's bed – the one the quartermaster had dismissed as unopenable – gave up more evidence than they could possibly have hoped to find. The pistol on the top was part of it, yes. But underneath that were a handful of letters: a few sheets of paper that were unambiguously the record of a man plotting murder. Another, stiffer document turned out to be a border pass in the name of Alezzandro Lepont. And at the bottom ... Caraway passed the last item to Bryan in silence. He didn't know a great deal about Kardise democracy, but he knew enough to recognise this when he saw it.

A government official's signet ring, with the Kardise lion stamped into it.

'So,' Bryan said softly. 'Looks like our Zander isn't from Mirrorvale after all.'

'No.' Caraway wondered why he felt so depressed about it. He should be glad – Ayla was safe. Everything could return to normal. And yet ...

'Not just any Kardise, either,' Bryan added. 'The Leponts are a big political family. Been involved in government for years. They're the closest thing Sol Kardis has to royalty.'

Caraway gave him a curious glance, and he shrugged.

'What? I've been in the fifth ring for nearly twenty-five years, student and teacher. I know these things. And,' he went on, gathering steam, 'you should know them, too. You're not just Captain of the Helm, Tomas. You're Ayla Nightshade's partner. You have to know what's beyond your borders, not just what's in Darkhaven.'

He's right. Again. Caraway nodded meekly. The day had knocked him completely off balance, and the worst was yet to come.

'All right,' he said. 'I suppose we'd better go and arrest Zander.'

The recruits had nearly finished their training session by the time Caraway and Bryan returned. Ree saw them walk up to Zander. She saw Bryan put a hand on his shoulder. Seized by the sudden knowledge that something was dreadfully wrong, she backed away from the boy she was sparring with and began to weave her way across the hall, dodging the combatant pairs of trainees. By the time she was close enough to hear what was being said, others nearby had also stopped what they were doing to listen, leaving a widening pool of silence into which Captain Caraway's words fell like stones.

'We have a witness, Zander. He says you tried to buy an illegal weapon from him. Described you in detail.'

'No, sir.' All traces of Zander's usual relaxed levity had vanished; he stood very straight and very still. 'He must be mistaken.'

'This your box?' Bryan asked him gruffly. Only then did Ree notice it at his feet: the carved, keyless box from under Zander's bed, wood splintered around the lock. Zander glanced quickly in that direction, too, and she caught the convulsive movement of his throat.

'Yes, sir.'

With his toe, Bryan flipped open the lid. There was a collective intake of breath as the nearer recruits saw what was inside. Zander frowned in apparent confusion, but he couldn't disguise the draining of colour from his cheeks.

'That isn't mine,' he said faintly.

'You just said it was.'

'The box is. The pistol isn't.'

The word *pistol* evoked another gasp from those who were too far away to see it. Ree bit her lip. *Secrets. That's what he said. But surely not –*

'You'd better come with us, son,' Bryan said. 'You're under arrest.'

Zander shook his head. 'What for?'

It was Caraway who replied. 'For the planned assassination of Ayla Nightshade.'

A pressurised whisper ran through the recruits, like the hiss of steam through a valve, but not one of them raised his voice. Ree's nails dug into her palms. Zander wiped drops of sweat off his forehead with the back of his wrist.

'I didn't – that's not –' With reluctant respect, Ree saw his shoulders straighten as he gathered himself together; the colour came back into his cheeks. 'Captain Caraway, that pistol isn't mine,' he said firmly. 'But even if it was, surely a pistol alone isn't enough to convict me?'

'Not alone,' Bryan said. 'But added to everything else in this box, I'd say it's more than enough.'

Zander shook his head, his voice dropping to a murmur. 'I don't understand.'

He looked lost. Automatically, Ree extended a hand across the space between them ... then let it drop back down to her side. *Assassination. He's been planning this all along. He's not your friend, and he never was.*

'Let me make it simple for you.' Bryan scooped up the box and began sifting through the contents. 'You say this isn't your pistol, but this is your ring, yes?'

'My father's,' Zander muttered.

'This is a border pass in your real name, issued by the Kardise government?'

Another hiss swept the room at the word *Kardise*; Zander flinched. 'Yes.'

'These are your papers?'

'Y-yes ...' Zander frowned. 'No. Some of them.'

'So you're saying that some of the contents of the locked, keyless box under your bed are yours, and some aren't?' Bryan snorted. 'I wasn't born yesterday, son.'

'Zander ...' Caraway stepped forward. He had stayed quiet most of the time, letting Bryan do the talking, but now he put a hand on Zander's arm and looked directly into his eyes.

'You need to tell the truth,' he said with soft intensity. 'I'll kill anyone who intends Ayla harm. You know that. So if there's any innocent explanation for this, anything at all ...'

Please, Zander. Ree clenched her fists, willing him to come up with something that made sense of the situation. But he only shook his head.

'I'm sorry, sir.' He sounded defeated. 'I just can't think of one.'

It didn't feel right. Even as he completed the arrest, Caraway knew it.

Zander looked bewildered and unhappy – that went without saying. He'd look that way whether he was guilty or not. And he must be a good actor to have fooled everyone for this long. Yet all the same, Caraway found himself responding to it. Because somehow, there was something missing. All the evidence, the gun-seller's testimony and the presence of the pistol itself ... it added up, and yet it didn't. That unease niggled at him all through the process of locking Zander in the cells. All through his report to Ayla – Captain of the Helm to Darkhaven's overlord – of what had taken place. And when he reached the end of his recitation, it hadn't gone away. If anything, it was stronger than ever.

'So that's it?' Ayla asked. 'I don't need to worry about being assassinated any more?'

She was looking hopeful, the haunted expression fading from her eyes. He didn't want to see it come back, but he had to be honest.

'I don't know.'

Her dark brows drew together in a frown. 'What?'

'It was too easy.' He ran his hands through his hair. 'I ... I don't believe it, Ayla.'

'But you found the pistol and the papers in his room.'

Caraway nodded. 'Exactly. No assassin would be that careless.'

'It wasn't as if he left them lying around,' she pointed out. 'You said you found them in a locked box under his bed. He probably didn't expect to fall under suspicion.'

'Yes, but Ayla ...' How to explain his misgivings? He grabbed the papers he'd confiscated from Zander's room and thrust them towards her. 'Read these. Why would he write these letters and never send them? Why? It makes no sense. A gun on its own wouldn't have been sufficient to condemn him outright, but with these ...' He shook his head, trying to find the words to explain his deep unease. 'It's as if they were written to be found.'

Ayla scanned the top page before looking up. 'He wrote them to send back to Sol Kardis. It says so right here.'

'It is possible that with our extra security, even after weeks in Arkannen, he still hadn't found any way of doing it.' Caraway sighed. 'Still, if it weren't for Klaus's account, I wouldn't hesitate to mark this as a setup.'

Setting the papers aside, Ayla reached for his hand.

'But Klaus had no reason to lie,' she said softly.

Caraway frowned down at their intertwined fingers. 'He lied about the pistol.'

'Of course he did,' Ayla said. 'He didn't want to be arrested for trafficking in illegal firearms. I have no doubt he sold Zander that pistol. Because how else would he have come into contact with any of your recruits? The only way he could have given such an accurate description of Zander is if the whole thing took place as he reported.'

That was unanswerable. A first-ring gun-seller and a fifth-ring trainee would not, in the normal course of events, cross each other's paths. One would have to deliberately seek out the other. And yet ...

'It just doesn't seem right to me,' Caraway said. 'I think we should keep operating at maximum security until we get a confession out of Zander, or until we find some kind of corroborating evidence.'

Ayla stared at him. Then, lips tightening, she pulled her hand away from his.

'No,' she said. 'No, you always do this. You always assume the worst.'

'Ayla –'

'We haven't been able to hire the servants we need. The Helm are stretched to their limit, watching every step I take. And I haven't left the tower for weeks, which means magistrates' cases are building up and state visits are going unmade. We're all at breaking point, Tomas. We need room to breathe.'

'I'm not doing it out of cruelty, Ayla!' he protested. 'It's for your own safety.'

She glared at him. 'My father kept me in this tower for eighteen years *for my own safety*. I don't expect the same from you.'

'That's not fair. I just –'

'Do you have any reason to believe Zander innocent, other than your own opinion of what it would be sensible or logical for an assassin to do?'

'No,' Caraway admitted, and she folded her arms.

'Then as overlord of Darkhaven to Captain of the Helm, I order you to stop! Call off the extra security and let things go back to normal.'

Caraway stared at her. He wasn't sure why her words hurt so much. She outranked him: always had, always would. It was just …

It was just, he hadn't thought the two of them worked that way. Not any more. Yes, she had her responsibilities and he had his, but within the small circle that encompassed the two of them, he'd always assumed they were a team. She hadn't given him a direct order like that since they'd embarked on their relationship. It made him wonder if she'd ever seen him as an equal, or if he would always be someone she thought she could control.

'And as a woman to the man who cares about you?' he asked softly. 'What do you say then?'

She shook her head. 'I say let it go, Tomas. Before you stifle me.'

'All right.' Suddenly he couldn't bear to be in the same room as her – not when he was suddenly doubting everything that lay between them. He leapt to his feet and retreated in the direction of the door. He considered saluting, but that would have been childish. 'I'll let the Helm know.'

'Tomas –'

'It's fine, Ayla.' He left the room. But as he headed for the guardroom, he already knew he wasn't going to obey her command. Whatever Ayla said, there was something wrong with Zander's arrest. And until Caraway knew what it was, he wasn't going to stop protecting her.

He'd just have to be a little more circumspect about it.

EIGHTEEN

Bryan sat at his desk and stared gloomily at the stack of paper in front of him. Miles was working at the university tonight – *A really fascinating experiment*, he'd said enthusiastically, *don't expect me before midnight* – and so Bryan had decided to use the opportunity to catch up on his never-ending paperwork. Funny thing about paperwork: no matter how much of it he did, he was always behind. He'd brought a pitcher of ale to keep him company, but he didn't expect it to make the time between now and seventh bell go any quicker.

Still, one page followed another, and after a while the tedium of it wasn't so bad. Bryan was almost enjoying the satisfaction of seeing the pile get smaller and smaller when his office door creaked open and a voice said, 'Art?'

Bryan raised his head to find Caraway standing in the doorway. His gaze brushed Bryan's face, before settling on the pitcher of ale.

'I couldn't sleep,' he said softly. 'Zander's arrest ... the more I think about it, the more I'm sure we've got the wrong man. But Ayla –'

'She doesn't agree?'

'She ... ah, forget it.' He looked up briefly, lifting one shoulder in a shrug. 'What does it matter?'

What does it matter? That wasn't a good sign. And even as Bryan watched, the lad's eyes turned back down in the direction of the pitcher, as though it held some irresistible fascination for him.

That wasn't a good sign either.

Privately, Bryan cursed himself. He was usually careful not to drink where Caraway could see him. Though it had been months since the captain's last bad night, Bryan had seen enough to know that the cravings of addiction never really went away. The best they could do was become less vivid over time, like the scar left by a near-fatal wound.

Trying to appear casual, he wiped his pen and stoppered the ink. He shuffled the papers on his desk into a neat stack. And then, finally, he shoved the half-empty pitcher into his cupboard and turned the key.

When he looked back at Caraway, the lad was gazing at the locked door with a bitter little smile.

'It's been three years, Weaponmaster,' he said. 'I think you can trust me to be in the same room as a drink without pouring it down my throat.'

Affecting ignorance, Bryan sat back down in his chair. 'No need to take offence, boyo. Just tidying up a bit.'

'Of course you were.' Caraway's voice was sharper than usual – and there had been that twist of sarcasm on *Weaponmaster*, before. Yet as the silence lengthened, Bryan allowed himself to hope that he'd read the signs wrong; that this was a fleeting temptation that would be forgotten almost as soon as it was born ... Then Caraway spoke again.

'As it happens, I was on my way to the warriors' mess hall. So you may have saved me a walk.'

Bryan had seen it coming, but still a cold weight of dread sank inside him. He knew Caraway didn't want to drink, not really. It would have been easy enough for him to hole up in an anonymous inn for the night and drink himself stupid before anyone who loved him even realised where he'd gone. No, he was warring with himself, and he wanted someone to fight for him. The fact that he'd come to a man who happened to have a pitcher of ale to hand was simply the garnish on the shit sandwich.

Of course, by rights it should have been Ayla here to talk him down from it. But as far as Bryan knew, Ayla didn't even know this side of her partner still existed. He did a good job of hiding it from her, and from his own men as well. Maybe Bryan was the only one who was allowed to see it.

It was a privilege he could have done without.

But Caraway had been his student, once. Quite aside from Bryan's personal liking for the lad, that gave him a responsibility that would never completely disappear.

'Well?' Caraway raised his eyebrows. 'Aren't you going to offer me a drink? Come on, Art –' cajoling now – 'that stuff is barely more than water. I could drink the lot without any risk of going back to what I was.'

No, you couldn't. You and I both know that. Bryan shook his head, assuming jocularity. 'Wouldn't bother if I were you. Tastes like piss.'

Caraway planted his elbows on the desk and leaned forward. One corner of his mouth lifted in a cynical smile. 'In that case, you won't mind if I take it off your hands.'

Bryan glanced across at the cupboard, wishing he'd removed the key from the lock. His attempt to wrench the situation back to normality clearly wasn't going to work; time to face it head-on.

'Tomas,' he said quietly. 'Don't do this.'

'Do what?'

'You know I'm not going to give you alcohol.'

'Do you think I don't know my own limits?' The edge revealed itself in Caraway's voice once more, a blade that was as likely to cut its wielder as the man who faced it. 'Like I said, it's been three years. I can handle it.'

'And then?'

'Then *what*?'

'What happens after that cup? What happens when it's another, and another, and another …?'

'I can handle it,' Caraway repeated stubbornly, and Bryan sighed.

'Tomas,' he said again, 'don't do this. You've made a good life for yourself. You have a family. You're well respected. You're Captain of the sodding Helm! Why would you risk all that for the sake of some cheap ale?'

'Because,' Caraway said, low and fierce, 'I'm Captain of the sodding Helm. Everyone is relying on me. Everyone thinks I'm something I'm not.' He scrubbed his hands through his hair. 'It's like duelling, Art. One wrong move and I die. Except the champion's sword everyone thinks I'm wielding is really a foot of broken steel carried by an idiot who bluffed his way to the top. And Ayla –'

'Yes, what about Ayla?' Rather bemused by the sudden flow of introspection, Bryan seized on the mention of their overlord. 'If you're not willing to keep it together for yourself, then do it for Ayla. She needs you, Tomas. Now more than ever, if you're right about Zander.'

'She doesn't need me.' The response was swift. Bryan frowned.

'Of course she does. She –'

'*She doesn't need me!*' Caraway's hands slammed down on the desk, hard enough to make the cupboard door rattle. 'She's made that very clear. So what difference does it make if I drink or not?'

Bryan looked at him for a long moment without speaking. Then he walked over to the cupboard, unlocked the door and took out the pitcher of ale. He set it down in front of Caraway, followed by a cup.

'There,' he said. 'Go ahead.'

Caraway looked at the cup, then back at him. 'What?'

'If you're so useless to the woman you love and the country you've devoted your life to,' Bryan said, producing each word with care, 'go ahead and drink.'

Silence. Then, hands shaking, Caraway picked up the pitcher. It chinked against the side of the cup as he poured out a measure of ale.

Bryan waited.

Caraway stared into the cup. His knuckles whitened on the handle of the pitcher. Suddenly concerned that he'd done something terribly reckless, Bryan opened his mouth to say something, though he wasn't sure what – and then Caraway's arm jerked to the side, sweeping pitcher and cup off the desk to explode against the wall in a shower of pottery shards and amber liquid.

'Damn you.' Caraway buried his face in his hands. His voice was a hoarse whisper. 'And damn her.'

Bryan watched the ale drip down the wall, and said nothing. He didn't see that anything he could say would be helpful, and it might very well make things worse.

'I'll never be free of it, will I?' Caraway mumbled. 'The … the *longing*.'

'No.'

243

The captain's shoulders shook in a mirthless laugh. 'The stupid thing is, I don't really want a drink. Even the smell of it turns my stomach. I just ...' He lifted his head, eyes full of stark self-loathing. 'I'm not good enough, Art. And I'm terrified that I'll screw it all up. That I'll fail again, that I'll fail *her* ...'

'Maybe you will,' Bryan said. 'But why let that stop you? There was a time, not so long ago, when you stood out there in the streets of the fifth ring and set yourself against twenty warriors for Ayla's sake. As I recall, almost certain failure didn't keep you from trying.'

One corner of Caraway's mouth twisted upwards. 'That was different. Back then I had nothing to lose. But now –'

'Now you're afraid of losing everything,' Bryan said. 'But that's the price you pay to have a life worth living. Fear just means that what you've got is worth holding onto.'

'Even if I don't deserve it?'

Bryan shook his head. 'That's not how it works. The world doesn't grade us like a pack of recruits and hand out rewards to suit. You deserve your new life no more or less than you deserved your old one. The only thing that matters is what you do with it now you've got it.'

Silence. Caraway glanced at the damp patch on the wall, the shattered pitcher beneath, and visibly suppressed a wince. Then, releasing a long breath, he reached across the desk to grip Bryan's arm. His eyes were clear.

'I'm sorry,' he said. 'For the mess. And for shouting at you.'

'It's all right.'

'I'll pay for the ale.'

'No need,' Bryan said. 'I should probably cut back anyway.'

Penn couldn't sleep. He'd found that to be increasingly the case, since he'd come to the city: every time he lay down, he was assailed by everything he'd managed not to think about during the course of the day. Whether he'd ever succeed in what he'd come to do. Whether his father would be satisfied, even if he did. Three years was a long time to be focused on a single goal to the exclusion of all else; Penn knew that first-hand, having had his father's purpose drummed into him every single day of those three years. Would his father find peace, when Caraway died? Would he return to being the man he used to be? Or would he forever chew on his own bitterness? In the dark of the night, alone in his room, Penn suspected the latter – in which case, he couldn't help but wonder what it was all for.

In the end, he headed down to the archery range, where he spent the next half-bell putting arrows in the centre of target after target. Penn liked archery more than any other discipline, because it was so precise. He fired the arrow, it hit the target, he knew instantly whether he'd got it right or not. It was like mathematics, the only subject in which he'd ever taken an interest at school: no room for ambiguity. Just a simple yes or no.

When he finally started to tire, he put his bow down and rolled his shoulders. For the first time, the vibrating thud of someone else's arrows caught his ear. Turning, he saw Ree a couple of stands along. Now he thought about it, she'd often been there before when he was practising. And he'd seen her coming out of the door a couple of times in passing, too. She was obviously pouring all the limited spare time she could snatch into it – and just as obviously, it wasn't doing any good.

She lifted her bow, set the arrow to the string, drew and released. It went wide, clipping the edge of the target, and she swore. The catch in her voice suggested tears, though he found that hard to believe. He'd never seen Ree cry.

She wiped her forehead with the back of her wrist, and then – as if aware of his gaze on her – she turned. He expected her face to crease into its usual defensive scowl, but she just shrugged wearily.

'Go ahead. Tell me how useless I am.'

He wasn't sure where his answer came from. Maybe it was an automatic response to the unfamiliar sadness in her eyes. Maybe it was the memory of how she'd put him forward in the strategy test, not because she had something to gain from it but because she genuinely believed he was the best. Whatever the reason, the words came out before he really had time to think about them. 'I can help you, if you like.'

'Help me?'

'Only if you want.' Already he half regretted the offer; opening himself up even that far was both dangerous and pointless, given his ultimate aim here. Yet something prevented him from taking it back. 'It can be hard to improve when you don't have anyone to point out your mistakes.'

She smiled, albeit shakily. 'Ah, now it makes sense. You want to be able to insult me without fear of retaliation.'

'If you're not interested …' He turned away and picked up his bow. But before he could leave, he heard footsteps behind him and a hand grabbed his elbow.

'Penn. I was joking. Come on …' She tugged on his arm until he turned to face her. 'I'd appreciate your help,' she said, very seriously. 'I really would. That is, if you're still willing.'

Was he still willing? He had no idea. 'I suppose so.'

So she fired a few more arrows, and he corrected her grip on the bow; and then she fired a few more, and he corrected her stance; and then she fired a few more, and he corrected the way she was aiming at the target. He wasn't the most patient teacher – he didn't have it in him – but privately, he had to admit that Ree was a very patient pupil. She soaked up advice and criticism without complaint, and though sometimes she looked as if she wanted to retaliate against his more astringent observations, she managed to bite her tongue. To his surprise, Penn almost found that he was enjoying himself.

By the time they'd finished, it was after midnight, and they had to be up again at dawn. Ree yawned and stretched, then looked ruefully at the wooden sword propped against the wall.

'I need to take that back to the weapons store in the training hall,' she said. 'I came straight here from the last session of the day, and somehow I managed to bring it with me.' She grimaced at Penn's expression. 'Don't worry, you don't have to come. Go ahead and get some sleep.'

If only. He shook his head: better to be as tired as possible when he finally lay down to rest, in the hope that sleep would catch up with him before his brain had a chance to avoid it. 'I don't mind walking with you. It's on the way.'

The startled glance she cast him said more clearly than words that she hadn't expected him to want to remain in her company, but she only nodded. 'Come on, then.'

The night was cold by now, and they huddled together as they made the short walk from the archery stands to the central training hall. They were nearly there when Ree said abruptly, 'Do you think he did it?'

'Do I think who did what?'

'Zander. Do you think he was really going to – you know.'

Penn hadn't been thinking about Zander's arrest at all. He was surprised to find himself feeling guilty about that, for an instant, before he pushed it away. It wasn't as if he'd ever done more than tolerate Zander. If anything, the arrest was good news for him, because presumably it meant they'd all be under less scrutiny.

But of course, Ree didn't feel that way, because Ree and Zander were close. Not that Penn would have noticed, but Saydi had speculated about the exact nature of their relationship on more than one occasion. And if she was right, that would explain Ree's unusual sadness tonight.

'I don't know,' he said cautiously. 'But it seemed like there was a lot of evidence. And they wouldn't have arrested him otherwise, would they?'

Ree sighed. 'I suppose not.'

She said nothing more until they reached the training hall – and even then, it was only to wonder aloud whether the door would be locked this late. Yet it opened to her touch, and the two of them entered together. Inside, the corridors and practice floors were dark and empty. Penn and Ree found their way to the weapons store using nothing more than the spill of moonlight through the high windows, but when they got there they found a second source of illumination: the door to Weaponmaster Bryan's office stood ajar, releasing a narrow beam of light.

He's up late. Penn waited a short distance away as Ree replaced the practice sword in the store. They were just turning to leave when a shout from within the office made them both jump. Instinctively they stopped walking and drew closer to each other.

'That was Captain Caraway,' Ree whispered. Penn put a hand on her arm, silencing her – and so they both heard the thud of the bottle on the table.

If you're so useless to the woman you love and the country you've devoted your life to, go ahead and drink.

A long, breathless pause, during which Penn could clearly hear the pulse of his blood in his ears – and then the smash of breaking pottery, and the spilling out of bitter words. Never in Penn's wildest dreams could he have hoped for such an honest display of weakness.

I'm not good enough. I'm terrified that I'll screw it all up. That I'll fail again.

'We shouldn't be listening to this,' Ree said in a tiny voice. Penn glanced down at her. She was pale, her eyes wide. For the second time that evening, she looked as though she wanted to cry. Of course, she didn't know what Caraway was. To her, those words weren't a potential weapon but ... what? The fall of an idol? Or something more complicated?

Fear just means that what you've got is worth holding onto, Bryan said, inside the office, and Penn grimaced. His own fear of failure didn't mean anything of the kind. It just meant he was more afraid of letting his father down than he was of killing a man. But if Caraway's greatest fear was losing the life he didn't deserve –

'Penn.' Ree whispered his name, tugging on his arm. 'We should go.'

Damn it, Ree! With a snarl, he rounded on her. He wasn't sure what was showing on his face, but she took a step back. For an instant they were frozen, staring at each other. Then the office door swung wider, casting a square of yellow light into the corridor where they stood, and Caraway's voice said, 'Ree? Penn?'

Slowly, Penn turned. The captain was standing in the doorway, one hand on the frame as if to support himself. He looked exhausted, but he managed something that appeared to be a genuine smile. 'Were you looking for the weaponmaster?'

Penn opened his mouth to say something blistering, but Ree spoke first.

'Oh, hello, captain.' She was close enough to Penn that he could feel the tension in her, but her tone was one of casual ease. 'I didn't know you were here. We were just dropping off a sword.'

'All right,' Caraway said. 'Well, it's late. You two should be getting some sleep.'

Again Penn opened his mouth to speak, but Ree grabbed his arm.

'Yes, sir. Of course.'

She turned and strode down the corridor, pulling Penn with her. He didn't object. She was doing him a favour. Though he'd wanted desperately to say something to Caraway, it could only have given away his own feelings towards the man – and now was not the time for that.

'You can let go of my arm now,' he said, once they were out of the training hall and heading for the barracks. Ree glanced up as if she hadn't realised he was still there, despite her death-grip on him; after a moment, she blinked and released him.

'Did you know?' she said softly. 'That he used to –'

I know more about your precious captain than you could possibly imagine. Penn shrugged. 'People don't remember that part of the story, do they? They want to make him into a hero, and the fact that he was really a second-rate alcoholic doesn't fit the narrative.'

Ree didn't say another word until they reached the turning to the women's barracks. Then she said softly, not looking at him, 'Maybe he was both.'

And before Penn could reply, she walked away.

NINETEEN

The address that Don Callero had given her was a warehouse down by the docks. Since there was never any point using stealth when openness would suffice, Sorrow tagged onto the back of a group of workers and walked straight in behind them. She'd dressed in the plain, hard-wearing clothing of a Kardise dock-worker, and with the battered bag slung across her body – emptied ready for the stolen ledger, in her case, rather than containing a midday meal and protective gear like all the rest – she could easily pass for one of them. The only difference between her and the others was the holstered pistol at her hip, but the bag concealed that well enough.

Once they were inside, the workers headed for the far side of the warehouse in a chattering stream, winding their way through the aisles created by stacks of crates and pieces of machinery. No-one noticed when Sorrow slipped away as casually as she'd arrived, turning down one narrow channel and then another until she was out of sight and earshot of the main group. Then she walked swiftly and silently back through the maze in the direction she'd come, towards the office she'd noticed on her way in.

A man was in there, making a note in what looked like the very ledger she'd come to steal. Sorrow found herself a hiding place behind some boxes, from which she could keep an eye on the door. When the man emerged, whistling, and walked off in the direction the workers had taken, she sauntered into the office and – with a quick glance around to make sure she hadn't been followed – flipped the heavy book to read the first page. Once she'd confirmed it was the one she was after, she stuffed it straight into her bag and left the office again.

Easy.

Too easy?

No such thing as too easy, she told herself. *You've got what you came for and now you need to get out.*

She was nearly back at the entrance when she spotted two more men approaching. One, the older of the two, was tall and stern-looking, with dark hair fading to silver at the temples. The other was a young, curly-haired man with an earnest expression. She whisked back round behind a crane, heart racing, and waited for them to pass. They were deep in conversation – probably too deep to notice her even if she stood right in front of them, she reassured herself – and as they drew level with her, she overheard a little.

'... why you agreed to see me now,' the younger man was saying.

'I felt it was time,' the older man replied. 'Goldenfire has already been set in motion, so there is no longer any need for secrecy ...'

As their voices receded, Sorrow found several different things clamouring for her attention.

Goldenfire has already been set in motion. She recognised that voice. It belonged to the man her employer had identified

252

as Eight – the man she'd stolen a document from, back when all this started.

You are involved in the Goldenfire business. And that was what the woman with him had said that evening. Goldenfire was their code name for the assassination of Ayla Nightshade.

It's important that you do as I've asked without deviation, Fourteen's voice added to the mix. He'd been quite adamant that she shouldn't use her initiative this time. Given her precarious position in Sol Kardis, it would be incredibly foolish of her to disobey. And yet she'd agreed to spy for Mirrorvale. What use would she be as a spy if she didn't take a risk now and then?

If there was a chance she could find out anything more about Goldenfire, she couldn't ignore it.

You're going to regret this, Naeve Sorrow, she told herself; but nevertheless, she turned her back on the exit and followed in the wake of the two men. They were heading in a different direction from the workers, so at least it was unlikely she'd bump into anyone else. She ghosted along behind the stacks, taking a parallel path to their own, until they walked through an archway into a part of the warehouse that was walled off from the rest. Sorrow waited to make sure they had enough of a lead, then followed.

On the other side of the archway were several large crates stamped with the same design that had been on the owner's sign outside the warehouse, and covered in labels that suggested they were due to be sent out of the country. Sorrow tipped her head and managed to read one of them sideways. *EXPORT: MIRRORVALE.* She snuck along behind the crates until she reached the last one, which she peered around cautiously. The two men were a short distance away, shoulder to shoulder, looking down at something in the middle of the floor. It was a trunk: an ordinary-looking wooden thing, rather battered around the edges, though still solid and sturdy enough for years of use.

'Here.' Eight gestured to the trunk, and the young man with him frowned at it.

'This is how you get firearms across the border?'

'Yes.'

'But –'

'Why don't you try and find the pistol?' Eight invited him with a smile.

Looking sceptical, the young man crouched down beside the trunk. He opened the lid and reached inside. After a very brief search, he straightened up with a thin, rectangular piece of wood in his hands.

'A false bottom?' He sounded disappointed. 'Hardly an innovation. The border guards must be asleep on their feet if they're missing that.'

Eight laughed. 'Really? Then where's the pistol?'

Leaving the false bottom to one side, the young man leaned back into the trunk. Sorrow heard the scrape of his nails against the wood, but the length of time he spent in there suggested that he couldn't find what he was looking for – and sure enough, when he emerged for the second time, he was empty-handed.

'I don't understand,' he said plaintively, and Eight clapped him on the back.

'The false bottom is just a decoy. Any guard worth his pay would notice the difference between the height of the trunk inside and the height outside, and deduce the presence of a secret compartment. When he opens it and finds it empty – or finds something private but innocuous inside, like a bundle of love letters – his job is done. But in fact, there's also a much subtler secret compartment on one side. Here, look.' He gestured to one of the trunk's thick walls. 'See if you can open it.'

There was a long pause whilst the young man ran his hands over the trunk, trying to find the catch that would release the secret compartment. Finally he shook his head with a rueful grin.

'I can't detect anything there at all.'

'Exactly!' Eight said with some satisfaction. 'It's a puzzle drawer. Only by pressing the right parts in the right order will it slide open.'

He began to demonstrate, his long fingers gliding over the wood. Sorrow risked emerging a bit further from the shadow of her concealing crates, but men and trunk weren't close enough for her to make out the details. Still, no matter. She had the most important piece of information; Caraway would have to work the rest out for himself.

The young man gave a low sigh of satisfaction as the drawer popped open. He reached down, then straightened up with a pistol in his hand.

'Another compartment on the other side, for the accoutrements,' Eight said. He opened the second drawer in the same way as the first, before passing its contents to the younger man. 'Balances out the design of the trunk, you see. Makes it less noticeable.'

I could use one of those trunks myself. Soundlessly, Sorrow retreated, one backward step at a time. She'd seen enough. Better get out before she was caught.

'Remarkable,' the young man said. With a click, he set his empty pistol to the firing position – and like an echo, a second click sounded behind Sorrow's right ear. Like an echo ... but not.

Someone was behind her with another pistol.

She froze. She knew better than most what firearms were capable of, after all. And the first step in any situation that involved someone holding a pistol to your head was *don't make any sudden movements.*

'Turn around slowly,' a female voice said. 'Hands where I can see them.'

Step two: cooperate fully and completely until the pistol is no longer in danger of shattering your skull like an egg.

Arms held away from her body, fingers spread, Sorrow turned. She didn't recognise the woman holding the pistol: tall, slender, dark brown eyes and hair to match. Yet her voice had been ... familiar. Almost. Like something Sorrow had heard once or twice before ...

The woman with the document.

Yes. She was the one who had been there that first night, when Sorrow found herself tangled up with the Brotherhood in the first place. She was one of *them.*

Which made it even more important to proceed to step three: *take control of the pistol.*

Yet before she could come up with a way of doing it without being shot, the woman gestured with the pistol, indicating that both of them should move out from behind the crates. Then she tweaked Sorrow's own pistol from its holster. By now, the man whom Sorrow had identified as Eight was alone beside his trunk, gazing in their direction; the young man he'd been talking to was nowhere to be seen.

'Five?' Smiling, Eight crossed the floor towards them. 'Have you got her?'

'Like a rat in a trap,' the woman – Five – said.

They knew I was here, Sorrow thought uneasily. *Which means –*

Yet she didn't have time to examine the implications. Her emergence from the shadows had brought her a step closer to the other woman, and that gave Sorrow her chance. Before Eight could reach them, Sorrow curled her toes to extend the blade from the sole of her boot, jabbing it swiftly into Five's shin –

But the other woman wasn't there. Even quicker than the weapon had moved towards her, she'd spun out of the way. Almost as if she'd known what Sorrow would do. And now she was behind Sorrow again, the pistol pressed to Sorrow's head.

That's not good.

'Do that again and I'll kill you,' Five said coolly, and Sorrow believed her. She'd made enough of her own threats over the years to know which ones were real and which were merely bluff. So she retracted the blade. With any luck, it had gone unnoticed and she'd be able to use it again later.

Of course, relying on luck in this situation would be a stupid thing to do. She couldn't fight someone holding a pistol to her head, so the next best thing was to try bluffing her way out. Spreading her hands again, she addressed Eight directly.

'Look, I'm sorry if I've intruded on private property. I didn't mean any harm by it. I only came in here because …' *Yes, why, Sorrow? What sort of shitty cover story are you going to come up with this time?* 'I thought you might give me a job.'

Five laughed; Sorrow felt it on the back of her neck, uncomfortably intimate. 'Really? Then I suppose we won't find stolen property in that bag of yours?'

Great job. Stick to the fighting next time and leave the bluffing to someone with a modicum of intelligence. Sorrow opened her mouth to begin explaining away the ledger, but the pistol dug harder into her skull and she shut up.

'We know exactly who you are, Naeve Sorrow,' Eight said. 'So you might as well save your breath.' His smile was unpleasant. 'You're going to need it.'

That didn't sound good at all. Sorrow could see her future rapidly diminishing to a single point – the point at which they shot her stone dead – and so she decided to cooperate. The chances were looking slim, but it was possible she'd find an opportunity to escape later on. Trying to escape now would only result in a bullet to the head.

That decision sounded sensible right up until Eight brought out a rope and she realised they were going to tie her. Since that would reduce her chances of escape to almost zero, she struggled after all. She couldn't help herself. Yet it did no good. The most she achieved was a few glancing blows before her own pistol came down hard against her skull and knocked her into darkness.

A week after Zander's arrest, Ree finally gathered enough courage to go and see him.

She wasn't sure quite why she was finding it so difficult. It shouldn't matter so much that he'd deceived her; after all, it wasn't as if she were in love with him. That would have been far harder. Oh, she liked him well enough, of course. She thought he was a good person –

Had thought.

And that was probably it, she reflected as she stood outside the jail. She didn't want to see Zander because that would force her to recognise the extent of her failure to judge his character. She'd have to admit to herself that she'd talked to, and laughed with, and slept with a man who was secretly plotting murder. No-one would want to accept that as a truth. Far better to stay away and pretend the whole thing had never happened than to hear him confirm it in person. As long as she didn't see him, she could convince herself that it had all been a mistake.

But that was the cowardly way forward. And Ree refused to be a coward.

After a final deep breath, she walked briskly through the entrance. Zander was being held in the fifth ring's tiny prison, a set of four cells that were usually used for warriors who'd breached the Code. Most people didn't stay in there long; they either admitted their transgression and did the kind of tedious penance that Zander and Penn had been given after their fight a few weeks ago, or – for a serious enough misdeed – were banished from the fifth ring for good or moved to another jail in the lower rings. Yet Zander was a special case. His crime was against Darkhaven itself, which should have meant the Helm took him into custody, but Captain Caraway hadn't wanted to move him any closer to Ayla. So he simply stayed where he was, waiting for the date of the formal trial that would determine his fate.

Ree realised, now, as the guard showed her past the three empty cells, that she didn't actually know what that fate would be. Anyone who killed a member of the Nightshade line would be executed; that went without saying. But a failed assassin? A man who'd planned regicide, but never carried it out? She didn't know, but she found herself hoping he might be deported from the country instead. Whatever he'd done, she didn't want him dead.

'Here you are,' the guard said. They'd reached the last cell in the row. Like the others, it was a small room with the closest wall made up of vertical bars. 'Not too long, now.'

Zander was sitting on the narrow cot that was the only item of furniture in the room, staring at his hands, but he looked up at the sound of the guard's voice. His eyes were creased with tiredness, and his usually bright and mobile face was set in solemn lines. Ree's anticipation and her nerves had been so intense, and her thoughts so turbulent, that it was a shock to see he hadn't changed at all – not beyond those superficial signs of strain. He wasn't a different person, the hard and mocking assassin of her imagination. He was just himself.

'Ree,' he said hesitantly, as she approached the bars and the guard walked away. 'What are you doing here?'

She shrugged. 'They searched me before they let me in, so you needn't think I'm here to break you out or anything.'

In response, the shadow of a smile touched his eyes. 'Wouldn't dream of it. You're far too law-abiding.'

'That makes one of us,' she retorted.

Zander got to his feet and came towards her, stopping within arm's reach to look at her appealingly. 'It's all a lie, Ree. I swear to you –'

She shook her head. 'I don't believe you. Because it makes perfect sense.'

'That I'm an assassin?' The hurt note in his voice sounded genuine, but it was hard to tell. It had always been hard to tell.

'No,' she said slowly. 'Not that. If anything you've ever said to me was sincere, it was all that stuff about not putting principles above people. But the secret identity ... I can believe that.'

'Really?' For some reason, Zander's smile was back. 'And I thought I was being so careful.'

She shook her head. 'You never talk about your home town. The rest of us talk about our families all the time. And for someone who's meant to be Mirrorvalese, you refer to gods an awful lot.'

260

'Clever,' he murmured. 'I always knew you were clever.'

She tapped impatient fingers against the bars. 'So? Who are you really?'

'Alezzandro Lepont.' He gave her a bow with a little flourish in it, incongruous in the dingy cell. 'My father is a councillor in the Kardise government.'

For a moment she didn't react. Then she reached through the bars and hit him as hard as she could.

'Ow!' He rubbed his upper arm and looked wounded. 'What –'

'That's for lying to me,' Ree said. 'And I'm still not sure I've got the whole truth. Those papers that were in your box – Weaponmaster Bryan said they showed you weren't who you said you were, and confirmed your plan to assassinate Lady Ayla. And with the pistol as well –'

'Partly true,' Zander interrupted. 'I pretended to be Mirrorvalese because I knew I wouldn't be allowed to train otherwise, and I used a different name because I didn't want my father to find out where I was. That's all. The rest of it – the pistol, and the letters ...' He gestured helplessly. 'I don't know where they came from. But I assume that if you find out, you'll find the real assassin in the process.'

'What about the ring? The one showing you were sanctioned by the Kardise government?'

For the first time, he looked embarrassed. 'I stole it from my father. I had to have something to convince them to let me out of the country. The children of councillors aren't usually allowed to go anywhere unattended.' A sardonic expression touched his face. 'Too much of an assassination risk.'

Ree regarded him without speaking. She wanted to believe him. She almost thought she did. But she wasn't sure how much of that was genuine instinct that he was telling the truth, and how much was her own desire not to have been so thoroughly fooled.

As the silence stretched out, Zander began to smile again, though this time it had a plaintive twist to it.

'Honestly, Ree,' he said. 'Do you really think they'd send a councillor's son to assassinate the overlord of Darkhaven? Assassins are trained not to leave a trail, so that if they're captured there's nothing to tie them back to their masters.'

She thought about that. 'But if you'd never been caught, it wouldn't have mattered who you were. So maybe they sent you for the very reason that if you *did* get caught, you'd be able to throw doubt on the situation by asking that question.' She raised her eyebrows at him. 'I could also add that you seem to know an awful lot about what assassins do.'

The plaintive smile became a fully-fledged grin. 'Fair point. I don't see that it's worth arguing about further. You'll soon find out I'm telling the truth when the real assassin goes after Lady Ayla. But, Ree –' and here he was solemn – 'be careful, all right? I wouldn't like to think of you getting caught in the middle of it all.'

Ugh. How many times? Ree punched him again. 'I can take care of myself.'

'I know you can,' Zander said. 'But the real assassin must still have a pistol of his own, don't forget. Even you can't fight a bullet.'

His hand reached through the bars, and she took it. The tension in the fingers clinging to hers told her that he was far more worried than he'd let on. If he was telling the truth, both their lives were in danger. Ayla's too. *Everyone's.*

If he was telling the truth.

'Why'd you have to make my life so difficult, Zander?' she muttered – and barely realised she'd spoken aloud until he replied.

'I've never lied to you about anything important, Ree. I swear.'

Except your name, and where you come from, and who your father is ... But even as she thought it, she dismissed it. Because it was entirely likely that those things weren't important to Zander.

'I have to go,' she muttered, unable to stand the confusion any longer, and turned away. He held onto her hand an instant longer before releasing it.

'Will you come back sometime?' He was trying to be cheerful, but she heard the note of misery beneath it. 'In case you hadn't noticed, it's kind of boring in here.'

'I'll try. It's the Helm aptitude testing in a few days' time, and –' But she stopped, because she was only flaunting his lack of freedom in his face. Yet she didn't know what to think, or whether she should come back, or ...

'I'll try,' she said again, and fled.

As she headed for the way out, someone touched her shoulder. The conversation with Zander had set her on edge; she spun, drawing a knife. But the man was already backing away, hands raised.

It was Captain Caraway.

'Can I speak to you for a moment?' he asked.

Unable to force words out through the pounding of her heart, Ree nodded.

'Er ... maybe better in private?'

She nodded again.

They walked in silence to Weaponmaster Bryan's small office, and all the while her heart kept racing – despite the lack of threat. She hadn't spoken to the captain properly since the night she and Penn had overheard his conversation with Bryan in that very same office. She'd been worried she wouldn't know how to act around him – that somehow, despite her best intentions, her opinion of him would have changed for the worse. Yet now she was face to face with him, it turned out that if anything, she admired him more than ever. Even she found that a little bit ridiculous, but it was true all the same.

When they finally reached the office, Caraway turned to face her.

'I need to apologise to you, Ree,' he said. 'I came to the cells to question Zander, but you were already doing a perfectly good job of it when I got there, so ...'

'You listened to our conversation?'

'Yes.' He gave her a shamefaced smile. 'Sorry.'

I probably should be angry about that. He doesn't have any right –

But even as she was thinking that, the rest of her said bashfully, 'It's fine.'

'The thing is,' Caraway said, 'this is why I asked Art – er, Weaponmaster Bryan to tell you all the details of our evidence against Zander. Just in case ...' His voice tailed off.

'In case what?' Ree prompted him, and his gaze refocused on her as though he'd momentarily forgotten her existence.

'In case it brought any worms out of the woodwork.'

'You're not sure he's the assassin either,' she said in sudden understanding, and Caraway shrugged.

'I don't know yet. But you've spent a lot of time with him. Did you believe what he said just now?'

'I'm not sure.' She closed her eyes, letting her memory of the conversation flow back to the forefront of her mind, and found the answer waiting for her. 'Yes. I think I did.'

'Mmm.' He frowned at her – no, not at her. Through her. As though he were trying to make a decision. Then his face cleared, and with a wry twist to his lips he reached into the bag on his shoulder.

'This is probably misuse of evidence or something, but … read these.' He passed her a handful of letters. 'It's possible he still intended to send them, once he found a safe way to get them out of the city.'

She scanned through them quickly, then looked up. '*These* are what proved Zander's intention to assassinate Lady Ayla?'

Caraway nodded, watching her face intently.

'But that doesn't make any sense!' she said. 'Writing this stuff and keeping hold of it when you were going to murder someone would be … well, it's just idiotic. Zander isn't stupid, Captain Caraway.'

He sighed. 'That's what I thought. But Ayla …'

He didn't finish the sentence, but his expression was troubled. Ree bit her lip and looked at the papers again.

'You know, Captain Caraway, whoever wrote these letters revealed more and more details as he went along,' she said. 'To start with it's all vague: *the threat, its source, my goal.* Doesn't tell you much. If you'd found just that one, you wouldn't have thought anything of it. But by the end, he's writing *shoot Ayla Nightshade between the eyes.* Um. Sorry.'

'Yes,' Caraway said. 'What's your point?'

'Only that it's consistent with the idea of a plant. The real assassin writes the letters over the weeks, never planning to send them, but including authentic details so they'll seem realistic. But he only includes the really incriminating statements on the day he plants the letters in Zander's room. That way, he can never be caught with anything too bad himself.'

'Except the pistol,' Caraway said. 'That's pretty undeniable.'

'Yes ...' Ree thought about that, then added slowly, 'Though if Zander is innocent, the real assassin must have another pistol. He wouldn't have used his only weapon as a plant. Which means he must have somewhere to hide them where he knows they won't be found.'

Caraway sighed. 'This is the problem, isn't it? We have Zander. We have the evidence. So on the face of it, Ayla is right. Certainly, as soon as she learns who Zander really is, she'll consider the case closed. Because to believe we don't have the right man, we have to assume the existence of a second pistol, an unassailable hiding place, an assassin who knew exactly when I'd arrest Zander in order to plant the papers on him at just the right time ... it's a lot to put our faith in, based solely on a feeling and an accused man's protestations.'

Dazed by his repeated use of the word *we*, Ree didn't reply straight away. But he was looking at her as though he hoped she could enlighten him – and suddenly, she knew just what to say.

'If the stories are true, sir, it's no greater a leap of faith than the one you made three years ago. You accepted Lady Ayla's innocence despite all evidence to the contrary, because you didn't believe she could be a murderer. So now –'

'You think I should extend the same belief to Zander? But I knew Ayla, Ree. I don't know Zander, not really.'

She shook her head. 'All I'm saying is that you should trust your instincts.'

He studied her face a moment longer, then smiled. It was a singularly sweet smile, and it set her heart pounding again. She dropped her gaze, trying and failing to prevent a blush. He must think she was a fool. He must think –

'Thank you, Ree.' His voice sounded so normal that it gave her the courage to peek upwards again. He was still smiling, as though he hadn't noticed her embarrassment. 'You've been a lot of help. And I appreciate it, I really do.' He touched her arm casually – something she had no doubt she was far more aware of than he was – before taking the papers from her loosened grip and packing them away again.

'We'd better carry on as normal, I suppose,' he said as he was doing it. 'Do keep an eye on your fellow trainees, won't you? And I'll expect to see you up at the tower in five days' time.'

'But – I haven't been tested yet –' Suddenly she was grinning wide enough to make her jaw muscles ache. 'You mean –'

'I hope so,' Caraway said. 'You're one of the best we have.'

'Even though I'm *still* useless at archery?' As soon as the words were out of her mouth, she wanted to call them back. What was she doing? Trying to convince him to revoke his high opinion of her? But he only laughed.

'I won't lie to you, Ree. Archery is important. Every discipline you'll learn here is important. But I would never exclude a promising Helmsman just because her aim was bad.' Opening the office door for her, he gave her a friendly nod. 'Just don't shoot me during the testing, and you'll be fine.'

'Thank you, sir!' She wanted to dance, or sing, or *something*, but she forced herself to walk out of the office at a sedate pace and head for the barracks as though her heart wasn't skipping about all over the place. *Just wait 'til I tell Zander* –

Reality slapped her in the face, and her stomach plunged. She kept walking, but now she wasn't sure whether to feel elation or guilt. And then the solution hit her.

Keep an eye on my fellow trainees, Captain Caraway said. *The real assassin must be one of them.* She lifted her chin as new resolve flowed through her. *I'll find him, and then the Helm will have to release Zander, and everything will be all right.*

TWENTY

The day before their trainees were due to undergo final testing, Caraway and Bryan met for a spot of decision-making. In the past they would have had a long, cheerful, rambling discussion about the current cohort: who had improved, who was likely to pass the test, who would have to pull something spectacular out of the bag to be in with a chance. Yet this time, after Caraway had related the conversation he'd overheard between Ree and Zander, and his subsequent exchange with Ree, the discussion had inevitably turned back to whether or not there might still be an assassin on the loose.

'All right,' Caraway said finally. 'If Zander is innocent, the real assassin must have planted the evidence. And he must have some hold over Klaus the gun-seller, to convince him to give me such a detailed lie ...'

Bryan nodded. 'So speak to Klaus again. Put pressure on his story, see if he breaks.'

'I tried,' Caraway said. 'But he's made himself scarce. None of his associates in the first ring have seen him for days.' He sighed. 'Which could be highly suspicious, or could just mean he's worried about being arrested for supplying firearms to an assassin. I have no way of knowing which.'

'Still,' Bryan said. 'If Zander is innocent, there are only so many people who could possibly have framed him.'

'It must be someone who would have a legitimate excuse for entering the barracks,' Caraway agreed. 'Since the assassin has presumably set himself up with a current or potential route into Darkhaven, that leaves … well, since none of the other weapon-masters or assistants have reason to believe they'll be given access to the tower, that leaves only the other trainees, pretty much.'

'Or you or me,' Bryan said, and Caraway nodded.

'Or you or me.' *Or Miles*, he didn't add – because ever since Miles had become the unofficial assistant weapon-master for firearms, no-one would be surprised to find him in the barracks either. But there was no point saying that to Bryan. 'So, given that … and given that unless the assassin is stupidly sure of himself, he must at least wonder if we still suspect him … how do we proceed with the selection process? Bearing in mind that the successful recruits are still expecting to be taken up to Darkhaven tomorrow.'

Bryan ran a hand over his face. 'Seems to me you have two choices. Call it off: that would nullify the immediate threat, but alert the assassin to your suspicions and leave him to find a way in that you haven't thought of. I'd say that was a short-term gain at the expense of a long-term problem. Or use the occasion to set a trap. There's risk in that, of course, but it would at least flush him out. And if you warn Ayla and have her properly guarded on the day –'

'Ayla is convinced that Zander is guilty,' Caraway muttered. 'She's insistent upon going about her life as normal.'

'Is she still expecting to address the chosen recruits up at the tower?'

'No.' They'd argued about it when he'd told her he didn't think it was a good idea, but he'd managed to prevail. Still, it was one more thing driving them apart. One more way in which she'd tried to assert her authority over his, leaving him doubting whether he would ever truly be her equal. Frowning, he changed the subject.

'What I can't work out is how the assassin intends to get his pistol into Darkhaven. It's not as if we're going to let the recruits walk through the Gate of Death without being searched. And the assassin must know that ...' Caraway hesitated, then asked the question he'd been tiptoeing around for a while. 'Art, don't take this the wrong way, but does Miles carry a lot of equipment to and from the tower?'

As he'd expected, Bryan bristled at the implication. 'You'd better not be suggesting what I think you're suggesting, boyo.'

'It's just that a pistol would be more easily concealed amongst an alchemist's trappings than on a person. And since Miles goes back and forth ...' He shrugged, then completed the lie that would make his question more palatable to the weaponmaster. 'I thought perhaps the assassin might be planning to slip something into one of his crates.'

'No.' Bryan's voice lowered again, though his expression was still wary. 'He took everything up to the tower that first time, and your men searched it all.'

'Right. That's that, then.' Caraway sighed. 'The whole thing is a mystery.'

'Then do you want to call off tomorrow?' Bryan asked, still gruff. Caraway hesitated, then shook his head.

'I think we have to go through with it. If there's a chance we can flush the assassin out and get this whole thing over with –' He scrubbed his hands through his hair. 'So now I just have to decide who should go on the list.'

'I think we have to assume the assassin is good enough that you'd have picked him for advanced training anyway,'

Bryan said. 'If not, then he won't gain access to Darkhaven tomorrow and the whole question becomes irrelevant. So I'd advise you to choose whoever you would have chosen if you didn't suspect that one of them was an assassin.'

'Right,' Caraway said. 'Then I suppose I'll proceed with the one-on-one testing as planned, and try to make my final selection without second-guessing myself.' He offered Bryan a rueful smile. 'Easier said than done.'

At home that evening, after their usual lavish dinner, Bryan looked over at Miles. Caraway had carefully not made even the suggestion of an accusation, earlier, but Bryan had heard it all the same. His first instinct had been angry rejection, of course, but now ... now he couldn't stop thinking about it. Because Miles had never been part of his life in the fifth ring before, and certainly not part of Darkhaven, and yet here he was: training the recruits, handling pistols, advising Ayla Nightshade. He had access to the target. He had knowledge of firearms. Albeit reluctantly, Bryan could see why Caraway might think him an obvious suspect.

Bryan could imagine how this would go, in another relationship. He would watch Miles in silence, letting the tiny uncertainty grow between them. Miles wouldn't understand why they were becoming distant from each other. Neither of them would confront the other. Until one day, whether Miles turned out to be an assassin or not, they found they were no longer what they used to be.

Because Bryan knew himself, and knew Miles, he decided to bypass all that nonsense.

'Milo, are you a traitor?'

Miles turned to him, a shade of alarm in his eyes. 'What? I do not –'

'Only Captain Caraway very politely *didn't* point out to me that you're a direct match with the profile of this damn assassin.'

Concern faded into a grin. 'Ah. I see. Then let me assure you that if ever I were to murder someone, it would not be for the benefit of Sol Kardis.'

'Of course,' Bryan said. 'You're a Parovian patriot.'

'Exactly. I am so patriotic, in fact, that I plan to stay in Arkannen for good.'

'You do?' That was news to Bryan. In the past, it had always been understood between them that Miles would be returning to Parovia once his five-year term at the university came to an end. Though that endpoint wasn't close enough to require any difficult decisions as yet, it had always been somewhere at the back of Bryan's mind. But now Miles was nodding very seriously.

'If I can be useful enough to Lady Ayla, perhaps she might employ me as the royal alchemist,' he said. 'Such a role existed, a few generations back. If she were to reinstate it ...' He shrugged. 'I would have no need to leave.'

'Then your research with her is going well?' Bryan asked, and Miles smirked at him like a well-fed cat.

'I have every reason to believe that we are close to a breakthrough.'

The door to Sorrow's cell opened with a bang, startling her out of a fitful doze. She was sore all over. There was only so long a person could sit on a chair with her wrists tied behind the back and her ankles fastened to the two front legs. They'd brought her food at one point – yesterday? It was hard to be sure – so she wasn't starving. The cell contained a single gas lamp, high up in an alcove on one wall, so she could see all right. And she'd shut up after they threatened to gag her if she didn't stop swearing, so at least her jaw didn't ache along with the rest. But those were very minor consolations compared to the fact that she was *tied to a chair in the custody of the fucking Kardise Brotherhood.*

Unable to wipe her grainy eyes, she contented herself with rubbing her cheek against her shoulder to rid herself of the patch of drool that had collected on it, before lifting her chin to face the woman who had just entered the room. It was Five, the one who'd captured her in the first place. In one hand she carried a pistol case, and in the other a lantern. Once the latter was hanging on a hook beside the door, the light in the cell was almost decent.

'What do you want?' Sorrow muttered, and the other woman smiled.

'Information, of course.'

It was a strange echo of that first overheard conversation, and Sorrow repressed a shiver. She couldn't afford to show any weakness.

'About what?'

Five put down her case and took out her pistol. Then she walked forward until she was just under an arm's length away: close enough to strike Sorrow, if she wanted to, but not close enough for any sort of retaliatory effort on Sorrow's part. 'You can start by telling me how long you've been working for the Mirrorvalese.'

'I'm working for Fourteen,' Sorrow shot back. It wasn't as if she'd be able to work for him any more, now that she'd been discovered, and better they think her a spy for one of their own than a spy for a rival country … but Five was looking amused.

'I'm sure a renowned mercenary like you is capable of having more than one paymaster, Naeve Sorrow.'

'Maybe. Maybe not. Why should I tell you anything?'

'It might be to your advantage.'

'Perhaps I could come up with something useful if you promise to let me go –' But she stopped, because Five was laughing.

'Come on, Naeve! Your death warrant was signed as soon as you showed Fourteen that you knew who he was. Seeing one of our faces is normally grounds for instant execution; if we hadn't thought you'd be useful to us, you'd already be dead. Surely you knew that.'

Actually, she hadn't. Yes, she'd heard that no-one knew who the Brotherhood were or what they looked like. She just hadn't realised that was because they killed anyone who found out. *Stupid, stupid, stupid.*

'In that case,' she forced herself to say coolly, 'what incentive do I have to tell you anything? Seeing as I'll end up dead anyway.'

'As I said, it might be to your advantage. Or, if not yours, then someone you care about.'

Rebellious, Sorrow shook her head and said nothing. Five sighed, her fingers moving slowly and almost caressingly over the pistol in her other hand.

'Let us come at this from a different direction. I already know you're working for Mirrorvale. The important question is, really, what do they know?'

Still Sorrow said nothing. With a shrug, Five smashed her across the side of the face with the butt of the pistol. It was like a miniature explosion going off inside her skull, rendering her temporarily unable to move or speak or do anything except suffer through it.

'I don't –' she began as soon as she could force the words out. Five hit her again.

'What do they know?'

'Nothing – I –'

Five laughed under her breath. 'Dear me, Naeve. Anyone would think you felt some kind of loyalty towards them.'

Then she leaned down and positioned the pistol just beyond the steel toecap of Sorrow's boot, the one with the retractable blade. Sorrow just had time to think, *So she did notice it* ... before Five pulled the trigger.

When the searing, white-hot pain faded to something on the edge of bearable – when the jagged lump in her throat subsided slightly and her vision began to return – Sorrow realised she was talking. No, not talking: swearing. An endless stream of bitter swearwords. Her interrogator slapped her, with detached efficiency, and the flow ceased.

'What do they know?' Five repeated with no change of inflection.

Gasping, Sorrow shook her head.

'All right.' The woman returned to where she'd left her case and began reloading her pistol. 'Then I suppose we'll have to pay the other one a visit.'

Other one? Even through the pain of her shattered foot, Sorrow felt her heart rate increase. 'What do you mean?'

'You know,' Five said. 'Your lover. That girl who looks so much like a *Nightshade*.' Her voice dripped scorn on the last word.

'I don't know what you're talking about,' Sorrow managed, then winced. *What a fucking cliché. Everyone knows people only say that when they mean the exact opposite.* Not her finest moment. And by Five's derisive expression, she agreed.

'Don't waste my time. The Brotherhood may not trust each other, but we trust the rest of the world even less. Particularly when they come from Mirrorvale.' She pulled a face of mock regret. 'Any normal mercenary would have fled as soon as they realised what they'd got themselves into. But not you. As soon as you agreed to do another job for Fourteen, he knew there must be a deeper reason for it. And so he had you followed.'

She'd finished reloading her gun, now; stroking it lovingly, she gazed into Sorrow's eyes.

'We know all about Elisse and her son, and the little house where the three of you play at happy families,' she murmured. 'So who is she?'

Sorrow pressed her lips together and said nothing.

'Let me tell you what I think,' Five said. 'Three years ago, a Nightshade baby was born in Darkhaven. Born, and lost. Very few people in Mirrorvale were aware that it had happened. Even fewer knew that he and his mother had fled the country. We heard of it only as a rumour, a suggestion that somewhere another Changer child yet lived. Until you came to Fourteen's attention. A mercenary in exile, carrying out one dirty job after another in our cities ... except for the infrequent weeks you spent in a cottage in the middle of nowhere, with a pale-skinned woman and a three-year-old boy. Even a child could put those pieces together, Naeve.'

Sorrow scowled. 'If you know, then why are you asking?'

'Because I want you to cooperate with us. You're already dead; you know that. But if you tell me the truth – confirm that Elisse is who we think she is – I'll convince the Brotherhood to leave her and her son alone. They're not doing any harm, after all. As long as we know where they are, I see no reason to bother them – particularly now that you won't be whispering in her ear any more.'

Shit. Shit, shit, shit. It was painfully clear, now, that Sorrow should have convinced Elisse to leave Sol Kardis as soon as she learned of the assassination plot, and left Darkhaven to fend for itself. *If I hadn't been seduced by just that little bit more danger, that little bit more recklessness –*

This isn't helping. Concentrate on deciding what to do.

She stared straight ahead, keeping her expression impassive, whilst thoughts whirred and bounced in her head like exploding clockwork. But in the end, it was very simple. The Brotherhood knew where Elisse was, and they strongly suspected who Corus was. If, by confirming those suspicions, Sorrow could preserve Elisse's liberty – temporarily, at least; she wasn't so naïve as to believe otherwise – then she had no choice but to do so. As long as Elisse and Corus remained outside the direct control of the Brotherhood, there was still always the chance they might escape back to Mirrorvale.

'All right,' she muttered. 'All right! I'll tell you whatever you want to know.'

Five smiled. 'You just have.'

Her long fingers reached up to turn the knob that would extinguish the gas lamp; then she unhooked her lantern and made for the door. Sorrow fought to go after her, but the ropes held her firmly in place.

'Wait. You said you'd leave them alone. You said –'

'Come on, Naeve. Where are those famous wits of yours? Our assassin will take care of Ayla and her brother's child. That only leaves your Elisse's boy.' Five shrugged. 'If it's any consolation, we would have gone after him whatever you said today. Your contribution has merely, shall we say ... *tipped the balance.*'

The door clanged shut behind her as she left the room.

TWENTY-ONE

Caraway always ended the seven-week assessment period with a series of one-on-one tests. They weren't the sole factor that determined which of the recruits he admitted to Helm training, but they made it easier to identify how each person had changed over the course of the seven weeks. Besides, it only seemed fair to give them all a final chance to demonstrate their skills.

Back when he'd done the testing for the first time, Ayla had unexpectedly announced that she was interested in coming along to watch. *If I'm going to be guarded by them*, she'd said, *I'd like to have some say in who gets chosen.* Caraway had been doubtful, but he'd agreed to it all the same. And so she'd sat quietly up at the top of the tiered seating in the demonstration hall, concealed in the shadows, and observed the day's testing. Afterwards, he'd asked what she thought.

I can't say much about their technical proficiency, she'd answered. *But I'd prefer you not to employ the tall boy with the reddish hair. I didn't like him.*

Caraway had been rather taken aback by that, because the red-haired boy was one of his most promising students. He'd made a noncommittal reply and admitted the boy to his training programme anyway – after all, he'd thought, it would be another year before any of them found a place in Darkhaven, long enough to see if Ayla's instinct was right. And sure enough, a few months into it, the boy had lost his temper with another recruit and beaten him almost to death.

Since then, Ayla – unseen – had attended every one of Caraway's testing sessions. And although he selected the trainees based on his own judgement, he always listened to what she had to say. So it was a shame she couldn't attend this time; he would have found it useful to get her opinion on the current cohort. But having her in the same room as a potential assassin and a whole lot of weaponry would have been foolish beyond belief, so he'd told her he thought it would be better for the trainees if she wasn't there on this occasion. She hadn't objected. Admittedly, he'd walked away before she had the chance, but what choice did he have? When it came to the subject of the assassination, she wouldn't listen to reason.

The door to the hall opened to admit Penn, the first recruit due for testing, and Caraway turned to tell him he was early. Only it wasn't Penn standing there with a chin raised in defiance. It was Ayla.

'What are you doing here?' he snapped. Her eyes narrowed at his tone, and he caught a fleeting glimpse of one of the contemptuous glances she'd been in the habit of giving him while she still blamed him for her mother's death.

'I came to watch the testing, as usual. I'll be in no danger. No-one will even know I'm here.'

He sighed. 'Go home, Ayla.'

'Don't tell me what to do.' She was cold. Haughty. Three years ago he would have backed down and let her overrule him. But that was three years ago.

'Do you want me to resign?' he said quietly.

'What?'

'I'm in charge of your safety. That's what being Captain of the Helm means. And I refuse to have the weight of another failure on my shoulders. So if you don't want me to do my job, I had better resign now.'

'Don't threaten me, Tomas.'

He shook his head in exasperation. 'It isn't a threat! I don't want to do it! But it's like you're asking me to fight a duel without giving me any weapons. How can I protect you if you won't let yourself be protected?'

'You're taking it too far,' she shot back. 'Do you think my father would have let Captain Travers control his every movement? No! He would have done whatever was necessary for the smooth running of his country, threat or no threat, and Travers would simply have had to deal with it. You're letting the Kardise win, Tomas, and they don't even have to kill me to do it!'

'Ayla –'

The door banged open again, and Ayla was up the tiered seating in a flash, concealing herself in the shadows at the top. Caraway forced himself to turn with a smile, despite his anger and frustration.

'Come in, Penn.'

He selected two practice swords from the rack on the wall and offered one to the boy, pushing every single bit of his argument with Ayla to the back of his mind. He couldn't fix it now. Time to find out what his trainees had learned.

He turned over the big glass-and-sand timer that stood to one side of the floor, and began the test.

Penn fought as if he took it personally – and maybe he did. Though the boy had become much easier to get on with since their conversation in the sixth ring, Caraway hadn't shaken the idea that Penn nursed a special hatred for him in particular. Yet he couldn't see why anyone would want to train under, and maybe even be employed by, a man they despised ... unless, of course, they were an assassin and were using it as cover to get into Darkhaven. Though if that were the case, then surely Penn would make every effort to hide his antagonism? Caraway couldn't work him out. But the lad was a good swordsman with the potential to be a brilliant one. If he hadn't still possessed a little of that prickly edge, he'd have been through without a doubt – and so Caraway couldn't in good conscience exclude him. All the same, it would be a good idea to ask Ayla specifically what she'd thought of Penn ...

Don't ask her anything! he reminded himself. *She's not meant to be here, remember?*

Exasperated with himself, he hit Penn's sword upwards and said, 'That's enough, Penn. Thank you.'

Penn didn't seem to hear the instruction. His mouth set in a grim line, he pressed forward, forcing Caraway to dance back a few steps. His eyes narrowed as he lunged –

'Penn! Enough!' Caraway used a move that he hadn't taught the trainees yet, sending the practice sword spinning out of the boy's hand. They stared at each other. Then Caraway lowered his own weapon and said mildly, 'If you want to kill me, you won't get very far with a wooden sword.'

Penn flushed and lowered his gaze. 'I just wanted to prove myself,' he mumbled.

'Well, I think you've done that. Go on back to the barracks. Test's over.'

Penn looked up, alarm creeping into his eyes. 'Captain Caraway, I didn't mean to – I wouldn't have –' He hesitated, then – apparently with great effort – got the words out. 'I'm sorry. Really. This won't make a difference, will it?'

Caraway regarded him in silence for a moment. 'Why do you want to join the Helm, Penn?'

'I –'

'You told me yourself that you don't like anyone very much. And though you've made an effort to get over that, I still see it in you. But my men are a team. They have to be. If you'd rather work alone, it's not the job for you.'

'I believe in the Helm,' Penn said fervently. 'I really do. Nothing else will be good enough.'

'Why?'

'Because I believe in justice. I want to become the best warrior I possibly can be, so that I can make sure justice is served.'

'That's a noble aim,' Caraway said. 'But justice isn't a solitary act. We make it together.' He crossed the floor to pick up Penn's discarded sword, and nodded at the depleted top bulb of the timer. 'Go on, now. The others are waiting.'

After the intensity that was Penn, Caraway was relieved to find the next few trainees straightforward. He got through a good handful of them before taking a longer break to rest and catch up on his notes. In the past he would have done that with Ayla, but not today. She stayed up in her place, and he stayed down in his.

He'd tested most of the trainees on their bladework, with some unarmed combat where appropriate, but it occurred to him that maybe in the future he'd be testing them on their accuracy with a pistol. Now that was a strange thought. It was possible that in a few years' time, everything he was teaching and testing now – everything he knew – would be obsolete.

Not so, he told himself. *There's far more to being a Helmsman than knowing one end of a sword from the other.* All the same, it was a depressing thought.

As his break neared its end, he checked the list. Ree was next, and he had every confidence in her ability to – *wait*. Slowly he lifted his head to look up at the shadowed corner where Ayla sat. He wasn't at all sure he'd raised the subject of female Helmsmen with her. And given that she was the one they'd be protecting, she'd probably want to have a say in it.

He climbed partway up the steps, and Ayla came down to meet him. Since their argument, she'd closed herself off; her expression gave nothing away. 'What's the matter?'

'I just thought you should know, the next one's a girl,' Caraway said. 'And another one later, too. We've had two female recruits this year.'

Ayla's eyebrows lifted, but apart from that faint indication of surprise she remained impassive. 'You're considering letting women into the Helm?'

'There doesn't seem a good reason not to,' he said tentatively. 'Is that all right?'

'All right? Of course it's all right. It's your Helm.'

Still unable to tell how she really felt, he scanned her face in silence until her cold expression melted into amused exasperation.

'I mean it, Tomas. Why should I mind? If anything, I'd welcome a few more women about the place. It gets a little lonely, sometimes, being surrounded by men all the time.'

She'd been completely lacking in female companionship after her mother died, Caraway realised. She'd never had a female friend. Or any friend, for that matter, apart from Myrren. For the first time, it occurred to him to pity her – and with that, his feelings for her changed. Not for the worse. Never that. But they splintered and reformed, like the patterns of a kaleidoscope, into something more complex and more real.

'I love you, you know,' he said softly, reaching across the gap between them to touch her cheek. Her fingers came up to cover his, but a small frown drew her brows together.

'Tomas, I –'

The door clanged on its hinges once more, startling them apart. Caraway turned to find Ree in the arena below, staring up at them. A slow blush spread up her cheeks, and she took a step backwards as if she wanted to retreat.

'Hello, Ree,' Caraway said cheerfully. 'You'll be pleased to learn I haven't brought a bow and arrows with me today.'

Ree mumbled something, but her gaze kept flicking between him and Ayla. He glanced at Ayla, afraid she'd think it impertinent, but her expression was soft.

'Just pretend I'm not here,' she told Ree gently, before returning to her hiding place. Caraway descended to the duelling floor and handed Ree one of the swords.

He was expecting an easy test, but to his dismay, Ree wasn't operating at anything like the level he knew she was capable of. The first time she made a silly mistake, he adjusted for it and went on as if nothing had happened. Just finding her feet, he told himself, but then it happened again. And again. After a while, he gave up on duelling altogether and got her to demonstrate some of the basic forms – the kind of test he'd give a complete novice after a month or two of using a sword. She knew them inside out. She'd demonstrated that the very first time he'd met her. And yet even on that simple test, she stumbled and got mixed up.

'All right, Ree,' he said finally. 'We'll leave it there.'

She looked up at him with wide greenish eyes. She knew she'd done badly – he could see it in the set of her jaw and the lack of colour in her cheeks. He suspected she wanted to cry, but she held herself steady. That was something, at least.

'Judging you only on today's performance, you'd have been lucky to get through the first week,' he told her sternly. 'I'm going to assume this was nerves on your part, but don't let it happen again.'

'No, sir. I'm sorry. I –' She hesitated, biting her lip, then said again, 'I'm sorry.'

She threw a quick glance up at Ayla's concealed seat, then another at him, before giving a wobbly salute and heading for the door. Caraway stared after her until Ayla emerged once more from the shadows and spoke softly.

'Is she usually that nervous?'

'No. She's one of the most competent new recruits we have.' He turned to look up at Ayla. 'Maybe female Helmsmen aren't such a good idea.'

'That's not fair,' Ayla said. 'I put her off. She'd have been fine if it had just been you.'

'She knows better than to be distracted by anything,' Caraway said. 'And if she's distracted by you, in particular, I don't see how she can do the job.'

'It wasn't me. It was us. We caught her by surprise, but I doubt it will happen again.' Smiling ruefully at his bemused expression, Ayla shook her head. 'Never mind. Just give her a chance. Now, I'd better hide again before I disconcert any more of your students.'

Caraway didn't have a clue what she was getting at, but that was fine. The important thing was that they were talking to each other properly again. He watched her retreat to the top of the stands, then turned to the door in time to see the next recruit come in.

The rest of the testing passed without incident. The only person who managed to surprise him was Saydi. She still wasn't perfect, but she'd improved a lot over the course of training. Every one of the mistakes he'd picked her up on previously had lessened, if not vanished entirely. She'd obviously been practising hard, and she was a fast learner – weren't those the qualities he wanted in a Helmsman? Not just technical proficiency, but dedication and adaptability. And since he'd more or less told Ree she had a place in the advanced programme, despite her poor showing earlier, why not two of them? Ayla had as good as said she'd like it.

As for the rest, they turned out to be quite predictable. Farleigh was showy but prone to over-reaching himself, as he had been throughout training; his estimation of his own abilities was always a little beyond reality. Timo wasn't decisive enough, but would have the makings of a solid warrior once the forms became instinctive enough that he no longer had to think about them. And so it went.

Once the last of them had left the hall, Caraway dropped his weapon on the floor and rolled his shoulders. It was harder than it looked, adjusting his style to challenge each trainee at the appropriate level. Letting mistakes pass, instead of following his natural instinct to take advantage of the smallest weakness. Particularly when he was using a damn wooden sword that left his palms covered in blisters.

'Are you all right?' Ayla asked, descending the stands to join him.

'Tired.' He hesitated, sensing the lingering remnants of coldness between them. But he'd had enough of fighting – of all kinds – for one day, so he gave her a rueful smile. 'I'm sorry, Ayla.'

She put her arms around him despite his sweaty and dishevelled state, resting her cheek against his shoulder. 'I'm sorry too.'

He kissed the top of her head. 'Can I ask you about a few of them?'

'Of course.'

'Then … Penn?'

'I don't think he wants to kill me,' Ayla said. 'But apparently he wouldn't mind killing you.' She pulled back so she could look up into his face. 'What did you do to make him so angry?'

Caraway shook his head. 'He's always been like that. Makes it very hard to tell if it's anything more than just his normal, everyday dislike of humanity. Farleigh?'

'I get the impression that Farleigh is too satisfied with the world and his place in it to commit so disruptive an act as murder.'

Caraway laughed. 'That's probably a fair assessment.'

'Ree is very sweet,' Ayla added, and he laughed again.

'She wouldn't thank you for that characterisation.'

Ayla gave him a surprisingly sharp glance. 'I daresay.' But she said no more on the subject, remarking after a moment, 'Saydi's an interesting one, isn't she? I must admit, I didn't expect her to do as well as she did.'

'Nor did I,' Caraway admitted. 'She's improved far beyond anything I could have imagined.'

'So that's it, then,' Ayla said. 'Women in the Helm.' Her smile held an edge of malice. 'My father would have had an apoplexy.'

'They still have to get through full training. A year is a long time.'

'But the door is open, now. That's what matters.' She leaned into him once more. 'Thank you, Tomas.'

'For what?'

'Breaking tradition with me.'

He grinned. 'I wouldn't have it any other way.'

TWENTY-TWO

The day after testing, Penn and Saydi got up early and went down to the yard outside the training hall. Weaponmaster Bryan had promised to post the list of those accepted for Helm training at the third bell, which was still some time away, but the two of them had agreed it would be impossible to focus on anything else that morning. So they sat in the yard, played skipping-stones, and waited.

After a while, the door opened and they both startled to their feet, but it was only Miles. He walked off in the direction of the Gate of Steel, not the Gate of Ice, so he clearly wasn't going up to the tower today. Penn was rather confused by Miles. He was an academic, not a warrior, yet every week he visited Darkhaven. Some kind of special research, was the rumour amongst the trainees. A secret project with Ayla Nightshade herself. But surely, if Darkhaven wanted to develop a new weapon, they'd be better off consulting a weaponmaster?

'What does he do up there every week?' he muttered, more to himself than to Saydi.

'Let's ask him!' Before he could stop her, Saydi rushed off in the alchemist's direction. Penn followed more slowly.

He liked Saydi a lot more than he had – *obviously* – but he still didn't understand her propensity to chatter. It was all he could do to muster the effort to string two sentences together for most people's benefit.

By the time he arrived beside her, she was already asking Miles a million questions about his research. The alchemist answered them guardedly – anyone could see, Penn thought, that whatever he was doing in Darkhaven was confidential – but that didn't put Saydi off. And when she discovered that it involved Ayla Changing, there was no stopping her.

'You've seen Lady Ayla's other form up close?' she repeated. 'I saw her fly over the city once when we were training – earned a nasty bruise for the distraction, too – but that's all. Is she very beautiful?'

'The most beautiful thing I have ever seen,' Miles said. Apparently this was one topic he didn't mind talking about. 'In creature form she is a horse made of burnished gold, though larger than any other horse in existence. Her wings are like two immense sheets of flickering flame. When she opens them wide, the whole world is filled with sunlight.' He looked thoughtful. 'Strange, that a creature of ice and ebonwood should have such a fiery exterior; but she has the Phoenix's colouring, I suppose.'

'Then where do you work together?' Saydi persisted. 'Surely to have space for her and all your alchemist's tools, you must need to be in a field or something.'

Miles smiled at her. 'Darkhaven is built on a far larger scale than most of us are used to. But we use the transformation room, the one just off the central courtyard. It is where Lady Ayla goes to Change anyway, so there is plenty of space.'

'Penn and I are hoping to visit Darkhaven tomorrow,' Saydi confided. 'If we get accepted for Helm training …

but let's not think about that now. Can you tell me what it's like up there?'

Before Penn knew it, they were off into a long conversation about the tower: how many rooms it had, their size, their furnishings, how many storeys there were and how they were positioned around the central square. As usual when confronted with information for which he couldn't see an immediate practical use, Penn's brain switched off. He did his best to concentrate – to distract himself from the forthcoming list of results, if nothing else – but he found it simply impossible to take an interest in something so irrelevant.

This, he thought with bitter amusement, *is why I never managed to learn much at school.*

Finally the conversation drew to a close, and Miles hurried off towards the Gate of Steel. *Probably made him late, the poor bastard.* Penn shook his head at Saydi. 'You talk too much.'

'I talk exactly the right amount,' she replied with dignity. 'He's a nice man, don't you think?'

'Yes.' But Penn disposed of the alchemist with a shrug. The third bell was about to ring, and he had no room in his mind for anything else.

Precisely as the temple bells began to chime, Weaponmaster Bryan emerged from the training hall with a sheet of paper in one hand. He cast Penn and Saydi an amused glance that gave precisely nothing away, before pinning it to the door and disappearing back inside again.

'Come on!' Saydi dragged Penn across the yard. Yet now the time had come, he was suddenly reluctant. What if he'd failed? What if that moment in the testing when he'd let his control lapse and his rage come burning through had cost him everything? He closed his eyes, not daring to look …

but at Saydi's intake of breath, he opened them again. He couldn't help it.

His name was at the top of the list.

'It's alphabetical, Avens,' Saydi said, nudging him with her shoulder. 'So don't go getting big-headed.'

Even before he found her name on the paper, the glee in her voice told him that she'd been accepted too. He turned his head, and they grinned at each other. *One step closer to taking my revenge. One step closer to upholding my family's honour.*

'That's it, then,' Saydi said. She sounded as jubilant as he felt. 'Let's go and celebrate.'

Later, back in Penn's room, she sat him down on the bed and fixed him with a determined stare.

'All right,' she said. 'You've got what you wanted. We both have. So now, you can tell me exactly what you're planning. How is Helm training going to help you kill Caraway? Because yes, you'll be around him a lot, but it's not as though any of us will have a lot of one-on-one time with him. If that's what you wanted, your best bet would have been to catch him off guard during the testing.'

Penn shook his head. Now that Saydi was forcing him to explain the details, he had a nasty feeling she'd laugh at him.

'I don't want to catch him off guard,' he admitted. 'If I stab him in the back or ambush him, he won't know it was me. It won't be enough. No, I want him to train me. Teach me everything he knows. And then as soon as I've learned enough to be sure of beating him, I'll fight him and I'll win.' He shrugged. 'That's why I wanted to be accepted for Helm training, and that's why I'm happy now.'

Saydi didn't laugh. She frowned at him as though he were a puzzle she needed to solve, and didn't reply for some time.

'It seems a very slow way of getting revenge,' she said finally. 'Months of training, for what? The chance to challenge a man to a duel you might not even win?'

'I suppose so.'

'Anyway,' she said, 'if I were you, I wouldn't be content with hurting Caraway himself. He's a soldier; he's used to pain. No – to make him suffer, I'd want to hurt someone close to him.'

'Who, Lady Ayla?' Penn asked doubtfully. 'She's even harder to get to than Caraway himself. He may be armed, but at least we see him regularly. She stays up in Darkhaven, guarded by the Helm. And anyway ...' He stopped, unable to articulate his deep unease about the idea of committing treason. It wasn't a prospect that should have mattered to him, given his intentions towards Caraway, but somehow it did all the same. Yet Saydi only laughed.

'I wasn't talking about Ayla. Unless you have a pistol stashed away somewhere, you wouldn't stand a chance. But Ayla has a nephew.'

'So?'

'It seems she doesn't care much for the boy.' She paused, smiling widely. 'But our Captain Caraway has taken to him like a father.'

You're suggesting I hurt a tiny child? Part of him shrank from Saydi at that, at the sheer disregard for common decency that had led her even to think of such a thing.

No scruples, remember? another part replied. *You're never going to be forgiven, no matter what you do, so you might as well do whatever will be most effective.*

And whispering in the wake of both came the dark part of him: *It could work. You already know his greatest fear is losing them – Ayla, Marlon, the whole life that was unfairly given to him. And at least there'd be no more waiting.* A spark of hope leapt in him at the idea, then just as quickly died.

'If Ayla's being guarded, even with the strength of her gift to protect her, I hardly think a vulnerable child will be less well defended.'

'Ah, but security has lessened since Zander's arrest,' Saydi pointed out. 'And that means young Marlon is allowed to walk outside the tower every afternoon with his nurse, just as he did before all those rumours came to the city.'

'Still beyond the Gate of Death, though ...'

'Yes, Penn,' she said patiently. 'And where is it we're being taken tomorrow?'

Of course. A slow smile spread across his face. 'You know, you're a lot cleverer than I thought you were when we first met.'

'You underestimated me,' Saydi said. 'A lot of people do.' She kissed him to soften the jibe. 'So it's settled, then? You'll take Marlon?'

'I suppose so ...'

'I'll help you. Provide a distraction so you can sneak away from the group to find him. Just think: no more waiting. Revenge tomorrow, instead of in a year. That has to be a good thing.' Her eyes narrowed. 'If I had a chance at revenge tomorrow, I'd take it in a flash.'

'Yes.' Fired by her enthusiasm, Penn pushed down his lingering doubts. 'Yes, I'll do it tomorrow. No more waiting.' He looked sideways at her. 'You do know that if I succeed in this, I'll probably be killed? Or even if I live, it will be inside a prison cell.'

'Well, then,' Saydi said. 'We'd better make the most of the time.' And she began to unbutton her shirt.

Yet afterwards, once she'd gone, Penn began to doubt himself again. Putting himself in a position to be trained by

Caraway, just so Penn could challenge him to a duel and beat him – that was fair, somehow. There was a symmetry to it that couldn't be denied. But using a child to get to Caraway, to make him suffer, was another thing entirely. *Hurt someone close to him*, Saydi had said. And she hadn't backtracked on that when she'd come up with the idea of Marlon. So although Penn tried to tell himself she only meant him to threaten the boy a little, to throw Caraway off balance so Penn would gain the advantage, he knew that wasn't the case. Though you wouldn't know it to look at her, Saydi had turned out to be the most ruthless person he'd ever met; to her, anything was acceptable in the name of vengeance. During all their discussions of what they'd like to do to the men who'd killed their kin and got away with it, it had become clear that she saw most people as belonging to one of three categories: targets, obstacles or tools.

Penn pushed aside the insidious thought that he probably fell into one of those categories too.

The point was, he'd done his best to convince himself he needn't have any scruples – that Caraway was a target, a monster to be slain. But he'd found that it was far harder to intend ill towards a man when you could see his face. When he became a person instead of an abstraction. And given that, it was hard to justify using an innocent child to get to him.

Yet despite all that … Penn just wanted it to be over. He'd expected his resolve to crystallise as soon as he reached Arkannen, yet instead it had twisted inside him. He couldn't live this way for months or even years, torn by the conflicting demands of his father's instructions and his own confused conscience. The idea of taking his revenge on Caraway tomorrow, instead of having to see the man every day until he finished his training – see and reluctantly like, until it became impossible to carry out his task – was a tiny gleam of hope in an otherwise bleak landscape. And if using Marlon as a tool was what it took to achieve that, Penn was willing to live with it.

Or die with it.

Preferably the latter.

Left alone in a lightless cell, tied to a chair and losing blood from her shattered foot, Naeve Sorrow swore fluently and with great vigour.

Once she'd run out of swearwords – which, admittedly, took some time – she began to list her assets. *List your assets and be thankful* was something her mother had always told her whenever a young Naeve complained about anything. Over the years, Sorrow had taken the platitude and made it her own. If she ever got into a situation she couldn't see a way out of, she mentally enumerated everything she had access to that might be usable as a tool or a weapon – and more often than not, that would lead her to a solution.

Unfortunately, the current list was a lot shorter than average.

She'd started with *chair*. Then *rope*. After a little thought, she'd added *darkness* – because at least by now her eyes were accustomed to it, which would give her an advantage over anyone who entered the cell. But that appeared to be it.

When she found herself seriously considering *broken foot* as a possible asset, she knew the list was as long as it was going to get.

So. She had a chair, some rope and darkness. Those were her assets. Unfortunately, they were also her constraints. Which meant the only way she'd be able to *use* any of them would be if she first got *out* of them. Of course, the Brotherhood were careful people, so they'd tied her far too tightly and securely for her to be able to work her wrists free. She wouldn't be able to escape the chair without someone else's help.

Which meant she needed to get hold of that someone else.

She threw all her weight over to one side, fighting against her constraints as much as possible. The chair rocked slightly.

All right. That was something. She could work with it.

She flung herself from side to side, ignoring the chafing pains at wrists and ankles as the motion pulled against her bonds. The chair began to rock more violently. Just a little longer, and she might build up enough momentum to tip it –

The chair teetered, legs scraping against the floor. Gritting her teeth, Sorrow put everything she had into the next rock. She felt her balance go. The world upended around her. And a swirling moment later, she hit the floor with a jarring impact that left her gasping.

Her ears were ringing, but as the dizzy noise subsided she heard approaching footsteps. There was a scrape as the small viewing panel in the door slid open.

'What's going on in there?' a male voice said wearily.

He wasn't stupid enough to come dashing into the room – and indeed, Sorrow hadn't dared to hope for it. But at least she had human contact now. That was another asset in itself, as long as she didn't screw it up; people were always the weak point.

She opened her eyes, but still couldn't see anything beyond a vague silhouette. His face must be pressed against the gap, looking in.

'Can you help me?' She didn't need any sort of fakery to sound feeble and breathless.

'Not likely. I know who you are and what you're capable of, Naeve Sorrow.'

'Please.' To her mingled delight and dismay, a sob shook her voice. 'I think I've broken something. Look – my hands are tied. My feet are tied. I can't do anything to you.'

He was silent, and she pressed home her advantage.

'They're going to kill me, you know. I don't want to lie like this until my execution.'

Without a reply, he slid the panel closed, and for a sick instant she thought she'd failed. But then she heard the scrape of a key in the lock.

As the door opened, Sorrow was immediately dazzled by the full brightness of the light that glanced in from the corridor beyond. *Didn't think that one through. Better strike darkness off the list.* She blinked and squinted at the guard as he walked towards her, stopping well beyond her possible reach.

'Oh dear,' he said, smirking down at her. 'You have got yourself in a tricky situation. But you're not fooling me, Naeve Sorrow. This is almost certainly some kind of escape attempt.'

Obviously. Sorrow increased the tremor in her own voice. 'I was trying to reach the door. But I couldn't do it.'

He snorted. 'Of course you couldn't.'

She gazed up at him pleadingly. 'So will you help me up? I promise I won't do it again.'

He hesitated an instant longer. But even if he did take a certain malicious delight in her discomfort, he wasn't a cruel man – and that, in the end, would be his downfall. Like plenty of men before him, he couldn't quite bear to leave a woman in pain, even if she was a prisoner. It was a dynamic Sorrow had taken advantage of in the past, and she'd gladly do so again now.

Shaking his head, the guard hoisted her chair upright. As he settled it back onto its four legs, his face moved closer to hers. And at that point she craned forward, sank her teeth into his lower lip, and pulled.

The guard lurched toward her with a strangled cry. Before he could right himself, she drew her head back and slammed it into his nose and mouth with as much force as she could muster. Even as he staggered back, reaching for a knife, she spun the chair on one of its back legs. Its weight and her own barrelled into his unbalanced body, bringing all three of them down. The guard landed hard on his back, head slamming against the stone floor, knife clattering out of his hand. The chair and Sorrow fell sideways next to him.

Ow. Fuck. She gasped as her whole body jarred with the impact for a second time, resonating in her damaged foot until she thought she was going to vomit. But when she'd finished gasping and swallowing and fighting for breath, the man was still motionless and the door to her cell was still ajar. And even more to the point, by the light from the corridor, she could make out the fallen knife on the floor.

New list of assets: chair, rope, open door, knife. Better. Now I have to make use of them before anyone else shows up.

She took a last, long look to fix the position of the knife in her mind. Then, with much jerking and wriggling, she managed to roll over until she was facing in the other direction. After that, it was simply a matter of shuffling backwards until she felt cool metal brush her skin. It took time to get the knife into her hand, and still longer to hack apart the rope that bound her wrists, but finally the job was done. And once her hands were out, it was a simple matter to sever the bonds at her ankles and clamber upright. Her wrists were bleeding from several deep cuts, and putting too much pressure on her damaged foot sent pain lancing up her spine to lodge in the base of her skull, but she'd done it. She was free. That was the only thing that mattered.

Of course, the whole thing would be in vain if she collapsed from her blood loss – so she took the time to examine her foot, wincing with every tiny movement. Her steel-capped boot and the metal structure that had housed the extendable blade had prevented the foot from being blown off completely, but it was still a shattered mess of flesh and bone, metal and leather. The bullet must be in there somewhere, too, but without the proper medical supplies, trying to locate it would only make things worse. Even removing the mangled leather of the boot would increase the blood flow. The best she could do was bandage the entire foot, boot and all, as tight as she could, and hope it held out long enough for her to reach a physician. To that end, she leaned down and cut the shirt off the unconscious guard's back, before ripping it into strips. It wasn't the most hygienic bandage the world had ever seen, but it was good enough for now.

When she'd finished, she considered the chair, the cut lengths of rope and the man on the floor. She was tempted to tie him where she'd been tied – the idea of the Brotherhood finding the cell exactly as they'd left it, save for the inhabitant of the chair, was a tempting one – but in the end, practicality beat poetry. As she'd just demonstrated herself, a person in a chair could create a disturbance that was loud enough to attract attention. What she really wanted was for her escape to go unnoticed for as long as possible.

To that end, she tied the man's wrists and ankles, and wadded up another piece of his shirt to stuff into his mouth. Then she dragged him into the corner furthest from the door. If he came round he'd have a long way to go in the dark, with no means of calling for help. And with any luck, once the door was closed again, no-one else would think to check on her.

Armed with the knife, as well as a leg wrenched from the battered chair, Sorrow crept out of the cell. Though the corridor beyond was illuminated, it was also deserted. She didn't know which way was out, but she had a vague feeling that the guard's footsteps had approached from the left, so that was the way she went. Her foot throbbed with each step; she looked down to see that she was leaving rusty smears on the floor. It was old blood, the blood that had pooled in her boot and was now leaking through her makeshift bandage. At least, she thought it was. To be honest, as long as the bandage kept her from bleeding out, it didn't really matter. What mattered was getting out of this building and reaching Elisse before the Brotherhood did.

Sorrow didn't hold out much hope for that, but at least she had to try.

TWENTY-THREE

Ayla took a roundabout route to the transformation room, one that allowed her to visit a particular part of the tower on the way. Tomas was down in the fifth ring, preparing those recruits who'd been accepted onto the Helm training programme for their afternoon's visit to Darkhaven; all the same, she looked both ways down the corridor before turning to one of her two guards – the ones Tomas had insisted on reinstating for the day, selected from a small group of his most trusted men. 'Unlock this door, please.'

He shifted uneasily. 'What do you want in the armoury, Lady Ayla?'

'Just open it.' She'd never been happy with the constant guards – as far as she was concerned, setting a man to protect a Changer against a pistol was simply a way of giving the assassin easy practice before he went for the real target – but it turned out this one would be useful after all. Though the Helm answered to Tomas, none of them would ever disobey a direct order from her. He had trained them too well for that.

Sure enough, though the Helmsman looked askance at her, he unlocked the door without further demur. With barely a glance at any of the weaponry hanging on the walls,

Ayla crossed the room to the safe into which she'd seen Tomas locking the pistols. She'd taken the key from him that morning, slipping it from around his neck whilst he slept. And yes, that veered from lying by omission to blatant dishonesty – but she hadn't wanted to break the fragile peace that had fallen between them, and she'd known he'd never agree to what Miles had requested.

That's crazy, Ayla. She could almost hear him saying it. *You can't go and see a man who could be an assassin with the very tool he can use to kill you. You promised to do everything you could to stay safe.*

But Miles had told her, last time they met, that he was ready to move to the next stage of experimentation. He had some possible solutions, and he wanted to test them properly. Which meant he had to shoot her.

'Lady Ayla ...' one of the two Helmsmen at her heels said again, fearfully, when she opened the safe. She ignored him, reaching in with utmost care to remove a pistol and one of the bags of accoutrements. As her fingers touched the chill metal, a shiver crawled across her skin. *Am I being stupid? Am I about to walk up to my killer and hand him his weapon ...?*

She shook it off. Zander was the assassin; there had been no sign of any other. And even if he wasn't the right one, she still couldn't believe that Miles would hurt her. She was almost positive that Miles liked her – at least, as much as it was possible to tell anything of the kind from a man whose speech was blunt to a fault and whose expression was set at gently mournful.

'All right,' she said, turning to her agitated guards. 'We can go. Would it make you two feel better if you were to carry these instead of me?'

One of them took the bag and pistol from her, gingerly, as if she'd handed him a live snake. She suppressed a sigh. It wasn't as if she liked firearms much herself – but nevertheless, the sooner Tomas started training the Helm to be comfortable around them, the better.

Well. Maybe not comfortable. But there had to be a sensible middle ground between terrified and over-familiar.

When they reached the transformation room, she took the pistol back from the Helmsmen and dismissed them to stand outside the door. They weren't happy about that, either, but they obeyed. Guilt squirmed in Ayla's stomach. She shouldn't be encouraging the Helm to go against their captain's orders. Tomas had taught them to respect her, to respond to her as they would to him, and this was a poor way to repay him for that courtesy.

Still, if Miles's experiments resulted in a way to shield her in human and creature form, Tomas would never have to worry about an assassination threat again. Surely he'd agree it was worth it.

Miles was already at the table when she entered the room, making incomprehensible notes in his usual scrawl. In lieu of a greeting, she handed him the pistol and accoutrements, trying not to reveal the edge of doubt that still cut her. He took them, murmuring absent-minded thanks, then promptly turned his back on her again. Yet once he'd checked and loaded the pistol, he turned to her a second time with something that looked very like a dog collar in his hand. 'Try this out, Lady Ayla.'

Eyebrows climbing her forehead, she looked from it to him. *Are you serious?* The question must have shown on her face, because he flushed.

'I – it needs to be something sturdy enough for your creature form to wear. I tried other forms of jewellery, but –'

'I understand,' Ayla said, putting him out of his misery. 'But won't it get left behind when I Change? Everything else does.'

'This will not – or at least, it should not, if I am on the right track. It is made from the pure elements of alchemy, just like a Changer creature.'

She looked again at the thing in her hands. It wasn't metal, as she'd thought at first glance – though it was dark enough to be iron. This material was less dense, and warmer to the touch. Ebonwood. And set within it, cloudy pieces of crystal like fragments of a winter lake. A beautiful thing. A creation of ice and ebonwood, like Ayla herself. It made her smile.

'Wood and ice,' Miles confirmed. 'Your elements. To enhance your strength.'

She lifted the collar to her throat, but stopped before it touched her skin. 'You know, Miles, my neck will get a whole lot bigger after I Change.'

He nodded. 'The collar should grow with you.'

'Should?'

'Er … I am almost certain it will. And if it does not, it will not choke you. Just fall to the floor.' He shifted uncomfortably beneath her stare. 'I think.'

'There seems to be a lot of speculation involved in this experiment, Miles.'

'Every step from theory to practice involves a leap of faith,' he answered. 'The question is really whether you trust me.'

In one smooth movement, he picked up the loaded pistol and cocked it. Ayla's pulse speeded up, her senses heightening automatically in preparation for the Change. But nothing happened. He simply stood there, weapon in hand, patiently waiting.

All right. If he was going to try and kill me, he could have done it already. She settled the collar around her neck.

The latent warmth she'd detected in it seemed to flare into heat, then subside – but the warmth was still there, running through her veins. *Something* was happening.

'When you are ready,' Miles said. She nodded once, then summoned the Change.

Once she'd settled into her other form, she snorted and tossed her head. The warmth in the collar was clearer now, spreading across her skin like a blanket. And yes, the collar had grown with her. Though it sat snugly around her neck, it didn't choke or constrict her.

Miles lifted his arm, pistol aimed at her chest, and instinctively she shied away.

'No need to worry,' he murmured. 'It will not be a fatal shot. If the collar fails to work and the bullet hits you, the worst you will be left with is a bruise.'

His arm swung round, finger tightening on the trigger, and Ayla braced herself against the deep-rooted urge to knock the weapon from his hand before running him through with her spiral horn. An instant later, the pistol fired. Her keen eyes saw the bullet approach her –

And hit.

She felt it, but it wasn't the impact she was waiting for. It was a slap rather than a punch, before the spent bullet dropped to the floor. All the same, she was knocked off balance, feet tangling, lungs tightening with the impact. While she fought to steady herself, Miles set the pistol to one side and peered down at the bullet.

'Well, now. That is interesting. It has flattened as though it hit a surface stronger than itself. The collar appears to have shielded you.'

He turned away, beginning to fiddle with the pistol again, as she returned to human form. Once she'd flung her robe back on and belted it tightly round her waist, she took a deep breath. 'What next?'

'Are you sure you are feeling quite well?' Miles still didn't face her.

'I think so.' She lifted a hand to touch the collar at her throat. 'This seems to work, at least in part. I didn't –'

Miles spun on his heel and shot her again.

This time, the bullet hit her properly. She just had time to be surprised before pain flared across her upper arm, incinerating all rational thought. Instinctively she clapped her other hand to the spot, backing away, summoning the Change –

'Lady Ayla.' Miles looked distressed, which gave her pause. 'Are you all right?'

She froze, teetering on the boundary between human and creature. *Of course I'm not all right!* she wanted to snap. *You shot me!* But when she took her hand away from the wound, peering at it to assess the damage, there was no blood. Her fingers were clean.

'It was a wooden bullet,' Miles said. 'I am terribly sorry. I just wanted to –'

'What?' she snapped. She might not be bleeding, but it still *hurt*. 'You wanted to what?'

'To be effective, the collar needs to work whatever form you are in.' He sounded apologetic, as well he might. 'It should have protected your human self from a bullet, just as it did your creature self. But it failed. And that is no good, Lady Ayla. We cannot neutralise this threat if all the assassin has to do is catch you in human form. If I were an assassin –'

'Which you're not,' she cut in pointedly, 'though I had my doubts there for a moment.'

307

He nodded. 'But if I were ... that is what I would try anyway. Because I know that is when you are most vulnerable. With or without alchemy.'

Ayla nodded; that was more or less exactly what she'd thought herself. Miles turned away to pick up something else from the table.

'Now, try this one.' He handed her another collar. This one was segmented, alternating dull grey metal, rich amber and pieces of clear glass. It looked more ... *dangerous* than the first collar, somehow. As soon as Ayla touched it, her skin prickled with reluctance.

'Wind, flame and steel,' Miles said, and she frowned.

'But surely, if my own elements strengthen me, these can only weaken me.'

He gave her an approving smile, tutor to student. 'That is one possibility, yes. But another is that they add what you lack. Knowing which possibility is correct will be key to any further work.'

'All right.' She unfastened the first collar and replaced it with the second. This one didn't feel warm against her skin; it sent a dizzy shiver deep into her bones. She pulled the collar of her shirt up around it, trying to block out the chill, and shook her head briskly as if she could rid herself of the sensation. 'I don't like it much.'

'You will get used to it, after a little while.' Miles was busy reloading the pistol, but he glanced over his shoulder. 'Will you Change again, Lady Ayla? We will test it on your creature form first.'

Ayla nodded slowly. She was tired, she realised. The energy required to Change, coupled with the stress of being shot at, had drained her. But they had to complete the experiment.

'Be careful, won't you?' she said faintly. 'If this collar weakens me in creature form, I'd hate you to kill me by mistake.'

He turned, pistol in hand, and smiled. 'No need to worry. I am a very good shot.'

'That doesn't really reassure me,' Ayla muttered. Still, they'd come too far for her to mistrust him now.

She summoned the Change – but something was wrong. The dizzying cold in her bones was getting stronger, swirling in her head. Her tiredness seemed to eat into the corners of her eyes, dissolving her surroundings in a wash of darkness.

The last thing she saw before she blacked out was the floor coming up to meet her.

Bryan rarely climbed up the hill to Darkhaven. Rarely went any higher than the fifth ring, in fact; temples weren't his thing. If Caraway wanted to discuss some matter of training or Helm business, he came down. But there were at least two occasions every year when Bryan passed through the Gate of Death: the days at the end of each assessment period, when Caraway invited the recruits he was considering for the Helm to see where they might end up in a year's time. On those days, it never failed to strike Bryan how bloody terrifying the tower must be to anyone who had never seen it up close before.

Blackstone was rare, possibly because the entire country's reserves had been depleted to build Darkhaven. He'd never seen any other building with more than a touch of it, and even then it was used in small pieces for decoration and enhancement, rather than great big chunks like it was here. And with good reason: Darkhaven *loomed*. It filled the sky like a vast, lightless tombstone. It probably wasn't as tall as it looked, but only because that would have been an architectural impossibility. And the inside was equally daunting.

Bryan had been into Darkhaven even less often than he'd visited the grounds, and it had mainly left him with a vague, uneasy memory of too many corners, as if the internal plan of the tower didn't match its exterior.

Yet Caraway never complained about it. Caraway lived there, and he didn't come down to the fifth ring with stories of losing his way along what should have been a perfectly normal, straight corridor. So Bryan was willing to concede that the whole thing was most likely just his imagination. Either that, or the Helm were given some sort of special knowledge that no-one else was allowed to share – because there was no denying that Bryan had got spectacularly bloody lost the last time he'd set foot inside Darkhaven.

'Amazing,' Penn remarked, far more animated than usual. 'It looks bigger, the closer you get to it.' But at the resulting jibe from one of the other recruits, his usual scowl returned to his face. 'I meant *disproportionately* bigger, Timo, obviously.'

All the same, he seemed happier than Bryan had seen him before. Maybe being accepted for Helm training had given him some kind of validation. Maybe he'd been a pain in the arse before because he was afraid of failure. Caraway must have seen past the attitude to something worthwhile, or the lad wouldn't be here at all.

When they reached the open ground in front of the tower, Bryan marshalled them into loose ranks to wait for Caraway. Once again, he found himself scanning their faces in search of … what? It wasn't as if an assassin would wear the fact on his face like war paint. They'd all left their weapons at the Gate of Death, aside from Bryan himself, so no-one could possibly break out a pistol and go rampaging up to Darkhaven with it. Yet despite that, Bryan realised, he was on edge. He was waiting for … something.

The postern gate creaked open, and he turned sharply, but it was only Marlon and his nurse on their usual afternoon walk. Bryan watched them disappear round the side of the hill, then glanced back at the recruits. They hadn't moved. He allowed himself a small smile. They were a decent bunch. Lot of potential between them. No doubt some of them would make fine Helmsmen in a year or two's time.

Assuming there's still a Nightshade overlord to guard, his doubts replied, but he shook them off. Ayla was in the tower. The trainees were unarmed outside the tower. The gate was guarded. He and Caraway were on the lookout for anything unusual. Nothing was going to go wrong.

The postern creaked again, and this time it was Caraway. He was wearing his full uniform for once, striped coat and all, with the captain's insignia on his shoulder and on the hilt of his sword. Out of the corner of his eye, Bryan saw several of the trainees straighten up in response.

'Welcome to Darkhaven,' Caraway greeted them. 'You're here because Weaponmaster Bryan and I believe that each and every one of you has the potential to become a member of the Helm. The year ahead of you won't be easy. The seven weeks you've just been through will seem like a summer picnic in comparison. But if you succeed, you'll win the right to walk through that gate in a Helmsman's coat. You'll win the right to do the most important job Mirrorvale has to offer, and protect those who protect us. There is no greater honour. There is no greater privilege.'

He'd given the same speech, or a variant of it, several times before; yet he always managed to sound sincere. One thing you could say about Tomas Caraway: he'd never stopped believing in the Helm, even when he wasn't a part of it. Bryan watched the bright, excited faces of the young people in front of him and wondered how many of them shared that belief. Most of them, presumably, or they wouldn't be here. Yet if his and Caraway's suspicions came to anything, one of those young people concealed a purpose that was the exact opposite of everything the Helm stood for.

It seemed that Caraway had been thinking along similar lines. When he'd finished his speech, he paused, then spoke again: slower, more hesitantly, but with even greater intensity.

'Usually this would be the point at which Lady Ayla came out to greet you. She needs to know your faces, after all, if some of you are to be her protectors one day. Yet given the ongoing threat of assassination, she thought it safer not to do that today.'

'But Zander –' Farleigh began, and Caraway shook his head.

'We have reason to believe that Zander may be innocent. And if that's the case, someone framed him. Someone who knew him. Someone who had access to his room. *That* –' his voice sharpened – 'is almost certainly one of you. So with that in mind, I would invite you all to look around you.'

Obediently, the trainees glanced at each other. Bryan searched each of them for a tell-tale sign, a hint of knowledge, but found only confusion.

'If you are standing here with murder in your heart,' Caraway said, 'I want you to know that everyone else on this hill is against you. These other men and women, whom you've trained with and eaten with and lived with – they're here because they want to join the Helm. They're here because they want to protect the Nightshade line from people like you. And so it's my prediction that I won't even have to lift a finger to stop you. Because I believe in your colleagues. I believe in their skill and their courage. They know you even better than I do, and I believe they will find you out.'

Dead silence. The recruits looked serious and uneasy. Bryan studied them again, feeling the tension rise in the air, feeling *something* about to happen –

And then, from her place in the middle of the group, Saydi screamed.

It was a harsh, ragged scream – a scream of intense pain. The trainees separated, moving away from her like a frightened flock of birds, turning to see what had happened. Bryan caught a glimpse of blood, shockingly bright.

'Out of the way!' he bellowed. The group scattered further, allowing him and Caraway to converge on Saydi. By now she was on the ground, rocking and moaning, clutching her side. Blood stained her fingers like a warning flag.

'Saydi.' Caraway crouched down beside her. 'What happened?'

'I – I –' She was hysterical. He gripped her shoulder. 'Don't panic. You'll be fine. Just breathe.'

Long moments passed, filled with nothing but her gasps as she fought for air. At one point Caraway appeared to make an attempt to examine the wound, but she flailed at him as if she thought he was trying to attack her. Finally she calmed down enough to force out a few broken words.

'S-sorry. I'm all r-right.'

'What happened?' Caraway asked again.

'I don't know. Someone – someone –' She took a deep, shuddering breath, then blinked at him with tearstained eyes. 'I think I was stabbed.'

Caraway looked up at Bryan, urgency in his face. 'Art – don't let any of them leave –'

It took some time for Bryan to get the shocked trainees into any semblance of order, and even then he wasn't immediately sure if anyone was missing. Yet before he could gather

his scattered wits enough to run through the list, Farleigh
piped up.

'Sir? Penn has gone.'

Penn walked away from the rest of the group as fast as he
could without running. He risked one glance back over his
shoulder, but no-one was watching him; they were all gathered around Saydi. He was impressed. When she'd offered to
cause a distraction that would allow him to sneak away, he
hadn't expected anything that dramatic. Still, she'd certainly
captured their attention. Now he just had to find Marlon –
and since he'd seen the boy leave Darkhaven with his nurse,
that shouldn't be too difficult.

Hurry, he told himself. *As soon as they notice you're gone,
they'll be after you.*

He was a little way round the hill, now, and he could see
the two figures ahead: Marlon, crouching down to examine
something on the ground, with the woman a short distance
behind him. *All right. You don't want to hurt her. And since
Saydi's provided the perfect excuse …*

He broke into a jog, putting a panicked expression on his
face – which wasn't hard. His heart was already pumping
like a piston.

'Excuse me?' he gasped as soon as he was close enough. The
nurse had already seen him coming; she'd stepped between
him and Marlon, a small knife in her hand. Penn hadn't
expected her to be armed. He concentrated on making himself
as unthreatening as possible.

'Excuse me?' he said again. 'Captain Caraway sent me.
You need to come quickly. Someone's wounded.'

Her expression changed from defiance to alarm. 'Wounded?'

'Yes. One of the other trainees.'

'You're here with the captain?' Her stance relaxed a little, and she lowered the knife. 'How on earth did someone get hurt with the captain around?'

'I don't know. An accident, I think. But please – he said you'd know what to do, and to come quickly –'

'What about the physician?'

It clearly hadn't occurred to her that both Caraway and Bryan would have plenty of experience at dealing with wounds. 'You were closer. Please hurry!'

She nodded, then glanced down at Marlon. 'What about –'

'I'll bring him after you,' Penn said. 'Please. She looked really bad.'

'She?' the nurse echoed, then shook her head as if to clear it. 'Never mind. I'll go. You're sure you're all right with –'

'I have little brothers of my own,' Penn said truthfully. He managed something close to a sob. 'Please – don't let her die.'

'It's that bad?' The alarm returned to the nurse's face, and she nodded briskly. 'Don't worry. I'll do what I can.'

She took off at a run, and Penn let out a long breath. Right. He'd done it. He'd got Marlon. So now what?

He looked down at the child by his feet, and the boy returned the gaze with a trembling lip. Renewed panic surged through Penn, because he hadn't planned beyond this point. And if Marlon started crying –

Ice and shattered steel, Penn. You really are useless at this. Why didn't you think it through before you had the boy within your grasp?

He fought back his sudden confusion and made himself consider the situation rationally. As soon as Caraway and Bryan had sorted out Lori's story, they'd be after him. Probably the Helmsmen from the gate, too, and maybe even more from inside the tower. That wasn't what he wanted. He didn't want to be forced to threaten Marlon's life in front of a whole group of armed men, only to end up being cut down by them before he ever had a chance to confront Caraway. Which meant ideally he'd get Marlon as far away from Darkhaven as possible, forcing Caraway to come after him. If he could get himself and Marlon into a position where they could only be reached by one person at a time, meaning that Caraway had to approach them alone –

A memory dropped into his mind with the force of a lightning strike, and he grinned. Of course. He should have thought of it before. It had, after all, been Caraway's own idea.

'Come on, Marlon,' he said, bending to scoop the boy into his arms. 'We're going on a little trip.'

TWENTY-FOUR

Penn has gone. Crouched on the ground beside the injured girl, Caraway heard the words, yet somehow he couldn't quite grasp what they meant.

For a moment, he and Saydi stared at each other. Her hazel eyes were already brimming with tears, but now they looked frightened, too. Then, slowly, he raised his gaze to Farleigh.

'Gone? Gone where?'

'I don't know,' Farleigh said defensively – and indeed, Caraway realised in some corner of his mind, he had spoken with more fire than usual. 'I just noticed he was missing, that's all.'

Shit. Caraway jumped to his feet, scanning the faces of the trainees. 'Did anyone see him go?'

They shook their heads. Caraway glanced up at the tower, but the two Helmsmen at the gate were still there. Penn couldn't have got into Darkhaven.

Maybe he's gone to relieve himself. Maybe Saydi's blood turned his stomach – it takes them that way sometimes. Maybe ...

But his heart told him something different. Because someone must have hurt Saydi, after all. And if Penn was the only one missing now, it must be because he was the one who'd wanted to cause a diversion. But why? If he hadn't gone after Ayla, where had he gone?

'Captain Caraway!' He turned to see Marlon's nursemaid, Lori, hastening towards him. He strode forward to meet her.

'Lori! What is it? Where's Marlon?'

'He told me it was urgent,' she said breathlessly. 'He said he'd bring Marlon after.'

'Who?' Caraway grabbed her shoulders, though he already knew the answer. 'Who said that?'

'Your recruit. Tall young man. Lightish hair, sort of an intense way about him ...' Her gaze flickered over the others, then settled on Saydi. 'I take it that's her?'

Caraway didn't answer. His whole being was focused on the desperate, plunging fear that clawed at his guts. *He's taken Marlon. Penn has taken Marlon. But why. Why?*

'C-Captain Caraway?' Saydi said. He glanced down; her lip trembled, but her expression was resolute. 'I – I'm afraid Penn means to hurt him.'

And with that, she fainted.

Means to hurt him. For an instant longer, Caraway was paralysed by fear. He concentrated on compressing it into a tiny, solid ball – one that sat in his stomach like a cold weight but no longer dragged every part of him down into inaction. Then he turned back in the direction of the Helmsmen at Darkhaven's gate and sent them the swooping, high-to-low whistle that would summon them to his side.

'Lori, look after Saydi,' he ordered while he was waiting for them to arrive. 'She wouldn't let me examine her wound, but now she's out you should have an easier time of it. The rest of you –' he glanced around at the trainees – 'spread out across the hillside and look for Penn. Stay in groups of at least three or four. If you find him, send a runner for me.

Don't try anything stupid. He's got Marlon with him, and I don't want anyone getting hurt. Understand?'

They nodded, wide-eyed. Several of them cast glances at Saydi's unconscious form as though wondering if they'd be next. But Caraway had no time to spare for reassurances, because by now the guards from the gate were at his side. He explained the situation to them in as few words as possible, before sending them off on their search. Then he and Bryan headed in the direction that Lori had come from.

They found the flower patch where Marlon liked to play, but there was no sign of either Marlon or Penn. Caraway turned in a circle, looking frantically in all directions, but saw nothing to indicate which direction they'd gone in. His thoughts were bouncing all over the place. Because he'd done this three years ago, hadn't he? Gone chasing after a kidnapped member of the Nightshade line. Only that time, it had turned out to be a decoy.

Of course, that surely couldn't be true this time. Marlon was gone. The nurse had last seen him in Penn's company. There wasn't any room for confusion. Yet all the same, Caraway's mind kept whirring. Was this a coincidence – two vendettas against Darkhaven, Zander's and Penn's, that had happened to coincide? Or was Zander innocent and Penn the real assassin? And if the latter, why had he gone after Marlon instead of Ayla? It made no sense from a tactical point of view. A child, even a Nightshade child, would have no part to play in the defence of Mirrorvale. Unless Caraway and Bryan had misunderstood exactly what it was the Kardise intended their assassin to achieve. Or unless Penn planned to use Marlon against Ayla in some way …

That brought him up short. He forced himself to stop and think. Penn couldn't hope to get into Darkhaven without being seen, not with the Helmsmen and his fellow recruits all searching the grounds. And he must know he stood no chance of defending himself against all those people out in the open, even using Marlon as a shield. So whatever his intentions, the chances were he'd have left the seventh ring as soon as he could.

Caraway gestured to Bryan, and the two of them ran down the hill to the Gate of Death. Sure enough, the guards at the gate had seen a young man and a little boy pass by. The young man had only lingered long enough to pick up his sword.

Caraway's fists clenched. 'Why didn't you stop them?'

The little boy hadn't seemed unhappy, the guards explained in some confusion. He was chattering away, something about an adventure. And they'd recognised the young man. He was the one who'd been given the freedom of the sixth ring by Captain Caraway himself. So it was reasonable to assume that Captain Caraway trusted him.

'But the boy!' Caraway protested. 'That was Marlon Nightshade. Surely you recognised him?'

The guards exchanged glances, then shrugged. It wasn't the city watch's job to prevent people from descending through Arkannen. They were only concerned with people trying to climb higher than they'd a right to.

Caraway shook his head in frustration. It was the same principle that had allowed Ayla to escape from Darkhaven, three years ago. And, in general, it was a reasonable one. But fire and blood! Why couldn't the watch use a little common sense?

'Come on,' Bryan said, calling him out of his fulminating thoughts. 'The lad's through the gate. Can't do anything about that now. So where will he have gone?'

320

'I don't know!' Caraway slammed his fist into his palm. 'I don't understand it! He's clearly not after Ayla. He wasn't mistreating Marlon –' But at that point his voice failed him, because Marlon was so very small to be out in the world with a stranger. If Penn wanted to hurt the little boy, kill him, there was nothing Caraway could do about it.

Yet even now, he didn't think Penn was a bad person. Angry, yes, and clearly harbouring a grudge against Caraway himself, but that didn't mean he was capable of the kind of cruelty required to injure a small child. No, this kidnapping was intended solely to provoke a response. Penn wanted to stage some kind of showdown, and taking Marlon was his way of ensuring that Caraway would come after him.

Some kind of showdown ...

The perfect place for a heroic last stand. The memory flared into life, and with it conviction. He set off again, moving at a jog.

'He'll have gone to the Spire of Air.'

When they got there, Caraway spotted Penn straight away. It wasn't exactly difficult. He and Marlon were up on the platform that sat halfway up the spire itself. The very high platform, separated from a vertiginous drop by a single rail that a child could easily slip underneath –

Dizzy fear danced in Caraway's head; he closed his eyes, willing it to pass. If only Ayla had been with him! With her wings, she could have been up to that platform and taking Marlon back before Penn had time to blink. He should have sent for her as soon as Marlon went missing. He should have brought reinforcements instead of trying to do everything himself. The similarities between this incident and the one three years ago had fooled him into thinking he was the only man who could do the job. Once again, he'd set himself up as the Nightshade line's last hope.

Stupid, he told himself. *Stupid and arrogant. If Marlon dies –*

But he shook his head to cast that thought away. Marlon wasn't going to die. He'd do whatever it took to get the boy back safely.

The high priestess met him at the door. Beyond her, a little huddle of priestesses were gathered at the foot of the stair that climbed up to the external walkway, peering upwards.

'Captain Caraway,' the high priestess greeted him calmly. 'I take it you are here to deal with this situation.'

'What happened?'

'The young man came running in here and made straight for the spire. Naturally we were unable to stop him. He has a sword.'

'He also has Marlon Nightshade,' Caraway said grimly. 'Leave it to me. Please make sure none of your sisters do anything rash.'

She inclined her head. 'Of course.'

Caraway and Bryan took the steps two at a time, but when they reached the roof of the temple and the staircase turned into the walkway that climbed the spire, Caraway turned to the weaponmaster.

'Art, please stay here. I'll handle this.'

'Tomas, are you sure –'

'I said I'll handle it,' Caraway said, more forcefully than he'd intended. 'He's my *son*.'

Bryan's heavy brows drew into a frown, but he didn't argue any further. He stood back, and Caraway began to climb the walkway alone.

When he reached the platform, he was confronted by the point of a sword. Penn's face was pale and set, but his grip on the weapon was perfectly steady. From somewhere beyond him, Marlon whimpered.

'Papa!'

Ignoring the sword, Caraway leaned to one side to catch a glimpse of the boy. He was standing by the guard rail, one wrist cuffed to it. When his eyes met Caraway's, his lower lip trembled. 'Don't like it any more. Want to go home.'

Caraway's fists clenched, but he forced all traces of anger out of his voice before replying. 'We'll go home very soon, Marlon. Don't worry. Everything will be fine.'

Scowling, Penn took a pace back and gestured with the tip of his sword for Caraway to come up. Caraway stood still on the last step of the walkway and just looked at him.

'Aren't you going to kill me, Penn? You've made it clear enough that's what you want.'

'I'm not a murderer,' Penn shot back. 'Not like you.'

What? Caraway shook his head in honest incomprehension. 'And who exactly am I supposed to have murdered?'

Penn's lip lifted in a sneer. 'You don't know who I am, do you?'

'You're Penn Avens ...' But Caraway fell silent as Penn shook his head.

'My name is Penn Travers. Owen Travers was my cousin.'

Sorrow lurked in the doorway that led from the stairwell to the roof of the warehouse, watching the scene before her. After a couple of near-miss encounters with guards and one lucky overheard remark, she'd found her way up here – where, as it turned out, Eight kept an entire fleet of two-man airships, the kind they would have referred to as balloons in Mirrorvale. The Kardise called them skyboats. There had been several of them tethered to the roof when she arrived, but they'd been taking off one at a time since then; the last-but-one was currently filling up with gas in preparation to follow the rest. They were going after Elisse. At least, she had to assume they were, or everything she'd done would prove futile. And so once there was only a single skyboat left, she'd have to incapacitate its small crew and fly it after the other craft.

Though Sorrow had many skills, hijacking an airship armed with only a knife and a chair leg wasn't one she'd had to use before.

Still, she had no choice if she wanted to stand any chance of intervening in Elisse's capture. Air travel was by far the quickest way of getting anywhere, so if she wanted to keep up, she needed to fly too. In which case, she'd better stop worrying that it was impossible and simply get on with it.

When the penultimate skyboat finally rose into the air – its warmed-up engines growling, the propellers spluttering into life – the two men left on the rooftop began to prepare their own craft. One of them climbed into the gondola to crank the engine and open the valves that would let more gas into the envelope, whilst the other began to release the tethers that held the ship to the ground. Sorrow took a moment to consider her strategy: since she was short on time and energy, swift incapacitation was the way forward. She'd just have to get it right first try.

As soon as both men's backs were turned, she launched herself on noiseless feet across the rooftop. Well, almost noiseless – her wounded foot dragged a little despite all her care, creating a faint scuffing sound that would have been audible were it not for the hiss of the gas entering the skyboat's envelope. She got nearly all the way to the first man before he caught the movement in his peripheral vision, and by then it was too late. He had time for no more than the start of a warning shout before the chair leg caught him on the temple, dropping him bonelessly to the floor.

Yet that cut-off cry might be her undoing, Sorrow thought grimly. It had alerted the second man, who'd turned and was looking at her from inside the gondola. If he decided his best course of action was to pull up the anchor and take off –

Fortunately, he didn't. Unfortunately, that was because he had a pistol and he knew that gave him the advantage. Had their situations been reversed, Sorrow would have shot him without a thought. She braced herself for the deadly impact, but it didn't come. Instead, he leapt nimbly over the side of the gondola with the pistol in one hand. Perhaps he wanted information from her, or perhaps he was just over-confident. Either way, in the instant it took him to recover from his landing, she swung the chair leg again and hit the pistol with it, as hard as she could. It flew from his hand and skittered across the roof, going off with a bang before falling over the edge.

Damn it. I could have used that pistol. With a resigned shrug, Sorrow brought the chair leg back round, this time into the second man's head. He crumpled beside the first. *Huh. I never realised a chair leg could be such an effective weapon.*

Despite that, she left it lying beside the two prone men when she clambered into the skyboat. The next part was going to require more than a chunk of wood to handle. She still had the knife, and that was a start, but with any luck she'd be able to retrieve her spare set of pistols from Elisse.

Before that, though ... She studied the controls of the craft before her in some bewilderment. *How the fuck do you fly an airship?*

TWENTY-FIVE

The two boys with Ree were bickering about the best way to search for Penn and Marlon, but she did her best to block them out. She needed to think. There was something ... *something* ... if she could only put her finger on it ...

Everyone has gone off after Penn. It came to her in a flash, from some hidden part of herself that was clearly more intelligent than she'd realised. *But if Penn has taken Marlon, he isn't the assassin. I don't know what he is – an accomplice? A stooge? – but he isn't that. Which means this whole thing could just be a cover.*

She nodded to herself. That made sense. Yet it wasn't the whole of what was bothering her. Because even in the throes of panic for his adopted son, Captain Caraway had done everything right. He'd called the guards off the gate, but he'd asked them to lock it behind them; so although it was only locked rather than bolted from the inside, it wasn't accessible to the casual intruder.

Zander could open it, the same small part of her observed. *Even you could open it. You've been carrying those lockpicks around with you for weeks.*

All right. So someone could get in, if they had the knowledge and the will. But Caraway had covered that as well. He'd kept the trainees in groups of three or four, ostensibly for their own safety, but also – and Ree knew this would have been deliberate – so that no single one of them could overpower the others. They were all on their guard. They'd be looking out for any suspicious behaviour. There wasn't any way an assassin could sneak off into Darkhaven under cover of Penn's inexplicable and reckless act.

But Penn wasn't the first distraction, her brain said. *The first distraction was Saydi …*

The revelation was coming. She could feel the shape of it up ahead. Her thoughts tumbled over themselves in their haste to get there.

Saydi was stabbed, and that's what allowed Penn to get away.

At least, we assume Saydi was stabbed. All we can really say is that there was blood.

And now she's up near Darkhaven's gate with only Marlon's nurse for company.

Which means it's likely that Saydi …

Saydi is the assassin.

The idea seemed ridiculous, but Ree forced herself to think about it rationally. And once she started looking for the evidence, it piled up thick and fast.

She's much better at swordplay than she looks. And probably even better than that; she made mistakes in training, but she must have done something right to get through the private testing.

She tried to get a job in Darkhaven before signing up for assessment. Which implies she wanted to get in there by whatever means she could.

She's the one who said it was impossible for anyone in the fifth ring to have a pistol without the weaponmasters knowing it, which may have been what sent Captain Caraway off to the gun-sellers the very next day. And that led to Zander's arrest.

She claimed to have been stabbed, yet she wouldn't let anyone close enough to examine the wound. Come on, Ree! That should have been suspicious in itself, only you were too stupid to notice.

She and Penn spent a lot of time together ... so she could have been aware of Penn's intentions and planned to use them as a cover ...

Ree stopped dead, her heart racing. 'I've had enough of this,' she called to the two boys in front of her. 'I'm going to find out how Saydi is.'

They returned absent-minded agreement without even looking up from their quarrel. Ree wanted to shake them. *We're supposed to be on the alert for a potential killer, and you're just going to let me wander off in the direction of Darkhaven by myself? What, you think a girl can't be an assassin?*

It's what you thought about Saydi, isn't it? the snarky, intelligent spark inside her replied. *The evidence was right there in front of your nose, and you didn't see it because she's feminine and giggly and good at looking helpless. You're an idiot.*

Ree was really beginning to hate that part of herself.

Still, there was no time to lose. Abandoning the oblivious boys, she turned on her heel and set off at a jog to where they'd left Saydi and Lori. The nurse had been kneeling beside Saydi, who'd been lying unconscious on the grass. But as Ree got nearer, she saw that only one prone figure remained.

Lori's sightless eyes gazed at the sky. The hilt of the knife still protruded from beneath her ribs. Saydi was nowhere to be seen.

Ree raised her head, and saw Darkhaven's gate rocking slightly in the breeze.

None of us came armed. But she's left the knife behind. Which must mean she has access to another weapon ...

She must have access to a pistol.

As if in a trance, she leaned down and pulled the knife out of Lori's body. She didn't like to do it, but if she was going to fight an assassin, she'd need some kind of weapon. It came free with a faint sucking sound and a fresh gush of blood. Ree winced, but she didn't have time to hesitate. If she wasn't quick, there'd be more death ahead of her.

Gripping the bloody knife, she ran after Saydi.

Kai slipped through the door into the transformation room and closed it behind her. She waited there for a little while, just in case anyone had seen her and followed, but no-one was even looking. They were all too distracted by Marlon's kidnapping to remember basic security procedures. Of course, as far as most of the Helm were concerned, the assassination threat had been defused; Captain Caraway and one or two others were clearly still suspicious, but Captain Caraway was far too concerned right now to be thinking straight.

Swiftly she unbuckled the small bottle that was strapped to her side. They hadn't been allowed to bring any weapons up to the tower, of course, but no-one had noticed the flat hip flask beneath her clothing. At the appropriate moment, she'd simply released the pin that held the cap in place and let the blood she'd bought from the slaughterhouse do its job. As she'd hoped, the apparent injury coupled with her fainting fit had led everyone to overlook her in the subsequent panic caused by Penn's actions.

Of course, she'd intended them to leave her alone where she'd fallen. She hadn't expected the nurse. And even though the woman hadn't been on her guard, making it easy for Kai to overpower her and take the very useful knife from her belt, she'd tried her best to fight back. Indeed, she'd done a good job of getting her nails into Kai's face before Kai stabbed her. With a frown, Kai touched the long scratch on her cheek, then let her hand fall. No matter. She'd succeeded. She was in Darkhaven.

As she moved away from the door and headed across the vast room to the table of alchemy equipment set out on the far side, she allowed herself a satisfied smile – because, all in all, it had been very easy to get here. A simple matter of making a few deliberate mistakes in training, then letting a hint of her real talent shine through at the final test. Caraway had been genuinely impressed by what he saw as her rapid improvement, and so he'd picked her to come up to the tower with the others. It hadn't even occurred to him that every single error had been finely judged to create the right impression: not skilled enough to be suspicious, but skilled enough to be worth teaching. He was a decent enough fighter, but he had no subtlety. None of them did. As far as her fellow trainees were concerned, she was exactly what she'd seemed.

She'd wondered from the start if a few of them would turn out to be of use to her, but she could never have imagined quite how useful. Zander had made the perfect scapegoat. A Kardise boy – the son of a government official, no less – hiding behind a false name, pretending to be Mirrorvalese … Kai couldn't have planned it better. And as for Penn, willing to do anything to satisfy his grudge against Caraway, he had proved to be an even greater piece of good fortune. Cultivating her relationship with him had been the best move she could have made. Not only would he provide her with the perfect distraction, but if he acted according to her careful suggestion, he'd end up killing Marlon.

It had frustrated Kai that she hadn't been able to see her way clear to disposing of Marlon and Ayla at the same time, given that they were so rarely together, so it pleased her greatly that Penn's involvement would swat two flies with one blow. Not that she had anything against the child, as such. But though Marlon wasn't a monster yet, no doubt he would be one day – and it would suit neither Kai's purposes nor the Brotherhood's if he survived to be concealed by Mirrorvalese loyalists until he reached his majority. A long-lost heir was a romantic enough figure that he could stir an oppressed people to rebellion, particularly if that long-lost heir was backed by all the strength and power of a Changer creature.

You care nothing for your country, then? her mentors had asked during the early days of her preparation. *If you perform this task, Mirrorvale will lose its main protection and be subjugated by Sol Kardis in perpetuity. You accept that?*

Kai had only shrugged. She cared less than the snap of her fingers for the fate of Mirrorvale, or indeed Sol Kardis. She just wanted to see the Nightshade line destroyed. After that, nothing else mattered. And her genuine indifference must have convinced the Brotherhood, because here she was: about to fulfil her childhood dream and slay a dragon. It was of benefit to them to send her, after all. If she were caught, there'd be nothing to link her to Sol Kardis. She was simply a disaffected Mirrorvalese citizen with a grudge against the throne. Though it was clear that rumour of Kardise involvement had come to Darkhaven's ears – and indeed, that was why she had fixed on Zander as a scapegoat – they would never be able to prove it.

Of course, that wouldn't be relevant once Ayla was dead. After that, Sol Kardis would be glad to show its hand. Because Ayla's death would reveal Mirrorvale as no more than what it truly was: a tiny country that was as capable of standing against the might of its neighbours as a babe in arms against a grown man. It might take a few months for Arkannen to fall, with its rings and its gates and the Helm in Darkhaven. But fall it would, in the end. What would the Helm have left to fight for, once their overlord was dead and gone?

Kai just had to get on with killing the monster.

Ignoring the glassware and other paraphernalia scattered across the table, she went straight to her small, carved travelling chest. It had been almost laughably straightforward to get it into Darkhaven. She'd seen Bryan and Miles enter the fifth ring together on the first day of training; having identified Miles based on the conversation she'd overheard between Bryan and Ayla the day before, she'd fetched the chest and pretended to be struggling with it as she left the barracks. By that time, Miles had left Bryan at the training hall and was busy pulling his wheeled cart full of alchemist's junk up towards the Gate of Ice. Once Kai had accidentally-on-purpose blundered into him and explained her intention to sell the chest in the first ring, he'd been more than eager to buy it from her – as she'd hoped. Because although the chest had been built to appeal to the Nightshade line, she'd guessed it would be equally fascinating to an alchemist. And although her original plan had been to send it to Ayla as an anonymous gift, sending it through Miles was far less suspicious. The Helm had searched it, of course, as they had everything else, but they hadn't found anything untoward. No-one ever did.

Then yesterday she'd asked Miles about the chest, casually, wondering whether he was finding it useful. Penn had been so reluctant to engage in any kind of normal human interaction that he'd missed that part of the conversation entirely. And during the subsequent chat, she'd learned all about Miles's work with Ayla and – more importantly – where they carried it out.

Now Kai opened the lid, pressed the hidden catches, and pulled her pistol from its weeks-long hiding place.

As she prepared it, checking each part carefully to make sure it was unaffected by its long sojourn in hiding, she found she was humming softly. An old song, one from her childhood: one her father used to sing her, before he was murdered. Fitting that it should have crept into her head now, when she was about to avenge his death.

She'd seen it happen. Her little family had all been at home, snug in their townhouse to the side of the market square, when the Firedrake came winging its way over the horizon. Just her father, her mother and her – that was how it had always been. Some of the other girls had siblings and cousins and aunts, but not Kai. *We don't need anyone else*, her mother always said. *We've got each other*.

That hadn't seemed enough for her father, lately. He looked worried all the time, a permanent frown between his brows. Once or twice he'd even snapped at her, which he'd never done before. He'd always been the most patient and gentle of men.

Don't fret about him, Kai's mother said. *It's just a bad business deal. It'll work itself out*. But the frown on her own face told a different story.

And then the Firedrake arrived in town. Kai watched from her window in mingled awe and dread as it landed in the square, vast wings cutting the air, talons scraping against the stone. She gasped as the beast dissolved in a swirl of black smoke, to remake itself as a tall man with black hair, pale skin and piercing dark eyes. The mayor came running to his side. The tall man gave his orders. And the town militia came for Kai's father.

There were four of them, in the end, standing in front of the tall man. Kai was still young, so she didn't understand everything that was said. Something about theft. Something about taxes. She huddled at her mother's side with the rest of the crowd in the square, letting the words wash over her, and wondered when her father would be free to return home and finish their game of skipping-stones.

The tall man said something. One of her father's friends raised his voice in answer. The tall man snapped something else, and now they were all shouting, her father's voice a familiar thread among the rest –

And then the tall man swirled and shifted back into his Firedrake form, and let out a long, fierce jet of flame that swept across the four men like a fiery wave. People screamed. The crowd became a herd, scrabbling to retreat from danger, each fleeing for his life without regard for anyone around him. Kai started towards her father, but her mother grabbed her arm and pulled her back. The Firedrake lifted a clawed foot and raked one of her father's friends from throat to guts. It seized a second in its mighty jaws, shaking him in a spray of blood. And then it reached her father –

Kai saw it in her nightmares for years afterwards. The tearing. The inhuman screams. The spattering blood.

She'd lived with her mother until the wasting disease took her, less than a year later. And then eleven-year-old Kai had turned her back on Arkannen, lair of the monster to whom she owed her vengeance, and travelled further south. Across the border to Sol Kardis, a country known for its hatred of Mirrorvale and Changers. She'd trained as an assassin for the Brotherhood in the mutual understanding that as soon as a way to kill Florentyn Nightshade was discovered, she would be the one to undertake the task.

Only by the time the relevant knowledge finally came to light, Florentyn Nightshade was dead.

Still, one Changer was much like another. A monster was still a monster, and the world would be a better place without any of them in it. Kai might not be able to revenge herself upon the man who'd killed her father, but she could certainly take his daughter's life in payment.

Once the pistol was primed and ready, she took the knife from the other secret compartment and slipped it into her belt; the pistol would do the job, but it was always wise to have a backup plan. Then she left the transformation room through a different door – the one that led deeper into Darkhaven, rather than back to the central square. Now all she had to do was find Ayla. And with the knowledge she'd gleaned from Miles, that wouldn't take long.

Time to slay the dragon.

TWENTY-SIX

By the time the hill that concealed Elisse's cottage came into sight, Sorrow's arms ached with the strain of keeping her unfamiliar vehicle on course, and her ears felt as if they'd never be free of the rattle and rumble of the engine – not to mention the continuous throbbing pain in her foot. One thing was for sure, these smaller airships weren't nearly as comfortable as their larger counterparts. Nor were they as easy to control as they looked. It was a constant battle not to veer off in random directions, or nosedive into the earth.

Still, she didn't think the occupants of the other craft had noticed anything wrong. It was very hard to tell at a distance who was inside the gondola of an airship, so the Brotherhood's men must be assuming that her skyboat was manned by the last two of their crew, as planned. And since the four or five craft that had taken off ahead of her had deliberately spread themselves out to make the journey – several independent ships being far less noticeable than a small fleet – they were unlikely to discover otherwise until they reached their destination. At that point, Sorrow would have to deviate from their path and land separately, but she hoped that because the Brotherhood were using unmarked skyboats of the kind that many wealthy people kept to travel swiftly around the country, they would simply conclude that they'd been mistaken regarding the identity of her ship.

There was certainly no chance she could follow them all the way. By now, it was clear they were going to cut their engines and vent gas to make a quiet landing at the top of the hill – the exact scenario she'd imagined the last time she was with Elisse, in fact, which both satisfied and annoyed her. Anyway, it would be suicidal for Sorrow to do the same, because the ambush party was bound to wait until all the craft were down before approaching the cottage. And if they thought she was one of them now, they certainly wouldn't think that once they saw her. So as she got nearer, she wrangled the airship round the side of the hill. She'd have to land in the meadow below the cottage, despite the steepness of the slope there. The trees and the building itself should conceal her from the party at the top of the hill, and with any luck she'd be able to get Elisse and Corus out before the Brotherhood's men arrived.

Great. Relying on luck again. Still, it's got me this far.

She circled round to approach the meadow from below, then – *no time to waste* – went in for the landing. But she'd misjudged it in the failing daylight, come in too fast. The skyboat bucked and plunged in the air like an unruly horse, before its envelope lurched sideways and the sheer weight of the gas dragged it off balance. Though she hauled on the controls with all her strength, nothing could stop the descent. And if the envelope ruptured and released its contents to be caught by a spark from the engine –

Time to bail. As the ground rose swiftly up to meet her, Sorrow released her flying straps, grabbed the unlit gas lamp that served as a headlamp at night, and dived over the side of the gondola. She hit hard, driving all the breath from her lungs, but did her best to turn the awkward fall into a roll. After a gasping interval during which it felt like every single part of her body was slamming into jagged rocks, she jolted to a stop and looked up. The skyboat hadn't met its end in a ball of fire, as she'd expected, but it was a wreck: the envelope listing and misshapen, the gondola crumpled beyond repair. She wouldn't be able to nip in, fetch Elisse and Corus, then depart as quickly as she'd come. She'd stranded herself in enemy territory.

A movement caught her eye, and she turned her head to see a couple of dark figures approaching stealthily through the trees that bordered the meadow. Either the ambushers had got down the hill really quickly, or the ones she'd followed had merely been the rearguard of a greater force. Still, she didn't have time to think for long. If they found her, she'd be screwed. If they found the ruined aircraft – the noise of which had clearly caught their attention – without a pilot, they'd come looking for her and she'd still be screwed. So she grabbed the sparker from the gas lamp she was still clutching in both hands, lit it, and threw it into the gondola. Then, as noiselessly as she could, she wriggled over to the stream and dropped over the edge to lie flat in the shallow water.

The airship exploded.

All right, perhaps *exploded* was a strong word. But the whole thing caught fire so suddenly and quickly that for the first time, Sorrow understood the true meaning of the phrase *burst into flame*. The heat of it was intense enough that it had its own sound, a sizzling roar that filled her ears. And then the envelope split open, releasing a further cloud of fire into the air, and bits of waxy-coated canvas rained down over everything. Sorrow put her hands on her head and waited for the world to stop burning.

Once her ears were no longer ringing, she was able to make out a few snatches of the conversation between the dark figures. As she'd hoped, their consensus was that no-one could have survived the crash and subsequent blaze. Less happily, she also gathered that the cottage was completely surrounded. The Brotherhood hadn't taken any chances. They'd sent enough snipers to cover every exit and more besides. The party she'd followed were tasked with entering the cottage and bringing out Corus.

'And his mother?' one of the men said.

'Expendable. They want her alive if possible, but better she dies than we lose the boy.'

Anger clenched Sorrow's hands into tight fists. She considered simply walking up behind him and stabbing him in the back – she'd probably be able to take out the other one, too, before he recovered from his shock – but she fought down the vicious urge with an effort. It was important that she didn't draw attention to herself. Maybe she'd have risked it if she still had her escape vehicle, but as it was …

As it was, she needed to reach the cottage first.

Of course, the entire Kardise attack team was between it and her, but she'd remembered the hole in the hedgerow. If she cut across the meadow and took down Elisse's barrier, she'd have a chance of getting ahead. So she waited for the men to leave, before wriggling out of the stream and setting off at a run, hoping the contrast between the blazing airship and the dim evening light would help to conceal her. She kept her head low and put a zigzag in her route, just in case one of the snipers spotted her, but it was an unnecessary precaution. Sooner than she'd expected, she was at the meadow boundary. She worked her way along it, cursing silently at the prickly thorns, until she found the patched-up hole. After that, it was a quick enough task to dismantle the barrier and push her way through to the other side –

But she was too late. The black-clad men were walking quickly and silently up the path towards the front door of the cottage. Even as Sorrow watched from the shadowed shelter of the hedgerow, they opened it and went in. She caught the glint of the covering pistols through the dusk. They were going to take Corus, and Elisse was bound to fight back, and then she'd end up being killed –

A whisper sounded, startlingly close, in Sorrow's ear. 'Naeve!'

Sorrow jumped and spun, knife at the ready, but her heart had recognised the voice before her brain did; it was already flooding her body with pure, joyful relief.

'Elisse!' she hissed. 'What are you doing out here? Where's Corus?'

'Hid him in the hay store, jus' like we said. The two o' us were picking berries in the top meadow when the first lot came. They didn' look ta me like people we wanted ta meet, so I figured we wouldn' go back ta the house jus' yet.'

'Perfect,' Sorrow said. 'If we can get away without them noticing us, they'll probably stay here all night, waiting for you to return.'

'Who are they, Naeve?'

'The Kardise Brotherhood. They're after Corus, just as we feared.'

Elisse's face paled, but her lips set in a grim line.

'We have ta go back ta Mirrorvale, don' we?' she whispered.

'It's what I've been telling you.'

'I know.' Elisse frowned. 'If they know Corus is in the country, won' they be watching the border?'

'Maybe not yet,' Sorrow said. 'At the moment they still think I'm locked up and you're out for the day. But that's going to change very soon. Sooner than we can get to the border, I reckon.'

'What if we wen' back to the city and caught an airship?'

Sorrow shook her head. 'It's not that easy. The Kardise place strict restrictions on who can fly where. All the captains are thoroughly checked and are only allowed to carry approved passengers. And I don't have any favours left to call in – not in Kardissak, anyway.'

'Then what? Are ya saying there's no way out o' the country?'

'No.' Sorrow grinned. 'I'm saying we indulge in a spot of theft. The Kardise came in small airships that are designed to carry two. And since I've already stolen and destroyed one of those today, I might as well steal another.'

'Oh. Right.' Elisse brought her right hand out from behind her back. 'Then ya might be wanting these.'

She was holding the case that contained Sorrow's spare pair of pistols.

'I could kiss you,' Sorrow muttered. And promptly did. 'All right, then. Let's go get Corus, and find ourselves a getaway vehicle.'

The Kardise had left a couple of armed men to guard their skyboats, of course – they weren't stupid. But they were watching for a mother attempting to flee with a young child, not a pair of women wielding pistols of their own. And besides, on their way to the hay store and back again, Sorrow had come up with a plan. As soon as they neared the bare crest of the hill, she swung Corus down off her back onto the ground.

'Are you ready?' she asked softly. Elisse clasped her son's hand and gave a grim nod; her free hand held one of the pistols, concealed in the folds of her skirt. Sorrow nodded back. Then she began to edge quietly along the treeline, whilst Elisse stumbled out of the shadows into the moonlight, head down, dragging Corus with her. Surprised at the sudden change, he began to wail. Immediately the guards set off down the hill towards them.

'Stop right there!' one of them called, raising his own gun. Elisse jerked her head up – Sorrow couldn't see the expression on her face, but she could imagine the shock and dismay; the woman was a damn good actress – and promptly tripped over her own feet, tumbling to the ground.

'Mama, get up!' Corus tugged at her sleeve.

'I can't, it's my ankle – run, Corus, remember wha' we talked about? Run!' And then, with an artistic flair that Sorrow couldn't help but admire, she pretended to faint.

When I tell you, she'd said to Corus earlier, *run as fast as you can back to Naeve. It's a game. You have to try and get there before the man catches you.*

So Corus ran for the spot in the woodland where he'd last seen Sorrow, and one of the guards promptly followed him.

What if they shoot him? Elisse had asked, and Sorrow had shaken her head.

They need him alive. At least until they know Ayla's dead.

Now, as the guard was about to pass her, she moved swiftly and silently out of the trees with her pistol trained on his head. 'Stop. Drop your weapon.'

He skidded to a halt, the pistol falling from his hand. Out of the corner of her eye, Sorrow saw the other guard – who'd holstered his gun and crouched down at Elisse's side – begin to straighten up; but Elisse's eyes opened, her arm came round to jab her own pistol into his belly, and her voice said in accented Kardise, 'Don't move.'

'Naeve!' Corus had veered off course as soon as he spotted her, and now stood at her side, grinning up at her. 'Did I win?'

Sorrow used her pistol to gesture the first guard up the hill. Beyond her, Elisse had scrambled back to her feet, the weapon in her hand never wavering as she directed the second man.

'Yes, son,' Sorrow said. 'You did.'

As well as Corus, the hay store had yielded some handy bale twine. Sorrow and Elisse herded the guards to the top of the hill, where Elisse kept them in place with both pistols whilst Sorrow began trussing them up. She'd been ready to kill them, earlier, but Elisse had dissuaded her.

Ya only kill if ya being paid for it, she'd said with unshakeable confidence – and Sorrow couldn't argue. It was, after all, one of the guiding principles of her life. So they'd agreed simply to gag the guards and leave them in the gondola of one of the skyboats.

'Naeve?' Corus said from where he was crouched on the ground, a short distance away. *Stay there and be good a lil' longer*, Elisse had told him gently. *And then we'll get ta have a ride in an airship. That'll be fun.* 'What are you doing?'

'Don't worry,' Sorrow told him, looking up from her second set of knots. 'It's all part of the game.'

Next moment, though, she regretted even that slight distraction. The man she was tying lashed out with his half-bound feet, catching her squarely in the chest and sending her flying backwards. Then he scrambled upright and made a break for it, shaking the twine away from his legs in a curious half-dancing step as he ran –

Elisse didn't hesitate. She swung one of the pistols round and pulled the trigger. The bullet took him squarely in the back; he staggered, pitching forward onto his face, where he scrabbled a little and then went still. Elisse cast the pistol aside and switched the other one to her dominant hand, swinging it back to point at the second guard before he could try anything. He stared at her mutely, not putting up any resistance. As Sorrow checked his bonds and then stuffed a gag in his mouth, she found herself smiling with an odd kind of pride. *A good actress and a good shot. She'd have made a damn fine sellsword.*

'We'd better be quick,' she said when she'd finished. 'They'll have heard that down the hill. We need to leave as soon as possible.'

'No need ta cry, sweetheart,' Elisse said briskly, handing Sorrow the remaining pistol before picking up a snivelling Corus. 'The man's only sleeping. Let's pick an airship, shall we?'

Whilst Elisse installed the boy safely into the gondola of their chosen craft, Sorrow dragged the living guard and the dead one out of sight. No time to conceal them properly, now; she could already hear faint rustles in the woodland below, some of the ambush party returning up the hill to find out what was happening, and she had another task to perform first. When that was done, she unhooked the skyboat's tethers as rapidly as she could, leaving it weighed down only by the anchor, then jumped into the gondola and sat down at the controls.

'Right.' She didn't bother telling Elisse that this was only the second time she'd flown an airship. Second was far better than first, after all. 'Let's get going.'

Anchor up. Crank the engine to get it running – though she wouldn't be able to steer until it had built up enough steam. Open the valves to replenish the depleted air inside the gas chamber and make the skyboat rise ...

As they lifted rather jerkily into the air, Sorrow glanced down and saw the first figures emerging from the trees onto the bare hilltop. She couldn't hear their shouts, but she saw one or two flashes as a couple of them fired on her. Since a bullet piercing the envelope would result in a second airship inferno, she was lucky it wasn't more – but then, it was their own craft. They couldn't be certain who was in it.

Soon enough, the shots became more numerous and Sorrow guessed that the ambush party had discovered their incapacitated guards. Yet by then, the skyboat was already out of range.

'Won' they come after us?' Elisse asked. Out of the corner of her eye, Sorrow could see her peering down at the scene on the ground.

'They would.' Sorrow grinned. 'But unfortunately for them, the rest of their craft have developed unfortunate gas leaks. The envelopes on these small ships are far too prone to damage from sharp objects.'

Elisse chuckled, and she was still chuckling as Sorrow swung the rudder round to point the nose of the skyboat north. It probably wouldn't be that simple, of course. The Kardise would fix the damage, or call for backup, and then they'd be in pursuit. But they were flying at night, and if Sorrow kept her craft's lights off and went as fast as she could, without bothering to conserve fuel ...

They'd make it. She was sure of it. They just had to reach the Mirrorvalese border.

TWENTY-SEVEN

Ayla opened her eyes to discover the familiar canopy of her bed above her. It wasn't morning, though, surely? The light was wrong. She struggled to sit up, but a gentle hand restrained her.

'Take it slowly, Lady Ayla,' a familiar voice said. 'That was quite a faint.'

She turned her head slowly in the direction of the sound, to find Darkhaven's physician sitting at her bedside.

'I fainted?'

'In the transformation room,' he confirmed. 'Your alchemist sent for me.'

Ugh. How embarrassing. Ayla let her head fall back on the pillow. The memory was coming back to her now, albeit in pieces. She and Miles had been performing tests. He'd shot her a few times. But after that, it was all a blank.

'The pistol?'

'Back in the armoury. The alchemist insisted upon it.'

Ayla smiled. She'd have to let Tomas know. After the day's events, he'd surely agree that Miles was wholly to be relied on.

'I'd been Changing back and forth a lot,' she said. 'Is that why –'

The physician nodded. 'It's highly likely that your condition makes you susceptible to overexertion.'

'My ... condition?'

'Yes, Lady Ayla.' He smiled at her. 'About eight weeks along, I'd say.'

Eight weeks along. Again Ayla tried to pull herself up to a sitting position, and this time she succeeded. 'I'm pregnant?'

'Yes.'

'I – are you sure?'

'As sure as I can be.'

She pressed the back of her hand to her mouth. A million questions clamoured for attention, but for some reason the one that came out was, 'Can I still Change?'

'I believe so.' The physician looked uncomfortable. 'The truth is, Lady Ayla, I have not had a great deal of experience in that area. The last pregnant Changer I attended was your late brother's mother, and that was a quarter-century ago. Besides, your father ...'

'Kept her in Darkhaven for her own safety,' she finished for him, and he nodded.

'Exactly.'

Ayla repressed a shudder, something coiling inside her that was too complicated to untangle. Sadness, on her predecessor's behalf. Guilty relief, that Florentyn wasn't alive to impose the same on her – and of course, if he had been, most likely her child would have been Myrren's, despite their combined protests against it. A far purer relief, that Owen Travers hadn't succeeded in his plan to incarcerate her and subject her to his own twisted desires. So many ways she could have been expecting a baby that she considered not a blessing but a violation of her will.

She was lucky.

And she really ought to apologise to Tomas. Because she'd accused him of stifling her – of being like her father – and yet Tomas would never use her pregnancy as an excuse to control her. She knew that before even telling him about it. In fact, she was pretty sure that after she'd delivered the news, he'd do anything she asked of him.

Since she wasn't her father either, she was determined not to abuse that power.

She wanted to run and find Tomas straight away, but by now it must be afternoon – which meant he'd be bringing the potential Helmsmen up to Darkhaven. And he'd asked her – no, *begged* her – not to make an appearance. *Please*, he'd said. *I know you don't believe you're in danger any more, but with so many new people up at the tower … please. Stay out of the way, and let me post a guard.*

She'd argued with him, of course, because she always did. Somewhere along the line, it had become less about what she actually thought was right and more about proving something to him. Proving that he didn't have the authority to keep her locked in Darkhaven, as she had been for the first eighteen years of her life. Only that was stupid, because he'd never claimed he did. He just wanted to keep her safe, because he loved her.

'Thank you,' she told the physician. 'Please keep this to yourself for now.'

'Of course. And I would advise you to avoid doing anything strenuous for the rest of the day. Perhaps stay here a little while longer.'

Ayla nodded meekly. In all honesty, she was still tired from the morning's activities. 'Don't worry. I'm not going anywhere.'

'Do send for me if you feel worse.' The physician stood up, giving her another kind smile. 'Your guards are just outside.'

'Thank you.'

He left the room, and Ayla heard him speak to the Helmsmen on duty. She lay back on her bed and took a long, deep breath. A baby. A cousin for Marlon. A niece or nephew for Corus, wherever he was. Maybe the Nightshade line wasn't doomed to extinction after all.

After a while, she sat up and reached for the pile of petitions at her bedside. *Might as well use the time.* But she couldn't concentrate. Her mind kept wandering with unabashed excitement to the baby, to what she imagined Tomas would look like when she told him – and then plunging into dread each time she recalled the possible lingering assassination threat, which had become all the sharper with the news of her pregnancy. If Tomas was right, there could be someone in the grounds of Darkhaven right now with the intent to kill her.

But they'd have to get past Tomas and Art and the rest of the trainees first, she reminded herself. *And then the guard at the gate. And then my own two guards.*

She considered those guards. They'd stood outside the transformation room earlier, when she was working with Miles, and now they were standing outside her bedroom. No doubt when they'd joined the Helm, they'd expected a little more swordfighting and a little less standing. Maybe she should send one of them for Tomas – but just as quickly, she dismissed the idea. Tomas was busy. The danger was no more acute now than it had been before; only her perception of it had changed. And besides, when she pressed her ear against the door, her sharp senses detected the rattle of dice on the other side of the thick wood. Not standing, then. They'd found something to do.

Leaving them to their game, she returned to the bed and, with a supreme effort of will, forced herself to concentrate on her petitions. Magistrates requesting that she uphold their judgement, a factory owner asking for a change in city regulations, the Captain of the Watch wanting her to sign a warrant of execution – all familiar tasks. And so she was able to lose herself in them, until she heard a soft thud on the other side of the door.

Again she crossed the room and put her ear to the wood: the sound of dice had stopped. She couldn't detect anything except her own blood rushing past her ears. Maybe they'd had enough of gambling for chicken stakes. Maybe one of them had gone to relieve himself. But Tomas had taught her caution, and so she retreated towards the window in search of a weapon. She carried a knife with her, sometimes, and she'd left it on the table this morning –

Before she was halfway there, a sudden volley of knocks on the door made her start. 'Lady Ayla! Lady Ayla!'

It was a girl's voice, light and urgent. Ayla strode back to the door and wrenched it open. One of Tomas's trainees stood on the other side, dancing from foot to foot in a state of panic. Her side and one leg of her trousers were drenched in blood.

'What's happened?' Ayla demanded. 'Are you hurt?'

The girl shook her head. 'It's not serious. I –'

'It looks bad enough. Let me call the physician back for you.' Belatedly, Ayla realised that the bloodstained trainee in front of her was standing there alone. 'Where are my guards?'

'I don't know! Maybe the assassin is here already ...' The girl glanced in each direction down the silent corridor, biting her lip. 'I came to warn you. Zander is innocent, and the real assassin is somewhere in Darkhaven.'

So Tomas had been right. The knowledge descended through Ayla's body like a stone through water, leaving bubbles of fear in its wake.

350

'Come in,' she told the girl, standing back far enough to admit her. 'Tell me everything you know. Hurry!'

The girl scurried in. Ayla searched her memory for the right name: not Ree, the small girl who very obviously had a crush on Tomas. The other one. The one who had surprised Tomas in the testing, the one who had been practising hard, the one who wore lace like a society lady yet fought with the determination of a soldier. Saydi.

'I'm glad I found you here,' Saydi said, her back towards Ayla as she pushed the door closed. 'For all I knew, you could have flown away from Darkhaven. That would have been the sensible option with a possible assassin at your door.'

The urgency and uncertainty had gone from her voice; she sounded calm, almost detached. Ayla heard the click of the key in the lock.

'But Captain Caraway wanted you here, I suppose. The bait in his trap. Shame he got distracted by the first diversion and left you alone.'

This wasn't right. This wasn't right at all. As Saydi turned, Ayla began to back away.

'I wouldn't, Lady Ayla,' Saydi said. 'Not if you want to draw your last breath with your guts still inside your body.'

And Ayla looked down to find a small pistol pressed against her belly.

Instinctively she summoned the Change ... but nothing happened. It was as if her skin were wrapped in a thick layer of glass, and her gift – the vast, expansive *freedom* of it – hovered just the other side. Within reach, yet untouchable. She tried again, but she might as well have been a butterfly beating its wings against a windowpane. She was trapped. She sought for her more recently discovered power – perhaps she could attempt to freeze Saydi's blood in her veins, or break a piece of furniture as a distraction – but that ability had deserted her too.

'How are you doing that?' she whispered.

'Surely you mean *why*,' Saydi said. 'You're wondering why I'd want to kill a woman I don't even know, for the sake of a country that isn't even mine. And more to the point, you're hoping you can get me to talk about it for long enough that your guards show up to take me in hand.' She laughed: a hard, bitter laugh that was as far from her previous girlish giggle as it was possible to get. 'I hate to disappoint you, Lady Ayla, but your guards met with a nasty accident.'

'Then there can't be any harm in telling me,' Ayla said – because even if the girl was wise to it, buying time was all she could do. Out of the corner of her eye, she could see her knife on the table by the window. If she could just get to it – 'Why *do* you want to kill me?'

'Your father killed my father,' Saydi said. 'That's all, and that's enough. There, did you enjoy the extra few moments of life that gained you?'

Ayla opened her mouth, desperately seeking for something else to say. Saydi's finger tightened on the trigger. And a loud, rattling thud shook the door.

Someone's come after her. Someone's here to stop her –

Even as Saydi turned her head in the direction of the noise, Ayla was across the room and running for her knife. She knew she wouldn't get there in time. She knew it wouldn't do any good against a pistol, even if she did. But at least she was doing *something*.

She heard the bang of the gun an instant before she felt the impact. Her outstretched fingertips were almost brushing the hilt of the knife, but the pain exploding in her lower back knocked her stumbling to her knees. She heard Saydi's low laugh close at her ear; the assassin must have followed in her wake, shot her at close range. She had to get away. She had to –

She tried to scramble to her feet, but her limbs refused to obey and somehow her cheek ended up pressed against the floorboards. The pain rose to an excruciating peak, clenching every one of her muscles in a wordless scream, then ebbed away into emptiness. Dusk fell around her, turning everything grey and silent.

Ayla closed her eyes.

For a moment after Penn had made his announcement, there was utter silence. Even the whine of the wind around the spire seemed to lessen. Then, frowning, Caraway stepped up onto the platform to face him.

'You're cousin to Owen Travers?' he repeated blankly.

'Yes.' Penn glared at him. Now, finally, Caraway would find his anger and attack him, and that would give Penn the strength he needed to hurt the little boy and make Caraway pay ...

But instead, the captain shook his head. His gaze met Penn's, steady and accepting. 'You must really hate me.'

Of course I do! Yet somehow, now that Caraway had acknowledged it, there was no longer any point in declaring it. Caraway had taken that from him as well. Penn scowled, tightened his grip on his sword, and said nothing.

'There I was,' the captain went on, 'going on about the Helm – the two of us looking up at this very building ...' He let out a long breath. 'Given the circumstances, I don't think you were rude at all. I'm surprised you didn't just tell me to shut up.'

Incredulity left Penn bewildered. *Why aren't you furious with me?* he wanted to reply. *I'm your enemy's kin. I've stolen your adopted son. What sort of coward stands there and takes that?* But again, he remained silent.

Yet in thinking of Marlon, he had involuntarily drawn the boy closer against his side – and Caraway didn't miss the movement. His gaze fell briefly to Marlon's face before returning to Penn's.

'You *could* have talked to me, you know,' he said mildly. 'I didn't know who you were when I made the offer, but I'd have kept to it all the same. We could have fought it out on the practice floor.' Almost imperceptibly, his expression hardened. 'You didn't need to involve a two-year-old child.'

'Hurting you wouldn't have been enough,' Penn muttered. 'But hurting someone you care about –'

He stopped at the look in Caraway's eyes.

'You won't hurt him,' the captain said.

'You don't know what I'll do,' Penn flung back, but Caraway shook his head.

'It's a promise, not a prediction. *You won't hurt him.*'

The shiver that tensed Penn's entire body at the last four words told him, without a doubt, that he'd been wrong to call Captain Caraway a coward – even if only in thought. Caraway wouldn't let him hurt Marlon. He'd kill Penn before that happened. And somehow, the knowledge left Penn relieved. No more incompetent plotting. No more trying to satisfy his father's desire for revenge. He'd face Caraway just as his cousin had, three years ago, and one of them would end up dead. That was what it came down to. That was what it had always been going to come down to. He wasn't ready, not even close – he hadn't started Helm training yet, after all – but he found he didn't care any more.

'Then fight me,' he managed. 'It's you or him, Captain Caraway.'

'Penn ...' Caraway didn't immediately reach for his sword. 'It doesn't have to be this way. If you let Marlon go and come down to the fifth ring –'

'Now.' Penn shoved the sobbing boy behind him, making sure the cuff still tethered one skinny wrist to the guard rail. He didn't want Marlon falling to his death.

All right, yes: that was contradictory. He did his best to ignore it.

'Fine,' Caraway said. 'Your choice.' And he drew his blade to meet Penn's.

Almost immediately, it became clear that every time Penn had seen Caraway demonstrate moves in training – every time he'd fought Caraway in a practice bout – the captain had been holding back. Penn had expected him to be good, of course; that was the whole point, that was why he'd originally planned to be trained by Caraway before he tried to fight him. But he'd hoped he might at least stand a chance. Maybe land a lucky blow, or use Caraway's fear for Marlon against him. Yet the reality was, Penn might as well have come up here blindfolded and unarmed for all the good he was doing with his sword. Because fear hadn't weakened Caraway, only focused him.

There was a lesson in there somewhere.

'Want a drink, Captain Caraway?' Penn panted, trying for a diversion, but Caraway's blade didn't falter.

'You'll have to try harder than that, Penn. I make no secret of what I used to be.'

'Still are, if what Ree and I heard is any guide.' Penn flung the words like weapons, and for an instant the captain hesitated. Desperate to seize the advantage, however slight, Penn pressed forward. 'Aren't you ashamed of it? The weakness?'

To his surprise, Caraway smiled at that, albeit sadly.

'Some things, you live with forever,' he said. 'That doesn't mean you have to let them define you. I think you'll need to learn that for yourself, one of these days.'

Then, with a fluidity that Penn both resented and admired, he turned his defensive move into an attack, and even that slim opportunity to disarm him was lost.

As the captain drove him back towards the edge of the platform, Penn risked a quick glance at Marlon. His only hope of fulfilling his father's wishes now was to use the boy. Stab him. Throw him over the edge. Anything to distract Caraway long enough for Penn to get past his guard.

Come on, Penn! he imagined Saydi saying. *If you want revenge, you have to be willing to do whatever it takes. You're going to be executed or thrown in jail for this anyway, so what difference does it make?*

And yet he couldn't do it. It didn't matter that he'd fail as a result. It didn't matter that his father would disown him. It didn't matter that his cousin's killer would walk free. He simply couldn't do it.

Frustrated with himself, he raised his sword and pressed forward for one last, forlorn attempt. And as if that were what the captain had been waiting for, he met the attack with that tricksy move of his own – the one that had disarmed Penn during the testing. Penn's sword clattered to the floor, the point of Caraway's own weapon settled just below his ribcage, and it was over. He'd lost. Though fear burned in his stomach like a hot coal, he glared into Caraway's face.

'Go ahead. Kill me. That'll make two of us.'

Caraway shook his head. His hands remained steady on the hilt of his sword, but he looked tired. Penn found that oddly incongruous. Surely the man who was about to gut him should be angry. Mocking. Anything but this ... weariness, as if the world had tripped him up one time too many.

'Do you know why I killed your cousin, Penn?'

'For revenge,' Penn spat. 'Because he threw you out of the Helm. Because you wanted his job.'

He braced himself for the final blow, but if anything, the blade holding him in place eased back slightly.

'If that's what you think, I'm not surprised you want me dead,' Caraway said. 'Listen, Penn. I deserved to be thrown out of the Helm. I failed in my duty. I didn't protect Kati Nightshade, and she died.'

'Farleigh told me that was an accident.' As soon as the words left his lips, Penn scowled. *Don't get distracted! There might still be an opening if he lets his guard down ...*

'It was an accident,' Caraway said. 'But that didn't matter. The Helm has one purpose, Penn, and one purpose only: to protect the Nightshade line. Remember that, when you're training. Reasons, excuses ... they make no difference. You do your duty or you pay the price.'

When you're training? The man must have forgotten who he was talking to. Unfortunately, that made it very difficult to argue with him. Ready to give it a go anyway, Penn opened his mouth to say something, but Caraway was already continuing.

'Your cousin forgot his purpose. He used his position as Captain of the Helm to make his men look the other way whilst he plotted against a woman he should have been willing to lay down his life for.'

Penn frowned. 'Plotted?'

'He locked Ayla up, in secret. He convinced himself that because she was only half a Nightshade, and because he wanted her, he could do whatever she liked to her. He did

357

this in Darkhaven, Penn, and not one of the Helm lifted a finger to stop him.'

It's all lies. Penn was ready to say it, but something kept him silent. He'd been brought up on the story of how his uncle had been murdered in Arkannen. How Florentyn Nightshade had executed the criminals and given Cousin Owen a place in the Helm. How dedicated Owen had been to the Nightshade line as a result. Penn was almost willing to swear that his cousin would never have done anything to hurt a woman of Nightshade blood.

Almost.

And yet, faced with this unexpected accusation, he found himself remembering a few odd things that hadn't seemed significant at the time. Snippets and observations from the letters that Cousin Owen had sent Penn's father, being passed across the breakfast table with the butter.

He says the daughter isn't a real Nightshade. A half-blood creature. The old Changer is ashamed of her.

Owen doesn't have much good to say about Lady Ayla. Which means, if I know the lad, he's probably half in love with her.

Hear that, Penn? Your cousin says the Helm will do anything he asks of them, even though he came to the captaincy young. Loyalty is more important than anything, Owen says. You remember that.

'She still has nightmares about it, you know,' Caraway said. 'What could have happened. But I wouldn't have killed him, all the same, if he'd only been willing to let her go when I caught up with them.' A shadow crossed his face. 'I'd never killed anyone before – or since, for that matter. It's not as easy as you seem to think.'

'I never thought it would be easy,' Penn mumbled. Caraway studied his face, then nodded.

'No. I don't think you did. And I respect you for that, at least. But I have to know, Penn.' Suddenly his voice was fierce. 'Do you believe, as your cousin did, that Ayla and Marlon are not worthy of respect, simply because they aren't full-blooded Nightshades?' He paused in expectation of an answer, eyebrows raised.

'N-no ...'

'As a Helmsman, would you be willing to protect them from any dangers that may threaten them? Would you defend Ayla against Tomas Caraway, Captain of the Helm, if I hurt her in any way?'

'Y-yes ...'

'There you are, then.' The blade aimed beneath Penn's ribcage retreated a little further. 'I may have been an idiot back then, Penn, but at least I got that right.'

They stared at each other. Into the silence, Marlon said in a small voice, 'Papa?'

'It's all right, son,' Caraway said. 'We're going home now.'

And with that, he sheathed his sword. Brushing past Penn, he walked over to where Marlon cowered by the railing and opened the Helm-issued cuffs with his own key. Then, without another word, he picked the boy up and carried him away.

Penn could have stabbed him. He could have retrieved his lost sword and driven it home. The man's back was exposed, he had his hands full – it would have been simple. Easy.

But once again, Penn couldn't do it.

What was more, he suspected that Caraway knew he couldn't. Why else would the captain have let his guard down so completely? To prove a point, to himself and to Penn. To show Penn that planning to kill a man was far, far easier than carrying it through.

Penn closed his eyes as the full force of his own stupidity struck him. The idea of descending the Spire of Air and showing himself to anyone in Arkannen filled him with the urge to flee. But he had nowhere to go. And so, slowly, feeling like the worst kind of fool, he picked up his sword and followed in Caraway's wake.

When he reached the bottom of the walkway, Caraway and Marlon had already disappeared down the staircase that led from the temple roof, but Weaponmaster Bryan was waiting for him. Relieved that he didn't have to face the captain again, Penn handed over his sword without waiting to be asked.

'Are you arresting me, sir?' he asked dully. 'Or is it to be immediate execution?'

'What do you think you deserve?' Bryan didn't shout, but somehow that made it worse. 'When Tomas was your age, they broke his sword and threw him out of the Helm for an accident that wasn't even his fault. So what do you suppose they'll do to someone who kidnapped and threatened a member of the Nightshade line, terrorised a sixth-ring temple, and challenged the Captain of the Helm to a duel?'

Penn's shoulders slumped. *At least I don't have to tell my father I failed.* 'Captain Caraway should have killed me up there,' he muttered.

'I agree,' Bryan said. Penn risked a glance at him, but the fury in the weaponmaster's face made him look away again quickly. 'But as it turns out, Captain Caraway has something else in mind.'

TWENTY-EIGHT

Ree was a couple of corridors into Darkhaven before she had to admit she had no idea where she was going. Ayla was in the tower, Captain Caraway had indicated that much, but as for where –

Movement caught her eye; she reached for the knife she'd taken from the nurse's body, but let her hand fall before it got there. It was only a woman carrying a tray, walking down the corridor towards her. Ree ran to meet her.

'I need to find Lady Ayla. Urgently. Where is she?'

The woman frowned at her. 'Is it the emergency?'

'Sorry?'

'The other girl said it was an emergency.'

The other girl. That must be Saydi. Dread churning in the pit of her stomach, Ree nodded. 'Captain Caraway sent me after them both.'

'Lady Ayla's in her room. Taken ill. So you oughtn't to disturb her, no matter how badly hurt this young man is.'

Young man? Briefly Ree wondered what sort of story Saydi had spun, but shook the curiosity off – it didn't make any difference. Instead she put her hand on the woman's arm. 'Please. I – it's life or death. Really.'

The woman studied her face a moment longer, then nodded. Ree listened to the directions, trying to keep control of her burning urgency long enough to commit them to memory. She stammered her thanks. And then she began to run. Along the corridor, through a door, up a flight of stairs, along another corridor. Her throat ached with exertion and with desperate anxiety, but still she kept running, until the door to Lady Ayla's chamber was ahead of her. She didn't slow down for even an instant, simply barrelled straight into it with as much force as her slight frame would allow –

And found herself on the floor, bruised and gasping. It was locked. Of course it was locked.

As she dragged herself to her feet, all tangled arms and legs as if her limbs were trying to climb over each other in their haste, a muffled bang sounded on the other side of the great wooden door.

Ree recognised it, though she'd heard it only once before. A pistol being fired – it couldn't be anything else. That was the whole point, that was what they'd been looking for all this time, that was what she'd raced up here to prevent. And she'd failed.

She'd failed.

She stumbled back to the door, dizzy with the bitter knowledge. Her hands shook with it. But she took out the set of lockpicks that Zander had shown her how to use – *you never know when you might need to become a criminal in order to catch one* – and manipulated them, mechanically, trying to suppress the one thought she really didn't want to think, until she heard the soft thud as the key on the other side fell to the floor, followed by the satisfying clunk of the tumblers. And then she opened the door.

The room was light. Thin curtains billowed in the breeze. Saydi stood in the middle of the floor, pistol pointing unerringly at Ree. Behind her, underneath the window, Ayla lay crumpled and still.

Maybe now he'll look at me, said the thought Ree didn't want to think.

The deep and utter shame of it got her moving. She didn't know how to fight a person armed with a pistol, so the obvious course of action was to get rid of the pistol – ideally before Saydi could shoot her with it. And to do that, she needed to get close enough to grab it.

So she started throwing things.

The silver hairbrush from the dresser went first, followed by the matching comb and a small hand mirror. Saydi backed away, around the bed, and lifted her free arm to block the onslaught, but made no other attempt to stop it. Then the dresser was empty, and Ree wasn't any closer to reaching the pistol than she'd been before. Panting, she stared at Saydi. *Why hasn't she shot me already?*

'It isn't loaded,' Saydi said. 'Any fool would have noticed me dragging all the accoutrements through Darkhaven with me. Even *you*.' She jerked her head scornfully in Ayla's direction. 'I only needed one shot.'

She threw the pistol on the bed, and pulled a knife from her belt. Mirroring the gesture, Ree raised her own blood-stained weapon.

'I don't understand,' she said slowly. 'I thought we were … friends.'

'No, you didn't. You thought you were being kind to me.' Saydi laughed, hard and bitter. 'You know, when I first heard about you, I was afraid you'd be my only real obstacle. Another woman in the same position, trying to prove herself – surely you'd see what the others didn't. Surely you'd be less quick to dismiss me as *just a girl*. But lucky for me, you were the most prejudiced of them all.' Her lip curled. 'I guess going *on* and *on* and *on* about wanting to be treated as an equal doesn't stop you being a narrow-minded bitch yourself.'

Ree flushed and didn't reply; that barb was too accurate to be easily ignored.

'The truth is, you ought to be thanking me,' Saydi added. 'Since I've freed your one true love to seek consolation in your arms. *Oh, Captain Caraway, I'm so sorry Lady Ayla is dead, why not let me comfort you with my –*'

Ree went for her.

It was a scrambling, disorganised attack, because the bed was in the way. By the time Ree got round the bedpost and into the space where Saydi was waiting, the assassin was more than ready for her. Ree had expected her to be more competent than she'd ever let on – after all, she'd hidden every other truth about herself – but the skill with which Saydi wielded her knife still came as a shock. Ree was used to seeing her in the training hall: a little clumsy, a little awkward, but with enough potential to become a decent warrior one day. Yet now, all that clumsiness was replaced by grace, and all the awkwardness had transformed into lethal intent. It didn't take long for Ree to become uncomfortably aware that she was outclassed in every way.

That, in fact, she stood little chance of surviving this encounter.

She tried one move, then another – drawing on everything in her limited repertoire of knife attacks – but Saydi countered them all with ease. Gradually, she forced Ree back towards the wall. And when she nearly had her pinned, she spoke.

'Let me tell you something about yourself, Ree,' she said. 'You're one of those girls who prides herself on being one of the boys. And you're so busy trying to prove something that you don't notice you're looking down on the rest of your sex far more than any man does.'

Her tireless blade darted forward again, and Ree barely managed to turn it away.

'And that's why you were willing to indulge your little dream about Captain Caraway, even though he was happy with someone else,' Saydi added. 'Because women don't matter to you. Even now, you're only fighting me because you want to impress him, not to avenge Ayla's death.' She sneered. 'I may be an assassin, but at least I have morals.'

Don't react. Don't react – But Ree's grip on her knife must have faltered, just a little. Enough for Saydi to notice and take advantage. She lunged forward, knocking the weapon from Ree's hand. Disarmed, Ree backed away until her shoulders hit something solid.

'But luckily for Caraway, you won't ever be a Helmsman,' Saydi said. 'You're simply not good enough.'

Then Ree was pressed against the wall, with the tip of Saydi's blade at her throat – she felt it break the skin –

Behind Saydi, something moved. *Someone* moved. *Captain Caraway*, Ree thought muzzily – but then she blinked and saw that it was Ayla. Ayla, pale and angry. Ayla, *alive*. She took something from around her throat – a collar or a choker – and cast it aside. Saydi's head whipped round at the sound, but Ayla had already gone. She was a swirl of black smoke, a falling robe. And then –

Ree swallowed hard, suddenly glad of the wall at her back. She'd heard people talk about Ayla's other form, of course, but nothing could have prepared her for being confronted with it. The golden unicorn filled the room, shimmering like firelight, and it was beautiful. Yet it was also terrifying. Ree took in diamond teeth and hooves like polished metal –the unimaginable sharpness of the spiral horn – and her insides melted in pure, abject fear.

She was barely aware of the knife stinging her throat as Saydi pulled it away. The assassin turned to face Ayla, gripping her weapon with white-knuckled determination.

'Monster!' she hissed. 'I'm not afraid of you!'

The unicorn flung back its head and let out a piercing, wordless cry. Ree clapped her hands over her ears, but she could still hear it inside her skull. Saydi's hands shook and her shoulders slumped – yet after an instant, they straightened again. Her grip tightened once more. And then she flung herself forward, her knife aimed straight at the unicorn's heart.

She's brave, Ree admitted to herself. *Braver than I am –*

Ayla lowered her head.

The spiral horn ran through Saydi like a sword through a strawman. Blood burst from her back, shockingly bright, and Ree flinched at the heat of it spattering across her own face. Saydi screamed, and she kept on screaming when the horn was wrenched back out of her body. Ree flinched down, covering her head with her arms and closing her eyes, as the assassin fell to her knees beneath the unicorn's rearing hooves –

Then Saydi's voice died into a gurgle, and it was over.

Slowly, Ree lifted her head. The girl's body lay in a bloodied heap on the floor. The winged unicorn stood above it, horn and front legs liberally splashed with scarlet. Ree didn't doubt the creature's ability to destroy her, too, if it chose. She froze, not blinking, hardly daring to breathe, wishing she could quiet the rapid thud of her heart.

This is why they rule us. What did you think they were like, you silly girl?

The unicorn stared at her as though it could read her mind. Then it shimmered, disintegrating into a swirl of smoke and remaking itself in the form of a woman. Standing barefoot in the spilled blood, but with no trace of it on her hands, Ayla looked down at Saydi. Then, abruptly, she reached down and closed the dead girl's eyes.

Ree took a deep, harsh breath. The sound made Ayla look up at her, expression fierce. Ree caught a shifting in her eyes, like a flare of flame. But then Ayla grabbed her discarded robe and backed away until she came up against a chair, where she sat down heavily.

'Well,' she said, her lips twisting in a not-quite smile. 'It seems I'm capable of retribution after all.'

'You're alive,' Ree said stupidly. She was relieved to find that her overwhelming sensation was gladness. 'I thought she'd shot you.'

'She did.'

'Then how –'

'That, I think.' Ayla's gaze rested on the collar she'd discarded earlier, and briefly her smile became something more genuine. 'Miles will be pleased.'

Ree wanted to know what Ayla meant, but didn't quite dare to ask. She'd just seen the woman kill someone, after all. If she closed her eyes, she could see it still.

Self-defence, she reminded herself. *And she saved your life.* A sudden blush heated Ree's cheeks as the truth of that hit her. Awkwardly, she cleared her throat.

'I never said … I mean, thank you.'

Ayla looked up at her, apparently glued to her chair as much as Ree was glued to the wall. 'Thank *you*.'

'Are you all right?' Ree asked, then winced. It was such an inadequate question. But Ayla nodded as if she saw nothing wrong with it.

'I've never killed anyone before,' she said softly. 'Training doesn't prepare you, does it?'

Ree shook her head. 'I didn't know you train too.'

Another singularly stupid remark: she didn't know anything about Ayla, not really. Not as a person, at any rate. Yet the overlord of Darkhaven only shrugged.

'Tomas has been teaching me. Not all of it, only how to defend myself.' Her gaze returned to the collar on the floor. 'But alchemy triumphed, in the end.'

Ree didn't reply. The unreality of the situation was beginning to bear down on her. She'd just duelled an assassin, nearly been killed, and now here she was, talking to Ayla Nightshade as if they were equals. She wasn't exactly sure of the correct etiquette at a time like this.

'Um,' she said. 'I should probably rejoin the others and –'

Ayla nodded. 'Of course. But Ree ... you did very well. Really. I think you'll be an asset to the Helm, and I know far more about these things than Saydi did.'

Ree blushed: out of pride, to start with, but then it deepened into embarrassment. Because if Ayla had heard everything Saydi said to her ... *Your one true love. You're only fighting me because you want to impress him. Women don't matter to you.* Ree winced. *I'm surprised she didn't run me through after all.*

She waited for Ayla to ask her what it had all meant. Maybe in a pointed manner that said she knew exactly what it had meant, and she was judging Ree for it. Maybe in a different kind of pointed manner that involved an actual knifepoint. But none of that happened. Perhaps she hadn't heard after all. Or perhaps – as Ree encountered a single penetrating glance from those green-washed Nightshade eyes – she had heard, but was choosing to ignore it.

'Come on, then,' Ayla said gently, as if to confirm that thought. She stood up and tied her robe close around herself. 'We'll go together. I expect Weaponmaster Bryan and Captain Caraway will want to hear our report, don't you?'

Captain Caraway ... shit. Ree bit her lip. What with everything that had just happened, she'd forgotten that Ayla didn't know about Penn. About Marlon.

'Lady Ayla,' she said helplessly, 'Captain Caraway may not be there. Before I came after Saydi, he had us all searching ...' She took a deep breath, trying to find the words, but there wasn't a good way to say it. 'Your – Marlon – he's been kidnapped.'

Kidnapped. The word was familiar, but somehow Ayla couldn't extract any meaning from it.

'What?' she whispered.

'Penn took Marlon.' The girl – Ree – looked even more scared than she had with the assassin's knife at her throat. 'But I'm sure someone will have found them by now.'

Ayla barely heard the reassurance. Her mind was full of images. Marlon, playing with Tomas. Marlon, touching the ice-crystals she'd made with a small, careful finger. Marlon, hurt and frightened ... A single sob escaped her lips, and she pressed it back with a fist. 'Where did he take him, Ree?'

'No-one knows. Captain Caraway had us all searching across the hillside.'

So she couldn't go after them. But nor could she sit and wait. It didn't matter that Marlon was one of a very few surviving members of a bloodline on the brink of extinction. It didn't even matter that he was Myrren's child. What mattered was that he needed her, and she wasn't there. Fierce love and bitter guilt lodged in her throat, almost choking her. Because she'd never been there, had she? Not really. Not in the ways that mattered.

'Take me down there,' she ordered Ree. 'Straight away.'

'Lady Ayla –' But whatever protest the girl had planned to make was lost in the sudden dull boom that split the air from somewhere nearby.

'Fire and blood,' Ayla muttered. 'What now?'

She snatched her knife from the table by the window, then – after a moment's thought – grabbed the discarded collar from the floor. Ree picked up her own knife and moved towards the door. And that was when a Helmsman arrived in a breathless rush.

'You'd better come quickly, Lady Ayla,' he gasped. 'An airship has crashed into Darkhaven.'

As it turned out, that wasn't quite accurate: the airship had crash-landed on the hill outside the tower. And it was only a small airship, a two-seater – practically a balloon – though it looked large enough on the ground. Even as Ayla and Ree arrived on the scene, a blonde woman was climbing out of the shattered gondola, hands raised in the air, a dirty and blood-soaked bandage wrapped around one boot.

'Don't kill me,' she drawled to the four or five Helmsmen who had surrounded the airship with weapons raised. 'This is the second craft I've crashed in as many days, and I'm really too exhausted to defend myself.'

'Sorrow!' Ayla strode forward to meet her. Her fear for Marlon still ran through her veins, sharp and urgent, but now she had a second little boy to think about as well. 'Where's Corus?'

'Elisse and Corus are safe within the borders of Mirrorvale,' Sorrow replied. 'I dropped them off before I came here. You'd have thought, having flown this piece of crap all the way from Sol Kardis, I'd have been able to make a further short flight well enough. But apparently losing half a foot screws with your spatial awareness.'

Ayla's fists clenched. *I want my family. Curse you, Naeve Sorrow, I just want my family back –*

'Where's *Corus*?' she repeated, her voice rising despite all her attempts to stay calm. 'If you think you can walk back in here without telling me *exactly* where he is –'

Sorrow lifted her chin and stared her down, though the effect was rather spoiled by the fact that she was swaying on her feet. 'Don't you want my information, Lady Ayla? I came a long way to give it to you. Oh, and I notice you haven't been assassinated. You're welcome.'

Ayla's hand tightened on her knife, lifting it half-automatically between them. Sorrow tensed in response. Ree shifted uneasily at Ayla's side. And then –

'Naeve!' A new voice broke into the charged silence, and swift relief left Ayla's knees weak. *Tomas. Does he have –?*

She turned. He was walking up the hill towards her. And there, in his arms ... The knife fell from Ayla's hand as she pressed a hand to her mouth once more. Tears stung her eyes. *Marlon. He's alive. He's alive.*

'What are you doing here?' she heard Tomas ask, somewhere beyond the roar of blood in her ears. 'Are you all right? Naeve?'

Sorrow sighed. 'I'd be better if everyone could get over this obsession with my first name.'

'Seriously, what are you doing here?' Tomas said.

'Mama!' Marlon called, holding his arms out to Ayla.

And Ayla began to cry.

It took a long time to sort everything out. Apart from anything else, Caraway wasn't sure what to do first: see Marlon somewhere safe, or fetch the physician to tend to Sorrow's foot, or find out why Ree was covered in someone else's blood – or, what he wanted most of all, comfort the woman he loved. But Ayla and Sorrow solved that between them, Sorrow by fainting dead away – which was such an unexpected vulnerability that he didn't quite know what to make of it – and Ayla by insisting that Marlon stay with her. So while the physician tended to Sorrow, and Ayla gave her nephew two years' worth of hugs, Caraway questioned Ree.

And he found out that Saydi had been the real assassin, and that Ayla had killed her.

After he'd recovered from that shock, he gathered up the scattered recruits and told them the bare bones of what had happened with Penn; they all knew the lad had snatched Marlon, so they had to be told something. Then he sent them back to the fifth ring, along with a Helmsman who'd been entrusted with a message asking Weaponmaster Bryan to release Zander from prison immediately. Caraway needed to apologise to Zander, of course, but that would have to wait for another day.

When Ree made to follow the others, he held her back.

'You did well today,' he told her. 'Very well. I'm proud of you.'

She blushed and nodded. 'Thank you.'

'I'll need the full story from you at some stage, I'm afraid.' Despite himself, he glanced at Ayla again – because it was important that she talk it through, too. She'd killed someone, and that was bound to affect her, even if she thought it wouldn't ... He dragged his attention back to Ree. 'Do you want to get it over with now, or leave it until the morning?'

Ree looked from him to Ayla, before giving him an oddly rueful smile that made her look, all of a sudden, much more grown up. 'Shall we leave it until tomorrow, captain? I'd like to see if Zander's all right. And ... and maybe Penn, too. I don't suppose he's feeling very good right now.'

'Of course,' Caraway said gratefully. 'I'll see you in training. Second bell. Don't be late.'

Once Ree had vanished down the hill after the others, he turned back to Ayla – but now Sorrow was awake, glaring at her newly strapped-up foot as if she took it personally. So he sat down and listened to her story. It was almost too much to take in all at once, but one fact stood out: Sorrow had discovered how the Kardise were smuggling firearms into the country. Maybe that knowledge would slow the growth of the gun trade in Arkannen for a few years. He'd have to send a message out to the borders and airship stations as soon as possible.

'Thank you, Sorrow,' he said once she'd finished her narrative. 'You risked a lot for this information.'

'It's going to cost you,' the sellsword said, no trace of a smile on her face. 'I had to leave everything I owned behind me, and so did Elisse.'

Caraway nodded. It was no more than she deserved – and besides, if she'd really meant to extort money from him, she could have kept secret what she knew until after he'd paid.

'Are Elisse and Corus all right?' he asked. 'It must be strange for the little boy, losing the only home he's ever known.'

Sorrow gave him a sly sideways glance. 'They'd have had to move anyway. Since you knew their old address –'

And then he had to explain to Ayla why he'd kept his knowledge of Elisse's whereabouts a secret. Once that was done, Ayla turned to Sorrow.

'Where are they now?'

'Elisse doesn't want you to know, Lady Ayla.'

'Please …' Ayla bit her lip, then said stiffly, 'I'm grateful for what you've done. Really I am. But surely such a narrow escape must have proved to you how dangerous it is for a Nightshade child to be out in the world without protection.'

Sorrow's lip curled, and she jerked her head in Marlon's direction. 'From what I overheard, living in Darkhaven with a bunch of Helmsmen didn't keep this one safe.' Her eyes cut towards Caraway. 'I did just as good a job protecting Corus as you did protecting Marlon, *captain*.'

'Yes,' Caraway admitted, ignoring the fierce glare Ayla directed at him. 'You did. But really, it's beside the point, isn't it? If I can find you in Sol Kardis, I can find you anywhere in Mirrorvale. It would save us all a lot of time and effort if you'd simply agree to give us your new address.'

'Corus belongs in Darkhaven!' Ayla snapped.

'That's for his mother to decide,' Sorrow shot back.

They were as stubborn as each other. Caraway rubbed his hands over his face and tried a compromise.

'Ayla … I don't see that we need to force Corus back to Darkhaven. He'll come to us of his own accord, when he's old enough to Change. In the meantime, surely you agree that Elisse has a right to determine his upbringing.'

Ayla's lips pressed tightly together. Fearing that she didn't agree, at all, Caraway ploughed on.

'But Sorrow … surely *you* must realise that we need to know where the boy is. We need to be kept informed of his progress. And we need to be assured that he'll learn about his heritage. It would be a strange and terrible thing, for a boy to reach adolescence and discover the gift in himself unawares. We can take a step back, agree not to interfere, but we need these assurances.' He paused, before adding, 'And Corus needs to be guarded by more than just you.'

Sorrow's chin shot up. 'I'm perfectly capable –'

'I know,' Caraway said. 'But you won't be there all the time. Unless you're telling me you plan to give up city life entirely for a farm and children? Because that's not what you did in Sol Kardis.'

To his surprise, a slight flush stained the sellsword's cheeks. She hesitated, then gave him a brusque nod. 'All right. I'll talk to Elisse. See if she'll agree to your terms.'

Ayla began to say something, but Sorrow shot her a fierce look. 'That's the best I can offer you, Lady Ayla.'

'All right,' Ayla said softly. 'But Sorrow, please … try to convince her. He's my brother.'

Clearly surprised by her lack of anger, Sorrow studied her for a good while without speaking, then nodded again.

'Will you stay tonight?' Ayla asked. 'We'll give you money for an airship in the morning –'

'I'd rather have it now,' Sorrow said flatly.

'But your foot –'

'It's fine.'

Seeing that she wouldn't be dissuaded, Caraway sent a Helmsman for some coin. Once the sellsword had departed down the hill towards the seventh gate, he turned to Ayla. She was sitting very still, Marlon on her lap. His head lolled against her shoulder, and he was fast asleep.

'Saydi killed the men you set to guard me,' she said quietly. 'And Lori. She fooled everyone, Tomas. Despite all our care. Despite everything.'

He nodded. 'But you're alive, and Marlon and Corus too. The Kardise failed, Ayla. We have to be thankful for that.'

She looked down at the sleeping child she was holding. 'Yes,' she said, so softly he could barely hear her. 'We do.'

TWENTY-NINE

Bryan sat behind his desk and fixed the lad standing in front of it with a glare. He still found it hard to believe what he was about to say, but Caraway had been adamant.

'All right, Penn. It turns out you have a choice. You're lucky to still have choices, but there it is.' He scanned the boy's face, waiting for his nod before continuing. 'Captain Caraway has made things right with the Spire of Air, but there's still the kidnapping. You can't threaten a member of the Nightshade line and get away with it.'

'I wouldn't have hurt Marlon,' Penn mumbled. 'Caraway knows that, doesn't he?'

Bryan snorted. 'It's the only reason you're still standing, boyo. If you'd so much as scratched young Marlon, *Captain* Caraway would have gutted you like a fish.' Shaking his head, he went on. 'Anyway. If you choose, you can leave Arkannen and never come back. That would have the effect of keeping you away from our overlords and from Captain Caraway himself, but you would be free to go anywhere else in Mirrorvale without restriction. It's a lenient punishment, and more than you deserve.'

Staring steadfastly at the floor, Penn nodded again.

'Alternatively –' and this was the part Bryan didn't approve of – 'if you want to stay here in the fifth ring and train as a Helmsman, you will still be allowed to do so. You'll be on polishing duty for months, and you won't have the freedoms the other trainees have. But should you wish to, you can still try and be accepted to the Helm.'

Penn looked up sharply. Bryan could almost have laughed at the expression of utter shock on his face.

'Are – are you sure, sir? I mean, Captain Caraway can't want me to –'

'This is Captain Caraway's decision,' Bryan said. *And one I don't approve of*, he didn't add. They'd had a brief conversation about it at the Spire of Air before Caraway took Marlon home and left Bryan to deal with Penn. Caraway had been adamant that Penn should be given the opportunity to stay. *Too forgiving for his own good, if you ask me.*

Now Penn frowned in confusion. 'I thought, after he left without speaking to me again –'

'Oh, grow up, son. The world doesn't revolve around you. Tomas has gone home to be with his family. Don't you think he has a right to that, after what you've done?'

Penn didn't answer, but the droop of his head spoke for him. Bryan sighed.

'Listen, boyo. If it was up to me you'd have been chucked out already, but Captain Caraway thinks you deserve a second chance. So bear that in mind when you're deciding what to do, 'cos I won't make it easy on you. If you still want to be a Helmsman, you'll have to work three times as hard as everyone else even to be considered.'

Penn nodded. His face was pale, his eyes shadowed. Genuinely repentant, or simply regretting his failure? Bryan wasn't sure.

'Captain Caraway says he knows what it's like to live with a terrible mistake, and it's punishment enough,' he said. 'Myself, I think what you did was more than a *mistake*. But he's in charge of the Helm, and he wants you to train. So give it some thought, and I'll hear your decision in the morning.'

'Y-you mean, you're not going to lock me up?'

Bryan gave him a look. 'Are you going to try and run away?'

'N-no ...'

'Well, then. Think about it. Sleep on it. And I'll see you again tomorrow.'

As the door closed behind the bewildered boy, Bryan sat back in his chair and ran a hand over his head. *What a day.* He couldn't imagine what Penn's decision was going to be – didn't have the lad pegged at all. It had always been difficult to see beyond the prickly exterior. But Caraway had, and apparently was continuing to do so despite the small matter of a kidnapping attempt. Which probably meant that Penn would surprise everyone and stay on. The fact that Caraway had offered it at all suggested he saw some metal in the lad that would be tempered by their encounter today.

Still, Bryan would have to wait and see. For now, he just wanted to get home, see Miles and have a cup of ale. He was locking the office door when a Helmsman arrived with a message from the tower.

'What now?' Bryan grumbled. He scanned the message quickly. Then he read it again more slowly. And then he began to laugh.

Art –

Saydi was the assassin. She tried to kill Ayla. Ree and Ayla between them finished her off. Please release

Zander from jail with our sincere apologies, and tell
him I'll talk to him as soon as possible.

In addition, you may want to let Miles know that
Ayla thinks his collar saved her life, and she'd like to
see him tomorrow to thank him.

Oh, and Naeve Sorrow has crash-landed an airship
in the grounds of Darkhaven.

Today has been interesting.
Tomas

'Interesting,' Bryan said aloud. 'That's one word for it.' He
nodded at the waiting Helmsman. 'You tell your captain he
can rely on me, and I'll see him tomorrow.'

And with a sigh of regret for the ale and Miles, both of
which would have to wait, he set off in the direction of the
cells.

Once Bryan had finished with him, Penn left the training hall
and tried to think what to do next. He didn't want to return
to the barracks in case he met one of the other trainees. He
certainly didn't want to see Saydi. Yet nor did he want to
descend into the lower rings and seek oblivion in one of
the many distractions available down there. He had a lot of
thinking to do, and he owed it to himself to be sober while
he did it. So in the end, he returned to the sixth ring.

The guards at the Gate of Ice waved him through as if
they didn't know what he'd done. In fact, they probably
didn't. Though he felt it must be branded on his forehead for
everyone to see, only the people who'd been up at the tower
that afternoon were aware of the truth. Captain Caraway
certainly hadn't had time to revoke the permission he'd given
Penn to visit the sixth ring. It made Penn uncomfortable, as

if he were adding insult to an already fatal injury. Yet the sixth ring was the only place in Arkannen he'd found where he could really clear his mind.

He didn't return to the Spire of Air; he suspected Air would never hold the same comfort for him that it always had, and he couldn't yet face the inevitable apology he'd have to offer the priestesses. Instead he walked slowly the other way until he reached an open space between two temples. The path terminated at a stone seat with a view out over the east of Arkannen. Penn sat down and tried to work out what he'd say to Bryan the next day. Would he accept Caraway's offer and stay to train, despite the taunts and dislike that would no doubt come his way? Or would he turn and run?

I was given a second chance. I try to remember that. Caraway had said that to him, up by the Spire of Air before any of this had happened. Before he'd given Penn the freedom of the sixth ring. *If you like it here, I see no reason to keep you from it.* Maybe if he hadn't offered that freedom, Penn would never have thought of taking Marlon to the Spire of Air. But then, Caraway wouldn't have guessed where to look for him, either. So it had probably all happened for the best.

Maybe.

Penn still had no idea how to feel about any of it.

He couldn't shake all his resentment of Caraway, even now. Whatever the circumstances, the man had killed his cousin. And Owen had been a good man, once. He'd overcome the tragedy that killed his father and brother – Penn's uncle and other cousin – and gone on to make a life for himself. *I always wanted to be of use to the Nightshade line*, Caraway had said; and the funny thing was, Penn had heard his cousin say something very similar on more than one occasion. Yet at the end, Owen's dedication had turned into something darker – so how could Penn blame Caraway for stopping him?

It was all very confusing.

And if Penn stayed to train, he'd have to see Caraway every day. He'd have to face the stares and taunts of his fellow trainees, who didn't like him anyway and who by now must know exactly what he'd done. Maybe he should just take his shame and go – not back home, to be shamed anew by a father who wouldn't understand why he'd failed to follow through on his oath, but ... somewhere.

Owen wouldn't have run away, the dark part of him said. *Whatever his faults, no-one could accuse him of cowardice.*

Penn shook it off. He didn't want to be like his cousin, subverting a decent principle to his own twisted ends. He didn't want to be like his father, either, consumed by anger and resentment. He wanted ... he just wanted ...

Before I can assess whether any of them would make good Helmsmen, I have to untangle their skills from all that wanting.

Penn sighed. He was remembering enough of Captain Caraway's words that they'd clearly made an impact on him. Maybe he should stay.

Maybe he should follow in his cousin's footsteps, but get it *right*.

Maybe his shame would keep him from going the wrong way.

Captain Caraway says he knows what it's like to live with a terrible mistake, and it's punishment enough. Yes. And somehow it was made even harder to live with by the fact that Caraway – the man against whom Penn had committed his crime – had forgiven him and wanted him to succeed. Retribution bred resentment; only mercy could breed genuine regret, and all the pain that came with it. A second chance could be a sharp-edged thing.

And that was the test, wasn't it? If Penn didn't seize the opportunity, even though it cut him, then he wasn't worthy of it anyway. Caraway didn't lose anything by this gesture. He either gained a potential Helmsman, or he lost someone who never would have been good enough.

Clever. Penn couldn't help but smile. And even as he thought it, he knew he was going to stay. His pride wouldn't allow anything less.

Now he just had to figure out how to live with it.

'Penn?' That voice was familiar. He glanced back over his shoulder to find Ree walking towards him. *What is she doing here?* 'Are you all right?'

He just looked at her.

'What?' she said. 'I know what you did. But Captain Caraway said he was letting you stay, so ...' She shrugged and repeated, 'I just wanted to make sure you were all right.'

He kept looking at her. She was a kind girl. A kind person. Not at all the shrill caricature he'd been so ready to despise when they first met. And he'd been nothing but dismissive of her so far. *Second chances.*

'Thanks,' he muttered, and made space for her on the bench. They sat together in silence, gazing out over Arkannen.

'I've already been to see Zander,' Ree said after a while. 'Weaponmaster Bryan let him out of prison after what happened with Saydi. Captain Caraway's going to let him stay on the training programme, even though he's not Mirrorvalese.'

'That's good,' Penn said, and meant it. Then, belatedly, the other part of what she'd said registered. 'Wait ... what did happen with Saydi?'

Ree froze, looking at him with the expression of a deer faced with a hunter's bow.

'I forgot you wouldn't know,' she said finally. 'Er ... Saydi was the assassin, Penn. She tried to shoot Lady Ayla while everyone was running around after you and Marlon. And, er ...' She hesitated, the panic intensifying on her face, then admitted, 'She's dead. Lady Ayla killed her, and I ... sort of helped.' She looked at him helplessly. 'Sorry. Really. I know you two were ... um. Close.'

Penn couldn't work out how to feel about that, either. He was already several straws past his last.

'Thanks for telling me,' he said uncertainly.

'I'm sorry,' Ree said again. There were tears in her eyes. And then both of them were crying, and it turned out he did know how to feel about Saydi's death after all.

Once the tears had passed, leaving them leaning rather drunkenly against each other like a couple of ships blown together by a storm, Ree said in a small voice, 'When we were fighting, she said some cruel things about me. Most of them were true.'

Penn nodded. 'I think she saw us all quite clearly.'

'Not clearly enough, though,' Ree said. 'I never would have wanted Lady Ayla to be harmed. And you wouldn't have hurt Marlon, either.'

Penn sat bolt upright and turned so he could look at her. 'You know that?'

'Of course.' Dislodged from his shoulder, she blinked up at him. 'You're a surly bastard, Penn, but you'd never have hurt a child.'

He didn't have anything to say to that. He thought he might cry again, but once in a day was enough for a grown man – even a grown man who sometimes made bloody stupid choices. So he leaned against the back of the seat once more, and Ree returned to her slumped position against his shoulder. Together, they gazed out over the flat grey roofs of the fifth ring.

'You know what?' Ree said after a while. 'Maybe we won't make such bad Helmsmen after all.'

Penn managed a shaky smile. 'Maybe you're right.'

THIRTY

Ayla and Miles sat in the library while she related the events of the previous day. When she'd finished, she handed him the iron collar she'd been wearing when it all happened. He took it from her with a grimace.

'I am sorry, Lady Ayla. I should have realised it would keep you from Changing entirely.'

She shook her head in disbelief. 'Miles, your collar saved my life. If I hadn't still been wearing it, the bullet would have killed me – whether I was quick enough to reach my other form or not.' On impulse, she leaned across the space between them and kissed his cheek. 'Thank you.'

The colour rose in his face, and he looked down. 'You are welcome. I assure you, it was entirely accidental. Ah ... not that I did not want to preserve your life, of course ...'

'Then you didn't expect the collar to have that effect? Do you have any idea why it did?'

As she'd hoped, the practical question distracted him from his embarrassment. 'It is an interesting problem. My current theory is that the elements to which you are aligned reinforce the alchemy in your blood, and so they have the effect of enhancing your strength in creature form. They amplify what is already in you, if you like. Whereas the rest ... they coun-teract your abilities, as you found, but they do not reduce you to mere human level. Instead, ah ...'

He gestured vaguely, seeking for words, then went off at an apparent tangent. 'In alchemy, we have stable pairs and volatile pairs. When you put a volatile pair together, something happens. There is a reaction, a change. Whereas when you put a stable pair together, they become inert – unchanging – but often very strong. I believe that is what that collar does to you. It takes away the fluid aspects of your gift, but it makes you harder to break.'

She nodded. 'Then why did I black out when the bullet hit me?'

'The collar was only a prototype, Lady Ayla. Clearly it was not enough to protect you fully. And I also suspect its effects were weakened by the initial blow. If the assassin had been able to shoot you a second time, the bullet might have found its mark.'

'I'm lucky Ree was there, then.'

'Yes.' But Miles showed little interest in anything other than the collar in his hands. He gazed at it in silence for some time before, finally, releasing his breath in a sigh.

'Prevented you from Changing entirely,' he murmured. 'Remarkable that such a small thing could have such a vast effect. Why, if people knew –'

He fell silent, but too late. Ayla was already considering it, a horrible plunging sensation in her stomach. Had she merely exchanged one threat for another?

But no. Even if someone knew that steel and glass and amber together could prevent her from Changing, they wouldn't be able to hurt her. The worst they'd be able to do was keep her locked in human form. Admittedly that would become an issue if Mirrorvale were to go to war, but her life was in no danger from this secret.

Not yet, a cynical part of her remarked. *But who knows what an alchemist might be able to develop?*

'I hope it goes without saying that I will keep this to myself,' Miles said, as if he could tell what she was thinking. 'And in fact, I owe you another apology. You say the red-headed girl was the real assassin, not Zander after all?'

'Saydi? Yes.'

'In which case, I did in fact smuggle a firearm into Darkhaven,' Miles said. 'Saydi is the girl from whom I bought my little carved chest – the one you and I looked at together in the transformation room. The pistol must have been in there all along.'

'Really?' Ayla wasn't sure how to react to that. Torn between unwilling admiration of Saydi's planning and shock that she'd unwittingly been so close to the weapon that had nearly killed her, she didn't realise she was staring at Miles until he cleared his throat.

'I am sorry. Very sorry. Do you want me to leave?'

Ayla came out of her trance. 'Leave? Of course not. It was hardly your fault.' She hesitated, but now was as good a time as any to make the first of today's proposals, so she added, 'In fact, I was hoping that you and Art might consider moving into Darkhaven.'

He gaped at her. 'Move … into Darkhaven?'

'Yes. Tomas has been stretched too thin for years, carrying out two sets of duties at once. And I know for a fact that Art has been invaluable to Tomas these past weeks. I was hoping that Art might take over some of the training for the Helm. And as for you …' She smiled. 'When you're not busy teaching, I rather thought we might continue our experiments. These collars need work, do they not? The vulnerability after the initial impact has to be addressed. And I can't switch jewellery every time I want to Change. I need you to find a way of ...'

But she stopped talking, because Miles was looking dazed. She'd been bombarding him with words. With an apologetic nod, she said, 'Anyway, I hope you'll consider it.'

'I have no need to consider it, Lady Ayla.' Suddenly and abruptly, he favoured her with a beaming smile. 'As long as I can convince Art it is a good idea, I would be very happy to live here.'

That evening, Ayla sat in the music room and waited for Tomas to come home. Nerves made her fidgety – she had several important things to say to him – but she tried to ignore the sensation. Going over and over the possible outcomes in her head would only make things worse.

To distract herself, she looked again at the carved wooden chest. After what Miles had said, she'd brought it up to her room and, after several attempts, found the hidden compartment that must have housed the pistol. The Helm had found a similar compartment in Saydi's trunk, containing a second pistol and a Mirrorvalese border pass stamped with the Kardise seal. Saydi's real name was Kai Sinder, and they'd located her father in the records. The family had lived in southern Mirrorvale until the elder Sinder had been found guilty of embezzling taxes. And for that crime, he'd been summarily executed by Florentyn Nightshade.

That didn't make Ayla forgive Saydi, exactly, but it was harder to condemn her outright. *If my father had been a little less quick to dispense retribution ...*

Of course – no doubt as intended – the fact that Saydi was a Mirrorvalese with a grudge would have made it hard to connect her crime to Sol Kardis. Even now, the only evidence was circumstantial: the fact that she'd spent a considerable amount of time there, the fact that the chest and pistols were Kardise-made, the fact that she'd been able to identify Zander and thereby select him as a likely scapegoat. Plus there was Sorrow's first-hand account, of course, but that alone wouldn't be considered reliable enough to take to the Kardise government. Besides, from what the sellsword had said, the Kardise government knew nothing about any assassination attempt; it was the power behind the government that had ordered it. So all in all, though it galled Ayla to admit it, Mirrorvale wasn't well placed to seek recompense from Sol Kardis. Still, with the knowledge of how firearms were being brought into the country, they'd be able to tighten controls at the borders and airship stations. And Ayla had to count it a victory for Mirrorvale. She was, after all, still alive.

'There you are, love.'

Ayla turned to find Tomas in the doorway. Straight away her heart began to pound, but she forced herself to appear calm. 'Well? Did Penn agree to stay?'

'Yes.' He walked over to sit beside her. 'Are you sure you're happy about it?'

'I trust you,' Ayla said. 'If, at the end of the year, you think he'll make a good Helmsman, I won't contradict you.'

Of course, she still secretly hoped that Penn wouldn't have what it took. She wasn't sure she'd get on well with being guarded by a man who'd once tried to kidnap her nephew. But she'd made a resolution to trust Tomas's judgement from now on, and this was a good place to start.

'Did the others accept him?'

'There was a lot of teasing. Some of it good-natured, much of it not. And let's face it, he deserves it. But he's got Ree on his side – and, funnily enough, Zander himself. I think he'll do all right.'

'Ree saved my life, you know,' Ayla said. 'If she hadn't turned up when she did, Saydi would have had time to check my pulse and find out I was still alive. And then, from what Miles says, she would have been able to stab me while my defences were weakened by the gunshot.'

Tomas frowned. 'It doesn't sound as if these collars of his are very reliable.'

'They still need work,' she agreed. 'Miles knows that. All the same, he saved my life too. He and Ree between them. And –'

She was going to say, *And it wasn't just my life they saved.* But Tomas spoke first.

'Assuming Ree carries on the way she has so far, I think I should admit her to the Helm, don't you? She's one of the best in the group, quite aside from our personal debt to her. And just because there's never been a female Helmsman before –'

'She'll make an excellent Helmsman,' Ayla said drily. 'Especially if she can get over her feelings for you.'

She watched Tomas carefully, out of the corners of her eyes, just to be sure; but the raw shock on his face was all the reassurance she needed. Not that she'd needed much. She trusted Tomas. She always had, even when she thought she didn't.

'Her ... what?'

'It's perfectly natural, Tomas.' Ayla gave him a benevolent smile. She was enjoying herself now. 'You do cut a romantic figure, you know. Captain of the Helm, the hero who single-handedly defended my honour with a broken sword – some of the stories they tell about you in the lower rings are really quite –'

'Fire and blood, Ayla! I don't want them to think that way about me! In fact, I specifically told them I *wasn't* a hero ...'

'Because there's nothing like a bit of self-deprecation to completely destroy a romantic ideal,' Ayla put in helpfully. He threw her a wild glance, then shook his head.

'Maybe I shouldn't allow girls into the Helm, if this sort of thing is going to happen.'

She couldn't let him get away with that. 'Who says it's just the girls?'

He stared at her for a moment before, reluctantly, beginning to laugh. When he'd finished, he wiped his eyes and sighed. 'Oh, Ayla. So you really mean to tell me that when I thought I was being honest about who and what I am, at least some of the trainee warriors I was addressing took that as a further sign of my heroism and – and –'

'And increased the height of your pedestal,' Ayla agreed. 'That's human nature for you.'

Tomas looked suddenly serious. 'So what do I have to do to convince them to take me off it? I don't want to end up like Owen Travers.'

'Tomas, you could never –'

He shook his head stubbornly. 'Just listen to me, love. Travers ruled the Helm through discipline and fear. He taught them to follow orders blindly, and we both know the result of that. But hero-worship is just another thing that stops people thinking for themselves. I don't want my Helm thinking they have to do everything I say, just because it was me who said it! Their job isn't to obey me, it's to protect you.'

'And our child,' Ayla said softly, getting the news in at last. Then she sat back in her chair, hands folded demurely in her lap, and enjoyed the range of expressions flitting across his face.

'You mean,' he said. 'I don't. Why didn't you. That's. Are you …'

Apparently giving up on the formation of a coherent sentence, he dropped to his knees beside her, took her hands in his and looked up at her. The pure joy in his smile made her want to cry. 'Really?'

'Yes, really.' And she kissed him.

After a time, with her head resting on his shoulder and her face pressed against his neck, she murmured, 'In answer to your previous question: I don't think you have anything to worry about. Travers chose his recruits for their biddability as well as their fighting skills. You'll choose yours for their intelligence. After all, despite Ree's feelings for *you*, she showed a good deal of initiative today when it came to protecting *me*. Isn't that so?'

'Yes,' Tomas said, winding a lock of her hair around his finger. 'I just don't like the idea of anyone thinking I'm something I'm not. My so-called heroism was a mixture of luck and idiocy –'

'And courage, and loyalty, and determination, and cleverness, and skill,' Ayla murmured.

'Do you really believe that?' His voice was teasing, but it also held a hint of surprise. If he still doubted himself, even after all these years ... She nipped at his skin with her teeth, hard enough to make him wince.

'*Yes*,' she said fiercely. 'And you should too.'

She hesitated, trying to find her courage; but there was no easy way to say what she intended, so she just went ahead and said it.

'I'm sorry, Tomas. I have a lot to make up for. I should have listened to you.'

'Of course you should,' he said, but there was a smile in his voice. 'About what?'

Ayla bolted upright. 'The assassin, of course! I was so afraid of being locked up in this tower again that I refused to accept your judgement over Zander.'

'Oh, that. It doesn't matter, love.'

'It does,' Ayla insisted. 'Apart from anything else, I called off the Helm and let Lori take Marlon outside again. If I hadn't done that, Marlon would have stayed safe and –' She swallowed, then finished in a low voice, 'And Lori would still be alive. I put their lives at risk through my own desire for freedom, and that's unforgivable.'

Tomas nodded. 'It was stupid. But I'm just as much to blame. I should have overruled you when it came to Marlon's safety. So we both have to live with Lori's death. But Ayla ... you didn't snatch Marlon, and you didn't stab Lori. You may have facilitated those events, but the fundamental choices were made by others.' His expression was warm with sympathy. 'You know, I gave Penn a second chance. I think we deserve to do the same for each other.'

'Yes ...' She hesitated, then said in a rush, 'I hope Marlon will give me a second chance, too. I haven't been any kind of mother to him. I was too wrapped up in my own grief over Myrren. But now ... I just hope it's not too late.'

'He loves you,' Tomas said softly. 'You'll gain his trust quick enough.'

'I hope so. I hope he comes to feel part of our family before his cousin is born. He'll be a big brother then, or as close as makes no difference.' Glancing up, she added shyly, 'He already thinks of you as his father.'

'I know.'

They gazed at each other. *This is it, Ayla*, she told herself. *This is as good a time as any*.

'Tomas, do you think –' Now that the moment had arrived, she was suddenly blushing. 'I mean, I should have asked you this before, but I was afraid you'd say no. I was afraid – Anyway. Never mind that. The point is, will you ... would

394

you consider … I'd be deeply honoured if …' *Fire and blood*. It was her turn to be lost for words. She bit her lip, trying to ask him the question with her eyes.

Apparently Tomas understood, because he reached out and touched her face, very gently, with his fingertips. His smile was radiant.

'Yes, Ayla,' he told her. 'Of course I will.'

Acknowledgements

This one's for Tiny, without whose naps it would never have been written; and for Small, who … didn't contribute a great deal, actually, but I love him anyway.

It's for the Digital Shadows, the most amazing group of little-known writers in existence, whose support, encouragement and ear for a good rant are second to none.

And it's for all of you who liked my first book enough to read this one too; who left a kind review; who passed on your recommendation to a friend. Without you, I lose my dream. So thank you.